"Paul Ricoeur once declared, 'The symbol gives rise to thought.' He probably didn't have Tolkien's Lord of the Rings in mind, but he could have. Austin Freeman here proves the truth of Ricoeur's adage, clarifying the system of theological thoughts that arise from trying to make sense of the symbols—people, places, things, events—that make up Tolkien's famous trilogy and other fictions. Freeman loves the stories too much to kill them by dull paraphrase. He does not murder (the saga) to dissect the (system of) truths that support it. Instead, he mines the stories and other resources, especially Tolkien's letters, in order to better understand the theological imagination of the man who created them. This is a well-researched, one-of-a-kind work that will appeal especially to those who have gone out the front door to engage in the dangerous business of walking the Way of Christ, pursuing their own adventures as inhabitants of the twenty-first century demystified Middle-West."

KEVIN J. VANHOOZER,
research professor of systematic theology, Trinity Evangelical Divinity School

"Among the many publications on Tolkien's theology, Dr. Freeman's study stands out since it provides a concise, comprehensive, and approachable primary-text based discussion of all important theological topics. His book is likely to become a standard text for interested laypeople and literary critics as well as professional theologians when discussing the theology of the maker of Middle-earth."

THOMAS HONEGGER,
Friedrich-Schiller-University, Jena, Germany

T0338822

"In this well-written, engaging, and theologically astute book, Austin Freeman, a clear-headed evangelical, has given us a sympathetic, thoughtful, and critical account of how Tolkien's devout Roman Catholic theology plays out in his stories. Freeman has accomplished something remarkable: arranging his material by the classical theological loci, he helps us to enjoy Tolkien's stories even more fully, while at the same time instructing us in traditional Christian theology. And as we see the theology and the stories intertwined, we gain a fresh admiration for that theology as it provides a comprehensive and appealing worldview."

C. JOHN ("JACK") COLLINS,
professor of Old Testament, Covenant Theological Seminary

TOLKIEN
DOGMATICS

TOLKIEN
DOGMATICS

*Theology through Mythology
with the Maker of Middle-earth*

AUSTIN M. FREEMAN

LEXHAM PRESS

Tolkien Dogmatics: Theology through Mythology with the Maker of Middle-earth

Copyright 2022 Austin M. Freeman

Lexham Press, 1313 Commercial St., Bellingham, WA 98225
LexhamPress.com

Print ISBN 9781683596677
Digital ISBN 9781683596684
Library of Congress Control Number 2022941648

Lexham Editorial: Todd Hains, Liz Vince, Jessi Strong, Cindy Huelat, Mandi Newell
Cover Design: Joshua Hunt, Brittany Schrock
Typesetting: ProjectLuz.com

24 25 26 27 28 29 30 / TR / 12 11 10 9 8 7 6 5 4 3 2

CONTENTS

ACKNOWLEDGEMENTS

This book took a long time to complete. It has been with me, to varying degrees, for almost half a decade now. As such, I'd first like to thank all of my family, friends, coworkers, and brief acquaintances for putting up with my shoehorning Tolkien into every conversation. Note well that I am thankful, not apologetic.

My wife, Mandi, has been my chief advocate in this as in all things. My editor, Todd Hains, saw the potential in this book long before there was any reason to give me a chance to write it. The other scholars of Tolkien I've met, and with whom I've collaborated, also deserve thanks here, but there are too many to mention by name, aside from Carl Hostetter who probably helped the most. The staff at the Rolfing Library in Deerfield, Illinois, deserve mention for their assistance in obtaining scans of material I couldn't otherwise have used, primarily from the Marion E. Wade Center at Wheaton. Finally, thanks go to Christopher Tolkien for the Tulkasian effort of collating, editing, and publishing his father's manuscripts, without which this book would be substantially slimmer.

PROLEGOMENA

The task of this book is in many ways an impossible one. J. R. R. Tolkien was not a professionally trained theologian, nor did he seek to construct a coherent "theology" in any of his published writing. But, as every individual does, *he had a theology*, a way of looking at God and the world, and it manifests in his writings, even in his fiction, by his own admission. One cannot, as with the work of Tolkien's good friend C. S. Lewis, simply read and digest a ready-made corpus of theological texts and provide a synthesis. It necessitates a thoroughgoing textual archaeology, in which interested parties must sift and sort through a variety of documents (letters, academic essays, poetry, fiction), with keen eye ready to discern telling phrases and connections. Tolkien's explicit theological statements (by far most prevalent in *The Letters of J. R. R. Tolkien*) are not generally sustained arguments, but passing comments situated within specific life contexts.[1] Nevertheless, a coherent picture does emerge, and in fact we shall find that Tolkien has something to say about virtually every aspect of a traditionally structured systematic theology. This is the sense in which we shall explore Tolkien as a theologian.

Tolkien is somewhat self-conscious about expressing theological opinions. While he appears to hold his views firmly, he does not often do so publicly. Two of his most significant theological writings, a letter to C. S. Lewis sharply criticizing him on divorce and marital ethics, and a lengthy apologia to a Catholic bookshop owner who calls him out on theological impropriety, are never sent.[2] But Tolkien's theology is not a background feature to his life. Even as a young man he claims religion as his moving force and foundation, along with love, patriotic duty, and nationalism.[3] Lewis writes to a friend that when he and his brother meet Charles Williams and Tolkien at the pub, "the fun is often so fast and furious that the company probably thinks we're talking bawdy when in fact we're v[ery] likely talking Theology."[4] Tolkien himself ranks his Christianity more significant than his historical context. Writing about the personal facts truly necessary to understanding his fiction, he explains that there are three tiers of importance to the facts of an author's life. After passing over lesser issues like personal foibles or moderate issues like his scholarship on language, he writes that the highest tier—those facts truly significant to understanding his work—include his birth in 1892 and experience of a pre-industrial age and, more importantly, his Christianity.[5]

Here he claims that his theology is both *the most important fact* in properly understanding his legendarium *and* clearly deducible from it. In point of fact, Tolkien comments that he will likely never write an ordered biography since such clear statement goes against his nature, which instead expresses itself about its deepest values in myths and stories.[6] As his daughter Priscilla writes, Tolkien rarely if ever spoke of dogma or doctrine intellectually or abstractly. "In fact," she asserts, "I do not think it was ever in his heart to write or speak of religion didactically: his mode was to express religious themes and moral questions through the medium of storytelling."[7]

This, and not because he seeks to preserve Middle-earth from Christian influence, is why he famously asserts, "*The Lord of the Rings* is of course a fundamentally religious and Catholic work;

unconsciously so at first, but consciously in the revision. That is why I have not put in, or have cut out, practically all references to anything like 'religion,' to cults or practices, in the imaginary world. For the religious element is absorbed into the story and the symbolism."[8] In other words, we should look for Christian theology not in the explicit elements of the tales (after all, they are set in a pre-Christian world) but in the deep structure of the story, in its metaphysics, ethics, and in the shape of its plot.

He claims that Middle-earth is meant after all to display the truth and encourage good morals in the real world, through the well-worn technique of clothing them in unfamiliar guises. After admitting that he could of course make errors, he nevertheless insists that he would have to be well and truly convinced that his fiction is harmful in itself (rather than merely misunderstood) before recanting any of it.[9] But since this is likely to be the greatest objection to the project of this book, we should devote some space to the propriety of mining Tolkien's texts theologically in the first place.

TOLKIEN: THE MONSTRANCE AND THE CRITICS

This introduction will be divided into three parts. First, in this section I will engage several objections to the propriety of the project—most importantly, whether Tolkien (or at least *The Lord of the Rings*) even ought to be read "Christianly." Next, I will explicitly lay out what I do and do not aim to accomplish in this book. Finally, I will briefly outline the methodology I have employed in reconstructing Tolkien's theology.

I have deliberately played upon Tolkien's well-known work *Beowulf: A Translation and Commentary* in titling this section.[10] Tolkien's interpreters can often fall into one of two equally unhelpful extremes.[11] On the one hand, there are those who see in Tolkien's fiction only a thin apology for Catholicism, in which the teachings of the church take center stage and other literary concerns take a backseat. We may call this the "monstrance" view. A monstrance is an ornate vessel used to publicly display an object of piety, usually the eucharistic host. This is its primary purpose; the art exists for the sake of the exhibition. For these readers, Tolkien's actual *creation* is only important insofar as it highlights the truths of the faith.

On the other hand, there are those of the "critical" school who, perhaps in reaction to the overzealous appropriation of Tolkien by the monstrance camp or perhaps out of a personal distaste for Christianity, seek to downplay the religious strands of Tolkien's thought. Seeing Tolkien's work as Christian does violence to his attempt to recapture ancient Norse, English, or other pagan myths. The essentially godless world of *The Lord of the Rings* demonstrates, to them, that Tolkien's work ought to be evaluated on primarily literary or critical grounds, rather than religious ones.

This latter point was more trenchant prior to the release of *The Silmarillion* and later materials with a more decidedly prominent theological flavor. The gods and demons of the Elder Days, despite being mythologically cast, gave the lie to Middle-earth as a naturalistic paradise. Nevertheless, the debate has continued. We shall see that the push and pull surrounding this issue crystallize many of the dangers inherent in the project of this book. They may perhaps all be gathered under the heading of "oversimplification," though in different ways. First, and most extensively, we will look at the debate over whether Middle-earth is a Christian realm. Second, we will caution against drawing too direct a link between the theology of Middle-earth and the theology of Tolkien himself. Third, we will ask whether Tolkien's constantly changing views exclude a single cohesive theological picture. Finally, we will relate the theology of Tolkien to the theology of Roman Catholicism.

CAN WE HAVE A CHRISTIAN TOLKIEN?

As previously stated, the legitimacy of an appeal to Tolkien's Christianity as a significant element in his fiction is often contested. The question here is largely moot. I am, after all, not talking about the legendarium as an isolated fact, but about the man—and the man was undoubtedly Catholic. I draw upon his fiction to illuminate his nonfictional statements and to demonstrate the way in which there is a continuity between the two. The emphasis here is on Tolkien as theologian, not on Middle-earth; this is distinct from offering yet another reading of Christian themes in *The Lord of the Rings*. But insofar as I will indeed be drawing on aspects of Middle-earth to paint the picture of Tolkien's theology, the issue must be addressed. Before we begin in earnest, we must therefore deal with the question: Why read Tolkien's fiction theologically?[12]

Literally dozens of books have touched on Tolkien's Christianity; some have made it their primary theme.[13] Often, however, writers fall prey to the criticism leveled by Drout and Wynne: "Articles on religion and Tolkien have a tendency to rely upon Christian theology as a received truth, which is no doubt true for many Christians, but exceedingly unlikely to be persuasive to scholars, Christian or non-Christian, who would like to see arguments grounded in rigorous logic."[14] Simply appealing to parallels between Aragorn and Christ, for example, will not convince anyone without argument as to why such a parallel is not merely circumstantial. Furthermore, an unreflectively Christian approach "totally ignores the vital epistemological fact that all texts must be interpreted. Finding a source merely defers the problem of interpretation; it cannot eliminate it."[15] Many scholars point out that making Tolkien into a purely Christian author writing unmixed Christian material is wrongheaded.[16] It ignores his deliberate intention to draw upon pre-Christian material in the manner of the *Beowulf* author, and reduces his stories into strings of allegories and typologies.

Perhaps the best single work to present both sides of the coin and to seek to render unto Caesar what is Caesar's is Claudio Testi's 2013 essay.[17] Again, as with all of the scholars mentioned above, Testi's focus is on whether Tolkien's legendarium can be considered a Christian work, not on Tolkien's personal theology. He presents a thesis ("Tolkien's work is Christian") and an antithesis ("Tolkien's work is pagan") and outlines the weaknesses of each. Reading Middle-earth as Christian (1) introduces truths into sub-creative reality that ought to remain in the primary world, (2) mistakes applicability for allegory and theorizes hidden meanings, (3) mistakes source for representation, (4) derives total identity from partial similarity while ignoring differences, and (5) diminishes the vastness of Tolkien's achievement.

Likewise, reading Middle-earth as pagan (1) diminishes the relevance of the texts that show the fundamental relation between Tolkien's work and Christianity, (2) considers some elements of the work as incompatible with Christianity when they are not, (3) creates contradictions between Tolkien's world and Christianity from what are only partial differences, (4) confuses historical paganism with "Tolkien" paganism, and (5) also diminishes the vastness of Tolkien's achievement.[18]

Testi synthesizes the two sides by proposing a distinction between "the plane of Nature" (that which is consciously available to the characters within the story, natural gifts) and "the plane of Grace" (that which is unknowingly available to the characters, supernatural gifts such as faith). He also distinguishes between an internal (pre-Christian) and external (Christian) viewpoint to the work.[19] Tolkien's characters live in a world that is chronologically pre-Christian but metaphysically Christian. That is, he has sub-created a fictional world in which Jesus Christ will one day become incarnate. Ultimately, Testi concludes that Tolkien is "a Christian author sub-creating a non-Christian world that is in harmony with the Revelation."[20] Middle-earth has a natural theology determined by the truths of grace. He theorizes that Tolkien's use of nature and grace within Middle-earth reflects his commitment to the theology of Thomas Aquinas, for whom this was a major principle.[21]

While very plausible, it might also be noted that the tension between natural and revealed religion was also the subject of a major essay by Cardinal Newman, Tolkien's grandfather in the faith.[22] Newman's 1833 poem "Heathenism" finds God's grace extended to non-Christians in a way that borders upon inclusivism. To this we might compare Tolkien's response to the monk Alcuin's challenge, "What has Ingeld [a pagan hero] to do with Christ?" Here Tolkien responds that Christians can find many useful and edifying things in non-Christian myths and, because of their insight into the truth of God, can in fact ponder such myths more deeply.[23]

Testi's essay has been well received. The subtleties in Tolkien's conception that he points out must be addressed by any scholar wishing to mine Christian truths from Tolkien's fiction. But Testi also demonstrates that such an attempt *can* be made, provided it is done carefully and critically.

TRUTH FROM FICTION:
THE PROBLEM OF INTERPRETATION

What of the issue of interpreting the meaning of a text or, even worse, the author's intention for a text? Can it be known? Does it matter?

Such issues have dominated literary criticism since well before Tolkien's death. For a certain group of readers, the text is a free and independent object once it leaves Tolkien's pen, and whether he did or did not intend it to reflect his theology is irrelevant; what matters is what readers (and communities of readers) do with the text today. Standard practice in literary criticism nowadays further dictates that an author can be mistaken in interpreting her own text, ignorant of the subconscious impulses that actually shape her work. Unfortunately, space does not permit a defense of the now controversial view that an author's intent ought to be, well, authoritative. For a theological defense of authorial intent and meaning, see Kevin J. Vanhoozer, *Is There a Meaning in This Text?*[24] Vanhoozer's hermeneutical principles will implicitly undergird much of my own.

Certain principles of interpretation are more directly relevant. We must, for instance, distinguish between narrator and author, between what is true in Middle-earth and what is true in the primary world. Tolkien acts at times as an unreliable narrator. What Elves or Men or even Valar think are not necessarily what Tolkien thinks. His creations have independent belief systems, and not all are reliable, as he points out.[25] Despite the fact that Middle-earth was intended by Tolkien to be our own earth in the distant and mythical past, the metaphysical apparatus that Tolkien created does not therefore completely correspond with what Tolkien believed about primary reality. Many of the internal explanations he gives for elements within his work are retroactive, outside-the-text justifications for inconsistencies. Different manuscripts become different textual traditions. Certain stories may be told from a human perspective or from an Elvish perspective.[26]

Tolkien explicitly denies specific metaphysical principles of Middle-earth, like a pre-creational fall of angels or Elvish reincarnation, as elements of his real-world theology.[27] We should therefore be cognizant that some differences may also exist unacknowledged. But overall, while he recognizes the freedom of a sub-creator to differ from the ways in which God operates in the primary world, he also intends that his depiction should be overall in line with it. He does claim that his fiction corresponds to Christian belief.[28]

What, though, of Tolkien's insistence that he is neither theologian nor preacher and that he is unqualified to speak theologically? He writes, for example, to W. H. Auden that he is not a sufficient enough theologian to assert whether his Orcs are heretical and that he feels no obligation to fit his world into formal Christian theology. He states elsewhere that his tale is built on religious ideas but does not mention them explicitly nor preach them since he is not fitted for theological inquiry.[29] At the same time, we have already seen that he is not at all reticent to defend his own views (informally, at least) and, immediately before the above passage, he claims that Middle-earth is theologically less dissonant from reality than many consider to be the truth.[30] Elsewhere, he admits that he is comforted by the fact that more learned theologians have given their approval to his stories.[31] To Peter Hastings, he strenuously rebuts the charge of bad theology by appealing to a writer's freedom. Perhaps in the primary world, he answers; but imagination can still reveal truth.[32] We can conclude, then, that while Tolkien claims no formal or professional theological training, he is a layman informed and opinionated enough to make theological judgments and implement them within his writing.

Not all ostensible theological analogues are valid. We should separate what is intended from what is manufactured by bad readers. Some would argue that it is precisely the *unconscious* elements of the work that reveal the most about the author, since such elements must by definition escape the desire for control with which the author dominates his text. Perhaps. But when Tolkien shuts down reading Tom Bombadil as Yahweh just because Goldberry says "He is," or denies any similarity between Moria and the Moriah on which Abraham begins the sacrifice of Isaac, we too should be cautious about seeing connections that are not truly there.[33]

Nevertheless, Tolkien sees his fiction as intrinsically theological, an echo of divine creation.[34] As Clyde S. Kilby reports, "When I raised the question of motive, Professor Tolkien said simply 'I am a Christian and of course what I write will be from that essential viewpoint.' "[35] He accepts (and intends!) theological readings and echoes when they are warranted by the text. *Lembas* is a prime example, as is the intercessory role of Galadriel or the threefold Christlike office of Gandalf, Aragorn, and Frodo.[36] In this book, however, Tolkien's fiction plays only one role. Other volumes have explored the theology latent in the legendarium itself; I am more interested in Tolkien's theology as a whole, and only consequently with how he illustrates this in his stories.

TOLKIEN: EARLY AND LATE

To the problem of interpretation we must add the problem of change. As anyone who has delved into the massive multivolume *History of Middle-earth* has realized, Tolkien's creative impulses leaned toward the protean. While some elements of the legendarium appeared in the very first versions and remained until the end, other elements (especially names) could shift from the top of a page to the bottom. How then is it possible to construct a single, coherent picture of Tolkien's theology? Should we not, as Christopher Tolkien did with his father's manuscripts, be forced to lay out Tolkien's thought in various stages of progression? In what sense is this project a compression and elision, a static presentation of a constantly evolving mind?

In one sense, this concern is of course completely valid. Tolkien's views on what a sub-creator may appropriately undertake altered over the course of his life. In *The Book of Lost Tales*, for instance, has the-Valar much more indebted to pagan mythologies. They have children; Morgoth sires a balrog son with an ogress. Ungoliant is an uncreated personification of Night. And the world begins as flat before being rounded at the fall of Númenor. By contrast, as Tolkien seeks to draw his sub-creation more into line with both Christian orthodoxy and the notion that Middle-earth is our own world, the idea that angels can have children drops away. Ungoliant is merely a rebel angel like Morgoth, not an independently existing evil. And if the Elves learn their astronomy from angels, they must have known the world was spherical from the beginning. If Middle-earth is our own world in a mythical past, then it must have the same metaphysical and cosmo-logical history.

Nevertheless, the cast of his thought had already in large part been set by the time of the *Lost Tales,* so that while Tolkien's *fiction* may have been in constant flux, his own view of the world, which to greater or lesser degrees underlies that fiction, remained relatively constant. He cites specifically his reverence for the Eucharist, for instance, as one he has felt for his whole life.[37] His creation myth, written as a young man, remained virtually untouched until his death. As such, though I take effort to clarify Tolkien's developing views, and prioritize later writing over earlier, the idea that there can be no overarching con-sistency or unity at all is ill-founded.

MIDDLE-EARTH OR THE MAGISTERIUM?

If one asked Tolkien, as an ardent Roman Catholic, to outline his the-ology, he might simply point to the Catechism. Tolkien desired to be in line with the Magisterium—that is, with the official and divinely

bestowed teaching authority of the church. He never made any indication that he intended to depart from the doctrines and creeds of the
church, so in what sense can Tolkien have a theology distinct from,
say, the theology outlined in the Catechism or in a papal encyclical?
Why is a book on Tolkien's theology not simply a book on Roman
Catholic theology?

As any well-versed reader knows, being a Christian (even a
Catholic one) does not entail mindless adherence to a static set of
rules; rather, it entails a living and active engagement with a vibrant
deposit of faith and practice.[38] While there is indeed a faith delivered
once and for all to the saints, this faith is in itself very much akin to
one of Tolkien's maps of Middle-earth. Certain boundaries and contours are definitively drawn, and yet there exist many spaces in which
readers can imaginatively explore and create their own landscapes.
We do not restrict ourselves merely to church teachings in interpreting
Tolkien's theology for the same reason Catholics today do not simply
content themselves with such documents. Alongside the Catechism
comes the work of Newman, Ratzinger, de Lubac, and von Balthasar.
Every thinker has a different contribution to make to the intellectual
life of the church, which does not contradict or replace doctrine but
complements and reflects it.

Theology is the truth of God applied to life—and not to life in the
abstract, but to concrete and specific problems and contexts. Tolkien,
living as he did within one of the most tumultuous times in the last
several hundred years, and as an idiosyncratic and complex scholar
of the highest caliber, used the tools provided for him by his faith to
construct a grand answer to the problems, concerns, and opportunities of his time and place. And while very many of his contributions
have been quite beneficially explored by others, he deserves a space
in which his unique vision of theology can be examined.

At the same time, Tolkien would be the first to affirm that where he might depart from the boundaries of theological orthodoxy, he ought to be marked and warned rather than followed. This book, though intended to be descriptive and not evaluative, is also not a hagiography. There are areas in which, at least in the extant writings to which we have access, Tolkien may fall short of the robust articulation of doctrine offered by the faith. This in itself requires two caveats. First, as we noted above, Tolkien never attempted to set out a systematic theology, so we cannot fault him for not hitting all the headings. To do so would be to misunderstand and distort him. Second, and as a consequence of the former point, to equate Tolkien's beliefs to Tolkien's written work would be misguided. To say, for example, that Tolkien wrote little about the authority of Scripture does not demonstrate in the slightest what his beliefs on that score may have been. It only demonstrates what he wrote about. Added to this, we should remember that not even all of Tolkien's writings have been made publicly available.

As such, readers should be mindful that this book is neither a systematic theology in itself, nor a completely accurate interpretation of Tolkien's private theology. It is only what it can be: an orderly presentation of Tolkien's published thoughts on various theological subjects. I have found that such a presentation has not so far been provided and that interested seekers must piece together many disparate resources in order to gain a picture of Tolkien's contribution to Christian thought. This brings us to the scope of the current project.

THE SCOPE AND USE OF THIS BOOK

Of the making of books on Tolkien there is no end. Many of them cover the same ground from slightly different angles. This book seeks to fill a specific niche that has so far been neglected in the scholarship, and it does not attempt to stray beyond that niche into a broader engagement with the field as a whole. *Reader, take note!* The fact that I leave aside much that was so central to Tolkien's thought must not be passed over. In seeking to understand the man, one must understand his relation to English history and literature, to linguistics and philology, to fantasy and myth, and much more. The very fact that Tom Shippey has not so far appeared in the footnotes should be evidence enough of this. This book will not, except when relevant, dip into any of these fields. I do not make any pretense at a comprehensive intellectual survey of Tolkien's thought. I do not even enter fully into the very fruitful discussions surrounding Tolkien and ethics or philosophy, despite their obvious connection to Tolkien's Christianity. This book is about Tolkien's theology—that is, about what Tolkien wrote regarding God, Jesus Christ, the church, and the other concomitant points that directly relate to God's relationship to his world.

A brief list, then, of what this book does not claim to do: This book is not a work of literary criticism, though literary criticism occurs. This book does not seek to evaluate or weigh the objective truth of Tolkien's theological claims, apart from noting where he departs from orthodox versions of them. This book does not trace sources, though it does sometimes comment on Tolkien's relation to other theological figures like Newman or Thomas Aquinas. This book does not claim that *The Lord of the Rings* or any other work in the legendarium is a Christian text, though it does claim that Tolkien's theology is apparent and many times even explicit in them. This book does not deny influences from other religious or cultural traditions, whether past or present; I am merely not examining them here. This book does not enter extensively into discussion of secondary literature or scholarly debates on Tolkien except when necessary. I have chosen instead to present Tolkien's theology as much as possible in his own words, which means engaging primarily with the primary texts.

As a result, the book may be profitably read from cover to cover, but it can also be used as a reference work and consulted at will on specific subjects. Each chapter and section, by its nature, covers pretty much exhaustively any citations in Tolkien's writings to that particular subject, and so it can act as a jumping-off point for further research on any element of Tolkien's theology. I also append a "Further Reading" section at the end of each chapter, with a selection of some (by no means all) secondary literature on the subject. I do not include relevant entries in the standard Tolkien reference works such as those by Drout, Hammond, and Scull. The works in these sections do not necessarily represent my views on the subject but are rather important or sustained engagements with the topic under discussion with which anyone seeking further information should be familiar. More circumscribed secondary sources are mentioned in footnotes.

METHODOLOGY

As I have already intimated, creating a cohesive, static, and unified picture of Tolkien's theology from the rapidly developing and widely disparate strands of his work requires explicit ground rules. Not all of Tolkien's works can be set on the same level, nor can truth be drawn from every document in the same way. Other Tolkien scholars may disagree with the picture I believe emerges, and that is their right, since in any such undertaking some level of personal interpretation is inescapable. I do, however, believe that the method here employed is a reasonable one.

I give more weight to Tolkien's nonfiction, and especially to his letters, than to his fiction. I allow the nonfictional writing to shape and interpret the fictional. The *Letters* receive pride of place, not only because in these Tolkien is more explicit than anywhere else about his theological commitments but because many of them are unguarded and personal. The *Letters* also provide authorial guides to the proper theological interpretations of much of his fictional world.[39] Some fiction, especially "Leaf by Niggle," I have given a more dominant role; the work is intensely autobiographical and thus merits being read as such.

I have given more weight to later works than to earlier ones, especially in the texts of the legendarium, since any thinker develops and refines their thought over time and the standard practice in historical theology is to consider the mature version of a thinker the more authoritative one. But as Christopher Tolkien notes, simply because his father did not retain elements of his earlier writings in later revisions does not entail their rejection, and those ideas may have remained as implicit elements in Tolkien's mind.[40] I have in general followed the principle that what is not explicitly rejected or replaced is implicitly maintained.

As Tolkien drafted and revisited his stories, he changed many elements. But much also remained the same. I do not feel bound to cite every variation from every parallel passage. On the other hand, sometimes even passages that have been struck out or altered can give insight. One need not restrict an examination to its final form. Clearly, Tolkien rejected these elements for some reason, but they remain evidence of his thought processes.

At places where the primary evidence has seemed thin, I have permitted myself to consult works of Roman Catholic theology roughly contemporary with Tolkien and especially aligned with the thought of John Henry Newman, that famous English Catholic who, indirectly, exerted considerable influence upon Tolkien's life.[41] I have tried to keep this to a minimum and, where such supplements are introduced, they are explicitly noted. Influence does not guarantee assent.

In the same vein, Tolkien undertook many translation projects throughout his career, virtually all of which are either directly theological (e.g., *Exodus, Pearl*) or theologically situated (*Gawain and the Green Knight, Beowulf*). Obviously, theological statements from these poets need not constitute Tolkien's own theological beliefs. I have therefore only borrowed from such texts when it seems fairly certain that Tolkien personally resonates with them (as, for example, his discussion of penance in *Gawain*). At the same time, much work could be done here. Why did he choose these particular texts? Not all were part of the Oxford curriculum. What of his choices in translating them? All translation is interpretation. But I am not a scholar of Old English and cannot comment on how an idiosyncratic rendering might illuminate Tolkien's theological understanding. Surely these texts are an influence on Tolkien's theology, but it is uncertain how.

Finally, this work is meant to be descriptive. I present Tolkien's views by and large without comment or evaluation, save for the exceptions noted above. I am a Protestant, and there are areas of Tolkien's theology with which I personally disagree. There are areas with which many Roman Catholics might disagree. Right or wrong, good or bad, weak or strong do not enter in here. I have sought only to set out as accurately as possible *what Tolkien thought*, without letting my or other people's views intrude upon the matter. As to authorial voice, it should be understood that any straightforward assertorial statements are from Tolkien's perspective, unless clearly indicated otherwise. The discussions that take place in the footnotes, in which I mostly engage with secondary literature, should be understood to be in my own voice.

Such are the preliminary issues we must address. If this task succeeds, then to the long litany of Tolkien's titles—twentieth-century English Catholic, survivor of two world wars, father, Oxford professor, lover of words, medievalist, husband, humorist, author—we shall feel entitled to add one more: theologian. Rather than being an unreflective receiver of Christian tradition, Tolkien absorbed and added to that tradition, becoming an original thinker with things to say in his own right. Tolkien, ever one for ancestry, might now be able to say of those fathers of the faith who preceded him what King Théoden of Rohan said after a battle well fought: "In their mighty company I shall not now be ashamed."[42]

I

GOD

Theology is the study of God and all things in relation to God, so it is fitting that our study of Tolkien's theology begins with the doctrine of God proper. But, before moving into these topics, it is usual to address the issue of the knowledge of God—that is, whether and how humans can know him.

THE KNOWLEDGE OF GOD

Within this section we include the questions of whether God exists, whether his existence can be demonstrated, and whether his existence is discoverable apart from the special revelation in Scripture and in Jesus Christ.

Tolkien does engage with the question of God's existence, but not for any doubt as to its answer.[1] Instead, he argues that the human mind looks to the universe and asks how it came to be. The appearance of design and pattern shifts the "how" to "why." But to him, such a question about purposes and motives can only be answered by appeal to a mind.[2] We are almost immediately, therefore, drawn to the question of God's existence by our contemplation of the universe around us. If one does not believe in a personal Creator God—a Mind"who has made ours and from which our own thought processes are derived—it is no use asking about a purpose for life. There is nobody there to answer you. The best one could do is accept the brute fact of existence.[3]

But if this is the case, and in fact the gods do not exist at all, then we invented them, and their stories need explanations. The most common is that ancient humans ascribed personalities to natural phenomena that inspired awe and wonder. If all we have, then, are stories arrayed around objects such as stars and waterfalls, it remains the case that they can only be given personal significance by a person.[4] So those personal figures that adorn the myths of every culture do not simply appear, but they originate from universal human impulses. This was the crux of the famous debate between Tolkien and C. S. Lewis on Addison's Walk. Lewis, at that time an ardent atheist, believed myths to be "lies breathed through silver."[5] Not so, said Tolkien. This universal impulse toward mythmaking and the construction of gods and heroes instead illuminates the existence of the true God. In the poem he writes to Lewis to epitomize his argument, he declares that our hearts draw wisdom from God and still reflect him, despite our simple wish-fulfillments and attempts to escape the dull materialist universe. Whence did the wish we want fulfilled come, and why? Whence came our notion of beauty and ugliness, or our imaginative desires?[6] Why, if materialism is truly the way things are, do we feel such a need for things to be otherwise—to be good and beautiful and personal as well? Yes, the gods may derive their glory from nature, but it was human beings who saw glory in nature in the first place and were able to abstract it from mere existence. This mental element, this intimation of divinity, comes not from the visible world but from the invisible and supernatural one.[7] So it remains the case that, even if humans worship false gods and construct false mythologies, something higher about ultimate truth sometimes shines through these mythologies.

Tolkien, an avid disciple of the older myths and tales, refuses to believe that they are simple fabrications devoid of deeper meaning; he also refuses to believe that one must simply abandon myth in favor of Christianity. Christianity is rather the fulfillment of myth—the True Myth. In the well-told tale, the human being glimpses divinity—which Tolkien defines as not only the possession of power but the *right* to such power, and to worship. In fact, says Tolkien, this is a glimpse of religion as such.[8] The great themes of sacrifice, heroism, love, and death affect us on a fundamental level because we are fundamentally storied creatures. We make according to the laws of our own making, Tolkien tells Lewis.[9] The story of the resurrection affects us so deeply because it bears all the hallmarks of both truth and mythology. Because its source is God, the supreme Author and Artist, this myth is actually true in the real world under the sun.[10] This is not surprising. Man, as storytellers, ought to be redeemed by a moving story; such a situation is most fitting to his nature.[11] Perhaps myth and religion, far from becoming slowly entangled with each other, were instead once the same thing, and only now begin to heal their deep fracture.[12] In what Tolkien calls the "Primary Miracle" of the resurrection (and in all other miracles) we can see not simply the truth that underlies the apparent vicissitudes of fate, but also a glimpse of light through the cracks of the visible universe.[13]

Sometimes, though, the knowledge of God is akin more to an immediate conviction than a process of reasoning. Tolkien describes the experience of once being bowled over with the obviousness of Christianity while riding his bicycle. Despite the sudden clarity of rational conviction, he could not reproduce a chain of argumentation. He theorizes that this may be due to a direct apprehension by the mind, standing momentarily outside of time. One perceives the truth apart from the sequential form of argumentation we must adopt in our temporality.[14]

However one is convinced, the train of reasoning must stop with God himself. To answer otherwise would require a complete knowledge of God, something patently impossible.[15] We cannot answer why God decided to create humanity, for example.[16] But despite being unable to go further back than God's own will, we still have an answer to the meaning of life: God himself. According to Tolkien, the chief purpose of life is to increase our knowledge of God as much as possible, according to our individual capacities, and in turn to respond to this knowledge with praise and thanksgiving.[17]

MIDDLE-EARTH AS MONOTHEISTIC WORLD

Tolkien engaged more extensively with the question of the knowledge of God outside of the church and the Bible. Theologians, working from the early chapters of Paul's Epistle to the Romans, have held that all people possess a basic intuitive knowledge of God, though this knowledge is often suppressed by sin and self-deception. This "natural" (from nature alone) theology may demonstrate God's existence, power, and rulership over the world, but it cannot offer salvation. This requires a special grace of God over and above the common grace given to all humankind. Tolkien, too, separates God's general revelation in nature and a special revelation addressed both to universal humanity and to specific individuals.[18] His views on the knowledge of God in the primal state of humanity, apart from the special revelation given in Scripture, may be gleaned from his fiction. He is very clear that Middle-earth is a monotheistic world in which the knowledge of God is limited to what can be gleaned by this natural theology.[19]

The decent and wholesome society of the Shire is based on a sort of natural law, and hobbits are examples of such natural philosophy and theology, Tolkien writes.[20] God is known by the enlightened and occupies a central place in history but has no organized religion, worship, or holy site. Tolkien's monotheists deny worship to any creature and especially to the devil, but they have not advanced to any positive faith.[21] The fact that only the supreme God Eru is worthy of worship, and monotheism is seen as the default state of humankind, is an insight that corresponds to the accounts in Genesis and Romans but which conflicts with much of modern anthropology and sociology.[22] The standard tale has been that humans rose from a primitive superstitious animism and a multiplicity of gods into philosophical monotheism. Tolkien, when given free rein to invent a history, adopts the biblical view instead. Here, the true knowledge of God is attained immediately, and there is rather a fall away from true worship into idolatry and polytheism. "Good pagans" might retain a sense of the ultimacy of God but, due to their very reverence, remain distant from him and eventually succumb to the temptation to worship more visible powers as false gods.[23]

THE BEING OF GOD

Tolkien's God is the supreme Being, which is to say that he is the only one to whom the term "Being" can be adequately and unreservedly applied. God has no cause or dependency but instead creates and sustains all other things. This is called by theologians the *aseity* of God, from the Latin *a se*, meaning "of itself." All other things depend on something else in order to exist, whether on their maker to bring them into existence, on their environment to sustain them, or on time to continue to endure. But God stands before all other makers, worlds, and times. At the back of everything is the single, ultimate fact of God. He is the "Prime Being."[24] Tolkien even notes that the Elvish word for "exist" does not properly apply to God, since one must distinguish the Creator's mode of existence from his creation's.[25]

God is so fundamental that of himself he can simply assert, "I AM THAT I AM" (Exod 3:14). When God identifies himself, he speaks in the first person, indicating his absolute oneness.[26] "The One" is the primary name of God in the legendarium. The oneness of God requires no special revelation but can be known to all. God *must* be one, not many, by definition. The old gods like Zeus and Odin show themselves not to have merited the term "God" because they lack this absolute supremacy.[27] Only One can be truly above all.

This self-naming of God demonstrates two further points. First, God is transcendent. He needs no predicate—he simply is. He is the only being without limits of any kind.[28] God's transcendence of space is called his spirituality, while his transcendence of time is called his eternity.[29] One can only dimly perceive what it might mean for God to exist completely *apart* from all things, including space and time; this perception is most often expressed by saying that God is *beyond* the world, with no physical or localized manifestation or presence within creation.[30] Since humans are limited by space and time, the beyondness in which God exists can be symbolically represented as heaven.[31] But God is not only apart from space and time; he is its ruler.[32] No authority or power can constrain or compass God, for he was there before them and made them.[33] The God who is neither in the world nor of the world has brought it forth out of love.[34]

Second, God's self-naming demonstrates that he is a person, an "I" and not an "it." We can face God, encounter him personally, as souls with free will.[35] Our relations to this person cannot be reduced to a relation with a mere object. As a person, God relates to each of his creatures in a unique and distinct way which can be pre-linguistic and non-cognitive. Tolkien insists that there is a fundamental distinction between "what-ness" and "who-ness" that can often be ignored. What-ness derives from webs of relationships, usually implying states of affairs in the world, while who-ness—personhood—is a naked fact, unique but inexpressible. It is so ontologically basic that in order to be articulated, personhood must borrow analogous language from (and thus confuse itself with) objecthood. And yet to say of my friend that "he is," conceived as a bare description of being, still does not approach the mystery of "I AM."[36] Our relationship to the personhood of God is thus also distinct from our relationship to other finite creatures.

This is because the transcendent and utterly unique God is, so to speak, on another level of being than his creatures.[37] While all being derives from him, he himself is derived from nothing. For Tolkien there is indeed a hierarchy of being, one in which all of God's creatures exist in a secondary and subordinate mode.[38] Unsurprisingly, Tolkien uses a literary analogy: God, as the author of reality, sits above and apart from it as the author of a story does.[39] God is more real than his creatures, just like an author is more real than his characters. They derive whatever existence they have from him. The difference in reality between ourselves and God is like the difference between an imagined world and the real world. But God actually brings his story *into* actuality, while remaining super-actual.

This distinction between the prime level of Being (God) and our level is known in theology as the archetype/ectype distinction. God is the archetype or universal model of all particular things, much like the platonic ideals stand behind their concrete instantiations. Rather than finding ultimate meaning in this level of reality, therefore, we each point upward toward the universal font of meaning that is God. For Tolkien, each person is an allegory embodying universal truth and everlasting life in the guise of particularity.[40]

God is the maker of all things, in a genuine sense.[41] He did not merely form, rearrange, or stitch together preexistent materials, but he truly brought new things into being from nothing through his thought and will alone.[42] God bestows upon the world a real existence, though this existence derives from God rather than itself.[43] God accomplishes this by *sharing* being with the world. This does not mean that the world is God or that God and the world form some sort of unity. Rather, Tolkien draws again upon what he calls the mystery of authorship. An author at the same time stands outside of his work while also indwelling it. But the work exists on a lesser plane than the author does and depends upon the author for its own existence.[44]

The whole world is not only created but also upheld by the word of God.[45] This ineffable principle of life is wholly and completely derived from the One, and its bringing forth is his sole prerogative.[46] Nor can creatures that now exist think themselves to be independent from their source of being: the entire world's continued existence may be likened to a burning fire at the heart of things, whose sole source and tender is the Lord.[47] He stands in an intimate relationship to his creation. He loves it, and it brings him joy.[48] He supports and nourishes us from behind, as it were.[49] For Tolkien, he can thus truly be called "All-Father,"[50] sanctifying that pagan title of Odin.

The world does not, however, merely exist, but it was created toward a specific purpose and end.[51] God, therefore, may also be thought of as a maker in the sense that he is a fashioner of artistic and creative work meant to communicate meaning.[52] As the originator of "Primary Art"—that is, of reality—God also intermediately authors the sub-creative imaginative works of his creatures.[53] Various creatures may possess fuller or more limited access to the mind of God in his purposes as author—for example, pre-Christian human beings might possess virtually no knowledge of God's story, while the higher angels might possess a great deal of it.[54] Nevertheless, the Writer of this story is not one of us, and he keeps his own counsel.[55] No creature can know the full extent of God's creative purpose, though we can know that creative work is a fundamental aspect of God's being.

THE TRINITY

The oneness of God's being is an element of natural theology. It requires no special revelation from God to discern but can be worked out from philosophical or observational principles. But the equally fundamental threeness of God cannot be so known. It requires special revelation. It could not have been known unless God himself were to reveal it. Tolkien realizes this. This is why God is only referred to as the One in the pre-Christian Middle-earth, and why the hints of Eru's activity within Middle-earth are so vague. The Trinity of God is a distinctly Christian concept, which cannot appear explicitly in Middle-earth, though Middle-earth must be made consistent with it. The Valar, for example, are presented as angelic powers rather than gods with the explicit purpose of harmonizing the legendarium with the doctrine of the Trinity.[56] This doctrine states that there is only one God, and that this God exists as three persons: Father, Son, and Holy Spirit. Each is fully God, and each is not identical to the other, and yet there are not three Gods but one.

Tolkien's own remarks on the doctrine of the Trinity are quite limited.[57] He only mentions the Trinity as such in four places, the first of which is merely that mentioned above in Letter 131. The second occurs in *Morgoth's Ring*. In his commentary on the story "The Debate of Finrod and Andreth," Tolkien describes the Elf lord Finrod's theological beliefs. After discovering that Men believe the One will enter into creation, Finrod reasons that, like an author, God will have to be both inside and outside of creation. As such, God would exist in two distinct modes while remaining "The One."[58] Once again, Tolkien foregrounds the simultaneous transcendence and immanence of God, but here he appeals to it to demonstrate philosophically that while God is one, he is one in a totally unique way. God's triunity does not compromise his oneness.

We find a more extended engagement in the allegorical and autobiographical short story "Leaf by Niggle" (written 1938–1939). Here, Tolkien features two Voices thought by the main character Niggle to be "a Medical Board, or perhaps a Court of Inquiry." This, along with the capitalization, indicates that the figures have great authority and knowledge.[59] One can presumably identify these as the Father and the Son, though they are nowhere so named.[60] The Spirit is totally absent. The first Voice is very severe and strict, fitting for a figure heavily associated in the popular consciousness with the Old Testament law and divine wrath such as God the Father. The second Voice is gentle without softness, conveys authority, seems exceedingly generous, and is simultaneously hopeful and sad.[61] This is an apt description of the Son Jesus who, while letting the little children come to him, nevertheless eschews all sappiness and takes the problem of sin and evil seriously. The paradox of hopeful sadness signifies Christ's acknowledgement of the present state of the world and his certainty of its mending.

The two Voices debate whether Niggle can be ascribed some virtue for helping his neighbor Parish without expectation of reward. The Son places great importance on Niggle's final sacrifice for Parish—resulting in his death—while the Father disagrees. "But," he remarks, "you have the last word. It is your task, of course, to put the best interpretation on the facts." This is a tonally appropriate way to assert that the role of the Son is to dispense grace, mercy, and forgiveness, and perhaps a reference to John 5:22. Since the Son's word is here taken as final, Tolkien here can also be seen to elevate mercy and gospel over judgment and law. After Niggle is caught eavesdropping, the two Voices are pleased to find that Niggle inquires after Parish's well-being. This convinces the first Voice that Niggle is ready to leave purgatory.

While one cannot forget the fictional nature of this debate, the highly autobiographical and transparent nature of the rest of the text should suggest that this exchange is a rough parallel to Tolkien's actual views. While he surely did not believe the Father and Son might exchange bourgeois remarks in the hallway, his characterizations of the Son as gentle but authoritative and the Father as stern and condemning are harder to dismiss. If this is the case, then Tolkien either here departs from traditional orthodoxy or, much more likely, displays mistaken understanding of the basics of Trinitarian doctrine. This would not be at all surprising—most laypeople have a remarkable unfamiliarity on this point. The image of the wrathful God of the Old Testament giving way to the loving Christ of the New Testament is a common, if ill-informed, one.

Tolkien has a proper view in this at least: he depicts the Father and Son as two full persons (in "Niggle," they are able to hold conversation with one another and can be distinguished). But in truth there can be no debate or disagreement. *Opera trinitatis ad extra indivisa sunt* (all the external operations of the Trinity are indivisibly united), the church would remind Professor Tolkien. This means that the Father and the Son never have two different opinions on things, nor does one person engage in an activity in the world without the other two. Neither is there a tension between law and gospel within the Trinity. There is no severe Father and merciful Son. It is the Father, for example, who sends the Son to save sinners (e.g., John 5:24). Likewise, it is the Son who judges the world (e.g., John 5:22).

The third mention of the Trinity occurs in a 1944 letter to Tolkien's son Christopher: he relates a mystical experience in which, sitting in church, he has a strong impression of the light of God as a guardian angel.[62] He muses whether the angel's existence as the personalized attention of God may not be a finite reflection of infinite truth—namely, that the love of the two infinite and equal persons, Father and Son, is itself a person. This third person is the Holy Spirit, and the idea that the Spirit exists as the love between Father and Son can be traced back to St. Augustine and has exercised a considerable influence on the history of Western theology.[63] Thomas Aquinas affirms it, as does Cardinal Newman, who writes, "He Himself … is the Eternal Love whereby the Father and the Son have dwelt in each other."[64] But this is not an entry-level statement of Trinitarian theology, and it indicates that either Tolkien is quite familiar with the tradition or was at least exposed to some teaching about this.

Immediately after Tolkien's statement about the Spirit above, he confesses to seeing his son's face shining in the light of God, though turned away from it as all our faces are. But, he says, we can see this light as it falls on the faces of others we love.[65] This image—Tolkien, sitting in a church filled with the sunlight that slants in through the windows—prompts not only his reflection on the light of God but also his analogy to the Spirit. In the same sermon quoted above, Newman proclaims of the Spirit that "He pervades us … *as light pervades a building.*"[66] Here Tolkien not only draws on Newman but strikingly illustrates a profound idea: all of us, turned away from God because of sin and the fall, may not be able to look directly into the light of God's face, but we can nevertheless see the presence of the Spirit of God indirectly in our love for one another, just as we might not face the source of the sunlight but see it filling the room. The community as illuminated by the Spirit is an avenue through which God manifests himself.

In this same passage, Tolkien not only affirms the full and concrete personhood of the Holy Spirit, but the infinity and equality of all three persons of the Trinity. Such comments show that he is by no means unacquainted with basic Trinitarian doctrine, and indeed this entire passage indicates that Tolkien might have had a well-informed view of the Trinity that belies the paucity of recorded mentions. His parenthetical aside here is not quite pertinent to the conversation, but he feels comfortable enough to make it. This stands in marked conflict with the apparent ignorance of the "Niggle" passage. A few things may explain this difference. Tolkien may have developed in this area in the five years between the two statements. Alternatively, "Niggle" could be less autobiographical here than it at first appears. Finally, it could be that Tolkien's comment about the Spirit was an anomaly—something he overheard in a sermon and remembered—and the doctrine remained generally foreign to him. Regardless, we do not have enough resources to make an informed judgment.

When we turn to examine each person of the Trinity individually, we see at once that Tolkien, as mentioned above, refers to God as "the One" (Eru) and "All-Father" (Ilúvatar) within the legendarium. Since Middle-earth is by and large a monotheistic world guided only by natural theology,[67] the term "All-Father" could here be taken to refer to the Trinity as such, God considered in his oneness, or to the special role of God the Father as "fount of deity." Augustine, Thomas, and Newman, who argued for the Spirit's role as the love between Father and Son, also affirm that "the Father is the Principle of the whole Deity."[68] But this is hardly firm evidence. In any case, the study of God the Father is a neglected area even in advanced theological study and lacks even a technical name.[69]

We shall discuss the Son in depth in chapter 9, so we will restrict ourselves here to those characteristics of the Son that have already appeared in "Leaf by Niggle." Here, the Son displays mercy with justice, generosity, and authority. Besides being biblical, these are also key markers of the good king in Old English culture. Compare *Beowulf*'s well-known kenning, "ring-giver," signifying generosity, or the last lines in Tolkien's translation of the poem: "He was ever of the kings of earth of men most generous and to men most gracious, to his people most tender and for praise most eager."[70] Here in *Beowulf*, Tolkien relates "that prime virtue of Northern kings, generosity," while in "Niggle" he writes, "Niggle thought that he had never heard anything so generous as that Voice. It made Gentle Treatment sound like a load of rich gifts, and a summons to a King's feast."[71] Jesus, the Son of God who became the Son of Man, is here clearly meant to recall the archetypal good king. Since the Son is theologically portrayed as the ruler of creation and of the human race in particular, we can assume that Tolkien too sees the Second Person of the Trinity as specially concerned with the rulership of creation.[72]

THE SECRET FIRE: THE HOLY SPIRIT?

The Third Person of the Trinity, absent in explicit form from "Niggle," is also virtually absent in Middle-earth, at least as a person.[73] While the Holy Spirit does appear as constitutive of the triunity of God in the passages mentioned above, Tolkien does not seem to have had as extensive a vision of the Spirit's work in the world as he does for the Father and Son. Some scholars, following the apparently straightforward report of Clyde S. Kilby, identify the "Secret Fire" or the "Flame Imperishable" as the direct fictional equivalent of the Holy Spirit. Kilby writes, "Professor Tolkien talked to me at some length about the use of the word 'holy' in *The Silmarillion*. Very specifically he told me that the 'Secret Fire sent to burn at the heart of the World' in the beginning was the Holy Spirit."[74] Just as Eru is actually the Christian God and no mere typology, and just as in "The Debate of Finrod and Andreth" Tolkien creates space for the actual incarnation of Christ in the future of Middle-earth, so too the Flame Imperishable is said to actually be the Holy Spirit, not a symbolic prefigurement. This view seemed to find confirmation when Tolkien's early Elvish lexicon was published in 1998, in which a word for ritual fire is also "A mystic name identified with the Holy Ghost."[75] But this does not specifically mention the term "Secret Fire."

Additionally, Newman speaks of the Spirit in strikingly similar language: the Spirit is "the secret Presence of God within the Creation: a source of life amid the chaos, bringing out into form and order what was at first shapeless and void, and the voice of Truth in the hearts of all rational beings, tuning them into harmony with the intimations of God's Law ... Hence He is especially called the 'life-giving' Spirit; being (as it were) the Soul of universal nature, the Strength of man and beast, the Guide of faith."[76] This idea that the Spirit is the giver of life receives not only biblical warrant but pride of place in the pneumatology of the Nicene Creed.

But the situation is immediately complicated by an examination of Tolkien's *use* of the Secret Fire in the legendarium. Most famously, Gandalf calls himself a "servant of the Secret Fire," but while one might suppose service is only rendered to a person, this is not necessarily true—one could be a servant of justice, for example, or of the crown.[77] God is said to have kindled his creatures with the Flame, the life-giving Fire.[78] After the Valar have sung a symphonic vision of creation, God tells them that he will send the Flame Imperishable into the void in order to give being to their thoughts.[79] So the "Secret Fire is sent to burn at the heart" of creation.[80] At the final consummation, God will again give the Secret Fire to the thoughts of the singers in the divine Music.[81] It is said that Melkor sought after the Flame but could not find it, since it is with God.[82]

The greatest Elvish craftsman, Fëanor, is said to have "a secret fire" within him.[83] After his prideful rebellion and subsequent curse, he proclaims that God may have set within him a fire greater than his enemies know.[84] Is this then the same fire as the Secret Fire discussed above? Fëanor could simply be making a pun on his own name ("spirit of fire"), but then why introduce reference to God? And in fact there are many other references to the fire of the spirit, the most significant of which is the discussion of home, fire, and "Dweller" in "The Debate of Finrod and Andreth." Here, too, the fire relates to the life-principle or spirit, as distinct from the home (body) or the "Dweller" (soul, personal agent).[85]

In speaking about the incarnation and the indwelling of God within the world, Tolkien himself says such an indwelling is glimpsed in the mention of the "Flame Imperishable," which Tolkien says appears to mean the creative activity of God. But here he emphasizes the *disanalogy* of the presence of the flame within the world to the bodily presence of Christ within the world. Instead, the Secret Fire is here the authorial presence of God, the sustained attention with which he continuously upholds the existence of the universe.[86]

These (and their equivalent forms in the various draft texts) are the only references to the Secret Fire/Flame Imperishable in Tolkien's work. There is therefore very little indication that the Secret Fire possesses any sort of distinct personhood or engages in any form of activity, and it is explicitly referred to by the impersonal pronoun several times.[87] Such a denial of personhood to one of the three persons of the Trinity would raise serious questions. Does Tolkien therefore have a deficient Trinitarian theology?

There seem to be three possibilities. First, Tolkien does indeed intend for the Secret Fire to be the Holy Spirit, and his pneumatology is thus defective, since the Spirit here lacks any personhood or activity. That the Secret Fire could be the "story soup" reminiscence of the real Holy Spirit seems unlikely given the context of the passages cited above.[88] In support of actual equivalence we could appeal to the explicit statement by Kilby, the strange Trinitarianism we already discussed in "Niggle," and the circumstantial similarity with Newman. One could imagine a layperson taking Newman's words above in a very different sense, imagining the Holy Spirit to be a sort of field or ground for the life-principle of the cosmos, and neglecting his personhood and full divinity. However, though Tolkien only mentions the Spirit twice in his letters, he clearly *does* see him as personal and evinces a completely traditional conception of his activity. In the first instance, he remarks that the Spirit sometimes inspires preachers beyond their natural ability and speaks through the preacher's mouth.[89] In the second instance, he asserts that the Catholic Church is the temple of the Holy Spirit (1 Cor 3:16), though the Spirit may choose to work outside the church.[90] So Tolkien is clearly familiar with the orthodox doctrine of the Spirit. For this reason, we must reject option one.

Second, the Flame Imperishable is not meant to be the Holy Spirit; it is instead the *esse* of creation, the mystery of being that only God can bestow. This makes good sense of the many usages above, as well as the story of Aulë's hapless attempt at creating the Dwarves.[91] This is also consonant with the explicit statement by Tolkien himself in *Morgoth's Ring*. The evidence provided by Kilby is debatable and the similarity with Newman circumstantial. But this interpretation founders upon Tolkien's definition in the "Qenya Lexicon." While not precisely equated with the Secret Fire or Flame Imperishable, it is hard to interpret the fact that the Holy Spirit is called "Fire" in any other way.

Third, Tolkien could intend the Secret Fire to be the Spirit, believe the Spirit to be personal and transcendent, but not expound enough on it within his fiction to make this evident. In this same line, Tolkien could have been deliberately masking certain elements in the doctrine of the Spirit in order to keep Middle-earth as a pre-Christian world. This would allow us to accept the note in the "Qenya Lexicon" and Kilby's statement at face value. It would provide a similarity with Newman and would acknowledge the narrow scope of the discussion in the legendarium while also affirming Tolkien's own remarks in his letters. Furthermore, the apparent sophistication of Tolkien's theological reflection elsewhere may suggest that sheer ignorance of this caliber is unlikely. A charitable interpretation of some of the above statements could imply distinct personhood for the Spirit.

At best, then, one could say that the Secret Fire is God in the mode of indwelling his creation as its ground of being, rather than in the mode of absolute transcendence (as the Father) or real, physical presence (as in the incarnation). It is both with God and proceeds out of God. His personhood remains inchoate at the point in the history of redemption at which the legends of Middle-earth take place. When he speaks of the creative activity of God or the mystery of authorship, he must be taken to refer not to the Flame Imperishable itself, but to *the mode of his presence in creation*. The activity and presence of the Spirit is thus necessary for life and being, and he kindles smaller derivative "fires" which are the spirits of rational creatures.

THE DIVINE NAMES AND ATTRIBUTES

When theologians speak of the doctrine of the names of God, they are referring to the knowledge of God we can gain through an examination of the words used to describe or name him. We will conclude our foray into Tolkien's understanding of God with a brief glance at his own divine naming and see that this principle still holds. For example, he seems to hold the oneness or supremacy of God in more esteem than his relationship to creation. Within Middle-earth, "Eru" (the One) is several times described as a sacred name reserved only for specially important occasions.[92] Ilúvatar (All-Father), by contrast, is the name of God used in common parlance.

The image of light is central for Tolkien, so it is no surprise that God is heavily associated with light, just as he is in the Bible. He is the "single White" light that contains all our many hues.[93] In Tolkien's fiction, God is said to turn the light of his face toward creation—an echo of the Aaronic benediction in Numbers 6:22–27.[94] In an intriguing phrase, the holy mountain upon which the Elder King Manwë sits shines whiter than snow and as terrible as the shadow of God's light.[95] Does this mean to convey the terrible shadow *cast* by the light of God, or does Tolkien here mean that though whiter than snow, Taniquetil is still only a shadow compared to God's effulgence? Or is Tolkien here using standard apophatic language to describe God's brilliant darkness?

He possesses all three of the classical "omni-" attributes.[96] Besides his omnipotence, already mentioned, he is omniscient, for he knows all things and sees even into the heart. What he finds there can please him or sadden him.[97] He is omnipresent and eternal. Tolkien on several occasions contrasts God's existence with sequential time.[98] God's "B-theory" relationship to time means that even those things that appear to have passed away remain in the mind of God.[99] God alone knows the future.[100]

God has a sense of humor and even smiles, but he also grieves and weeps.[101] He is longsuffering but does exercise wrath; he judges, but not without mercy and not without a recognition of the good mixed into the evil that has been done.[102] Everywhere mercy is combined with justice. The Elves say that God's punishments are healing and his mercies stern.[103] Indeed, Tolkien especially emphasizes pity. Pity and mercy are absolute moral requirements for judgment, since they are present in the divine nature.[104] But the mercy of God is genuinely directed toward the good of the one being pitied, for pity lacks all worth if only undertaken to keep oneself from being sullied by injustice (despite this being a good motive in itself).[105] He is therefore genuinely the "Healer" of defects.[106]

We have already noted that God is the absolute king.[107] This is surely one of the more predominant descriptors in Tolkien's thought. But the king is a complex personality. Tolkien, for instance, wavered between having Ilúvatar address Aulë with the formal pronoun "you" or the familiar pronoun "thou," indicating that he was unsure whether it is more appropriate to portray God as regal or as familial.[108]

However, Tolkien also insists that our attempts to name God cannot get us any closer to the actual *idea* of God, which is independent of the conventional shorthand signs by which we may refer to him. The *logos* (or idea) is in the end independent of the *verbum* (or word).[109] The facet of a word by which we may pick out a certain element of God's nature does not exclude other elements which may be equally present to our minds, yet unexpressed.

How, though, do we come to know anything about God at all? If God so transcends human capacities, how can Tolkien so confidently declare on his nature and attributes? Would it not rather be better for Tolkien to keep religion a private enterprise, amounting as it must do to no more than mere speculation and opinion about issues by definition irresolvable? Not so, for Tolkien also believes that far from human beings fumbling blindly about in the metaphysical dark for

God's existence, God has taken the initiative in revealing himself to his creatures and in giving them an authoritative account of his being and activity. God speaks and acts in the world. To this, the doctrine of revelation, we now turn.

FURTHER READING

Any work dealing ostensibly with Tolkien's Christianity will make mention of God. As far as a sustained engagement with the doctrine of God proper goes, and despite the prevalence of theological engagement with Tolkien's work overall, this area is somewhat underresearched. Of forty-four entries in Drout's *Tolkien Encyclopedia* dealing with religious or philosophical themes, neither "God" nor "Trinity" is one of them. As such, apart from scores of blog posts or other informal treatments of the way, for example, the Trinity appears in Middle-earth, which I do not list here, readers should consult:

Kreeft, Peter. "Philosophical Theology." In *The Philosophy of Tolkien: The Worldview behind "The Lord of the Rings,"* 49–70. San Francisco: Ignatius, 2005.

McIntosh, Jonathan S. "The Metaphysics of Eru." In *The Flame Imperishable: Tolkien, St. Thomas, and the Metaphysics of Faërie,* 29–72. Kettering, OH: Angelico, 2017.

Coutras, Lisa. "The Light of Being." In *Tolkien's Theology of Beauty: Majesty, Splendour, and Transcendence in Middle-earth,* 47–64. New York: Palgrave Macmillan, 2016.

II

REVELATION

In this chapter we shall deal with several aspects of Tolkien's doctrine of revelation. Revelation, theologically defined, is some form of communication from the divine that gives a truth otherwise unknown to the recipient. In many cases in Christian theology, this truth is impossible to know unless God reveals it, although there are instances of divine revelation in which the recipient merely gains knowledge that was humanly accessible but personally unknown. There are two broad categories of revelation: general and special. *General revelation* includes truths that can be approached through science and philosophy, without the Bible. This information is a very large-scale gift, but it is still given by God. *Special revelation* is anything that could not be deduced from an observation of God's ordinary world. It requires theology. Tolkien also reminds us that we can distinguish between revelation addressed to particular people and that given to all humankind.[1]

This chapter will be broken down into two major sections based on these divisions. We will first deal with general revelation—here, with how much Tolkien believes pagans might know of the true God apart from Scripture. We will next address Tolkien's views on special revelation in Scripture and his attitudes toward the Bible, then specific extraordinary revelations such as dreams and visions, and finally his views on the (perhaps) supernatural provenance of his own work.

GENERAL REVELATION

REVELATION AND NATURAL THEOLOGY

We mean by "general" or "natural revelation," again, that which non-Christians can know or learn of the true God and his works. But what of the content of natural theology, and what is its relationship to saving faith? Tolkien provides an example of natural theology of Middle-earth in "Fíriel's Song"—it progresses from the existence of God through creation and fall and ends in a hopeful question about the possible redemption of the world, but it cannot proceed further than that.[2] Merry and Pippin, in a more limited sense, reflect on their own small knowledge and its relationship to a fuller account of the truth after witnessing Aragorn's regal display in the houses of healing. Hobbits aren't made for high and mighty affairs, Pippin remarks. Nevertheless, says Merry, they have been given a glimpse, enough now to see and honor them. Best to begin by loving what you're fitted to love, like the Shire; but there are deeper and higher things on which the peace of the Shire depends, and it is gladdening to acknowledge them.[3] God does not leave himself without a witness, even if a brief one. The hobbits recognize there is more to the truth than they can currently access, but they appreciate what light they have.

What, then, of the knowledge of God among non-Christians today? Tolkien seems to adopt the basic outline of general revelation given in Romans 1. All people possess an innate knowledge of the true God to varying degrees. This innate knowledge can include God's existence, power, and moral character, but it is not *saving* knowledge.[4] People can also forsake what knowledge they have and position themselves as pawns of the devil, only able to be freed in the light of Christ. Genuine saving knowledge exists only as the true God specially reveals the means by which creatures might be reconciled to him. This occurs through the person and work of Jesus Christ.

Tolkien admits that truth may be found outside of the church, since God cannot be limited and can choose any means by which to dispense his grace.[5] All truth is God's truth, as Augustine reminds us. And yet all truth is ultimately drawn from the same source and depends on that source for its existence. There is moonlight as well as sunlight—sometimes quite a lot of it—but the light of the moon depends on the existence of the sun.[6] Any and all reflections of the knowledge of God in his beauty and goodness are fulfilled in Christ and preserved by his witnesses. As such, a quest for truth will eventually lead to the church. God is gracious, and we should trust that he will provide genuine seekers an opportunity to find him.

VIRTUOUS PAGANS

One might gain insight into Tolkien's views on natural revelation by reading his thoughts on the way in which the *Beowulf*-poet relates to his pre-Christian ancestors. Tolkien's disquisitions on the poet's use of Scripture in a work set in the pre-Christian world ought to be read with an eye to Tolkien's own fiction; he holds the *Beowulf*-poet specially close to his heart. In short, Tolkien appears passionately to endorse Christian inclusivism, as does the *Beowulf* author under his analysis. That is, while Christianity is absolutely true, other religions are not entirely false. They can, by dint of natural revelation or common grace, come to a limited but accurate understanding of God.[7] This is not surprising; it is the standard Roman Catholic view and was also shared by C. S. Lewis.

Christian inclusivism does not mean syncretism or universalism. The *Beowulf*-poet, according to Tolkien, holds that where pagan myth and Scripture differ, Scripture is truer.[8] Some non-Christian theology may simply be wrong. Tolkien's pagan narrator Eriol betrays total ignorance of Eru the Supreme God and of the truth about the creation of the world.[9] His Germanic gods are not true divinities. When the Elf Lindo informs him that Men tell strange and garbled tales of the Valar full of falsity, Tolkien obliquely affirms that non-Christian theology can be badly mistaken.[10] At the same time, one can adopt the best elements of pre-Christian culture. The basic theological worldview of the Anglo-Saxon world is consonant with the truth: humans are engaged in a struggle we cannot win on our own power, but we are assured that our enemies are also God's enemies, meaning that our courage in the face of such foes is good in itself and a demonstration of the highest form of loyalty to God.[11]

How, then, can a Christian appreciate the truths of general revelation that can be gleaned from other times and cultures? Again, *Beowulf* leads the way. The poet, says Tolkien, must decide how to deal with his own cultural history and the impulses toward the true and good that arose from them. What are we to do with all the heroism and nobility of previous cultures? Was it all worthless, evil, and condemned?[12] No, rather, the inborn imagination of the English nation underwent a dramatic alchemical transformation when exposed to the Scriptures, creating at once the Christian works of Caedmon and others while altering the memory of older traditions into something darker and more alien.[13] Tolkien repeatedly describes this as a sophisticated fusion between Scripture and existing legend.[14] The poet, for example, is free to adopt a pre-Christian tale about giants and monsters of old as long as he can find a source for them in the

Bible. This is why the author locates the origin of such monsters in the genealogy of Cain.[15]

Beowulf's King Hrothgar is the archetypal model of the virtuous pagan, a monotheist who acknowledges God's power and mercy, giving him thanks at all times.[16] Hrothgar, as a natural theologian, knows that God exists, that he is the giver of all good gifts, and that he accepts the upright in heart. Hrothgar desires the good and the true, and he is equivalent to the patriarchs and kings of Israel.[17] Far from merely being written off the Christian stage, Hrothgar and the heroes of old can be thought to occupy an unwritten chapter of Old Testament history.[18]

Tolkien reminds us that all peoples pass through a stage of ignorance before coming to a saving knowledge of God, so the *Beowulf*-poet's own people should not be judged any more harshly. The ancient Israelites, though part of the chosen people, were still damned because of sin and the fall. They too forsook the true God in times of trial and turned to heathen idols.[19] These idols were, to the *Beowulf*-poet, not merely graven images but snares of the devil.[20] In this way, while even the noble Hrothgar, with his knowledge of God's basic character, could deny his knowledge of God and worship the devil instead, Hrothgar is in no worse a position than many other figures from the pages of Scripture. A serious fault, yes, but a familiar trope in the history of redemption. And Tolkien argues that Christ's redemption might work backward in time and provide at least an opportunity for salvation to pre-Christian souls.[21] Traditionally, the Old Testament saints were given just such an opportunity to trust in Christ when he descended into hell. If this is the case, then why shouldn't Hrothgar also be among those Christ rescued in the harrowing of hell?[22]

SPECIAL REVELATION

Special revelation, as we have said, deals with those matters that could not have been known through natural processes but must come directly from God. All knowledge comes either through reasoning or receiving from an authority, and special revelation is no exception. Forms of divining are in fact simply swifter forms of receiving from an authority, whether angels or God himself, in direct mental contact. Tolkien directly calls this "inspiration."[23] There are several examples of such extraordinary revelations present in Tolkien's writings. But the preeminent form of special revelation, apart from Jesus himself, is the Bible.

SCRIPTURE

Tolkien believes in the inspiration of Scripture—this is a surmise, but a safe one. While he nowhere explicitly states this, it is Catholic dogma and defended by Newman.[24] But his views on the exact *nature* of this inspiration are unclear. As to the trends in biblical interpretation, Tolkien understands the complexities of the issue. He does not go along with higher criticism; if the Gospels are not true, they can only be the distorted stories of an insane megalomaniac.[25] Echoing Lewis's trilemma, there can be no simple moral teacher hidden underneath the Christ of faith, given what he claims about himself. Nor, "Philomythus" that he is, does Tolkien believe the New Testament to describe anything other than events which actually occurred. Doubting Jesus' historicity is absurd, as is doubting that he said the things recorded in the Gospels, since they were so foreign to the thought-world of the time (he mentions specifically John 6:54; 8:58; 14:9).[26] As a result, one must either accept Jesus and his message or reject it and suffer the consequences.[27]

But, also like Lewis, Tolkien distinguishes between different levels of historicity. He can write of Genesis 3 that it is not the same sort of history as the New Testament, since the latter is composed of basically contemporary documents and Genesis is separated by an unknown span from the time of the exile from Eden. But he does, nevertheless, affirm that Eden existed in the first place.[28] While he therefore reads Genesis as a different, more "mythological" sort of document than Acts, perhaps incorporating literary elements, this does not mean he divorces it from fact.[29] Indeed, he speculates whether most Christians have tried to forget about Genesis as an unfashionable and somewhat embarrassing element of the faith, and whether those who have not rejected it outright might now even deprive themselves of its benefits as a spiritually nourishing story. On the contrary, he asserts that the beauty of the account, while it does not guarantee historicity, is nevertheless intimately linked with it. Readers should appreciate both its beauty and its truth. Tolkien credits Mother Church, C. S. Lewis, and his own work with clearing away his doubt and shame about Eden.[30] He also accepts the thousand-year rule of the saints on earth at the end of time (what Christians call the millennium).[31]

But we can also see that the story of redemption set forth in Scripture takes a much more central place in Tolkien's thought than may at first appear. In the epilogue to *Tolkien On Fairy-stories*, Tolkien comes closest to giving that thing he is always so keen to avoid: a sermon. While the passage should be read in its entirety, its thrust is that the story of Jesus recapitulates and completes the best elements of every fairy tale, but on the level of reality rather than fiction. The art is in the plot of the story itself, the author of which was not the evangelists but God.[32]

Thus, the narrative of Scripture contains the central narrative of all narratives, in both fact and fiction. Christ's birth and life is the eucatastrophe of human history; his resurrection is the eucatastrophe of his incarnation. Both beginning and ending in joy, it also bears the indelible stamp of reality. Indeed, there is no other story we would rather find to be true, or which so many skeptics have instead chosen to wholeheartedly accept.[33] Tolkien can therefore write, joyously, that God has redeemed his sub-creators through a sort of fairy story, or at least a larger sort of narrative which retains the essence of a fairy story.[34] He locates the crux of all human history and human artistic endeavor in the revelation of God in Jesus Christ and in the story recounted in the Gospels. In fact, says Tolkien, the human writer can *participate* in this grand narrative through his or her own creative work.

But what of Tolkien's personal use of the Bible? How familiar with it was he? Tolkien only knew a smattering of Hebrew and found it frustrating, though he enjoyed the sense of antiquity it conveyed.[35] He was at least familiar with biblical Greek.[36] Tolkien worked on the Jerusalem Bible as a translator for the book of Jonah[37] and shows interest in questions of biblical translation at other points.[38] He also refers to Scripture several times in his academic writing.[39] We must be careful not to deduce from a particular biblical reference that Tolkien always thinks of it himself, however. It may be a result of linguistic research rather than personal piety.[40]

Nevertheless, his private writings bear several scriptural allusions and quotations, some flippant, some serious.[41] When explaining the book of Jonah to his teenage grandson, Tolkien sets aside the great fish and focuses on how the story reveals God's character. "The real point is that God is much more merciful than 'prophets,' is easily moved by penitence, and won't be dictated to even by high ecclesiastics whom he has himself appointed."[42] In a poignant reflection on the difference between converts and "cradle Catholics," he writes that the church has a special sanctity and value for those who came to it from outside, using the biblical analogy of coming to Canaan from the desert or from Egypt.[43] When he advocates for prayer and praise, he cites Psalm 148 and Daniel 2 as models.[44] We know that the Inklings frequently discussed Scripture.[45]

Tolkien can also reason from Scripture and appeal to Scripture to buttress his reasoning. He muses whether a desperate loyalty for a seemingly hopeless cause might not have also dwelt in the hearts of the disciples during Jesus' earthly ministry.[46] He refers to the feeding of the five thousand to argue that not every Eucharist has to be a mystical experience,[47] and he argues from Paul's strictures on the Eucharist that clerical abuses are no recent fad.[48] He claims he is a Catholic because the Roman Catholic Church puts the sacrament at the center, as Jesus clearly intended. Arguing that Christ's words are always meant to be understood literally if possible, he argues that the injunction to Peter to "Feed my sheep" was meant to refer to the "Bread of Life," the eucharistic loaf.[49] Tolkien further cites the parable of the mustard seed to support Newman's account of the development of doctrine and of ecclesiastical structures.[50]

He offers an extended meditation on the passion story in the context of Christian failure. If, he argues, Christ was a liar, the whole church is naught but a gigantic fraud, and moral failure ought not be a surprise. If, on the other hand, Christianity is true, failure is not unknown here either: the disciples failed Jesus before the first Easter. The failures of the church ought to grieve us, but we should be careful to see ourselves properly. We ought to identify ourselves not with Jesus but with the scandalizers like Judas and Peter.[51] Here Tolkien moves from narrative to personal application, not only reading but meditating on Scripture to draw spiritual lessons from its words.

Scriptural Influences on Middle-earth

The view of Genesis as some form of history exercises massive influences on Tolkien's fiction. He places Middle-earth in the mythical (pre-Abrahamic) past of our world and desires that it be consistent with this world. He even avoids post-Abrahamic biblical names in his fiction, for artistic reasons.[52] But while Middle-earth might be set before God's call to Abraham, it is certainly *not* set before the creation of the world or the advent of the first humans. Tolkien thus feels the need to account for Genesis in the stories of the First Age and to tie it to existing knowledge of ancient human history. We shall see in other chapters that Tolkien was deliberate to portray human origins in Middle-earth as consonant with Genesis to a certain degree, especially as relates to the fall. Elendil is a Noah figure.[53] Tolkien even toys with having the Edain descend from Shem or Japheth, the sons of Noah.[54] The Númenoreans have some connection to ancient Egypt, while in *The Book of Lost Tales* he places Gondolin beside the great cities of the world, including Rome, Babylon, Nineveh, and Troy.[55]

Other merely tonal allusions to biblical passages occasionally come through.[56] He himself characterized the style of *The Silmarillion* as "quasi-biblical"—and his best.[57] The song of the Eagle in the chapter "The Return of the King" sounds like it has been lifted from the last pages of the book of Revelation.[58] It borrows the defeat of the devil, bright sunshine, a tree, a river, glad song, and the glorious reign of a king. Likewise, when the chronicler of Númenor writes the summary of the reign of Ar-Pharazôn, one thinks of the similar annalistic accounts of the kings of the Old Testament.[59]

SPECIAL INDIVIDUAL REVELATION IN MIDDLE-EARTH

Middle-earth also plays feature to more unusual forms of revelation, such as prophecies or visions. While obviously not as prevalent in

Tolkien's nonfiction as discussions of natural theology or Scripture, Tolkien finds a prominent place for these special communications from above in his fictional writing. In what follows, we will briefly examine some ways in which characters in *The Lord of the Rings* receive special supernatural revelation.

It should be evident that the gap between Tolkien the writer and Tolkien the theologian will be wider here than elsewhere. While we cannot expect to learn much from this about how Tolkien perceived supernatural revelations of this sort in the primary world, we can expect that these methods are not disconsonant with what Tolkien believed could happen. They contradict neither Scripture nor Christian history, and the general tenor or mode in which they occur seems in keeping with Tolkien's thought about the primary world.

Most of the following instances are revelations from the Valar rather than from Eru himself. This too may point to a distinction between Tolkien's fictional account and his primary belief: one would expect divine revelation to proceed from God rather than created beings. But the church has a place for angelic and even saintly revelation to human pilgrims. Indeed it is implicitly understood that such communications take place at the behest and approval of God, with creatures as intermediaries. As such, one can be justified in taking Tolkien's angelic revelators to act in accord with the designs of Eru, that character always present yet never named.

Prophecy

The gift of prophecy seems almost common in Middle-earth. Tolkien defines foretelling as speech that does not depend on reasoning from evidence or prior knowledge.[60] Much of the so-called prophecies of the wise are in fact the deductions of powerful minds. True foresight, a glimpse of the future as such, is a gift of inspiration.[61] No being other than God knows the future directly. All beings, such as angels, who have insight into the future have received this knowledge indirectly from God. But mortal beings might also receive such direct divine revelation.[62]

Not only are whole races (such as Elves and Númenoreans) gifted with foresight, but even Samwise Gamgee is numbered among the prophets.[63] The ability to see the future is the centerpiece of the chapter "The Mirror of Galadriel." Such foresight can be blocked (especially by the shadows of Sauron) and is never guaranteed; Gandalf admits his vision is limited.[64] Other prophecies include Elrond's remark to Frodo that he should find strange help on the way (fulfilled in Faramir),[65] Galadriel's declaration that she and Treebeard may meet again in a restored Beleriand,[66] and Saruman's hint that Frodo will not be content in Middle-earth.[67]

Tolkien's prophecies almost always center upon major plot points in the web of story, such that certain foretellings enter the public consciousness and many wait for their fulfillment.[68] Famous seers, such as Malbeth, are remembered for many years.[69] Prophecies are never frivolous but hold fast to the Old English concept of doom and fate. Even when Galadriel literally tells Gimli's fortune,[70] there is a strong moral element centered upon destiny rather than mere material circumstance. Tolkien himself may believe that God keeps future knowledge mostly hidden in order to amplify his own glory, if Gandalf's remark to Frodo be taken as truth.[71]

While Gandalf is the subject of much prophecy-talk,[72] and he himself foretells many things, such as Gollum's eventual part in the story,[73] the central subject of prophecy in *The Lord of the Rings* is Aragorn. His whole life seems the subject of a high destiny.[74] Aragorn himself foretells Gandalf's fate in Moria twice, though he is pained by his prophecy. He also foresees that he and Éomer should meet on the field of battle and prophesies the passing of the Elves to Elrond.[75]

We ought to expect Gandalf's supernatural knowledge based on his divine origin, which makes the prophetic nexus around Aragorn even more interesting. A comparison to the prophecies of the Bible is illuminating here. The majority of biblical foretellings fall into a few basic categories: oracles of judgment, promises of eschatological restoration, and messianic prophecies. Aragorn is both a messianic and a restorative figure. He is the long-awaited king who will restore the exiled kingdom and who ushers in a sort of demi-paradise with the fall of Sauron. He is the culmination of angelic, Elvish, and human lineages, and the ruler who oversees the end of the mythological era and the beginning of ordinary history after the departure of the Elves and the fading of magic. He is a focal point for providence, while Gandalf is its agent. Aragorn is Tolkien's literary echo of the Davidic king of which so many biblical prophecies speak, and, similar to David himself, he is both the subject and speaker of prophecy.

Visions and Voices

Direct and waking visions or auditions are rare in Tolkien's writing. The most prominent is Faramir's vision of Boromir upon the River.[76] Apart from this, Pippin is inspired to leave his Elven brooch on the Uruk-Hai trail, without knowing why, when he seems to see Aragorn following behind.[77] Frodo once feels Gandalf's thought upon him at a distance, unknowing.[78] Three times characters seem to hear things in a supernatural way: Denethor hears Boromir's horn all the way from Minas Tirith,[79] Frodo seems audibly to hear his conversation with Gandalf and has mercy on Gollum,[80] and Sam likewise again hears his own prophetic words in Rivendell that he has a job to do.[81]

In a metafictional instance, Bilbo sings about Eärendil, who hears and sees things forbidden to mortals.[82]

Virtually all of these instances serve to guide or encourage good characters to remain faithful and press on. The only exception, Denethor's hearing of the horn of Gondor, seems to owe its force to the horn as a magical artifact itself, whereas the other occurrences are not tied to any sort of magic. Frodo and Sam's auditions are not *new* knowledge, but powerful impressions of memories, dredged up and strengthened at just the right moment in order to non-coercively stiffen a character's resolve. Each subject can choose whether they will remain committed to their previous choices.

Dreams

In his introduction to the poem *Pearl*, set within a dream, Tolkien writes that the Middle Ages were a time when people still considered that dreams could at times give glimpses of truth. Their imaginations were full of symbol, allegory, and scriptural allusions. Sometimes, amidst all the nonsense of dreams, saints and prophets might speak.[83] He seems to take the same view as the medievals, writing that one can both pray and praise while the body sleeps, though such activities are not dreams but pure acts of the soul.[84] Faramir and Boromir both receive recurring dreams summoning them to Rivendell for the Council.[85] Frodo experiences *seven* revelatory dreams, in which he sees things he could not have seen while waking.[86]

None of these dreams, however, cause any direct action on Frodo's part, and most are not even explicitly mentioned as corresponding to real events, save for when Frodo recounts his dream of Gandalf (which surprises the Wizard greatly) and when his dream of Valinor comes true at the very end of the story. We as readers know the dreams are true dreams, but Frodo is usually none the wiser. Dreams occupy an ambiguous conceptual space, then, neither directly recognized as revelation, as are prophecies, nor leading to immediate action, as do visions and voices.

Divine Guidance

In various ways, characters either feel or discern supernatural promptings or openings at crucial times. Aragorn and Sauron study signs to determine their course of action, and Aragorn at least explicitly ascribes purposiveness to such signs.[87] Frodo and Sam often feel guided but have no categories with which to understand these events.[88] After their "chance" meeting in Bree, Gandalf and Thorin reveal that each seemed bidden to seek and think of the other.[89] Pippin receives two alien proddings that ultimately save his life.[90] And at times, characters seem to look inward for guidance, hoping that the movements of their own hearts reveal the right course of action.[91] Here we must correlate such soul-searching with other passages in which the will of Eru can be revealed through an inner communication.[92] According to the appendices, the revelation of the Ring as such is also implied to have been supernaturally guided.[93] *The Lord of the Rings* is therefore not nearly so deistic as many critics assume, whether or not the Valar act as intermediaries for Eru.

Inspired Speech and Tongues

Tolkien explicitly speaks in categories of divine inspiration when Sam uses Galadriel's star-glass and invokes Elbereth without knowing Elvish—here, not only a miracle of inspiration but of tongues as well.[94] Again, while the source of such inspiration remains unnamed, it is clearly the Valar, and, if the Valar, ultimately God. The Valar are explicitly named as inspirers of speech in the tale of Beren and Lúthien.[95] The Valar likewise probably inspire Sam's song in the tower of Cirith

Ungol: it is the only way he finds Frodo.[96] Frodo himself invokes both Elbereth and Eärendil, without consciously seeming to have chosen to do so, yet with powerful results.[97] When Frodo accepts the Quest of the Ring in the council of Elrond, Tolkien writes that it was as if another will were using Frodo's voice.[98] Frodo's inspired speech is highlighted when Elrond remarks that the task seems appointed to him. Faramir also wonders to hear himself mention Númenor to Éowyn.[99] Other more dubious examples include Pippin's impulse to swear fealty to Denethor and Frodo's unconscious invention of the walking song.[100]

Tolkien is therefore very comfortable with inserting revelations both subtle and explicit into his narrative. But what of the narrative itself and Tolkien's own opinion of revelation in the primary world? There is at least one instance in which Tolkien appears to accept personal revelation or inspiration, and to this we now turn.

WAS TOLKIEN INSPIRED?

This section explores Tolkien's views on one aspect of an extracanonical special revelation addressed to the world: his own writing. While grading student exams one day, Tolkien wrote down ten fateful words without any clear meaning behind them: "In a hole in the ground there lived a hobbit." Whence did this sudden impulse come? Tolkien seems to have explicitly admitted he believed his work to have been inspired in some sense.

In a letter from 1971, two years before his death, he recounts a strange visit. A man had come to see him with some old pictures which seemed to have been made to illustrate *The Lord of the Rings* ages before it was written. The man wanted to know whether Tolkien had drawn inspiration from such images. When Tolkien revealed he had never seen them before, the meeting took a strange turn.

His visitor asked him whether he believed he had really written the whole work on his own. No, Tolkien had answered, not anymore.[101] Tolkien then tells his correspondent that he has never since been able to believe that *The Lord of the Rings* was purely his own invention. Recognizing that this is a somewhat alarming and possibly arrogant conclusion, he reasons that God after all uses quite imperfect instruments all the time.[102]

We must make clear from the outset what Tolkien did and did not believe here. He did not believe his fiction was true in the primary world, though he did believe it was not entirely false. He did not believe he was writing Scripture, or some special basis for a new religion or teaching.[103] He did not believe his work ought to be considered "inspired" in the same sense as the Bible or the church's teaching. But he *did* seem to eventually believe that he received large portions of it from God by the ministry of angels operating on relatively normal authorial processes—that is, not by means of an Islamic angelic delivery, but in a more subtle and synergistic manner.

Tolkien can speak of a sermon as requiring a special grace which does not set artistic effort aside but attains the goal of that effort through instinct or "inspiration." He makes clear that the use of this term is deliberately theological: on rare occasions, the Holy Spirit can seem to speak through a human mouth by providing skills and capacities that person does not otherwise have.[104] This is more or less the mode in which Tolkien believes his own work is inspired. We shall first outline the evidence for this claim and then compose a synthetic account of Tolkien's views.

The argument here depends upon taking certain remarks in *The Lost Road* (1937) and "The Notion Club Papers" (1945) as basically autobiographical.[105] This is not without risk, but not without basis. Christopher Tolkien himself concludes that Alboin's biography is strongly modeled on the senior Tolkien's own life, though not exact-ly.[106] Likewise, both the visionary Michael George Ramer and the translator of his revealed manuscript, Professor Rashbold, were in some sense based on Tolkien.[107] In general, we must also remember that while Tolkien did, to be sure, draw distinctions between his fic-tion and his belief, these distinctions do not always occur as strongly or as obviously as we might expect. For example, when confronted, Tolkien hesitantly admitted that he believed something like the Valar probably exist in the real world.[108] The picture he paints of Middle-earth is said to be theologically closer to reality than many expect.[109] "[A]lways I had the sense of recording what was already 'there,' some-where: not of 'inventing,' " he writes.[110] Stories have grown up rather than been constructed by him.[111] Interestingly, he recognizes that not all of his work partakes of this gift. His children's stories, "Leaf by Niggle," and "Farmer Giles," were merely invented. *The Hobbit*, on the other hand, while begun under the guise of invention, gradually showed itself to have been an integral part of this "revealed" work.[112]

He frequently explains that his writing seems to proceed quite apart from his intentions. The visionary Ramer gives a summary probably quite apt for Tolkien's own creative process. He says his visu-alizing seems independent of his conscious mind or will, and appears all at once, fully formed. He finds it difficult to alter such pictures, in fact, and concludes that it is better and more right to alter the story to fit the pictures instead.[113] Tolkien similarly expects that the work will not always obey his designs for it. It seems to write itself, as if the truth finally appears after his imperfect sketches.[114] He says he no longer "invents," but instead waits until he seems to know what really happened.[115] This sort of independent development is a large impetus for his conclusion that parts of the story seem revealed *through* him rather than *by* him.[116] He deliberately chose to work with archetypal motifs, and sometimes characters intrude out of narrative necessity. But he describes the full characterization of Aragorn in tones of awe as a revelation.[117] He admits that he neither invented nor even desired the character of Faramir,[118] though Frodo later tells Faramir that their meeting was the fulfillment of Elrond's foretelling of strange help on the road (a passage written many years before!).[119] Tolkien often singles out the Ents as a particular example of an unexpected addition.[120] He can at the same time comment that he likes Ents because they seem to be totally independent from him, and then immediately speculate on their possible source in a mixture of his own interests, desires, and impulses.[121]

One should not picture Tolkien sitting at a desk while an angel dictates plot points over his shoulder. The inspired elements, to him, are always mixed in with the deliberate, and frequently with everyday activities. Tolkien here includes sleeping but understands himself to be not simply dreaming but *receiving*.[122] His fictional stand-in Ramer likewise distinguishes between dreams and the realities that may be communicated through dreams. Sometimes a blessedness from beyond the region of dreams soaks into the mind and illuminates the scenes within it, flowing thence out into waking life.[123] In these rare instances, the sleeper is taken out of ordinary dream and can receive insights or even specific words from other minds, either human (dead or alive), alien, angelic, or demonic. These dream recollections and visions form the basis for Ramer's interplanetary voyages, but he ponders whether writing them down somehow anchors them in the everyday and flushes them of some of their potency.[124]

Here we find another connection between Ramer and Tolkien. It is well-known that for as long as he could remember, Tolkien was plagued with a recurrent dream of a great wave towering over green fields. When he bequeathed the dream to Faramir in *The Lord of the*

Rings and incorporated it into his Númenorean myths, the dream ceased. Most strangely, his son Michael revealed in 1955 that he had the same dream, though neither had ever before spoken of it to the other. Tolkien assumes from this that he may have in turn inherited it from his own parents, as an echo of their ethnic past.[125] These remarks occur almost a decade after "The Notion Club Papers."

If one continues to assume that Tolkien uses Ramer as a mouth-piece to express his own experiences—experiences most people would consider outlandish—we have a much larger window into the way in which Tolkien believed he received his revelations. Notably, his remark about ceasing to invent and waiting for truth takes place immediately after his remark on dreams. But are we to believe that Tolkien was merely speaking poetically about normal authorial inspiration, or instead that his experiences more closely paralleled actual supernatural and physically perceptible interventions? Ramer again, quite humbly but seriously, admits that he feels he has been visited and spoken to.[126] In these instances, the meaning was direct and immediate, while the translation followed shortly thereafter, though audibly. He recognizes other accounts of a similar kind.[127] Here Ramer (Tolkien?) probably means mystical visions of some sort—something that actually interrupts the everyday element. This, at least, is how Ramer's friends understand him. They take him to imply something like hallucination. Ramer immediately accepts this diagnosis, with the caveat that while the process might be the same, the purpose is not: there is actually something external being communicated.[128] Tolkien does not mean to suggest that every such communication takes place in this way, nor that every element in his writing is a result of such communication, but it seems not to have been uncommon. They may occasionally have been more than auditory.[129] He admits to at least one mystical vision in his letters.[130]

The central aspect of Tolkien's whole legendarium—his languages—also seem not to have been so much invented as received, at least partially. The character Alboin receives supernatural communications of specific words, which seem real and not merely made up to please himself. The name Númenor is one of these.[131] Compare this with Tolkien's remarks in *Letter* 163: he asserts that he knew most of Gollum's part in the tale, but "nothing of the *Palantíri*," though when one appeared he recognized it as the object of a preexisting rhyme that had been running through his mind.[132] He did not at first place much weight on these recollections but eventually began to consciously note and use them. They did not fit his private hobby-language, but instead began to control and alter it, such that the language became more and more a collection of these "real" words and less his own invention.[133] These words were not confined to one language only, but influenced both Quenya and Sindarin.[134]

Notably, Tolkien's Alboin is quite self-conscious about the whole situation, even toward his most intimate confidants who believe him to be simply imagining things. Though he wishes he could stop it and save face, he cannot.[135] Importantly, despite any awkwardness, Tolkien often reminded others that he did not walk about with his head in the clouds and was not obsessed with his private communications. He was not mentally disturbed and could readily distinguish between his revelations and reality.[136] To one already self-conscious of his "secret vice," it does not seem far-fetched that he would avoid also admitting he believed it to be supernaturally received, and might instead reveal such information through a fictional stand-in.[137]

But is not all this making rather too much hay from very little seed? Tolkien does make several statements that seem to complexify things. In contrast to the thesis presented here, Tolkien could claim in 1958 that he had no conscious message or sermon to deliver, in the sense of a specially revealed vision of truth; *The Lord of the Rings* is just a good story, though his own ideas inevitably peek through.[138] In another contemporaneous letter he remarks that Middle-earth is no new religion or vision, but an imaginative story meant to express his dim apprehension of the world … as far as he is aware.[139] He can speak of making headway in his authorial process as releasing the "demon" of invention—surely an odd turn of phrase to fit into our thesis![140] Clearly Tolkien did not mean to preach, but an avoidance of authorial message in the sense of setting up some new religion does not exclude a burgeoning sense of revelation. Tolkien tells one correspondent, in answer to a question about God, that he will not venture onto a theological disquisition.[141] This at least implies that such a disquisition *might* be undertaken. He has opinions but holds them in check.

Shortly before the statement above, he writes that he does not know all the answers to his readers' questions. His own work often puzzles him and is now so far back in life that it seems written by someone else.[142] These sentences bear unpacking. On the surface, it seems that Tolkien ascribes the work's independence to normal authorial processes undergoing the vagaries of time. It is merely as if by a strange hand, because of the distance. But he contrasts the first and the second clauses. It (1) puzzles him, and (2) was written so long ago he can take an objective stance on it. The sense of objective distance and the sense of puzzlement are not identical. Whatever puzzles Tolkien about his writing, it is not merely because he wrote it long ago.

Finally, in a 1967 interview, Tolkien touches again upon how the story takes on a life of its own. Explaining that long tales take multiple writings and must often be worked backward, he says that in so doing, characters and events will pop up. "People will occur. One waits to see what's coming next. I knew there was going to be some trouble with treelike creatures at one point or another."[143] This at least sounds like standard authorial flexibility. Every writer knows their work can take unexpected turns; this doesn't mean an angel is whispering in their ear. It simply means their ideas may be inchoate. But Tolkien's apparent nonchalance about the subject may have many causes. He might have wanted to avoid being seen as any more eccentric than he already was; perhaps a tone of seriousness belied by this phrasing was lost in the transition to print. But, most likely, this is an exhibit of the quite complex view he takes on the way his own work develops. It is not an either/or formula; his communications become inextricable from his own invention. And in this particular example, the Ents bear very little similarity to the evil Giant Treebeard from Tolkien's first drafts.

Tolkien does not believe he receives his gifts in a single standard way. Sometimes he simply writes what he wants. Sometimes his plans deepen and take on meaning as they go, or shift significantly in a way that surprises him. Sometimes entirely new elements might be introduced that astonish their author. And in among all of these events, there might be some snatch of verse or evocative word pulled from the depths of dream as if it were a message from another time. These too he weaves into his own work. While Tolkien seems to have been conscious for most of his life of this last sort of phenomenon, and may even have early understood himself to be specially tasked by God for some great mission in his time, it is likely that he only came to hold that the other such instances ought also to be included in the same rubric sometime between 1967 and 1971.[144] This could very well have been due to the ostensible external confirmation of his fancies he found in the strange visit described in Letter 328.

We return to the question with which we began: Was Tolkien inspired? No—not if one means by this that Tolkien was somehow bestowed inerrant divine authority to deliver a message purporting to be from God. But, in the Catholic milieu of which Tolkien was a part, it is not unusual to find persons specially gifted or guided by God outside the pages of the holy Scriptures. The first known English poet, Caedmon, received his poetical skill from an angel in a dream—something Tolkien surely took to heart. One might speak, therefore, of Tolkien's work as arising from revelation in this sense—revelation as a special and direct gifting whose ultimate source is God, and meant in some sense to "testify for God and Truth" and to "rekindle an old light."[145] Many, including himself, felt as if hope were returning to the world.[146] It remains a work of art and not a gospel, however. While Middle-earth might awaken a religious impulse in some readers, Tolkien is quick to point away from himself and toward God. Speaking about any person said to be used by God, Tolkien demurs: any sanctity in the work comes not from him but through him.[147]

CONCLUSION

Within the realm of natural theology or general revelation, the first of the two major divisions in the doctrine of revelation, we have seen that Tolkien likely adopts a Christian inclusivist view in which non-Christians may apprehend God under various guises, yet need the fullness of truth in Christ. Pagans may deny their innate knowledge of God, and not all of their notions of God are correct. Yet there is much to appreciate and adopt into the fold of the church that began outside it.

Tolkien divides special revelation into two categories: that which is addressed to particular individuals and that which is addressed to the world. The supreme form of special revelation is the Bible, and we saw that Tolkien is highly familiar with the Bible and uses it to found theological claims. He is not any sort of fundamentalist literalist and can assert that the Bible includes accounts of varying historicity. It is nevertheless based firmly in fact. Within his fiction, Tolkien includes several kinds of supernatural revelation, including dreams, visions, and inspired speech. Tolkien himself came to believe his own work to have been inspired or gifted to him by God, perhaps to fulfill a mission of renewal in the world. Here God works through sub-creation to restore creation, and in order to understand these three ideas—divine providence, creation, and sub-creation—more fully, we must explore the doctrine of creation in more depth.

FURTHER READING

The issue of natural theology, and the relation between specifically Christian revelation and the inbuilt glimmers of the gospel in pagan times, is a major theme in most discussions of Tolkien's theology. Apart from the primary sources, Testi provides the best overview of this discussion. Tolkien's biblical influence is an area particularly rife with misinterpretation or sloppy exegesis.

Greene, Deirdre. "Higher Argument: Tolkien and the Tradition of Vision, Epic and Prophecy." *Mallorn* 33 (1995): 45–52.

McBride, Sam. "Divine Intervention in the Third Age: Visible Powers" and "Divine Intervention in the Third Age: Invisible Powers." In *Tolkien's Cosmology: Divine Beings and Middle-earth.* Kent, OH: Kent State University Press, 2020.

Murray, Robert. "J. R. R. Tolkien and the Art of the Parable." In *Tolkien: A Celebration*, edited by Joseph Pearce, 40–52. New York: HarperCollins, 1999.

Shippey, Tom. *The Road to Middle-earth*, 3rd edition. New York: HarperCollins, 1993, 222–31.

Testi, Claudio A. *Pagan Saints in Middle-earth.* Zurich and Jena: Walking Tree Publishers, 2018.

Wolfe, Brendan. "Tolkien's Jonah." *Journal of Inklings Studies* 4, no. 2 (2014): 11–26.

III

CREATION

F ollowing the biblical paradigm, Tolkien's doctrine of creation is almost inseparable from his doctrines of humanity and the fall. God is fundamentally a creator—for Tolkien, this is one of his primary attributes. Humans, in the image of God, are thus sub-creators. The precise meaning of creation/sub-creation, and the uses to which Tolkien puts them, have been thoroughly explored elsewhere. This chapter will confine itself only to the theological aspects of his thought on creation and sub-creation, while subsequent chapters will address humanity and the fall.

The idea of a fallen yet noble drive toward creation and creativity undergird Tolkien's entire anthropology, sociology, and psychology, as well as his philosophies of art, literature, and culture. Tolkien stresses the importance of this concept to his thought life. He goes so far as to say that his entire fictional output is about the relationship between art and reality in a fallen world.[1] His comments on creation within his fiction must be taken quite seriously by any who wish to mine Tolkien's insights on the doctrines of creation in the real world, and Tolkien himself encourages us to do so. From beginning to end, he says, *The Lord of the Rings* is about the relation between divine creation and non-divine making and sub-creation, which means that any reference to these matters is absolutely central.[2] This chapter therefore relies quite heavily on Tolkien's highly intentional mythical reflections, assuming as a rule that his comments hold true for his theological beliefs. Where this is less than clear, fictional names will be retained (thus, for example, "Eru" rather than "God").

CREATION FROM NOTHING

As stated above, God, existing eternally before the world, brings the world forth by his will and his word. He exists in a relation of absolute freedom to the world. God is the almighty Lord of all, reigning above all other rulers forever.[3] God's authority inheres in him by nature rather than accident; Tolkien equates divinity with an entitlement to be praised, adored, and obeyed.[4] God alone has a right to divine honor, and all other authority is derived from him.[5] God's absolute right to rule stems from his role as the sole creator of all that exists. As creator and ruler, God institutes a natural law in both senses: the laws of nature against which it is impossible to rebel, and a moral law inherent in the universe. They are an eternal reminder of God's existence and invincibility.[6]

Tolkien does not explicitly speak of creation ex nihilo, creation from nothing, outside of his fiction. We must turn primarily to Tolkien's creation myth, the "Ainulindalë" (or "song of the angels"). This is one of the richest sources for Tolkien's theological and metaphysical thought and ought to be read in full by anyone interested in Tolkien's theology.[7] It influences the doctrine of creation found throughout the rest of Tolkien's corpus. Here, the one Creator God designed but is distinct from the world.[8] Time is a part of creation, and God's throne lies beyond it in the "Timeless Halls."[9] God therefore existed before anything else. To attempt to pry behind the sheer fact of God's existence is impossible. No wisdom can go beyond the beginning of creation.[10]

When we speak of creation ex nihilo, we must include not only the physical but the spiritual world. Tolkien is clear that, just as is traditionally held, God made first the angels and then the physical world. He directly creates the spiritual world from nothing, without intermediary. However, in Tolkien's myth, God accomplishes the creation of the physical world by first showing the angelic host (the Ainur) a theme for a great Music that his angels carry out and even augment.[11] But despite the mediatory role played by Tolkien's angelic demiurges, only God possesses the power to truly bring something into existence, to give it being in an absolute sense. All existence, even that of the angels, shares in the being of God himself.[12] Notably, the Ainur are the offspring of God's thought and thus are not shaped from any preexisting material—though they are never called his Children, as Men and Elves are.[13]

Tolkien distinguishes (in Middle-earth at least) between creation, an act of God's will to give reality to ideas, and making, by which God permits others to work upon his materials. Tolkien here wishes to preserve the equivocal usage of "creation" and "making" within standard Christian discourse—in other words, "I believe in one God, the Father almighty, *maker* of heaven and earth."[14] Angels and mortals can shape preexisting material, but only a direct act of God can give reality. Even after the Ainur do their work, they consider God and not themselves to be the world's true creator.[15] God's great pattern exists not in the contributions of the angels but in his own mind from eternity. In particular, the Valar did not make bodily life; the idea of life and growth belong only to God.

Again, while Eru brings forth the general outline of the tale of the world, he leaves space for his creatures, empowered by the Holy Spirit,[16] to work in adorning the creation with their own sub-creations.[17] While the Valar were permitted to give shape to the forms of living things, these designs were implemented by God by means of a principle of growth and evolution over time. But he is also free to intrude other things into creation according to his will, even new intelligent creatures.[18] Though Tolkien grants the angels a more central role in the creation than is traditionally done, he still affirms that theirs is only a secondary causation.[19] This is not as clear in the final published version as in the original manuscript. Tolkien originally has it that "*through you I have made* much beauty to come to Song,"[20] while in *The Silmarillion* there is only the passive "through you great beauty has been wakened into song."[21] There is a much greater stress on the real creative agency of the Ainur. The plan of creation is initially perfect, and just as God declares what he has made "very good," Tolkien also says that the Music seems good to Eru because there are no flaws in it.[22] Satan, however, corrupts the Music with his own designs and introduces evil into the creation. This disruption will be covered in the following chapters.

Tolkien asserts a single act of creation. All creation proceeds from God in the same way and is in that sense on the same order of being.[23] He does not believe in the multiverse or alternate dimensions, since they are by definition unknowable. If they do exist, they are provinces of the one singular existence, perhaps wider than we previously knew, but still part of the same creation.[24]

Tolkien (and Eru) recognizes the natural desire of a maker to participate in the thing made, to go inside the story. He allows his angels to enter into their own story on the same level of existence as their own, kindling it with the Flame Imperishable and giving it true being.[25] Tolkien here retains and reframes the declaration "let there be" of Genesis. The music goes "out into the void," and it is no longer void.[26] The speech-act of God, here shared with the angelic Ainur, effects creation from nothingness.

The drama as revealed to the Valar is incomplete, however. Even if all their collective knowledge were pooled, the Creator keeps his secrets. He alone understands the full and complete detail of all things.[27] Eru already knows what history will look like, but, in an act of condescension, he allows his creatures to participate in its achievement, as secondary causes. Importantly, God's plan seems actually to already include the additions the Ainur make to the original music, since he works all things into a single overarching unity.[28] This is called God's providence.

PROVIDENCE

There are three elements to God's providence: his conservation of the world, his concurrence with secondary wills, and his governance of all that occurs. God holds all of existence in his thought, and it is only by this that it continues. The earth is set in place by God and hangs in space according to his will. But his concurrence with and governance over other wills requires further explanation.

Though God has determined and ordained a certain course of events that are visible and knowable to his creatures (what Tolkien calls fate), he retains the prerogative to introduce new designs into creation and to hold in certain of his plans a secret known only to himself.[29] He sets certain bounds on what creatures can or ought to accomplish.[30] Only God, for example, can change the shape of Middle-earth, and the Valar must lay down their delegated power in their appeal to him to do so.[31]

But God also grants his creatures a share in his rule. In Middle-earth, the Father gives the world to the Valar to govern as seems good to them, but only under his ultimate authority.[32] These Powers, which pagans call "gods,"[33] distribute God's gifts to the world, though some still realize that the ultimate giver is God.[34] Sometimes Tolkien speaks of God's permission of events, especially in relation to the Valar's interference in the destiny of Elves and Men, entailing that he takes a more active role in governance.[35] His counsel can even be changed by appeal, as it appears in Genesis 18 or Exodus 32.[36]

Sometimes God controls the course of things by direct decree. For instance, he forbids the Valar from intervening in world history by force and forbids any to deny the "gift of death" to Men.[37] In other instances, God takes up and enlarges the plans of his creatures, such as when the Valar send Gandalf to Middle-earth.[38] On rare occasions, Tolkien even speaks in the language of election, with Gandalf declaring that Bilbo was "chosen."[39] But most commonly Tolkien writes of things being appointed or ordained by God. God has designs and desires for the world and the specific persons and periods that constitute it.[40] Nothing can happen that does not work to God's intention, even those done by creatures actively seeking to rebel against God.

All creatures are actually helpless to subvert the divine design. Ilúvatar avers that no Music can be played that does not have its ultimate source in him, and none can change the Music if he does not will it. Instead, they are only aiding him in devising things more wonderful than they ever intended.[41] All the evils of pain and cruelty and chaos serve only as triggers to new developments that beautify and enrich God's world. Tolkien even provides fictional examples of this. Ilúvatar shows Ulmo, the Vala of water, the way in which Melkor's inordinate making has, far from destroying Ulmo's creativity, in fact accented it. Extreme cold brings forth frost and snow, while extreme heat produces mist and cloud and rain. In these, Ulmo is even brought nearer to his brother and friend Manwë, the Vala of the air.[42] Tellingly, despite God's special gift of freedom to Men, even these will find that their ugliest works result in his glory and the increase of beauty in the world.[43]

Tolkien is committed to the notion that the worst evil is in the end subservient to God's good purpose. And lest we are tempted to accuse Tolkien of naïve optimism, we see that, in the midst of a world at war, Tolkien can write that he is in God's hands and that even their evil days are not mere bad luck.[44] God does nothing without purpose, although the purpose may not be made manifest for centuries.[45]

It is important to stress that God does not create evil, nor does he desire it, nor is evil simply good improperly considered. Evil is genuinely evil, and is opposed to God. It grieves him.[46] But God is sovereign enough to *use* evil as a soil from which unexpected good can sprout.[47] Sometimes Tolkien goes further and actually implies that certain seemingly needless evils are part of the desire and will of God, rather than something he merely takes into account.[48] For example, when speaking about death, Tolkien writes that a divine punishment is also a gift if it is accepted willingly, since God's punishments are intended for ultimate blessing. God's supreme creativity can turn these changes of design into sources of good that cannot be attained otherwise.[49] Looking back on our own trials—and on the evils of the world in general—from eternity, we shall have the proper perspective to understand each evil's part in the larger story.[50] The mortal Man has a higher destiny than the immortal Elf, for instance.

DIVINE FOREKNOWLEDGE AND HUMAN FREEDOM IN MIDDLE-EARTH

But in contrast to this, there are points at which Tolkien seems to deny God's omniscience in the interest of freedom. In a somewhat illegible note, he explicitly writes that at the time of the movie-like Vision of the world God gives to the Valar immediately prior to its actualization, "Eru had not [?complete] foreknowledge, but [?after it His] foreknowledge was [?complete] to the smallest detail."[51] This evidently seems to imply that even God did not know what would happen as a result of the choices of his creatures prior to seeing it play out in the vision. He gave the plan of the Music, but his creatures introduced new elements he did not know and only learns about when the Music is made manifest in the pre-creative Vision. If true, this is highly unorthodox on Tolkien's part. Were such comments limited to a single instance, we might dismiss them, but in fact they form a larger pattern.

Tolkien has his Elves present an admittedly limited analogy between an author and his story. He is both present (in that everything in the story proceeds from him) and not present (he is not "in" the story). The author might have general purposes for how the story goes and specific ideas about each character, but, in the process of writing, characters and events come alive and do things that were unforeseen by the author in his original conception. These may even greatly alter the plot, although such alterations become integral parts of the plot once it is finished. Tolkien concludes, "[W]hen that has been done, then the author's 'foreknowledge' is complete, and nothing can happen, be said, or done, that he does not know of and will/or allow to be."[52] We might assume that all such character developments happen at the Music stage, save for a comment by Ulmo in *Unfinished Tales*, in which he remarks that Doom seems not to be completely set until the end of time.[53] This would imply that characters still have such freedom even after the Music and the Vision.

The chronology of events appears to run as follows: God gives his theme to the Powers to perform. As they perform, they each add their own embellishments to the theme—this is the Music proper. In response to these unforeseen alterations during the Music's performance, God brings forth his own alterations, secretly introducing his Children and granting free choice to Men. Then, when the performance is complete, God shows the Valar their achievement as a sort of movie—this is the Vision. After the completion of the Vision, the Powers receive limited foreknowledge, while God receives complete foreknowledge. During the actual unfolding of the Music/Vision as history, in response to the free choices previously foreseen, God again intervenes to alter history at various points and take new developments into account in various ways.

But what does it mean that the author only has foreknowledge once the tale is complete? How can it be *foreknowledge* if it only arises *after* everything has taken place? And, more importantly, how can Tolkien's fictional conception of God's limited foreknowledge post-Music but pre-Vision be reconciled to the truth of things in primary reality, where no such preview screening has taken place? He does not answer any of these questions.

What then are we to make of this? On the one side, the will of Eru cannot be contradicted.[54] On the other side, Tolkien writes that he believes each individual and even the entire human race's destiny is always subject to the mystery of free will (even to the extent of losing salvation), in response to which choices God would arrange things differently![55] To make matters worse, elsewhere Tolkien says that these *free* acts toward salvation or damnation are subject to God's *permission*![56] One of his characters muses that freedom may be like fatherhood: a choice, but not entirely by one's own will.[57]

We might resolve these statements with the observation that God seems to rule Middle-earth as a sort of master strategist, ready with move and counter-move to realize his plan in response to the free choices of his creatures. And, ultimately, God is powerful enough to accomplish his purposes in the face of any creaturely opposition. For example, Tolkien writes that if Bilbo had refused to surrender the Ring, another way to defeat Sauron would have presented itself. When Frodo does in fact refuse to destroy the Ring, Gollum immediately appears in a eucatastrophic moment to accomplish the deed regardless. Tolkien even describes Gollum's intervention as "kept in reserve" by God.[58]

So while creatures may, through use of free will, alter the plot of God's story in one sense, these alterations themselves seem to be foreseen and under the control of God. Or, as Tolkien writes elsewhere, all things on all worlds in all planes are under God's will.[59] Being under God's will implies a permissiveness rather than a determination. Due to God's non-determinative foresight, he knows what his creatures will freely choose and arranges things accordingly. If they had freely chosen differently, then he would have likewise arranged things differently. This is very close to what philosophers have dubbed "middle knowledge."

Additionally, we see Tolkien distinguishing between different levels of divine purpose. He writes that the Valar may have strayed from Eru's purpose in bringing the Elves to Valinor and that this was the cause for much evil in the world afterward. But, since this set of events happened and not another, this must ultimately have meant that it was fate that they should disobey, since nothing can in the end go against Eru's design.[60] In other words, one's failure to follow God's plan can itself be a part of that plan when considered from a larger perspective.

It seems as if we may be able to speak of two elements of God's will—one which responds to creatures and adapts to changing circumstances, and one in which even the free acts of creatures are foreseen and taken into account. Rather than speaking of a free world in which God sometimes intervenes, we ought rather to say that for Tolkien, God's sovereignty is absolute, but that he deigns to grant freedom in certain cases. Even in the prime case of human free will, for example, this freedom is a *gift* that God must bestow.[61] It is not the natural right of any element of his creation. As Tolkien avows, free will is derivate and only operates within the circumstances God provides. If it is to exist, then God has to guarantee that it continues even when it violates his wishes from our finite perspective.[62] When Aulë fashions the Dwarves, for example, Eru says that he has taken Aulë's disobedience into his design, but he places his own limits on the way Aulë's freedom impacts God's story. The Dwarves will exist, but Eru decides the time of their awakening.[63] This demonstrates that, far from being subject to his creatures' decisions, God actually *controls* the way in which he allows these decisions to influence his plan.[64]

The difficulty in dealing with this issue arises in large part because God stands in a completely different relation to time than his creatures do.[65] In a late manuscript, Tolkien implies that we only perceive history to change because we exist in a linear relation to time. In speaking about personal identity across time, he compares a person to a river: it runs its course through many lands, and its water always changes, but its true identity is at once the entirety of the river, throughout both time and space. We may speak from our perspective of the river changing, growing broad or narrow, beginning or ending, yet the river exists all at once, beyond our immediate perception. A tree may change many times in its long life, from acorn to full growth to dead wood, but its identity remains the same. Its network of relations also remains the same—each differing tree shaped by its circumstances but all sprung from a single seed.[66] God, by implication, sees past, present, and future at once, so that a change in the course of our lives takes him no more by surprise than does a bend in a distant river seen from a mountaintop.

TOLKIEN THE DEIST?

By now it should be clear that one of the major charges leveled against Tolkien's depiction of God must be false. One *could* appeal to specific instances in Tolkien's corpus to argue that, far from the active and interested God of Christianity, Tolkien's Eru is a detached and deistic god. The most famous such line is that to Robert Murray, in which Tolkien explains Middle-earth's lack of visible religion. It is a purely monotheistic world where even the Valar are not to be worshiped, being only creatures of the true God, who is "immensely remote."[67] Creatures know that God exists, and that he alone possesses authority, but he is distant, far outside the world, and accessible only by the ruling powers or angels.[68] This notion of distance, however, is probably more to set a contrast between the physically embodied Powers, living in a literal place to the West, and the exalted God who has no image or circumscribed body.[69] Even this remoteness, however, cannot be termed "deism" in any meaningful sense for several reasons.

First, unlike deism, in Middle-earth God's remoteness is undesirable because, though Men in the first Ages might have *wished* to pray directly to him, they feared to do so.[70] Humans have an impulse toward God which at the time of these tales remains unsatisfied.[71] Thus, rather than demonstrating an incipient deism, the problem of God's remoteness in Middle-earth demonstrates instead the necessity of a mediator in approaching the divine. We will take up this theme in chapter 8.

Second, Middle-earth is not a materialist realm in which God winds up the clock of the world and lets it run. God might be *inaccessible* to mortals, but he is not uninvolved or uncaring. Humans are unable to reach up to God, but he constantly reaches down to them. He can even reveal his will internally, in a person's innermost being.[72] Tolkien explicitly states, "The Creator did not hold himself aloof."[73] God's perpetual production of the drama of history seems to imply a sustaining aspect to creation, sometimes called God's "preservation of creation" or "continuous creation."[74]

Thus, God not only calls the world into being by his word, but he actively wills that it continue in being. Were he to cease willing it, existence would vanish.

Even those things which appear to be laws—that is, unbreakable modes of operation by which the world must abide—are in actuality merely rules which God is free to follow or to bend.[75] Eru introduces many events and designs unforeseen by the Powers. Tolkien explicitly denies that the world is some sort of machine that makes other machines—that is the way of Sauron, not God.[76] God is the *author* of the rules, active to sustain every element of the cosmos. And indeed, God's operations in suspension of these rules—what we might call miracles—provide insights into the meaning behind the story he tells with the world.[77]

MIRACLE

Tolkien believes that God can freely intervene in creation through a *miracle*: a thing of awesome and overwhelming holiness.[78] He is usually reticent to use the term "supernatural," as it is a dangerous and difficult term. Human beings are, after all, supernatural in a sense.[79] We are not purely material. But a miracle comes from outside the world, from God, and is therefore properly *super*-natural.[80] He defines a miracle as God's freedom to produce realities that one couldn't deduce from past events and which, unlike illusions, continue to exist as permanent elements of the world.[81] Miracles can be both creative or recreative.[82] These acts are not intrusions in the sense of unlawful entries, but they do crop up into real ordinary life, into the chain of cause and effect and materiality.[83] Miracles are only unexpected when viewed serially in time. From God's perspective, they would always have happened.

Miracles are effected *only* by God the transcendent Lord, either directly or—less frequently, through his authorization—by an angel or human as the agent of a specific divine purpose while wholly absorbed in doing God's will.[84] They can therefore only be good and moral in purpose, effect, and nature, neither frivolous nor ethically ambiguous. Even the seemingly slight miracles featured in saints' lives and legends still have an ultimately moral object: testimony to God. And Tolkien further explains that when God answers a specific prayer miraculously, such miracles are the flower of the holiness of that saint borne from close union with God. Alternately, they could be performed unasked in order to bear witness to that holiness.[85]

Miracle is distinguished from mechanism, the mere illusion of stage magic, and marvel, that which is simply unfamiliar and therefore bewildering. Miracle is also distinct from magic and Faerie, though miracle and magic are so similar that they can only be distinguished by Christian theology.[86] The effects may seem identical, but the context and motive are totally different. The supernatural religion of Christianity lifted the shadow of fear that lingered over cultures in dread of malicious or arbitrary magical power by its insistence that the good and holy God's sovereign will rules all that happens.[87]

This is evident in the miracles of the Scriptures. The Gospels contain miracles which are not mere literary devices but actually occurred in history, and these miracles are demonstrations of Christ's true identity and of the power of God for redemption.[88] Here the author and hero are the same being—the one God.[89] Apart from this primary instance, Tolkien admits to being deeply moved by certain miraculous stories which display the eucatastrophic turn of which he is so enamored. Tolkien compares miracle and eucatastrophe to seeing sunlight through the chink in a wall or a gap in the threads of fate. This idea of a chink or gap through which the light of God pours occurs three times in Tolkien, both in his fiction and in his nonfiction, and it might be the best image with which to illustrate his ideas of God's relationship to the world, alongside the image of the author.[90] Indeed, in Tolkien's discussion of miracles as glimpses of light, he relates that such events reveal the plot of God's story of the world.[91]

THE WORLD AS STORY

When he writes that God creates the world, Tolkien does not only mean that he creates matter and time. The creation of the world is also God's authoring of history. Indeed, the history of the world *is* a story, a cosmogonical drama authored by someone else.[92] The design for the "Great History" of the world is also what the Elves call God's "production" or "management" of this drama.[93] Tolkien explicitly calls it the "Creation Drama"[94] and affirms that Eru has a "Divine Plan"[95] which informs the mythological-theological situation at any moment of history.[96] Earth is the central stage of this drama, which Tolkien conceives as the battle of God and his Children with Melkor (the devil).[97]

Tolkien's description of the Music in the Ainulindalë is actually a microcosmic tonal description of the very story of creation itself. When Ilúvatar adds a second theme to combat Melkor's dissonant sabotage, the theme begins as soft and sweet ripples of gentle, delicate sounds, which grows unquenchably into a song of power and depth. Its beauty stems mainly from the profound sorrow with which it is blended, and the most powerful notes from Melkor's chaos serve to supplement it rather than replace it.[98] Melkor's pseudo-creation comes merely through him rather than by him.[99] He is merely a secondary cause, whose every work only makes the design of the Primary Creator more intricate and wonderful. Echoing the biblical refrain "So you may know that I am the Lord," Eru declares that all the sorrow and evil of the world redounds only to his glory and to the enrichment and wonder of life. Indeed, he even says that in the end the allowance of evil will be called the mightiest and loveliest of all his deeds.[100] This is a powerful statement of theodicy.[101]

This history therefore includes an element of danger, to some extent.[102] Without taking too much away from our discussion of theodicy in chapter 7, we should note here that Tolkien sees the essential process of history in the constant rise of evil and the equally constant rise of goodness out of that evil.[103] A perfectly safe story rings false, whether in fiction or reality.[104] When the Elves become obsessed with the stasis of time, Tolkien says it is as if a person hated the progress of a book and the disruption of the status quo and, rather than continue, simply stays in a favorite chapter.[105] Denial of this storial aspect of reality is sinful.

Gandalf intercedes in the culture of the Shire because the hobbits had begun to forget their own stories of daring and danger and therefore their sense of the world's greatness. They needed to renew their memory of the high and the perilous.[106] The hobbits *must* be reminded of an element of danger in order to appreciate what they have. The good things that make hobbit society valuable, such as freedom and peace and pleasure in ordinary life, require a greater and more dangerous world outside their borders in order that they not grow stale.[107] The richness and depth of our world come from this relationship between the ordinary pleasures, such as food, drink, and family on the one hand, and the longing for transcendent beauty, quests, and noble sacrifice on the other hand.[108]

This is as true in the primary world as it is in Tolkien's fiction. Tolkien compares our enjoyment in reading about Sam and Frodo on the steps of Cirith Ungol (a terrible place for the characters themselves) with our satisfaction in reflecting on the dangers and even horrors of our own lives.[109] And even Sam, no erudite literary critic, knows that what is good inside a story is not always good outside of it. Nobody enjoys a story without conflict, except the person living it. Nor do we want our characters to have certainty of a happy ending—it spoils the frisson.[110] Sam realizes that the rule of the Shadow is actually a localized evil and that goodness and beauty live eternally; likewise, the soul possesses an eternal element free from the disturbing evils and cares of life, which can at times survey tragedies undismayed.[111]

Every bit of history, every grand myth, re-narrates the same— ultimately theological—story. Time and story are fractal, and both creation and sub-creation echo the original strains of the divinely bestowed music. As Tolkien says pithily, history often resembles myth because they are made of the same stuff, and they come together in the plan of redemption.[112] Even Aragorn recognizes the permeability of the boundary between legend and fact; the green earth itself is a prime example. Creation is the "Primary Art" which irresistibly influences all creaturely myth- and meaning-making activities.[113] Allegory and story converge with one another as they both travel toward truth. Real life is the only perfectly consistent allegory, and the only perfectly understandable story is allegorical.[114] In other words, the better an allegory is, the better it functions as a story per se, while the deeper a story is, the more easily one can project allegory onto it.[115] The stark good and evil of romance, for instance, rises from its origin in allegory and in the interior war between the soul and sin.[116] Each individual, like the instantiation of a Platonic Form, contains universal truth and exemplifies part of the overarching pattern of truth, but they are not identical to it.[117] Each individual has a story, but they also participate in the "Whole Story."[118] And the whole of a story is greater than the sum of its parts.[119] The Ainur are privileged to gain a glimpse of the sweep of the whole creation story at once, as they see a vast and majestic history with a glorious beginning and a splendid ending, and it leaves them speechless and worshipful.[120]

THE ORDER OF BEING

Unsurprisingly for a conservative Catholic and medievalist, Tolkien's is a hierarchical universe, both in terms of human political structure (monarchy and episcopacy) and metaphysically as a great chain of ordered relations. However, Tolkien seems to distinguish between at least three sorts of hierarchy: those of existence, authority, and love.

In the hierarchy of existence, creatures are more real the more closely they participate in God's own being. An elm tree or a horse is more real than a chimney or a car. The clouds are more real than the roof of a train station.[121] This is because the former are God's creations, while the latter are creations of creations (sub-creations).[122] Yet what does it mean when Tolkien asserts that an imaginary giant's castle is more real than a non-imaginary robot factory?[123] Both are sub-creations and, as such, on a lower level of reality, but one is at least a physical object in the world. We may presume that whereas the robot factory has as its purpose the efficient production of tools for the commodification of the natural world, the giant's castle is primarily meant to be a beautiful place to live. As such, the castle is a better exemplar of God's purpose for our own creative endeavors, and therefore closer to God himself, and therefore more fully participant in God's fundamental existence.

Distinguishing between creation and sub-creation, as above, Tolkien denies a chain of being among created realities themselves and writes that Men and Elves have a relation to the Creator equal to that of the angels, if on a smaller scale.[124] All proceed directly from God, rather than as creations of creations. The Valar are said to be hierarchically on par with the physical world. Yet they are clearly more exalted than any other creatures.[125] This second sense of hierarchy, then, seems to refer to a rank of status or authority. Manwë and the other Ainur are at the top of this scale, followed by the Elves, then Men, and so forth.[126] Within Middle-earth, while Elves and Men are both physically and spiritually far closer than any other created beings, the Noldor have a certain prestige as the noblest of the physically embodied creatures, more elevated than their wild kin or than Dwarves, Men, and other races.

There is apparently one further division, not of authority or reality but of love. Finrod, for example, tells Andreth that sentient beings are more properly to be loved than non-sentient creatures such as animals and trees.[127] And, as mentioned above, the Valar are never called "God's Children" as Men and Elves are—surely a mighty title. Here the Elves and Men are at the top; the Children are the purpose of the whole creation drama, and the Valar exist and rule only to prepare and protect them.

Within the hierarchy of love, though, there is an element of mutuality. Every order of creature has a special purpose and gift unique to itself, which may even be admired by beings of higher orders.[128] Both the upper and lower ranks need each other's mutually beneficent influence. Simplicity becomes baseness without the high and noble; heroism is meaningless without its defense of the ordinary.[129] Human ethics bases itself on the varying bonds between all other things on this scale of being, up to the absolute bond between humans themselves and, presumably at the summit, one's duty to God.[130] Kings and priests both act as intercessors and mediators between higher and lower orders, which is perhaps why Tolkien is so fond of them.[131] The interrelations between nobility and commonness, and especially the ennoblement of the ignoble, are important tropes for Tolkien.[132] This is because he finds in them an echo of the character of God, who exalts the humble and unseats the powerful from their thrones.[133]

THE NATURAL WORLD

Tolkien's love for the natural world is well-known. He was at one point actually more eager to study nature than fairy tales.[134] For him, our relationship to the natural world is part of our metaphysical makeup. We cannot fully flourish apart from it.[135] All living things depend on the natural world, even the twisted monsters of Sauron.[136] We can in times of joy call on the created world to join us in praising God, echoing Psalm 148 and the song of the three children in Daniel.[137]

Though Tolkien's love for the landscapes of the English midlands is well-known, he in fact values vast space most highly. The tracklessness of seas and mountains gives beauty to the cultivated lands carved out from them.[138] This is likely why he feels drawn to the poetry and legends inspired by the desolate landscapes and sea voyages of the North. This is also why he so deplores the space-devouring transportation infrastructure infesting Britain and the destruction of the wilderness or of quaint and simple structures in exchange for more crowded, more efficient modernities. Even the fancies of our imagination are more connected to true being than the dead technology that separates human beings from the world.[139] He admires those who have never bowed their hearts and wills to the evil spirit of the world, defined here as mechanism and scientific materialism.[140] Each of these is an attempt at idolatry, at the denial of God's creation and the exaltation of human power structures instead. Machinery is distinguished from art by its attempt to actualize the desire for power in the primary world, rather than resting content with the construction of a secondary world and the God-given stewardship of creation.[141]

Our responsibility toward creation may be summed up in this term: stewardship. In Genesis God gives Adam and Eve dominion over all creatures and tasks them with dressing and keeping the garden of Eden. God's first commission to the newly created humans in Tolkien's version of the Genesis story is very similar. "Ye are my children. I have sent you to dwell here. In time ye will inherit all this Earth, but first ye must be children and learn. Call on me and I shall hear; for I am watching over you."[142] Similar to the creation anthropology of Irenaeus of Lyon, Tolkien combines regency over the earth with a probationary period of childhood and growth.

Stewardship is no uncommon theme in Tolkien's writing. Sam embodies this philosophy well: "The one small garden of a free gardener was all his need and due, not a garden swollen to a realm; his own hands to use, not the hands of others to command."[143] Denethor, of course, is the steward of Gondor, who holds and protects the realm in place of its true king. Aragorn's role as a type of Christ only makes the term more meaningful. Gandalf, too, exercises a more forthrightly creational stewardship. "All worthy things that are in peril as the world now stands, those are my care. And for my part, I shall not wholly fail of my task ... if anything passes through this night that can still grow fair or bear fruit and flower again in days to come. For I also am a steward."[144]

Stewardship means balancing our right as regents with the rights of nature's true Owner. Man holds dominion over creation in trust from God. We do evil by abusing nature, not just to God but to our neighbor who might have enjoyed it. Misusing fruit by destroying it before it ripens, for example, is more than just robbing its owner. In fact, it robs the world by preventing a good thing from its fulfillment. Some might say that to cut down any tree is an evil, but trees are not our judges or masters. God has placed human beings above the plants and animals. Because we are God's children, we have the right to use all that we find in the world, which he has made for our own good, provided that we do so in the proper way.[145] We ought to show reverence, respect, and gratitude rather than pride or needless destruction.[146] Tolkien rakes Americans for their treatment of their natural resources but believes we have all become increasingly alienated from this aspect of our created nature. Men have less love for the earth and instead busy themselves in destroying and dominating it.[147] He calls pollution orc-work.[148]

The appearance of struggle and of a sort of Malthusian zero-sum game in nature itself is misleading, says Tolkien. God attends to every detail of the creation Music, even to those aspects unheeded by the great.[149] The patterns willed by God unfolded not according to their own will or awareness but as a result of their unknowing movement toward conformity with God's design. This does not mean, however, that such conformity is always perfectly achieved. The proper design of God's creation is harmonious and peaceful, but nature's redness in tooth and claw stems from the fall. Yet despite this, the world is still good at a fundamental level, turning by nature toward the good, healing itself from within.[150]

SCIENCE AND FAERIE

The scientific study of creation can be an act of religious contemplation and an avenue toward knowledge of God.[151] The natural world is important for theology, since our ideas and language about God will be mostly drawn from our observations of it.[152] Far from separating one from the other, Tolkien integrates science and religion, though science remains the handmaiden to theology, not the mistress. He recognizes that biological science is a work in progress rather than a fixed star.[153] Perhaps echoing Chesterton's *Everlasting Man*, he is somewhat skeptical of the semi-scientific prehistoric mythology, for example.[154] He can both adopt and depart from the reconstructed deep history of the earth.

He begins with the observation that God's design of the world is evident in its structure. Going up the scale of being from rocks to plants to animals, we begin to notice patterns exhibited by kin and off-spring, displaying shape, organization, and purpose.[155] This patterning of the universe suggests intelligent design by something vastly more powerful than we are.[156] While each living thing has an ideal pattern, the limitations of a finite (and fallen) world mean that imperfections and variations exist. We can observe in our own day species akin to one another and surmise common descent.[157]

But here theology begins to exert its influence. It is not clear that Tolkien believes in a single common ancestor for all living things. He can speak at the same time of the evolutionary process using the metaphor of a tree or river arising from a single source but also of all existing patterns arising from a few (meaning *not* one) original patterns.[158] He is clear that human beings are not descended from the beasts but *are* akin to them in the mind of God, given their shared characteristics.[159] While Tolkien acknowledges the impulse of vegetarianism—that animals are too similar to us to be the subjects of such violence—he does not agree with it or view killing animals as sinful.[160] As a result of life in a fallen world, creatures cannot live without causing violence or death.

We can see the interplay between science and religion in other areas of Tolkien's work. He finds the scientific and biological questions of Elvish-Human intermarriage just as concerning as the metaphysical and theological ones, for example. An avid science fiction fan, Tolkien also engages the question of Christianity's response to life on other planets. The earth, regardless of size or astronomical importance, is the dramatic center of creation, he says. Even were we to discover other life forms out in the universe, this would not invalidate our concept of redemptive history. God may decide to write other stories, or perhaps the scope of our own story is wider than we know. We are nevertheless unique.[161]

Science has a noble origin and purpose, but as a product of fallen human beings, may be turned to evil. Tom Bombadil allegorizes or exemplifies pure natural science, knowledge of nature for its own sake rather than for instrumental use.[162] We ought to recognize that non-human things possess intrinsic value, apart from our use or study of them.[163] The failure to acknowledge this can result in twin sins that arise from the same impulse and go astray in the same ways. Both scientists and magicians use the inherent powers of the world (themselves ultimately derived from God) in order to create a desired effect. Much like the parallel developments of alchemy and chemistry, the concern is with what works, and with the power being relied on. Scientific, mechanical power relies on the opportune arrangement of objects—a kettle placed on a fire will boil—while magic relies on spells and rituals that postulate the same relationship.

The difference is that such spells are often only means by which the powers that lie behind the visible appearances are compelled to manifest. Tolkien labels this hidden power Faerie. It has an existence independent of the magicians and whatever wicked use is made of its power, and its proper denizens may use this power without exploiting it as the magician does. Faerie is in essence the land of wonder, the place in which one receives the power to achieve beauty directly through the effective operations of will and desire, yet within the limits of the created order. Faerie insists that our normal visible world is only a mask hiding a reservoir of power into which we can drill down, tapping this power so that it spouts up in the metamorphoses of existing forms as well as an endless and unimaginable wealth of new forms yet unknown.[164]

The march of science may be unstoppable, at least by science itself. But for all this, it is not science but fantasy which has kept the light of truth alive, since there the mind is preeminent.[165] Tolkien believes his own work expresses a love for God's creation and that the Elves, as created things, express a mystical truth about nature that science cannot capture. Nature is a life study, or perhaps a study for eternity for those gifted to see it. But there is a part of us that does not exist as a simple material element in the world. As such, if we seek to understand what it means to be human, we are not obligated to study nature and are in fact wholly unsatisfied with purely natural explanations.[166] Elves are "better, warmer, fairer to the heart" than the laws of physics and chemistry.[167] This leads us to Tolkien's doctrine of sub-creation, which we have already had cause to mention but will now address directly.

SUB-CREATION AND ART

Sub-creation is any form of artistic production which uses preexisting matter. God alone actually makes in the proper sense. The world is a work of art which the Creator has made real, giving it the secondary and subordinate reality under God's own reality that we call primary reality.[168] Sub-creation ranges from the Valar who shape the world down to the human author who writes works of fantasy literature. This latter work is our focus here.[169] Fantasy is emphatically not escapist in a pejorative sense; fairy stories and their contents do not denigrate but enrich and ennoble the real world.[170] Human beings, now alienated from their environment due to the fall, still feel a deep desire for communion with other living things.[171] Fantasy fills this need. The magic of fantasy is in fact intimately connected with nature and with our appreciation of it.[172] It helps us to recapture the wonder of the primary world. This is what Tolkien calls "recovery."[173]

As Tolkien has it in his poem "Mythopoeia," we make because we are in the image of a Maker. We are created creators.[174] All art comes ultimately from God. Our own ability is infinitely derivative of God's creative power. We need not only God's grace to achieve art, but grace to cooperate with that grace. While we may derive our building blocks for fantasy from the sensory world, both the final product of the imagination and the faculty of imagination itself come from the original Source.[175] Tolkien's daughter Priscilla describes her father's "Christian belief that without our lives being seen as a journey to God our artistic or other talents will come to nothing."[176]

As is therefore proper to an activity that arises in and is sustained by God, the most basic function of sub-creation is to pay tribute to the infinite potential variety of God's creation, to affirm the basic goodness of the world and of many other worlds that could have been.[177] Tolkien stresses the plural of the word "metaphysics." There is not a single metaphysic, but many, and perhaps an uncountable number.[178] God's creativity is infinite and could have taken many other forms than it in fact has.[179] Based on our finite and limited knowledge, how can we assert that the rules of the existing world are the only possible rules, or the only rules acceptable to God?[180] Our own creativity is in a sense a celebration of these alternate forms; sub-creation is a way of glorifying God for the many *other* ways form, matter, and time might have been put together.[181] In this sort of possibility-play, an author is not bound by any law except that of her own finiteness and the law of non-contradiction.[182]

The goal of sub-creation is art rather than power, which is ultimately the same as a domination and tyrannical reformation of God's good world.[183] Though the Valar, for example, are powerful sub-creators, assisting in making and ordering reality, they cannot change its fundamental laws.[184] Eventually, Tolkien comes to believe the same thing of human sub-creators. An artist working within the mythical past of our own world ought not to introduce principles which are known to be false in the present day. A flat earth cannot exist, even in a myth.[185] This does not mean, were one to write about another world, that different rules might not apply. Tolkien merely believes that an author is not at liberty to distort the truth of the real world while still passing such a picture off as true, even in a sub-creative sense.

Fantasy is in fact the purest, highest, and most potent form of art.[186] Consequently, this ability for sub-creation, though God-given, is not without risk. Any sub-creator ought to approach the task with humility, aware of the great danger in such an enterprise. In attempting to communicate truth, one may end only by spreading one's own form of error which, encased as it is in such a powerfully affective medium, is terribly perilous.[187] Now, importantly, sub-creation as such is a good impulse and not a result of the fall. The Vala Aulë, for instance, shapes the Dwarves not out of a desire to dominate others, but because he wants to imitate his Father in loving the things of his own making.[188] The unfallen humans of Tolkien's temptation narrative already possess the impulse to make, just as the Elves do. They greatly desire knowledge to fill their ignorance and hasten to make the things that arise in their minds.[189] Creative desire seeks shared enrichment and partnership in the delight of making, not delusion or dominion.[190] But this drive is easily corrupted into sin. Nevertheless, God, in order to uphold the great good of free will, even allows the misuse of sub-creative activity in the production of horrors.[191] When we realize the power that a story holds and our own absolute power to shape the world of our imagination, we also begin to desire to wield the same power in the primary world.[192] This way, too, lie the dangers of magic and the machine.

Tolkien presupposes that our sight has been clouded by the sin of domination, one of his prime theological enemies. As such, fantasy in fact cleans our window on the world, clarifying our view of reality and helping us to regain our sight of creation, as it were. We see things as we are meant to see them, as independent from us, and we free ourselves from the obscurity of triteness, familiarity, and ultimately possessiveness.[193] The beautiful peril of fantasy reminds us that nature is God's world and not ours. Story-makers that can depart from nature into imaginary realms are her lovers, not her slaves. And these departures can instill in us the power of language as such, able to conjure the wonder of the presence of things like stone, wood, iron, tree, bread, and wine.[194]

One of the most potent tools of the sub-creator is the word. Tolkien sees language as intrinsically creative, and even magical. The mind, the story, and the language all arose at the same time. We can generalize and abstract from our senses, seeing not only grass but greenness.[195] The adjective is a powerful spell. With it, one can think of golden grass, or of green suns. We are like enchanters, able to take the blue from the sky and the red from blood, and to give it to the eyes of Elves and the scales of dragons.[196] Many critics have tried to account for the effect a good story has on us with terms like "literary belief" or "willing suspension of disbelief." But Tolkien demurs. We instead become successful sub-creators, making a secondary world that other minds can enter into. There are then things which are true within that world—that is, which accord with its laws. That is why we believe it when we are inside it.[197]

Because of the way Tolkien has structured his metaphysics, he can appeal to the image of God in order to grant a much more sweeping power to art than would otherwise be available. But this is simultaneously why he does not approve of mixing sub-creative realities with theological elements of the real world, such as occurs in the Arthurian romances. These reminders of the real truth shatter the illusion and shine a harsh light on the inadequacies of any fictional realm.[198] Tolkien comes, then, to the paradoxical conclusion that the best way to shine the light of holiness through fiction is to separate it almost entirely from direct theological concerns. But this does not mean sub-creation cannot be intensely theological. The many spiritual readings of Tolkien's corpus attest to that.

All artists desire that their work should partake of reality.[199] Such a desire is at once powerfully in love with the real world—with its colors, textures, histories, landscapes—but at the same time unsatisfied by it, yearning for something more.[200] The sub-creative desire indeed has no apparent biological function and can sometimes be at strife with the basic needs of the body (the term "starving artist" comes to mind here). But might we surmise that the purpose of the human impulse is the enrichment of creation—that God might take our small offerings of art and grant them true being?[201] In the Ainulindalë, the Art in which the Valar aided now exists on the same plane as themselves in the hierarchy of being.[202] This is perhaps the ultimate dream of the sub-creator—to enter into the world one has made. Tolkien toyed with this dream himself many times. But further discussion must wait until the final chapter.

THE ENDS OF CREATION

What is the purpose and destiny for creation and for its chief feature, humankind? Presumably, that human beings inherit the earth, as the first Men were promised in the "Tale of Adanel."[203] But more fundamentally, our destiny as creatures is wrapped up in the contemplation of God's uncreated beauty. This, in turn, makes creation itself beautiful by reflection. God created us because he delights in looking at us as we reflect his own beauty and blessedness.[204]

This involves not only a passive gazing but an active working. Much like the artist constantly gazing at his muse, we gaze at God in order to bring forth creations of our own. Our sub-creative tasks are in some sense foreordained as part of the singular prime creation, and thus a fundamental element in its purpose.[205] Sub-creative art may assist in adorning the "Primary Art" of reality, the evolution and enrichment of creation, as Tolkien calls it.[206] God gives human beings free will so that through our operations everything may be completed to the smallest degree.[207]

The secrets of the Music are also equated with the purpose of the world.[208] Creation begins with that vast and splendid music, and it shall end with one mightier still—one in which Men will now join, knowing God's heart, mind, and intentions to the best of their capability.[209] This is similar to Irenaeus's recapitulation theory, in which the history and purpose of the world operates on a symmetrical pattern. Tolkien hints that the whole of history is but the great rehearsal for the second performance of the Music, which God too will grant reality as the new creation.[210]

The great tales never end; their characters merely come and go.[211] The world is an age-long battleground between the forces of good and evil because earth is the jewel of God and the home (sometimes the mansion) of his Children.[212] This is, in part, what Tolkien means by "The Tale of Arda" or the story of the world. It is called such because it is finite and bounded, with beginning and end. It is a work of art, a finite story which can be contemplated with pleasure and awe by the blessed who have taken part in it, as well as by God himself.[213]

Perhaps not even the Powers know the end of this story. If the world is indeed a great tale, then God may, like a master artist, keep the greatest moment hidden. Those who have been listening carefully may catch foreshadowings and hints, as the author desires. And when those foreshadowings are fulfilled, this does not diminish the surprise, wonder, or satisfaction. The response of the audience is in a way a part of the story itself. We share in his authorship, as Finrod realizes. But such a perlocutionary effect could never come about were the whole tale told in a preface.[214] Living as they do in the distant past of Middle-earth, neither Finrod nor Andreth know what the supreme moment of the story might be, but we realize it is the incarnation of Christ, as will be discussed in chapter 8. This is the axis around which creation revolves.

FURTHER READING

His work on the doctrine of creation stands as one of Tolkien's primary contributions to modern theology. As such, there are several excellent resources available. Ecocriticism in general has become one of the standard subfields surveyed each year by the journal *Tolkien Studies*. The following studies focus not merely on Tolkien's environmentalism but on the Christian doctrine of creation as such.

Curry, Patrick. "Middle-earth: Nature and Ecology." In *Defending Middle-earth: Tolkien: Myth and Modernity*, 48–86. New York: Houghton Mifflin, 2004.

Dickerson, Matthew, and Jonathan Evans, eds. *Ents, Elves, and Eriador: The Environmental Vision of J. R. R. Tolkien*. Lexington, KY: The University Press of Kentucky, 2006.

Hood, Gwyneth. "Nature and Technology: Angelic and Sacrificial Strategies in Tolkien's *The Lord of the Rings*." *Mythlore* 19, no. 4 (1993): 6–12.

Larsen, Kristine. "Medieval Cosmology and Middle-earth: A Lewisian Walk Under Tolkienian Skies." *Journal of Tolkien Research* 3, no. 1 (2016): Article 5.

Lawhead, Stephen R. "J. R. R. Tolkien: Master of Middle-earth." In *Tolkien: A Celebration*, edited by Joseph Pearce, 156–71. San Francisco: Ignatius Press, 2001.

McIntosh, Jonathan S. "The Metaphysics of the Ainur" and "The Metaphysics of the Music and the Vision." In *The Flame Imperishable: Tolkien, St. Thomas, and the Metaphysics of Faërie*, 73–156. Kettering, OH: Angelico, 2017.

McBride, Sam. "Divine Intervention in the Third Age: Visible Powers" and "Divine Intervention in the Third Age: Invisible Powers." In *Tolkien's Cosmology: Divine Beings and Middle-earth*. Kent, OH: Kent State University Press, 2020.

Whittingham, Elizabeth A. "Tolkien's Mythology of Creation." In *The Evolution of Tolkien's Mythology: A Study of the History of Middle-earth*, 37–63. London: McFarland, 2007.

Wood, Ralph C. "The Great Symphony of Creation." In *The Gospel according to Tolkien: Visions of the Kingdom in Middle-earth*, 11–57. Louisville: Westminster John Knox, 2003.

IV

HUMANITY

Tolkien's most frequent theological designator for humanity is the Children of God.[1] The concept of a child implies a likeness to the parent (thus, Son of God), though in our case such likeness is derivative. That Elves and Men are the lone Children of God within Tolkien's legendarium—excluding other creatures such as Dwarves and Ents—therefore means that God's likeness resides in these creatures in a mode unavailable to other such beings.[2] This is the doctrine of the *image of God*.

THE IMAGE OF GOD

The image of God, taken from Genesis 1:26, is the central tenet of Christian anthropology. The image is that which makes us like God; it is the essence of humanity. But in what, exactly, the image *consists* is never defined in the biblical text. Thinkers throughout history have parsed it in many different ways. While Tolkien does not speak about the image of God directly at much length, it retains a prominent if implicit place in his thought, and he is quite vocal about those things that make human beings distinctly themselves: the image of God in so many words. We can divide Tolkien's position on the issue into a positive and a negative aspect. If the human being is *like* God rather than *identical with* God, this means that the human being is both similar and different to her Creator. This positive similarity Tolkien defines as freedom and creativity.[3] The negative difference Tolkien posits as mortality and homesickness.[4] We will explore each of these in turn.

FREEDOM

Free will is perhaps the most prominent of the distinctly human characteristics Tolkien emphasizes. We have already discussed human freedom in relation to God's providence in chapter 3. As has been demonstrated, Tolkien does not deny God's influence over human life, but he does conceive of the world as the interplay between fate, freedom, and chance. Here we examine free will from the human perspective rather than the divine, with emphasis on these three aspects.

Human beings possess a basic character with considerable diversity in behavior.[5] Tolkien compares a human being to a seed, with inborn traits and predispositions yet with a capacity to grow and develop into a totally unique specimen.[6] What we conceive as changes are actually the outworking of the hidden patterns embedded in the seed's nature, although modified by the situation and circumstances in which the seed is planted. This sort of determination—between created character and experiential modification—is on a different plane from the purely physical chain of cause and effect Tolkien labels as fate.[7]

Fate is the network of physical chances in the world able to be used by free persons.[8] It deals only with the backdrop of the world, the setting in which the drama of freedom plays out, and never to personal decisions themselves.[9] This setting is impossible to change, but the use that free agents make of their circumstances is up to them. Will is the force that galvanizes the whole production.[10] Bilbo was fated to find the Ring but not to surrender it. He could have chosen otherwise. One might be fated to encounter his enemy, but the way he treats him when they meet is his to decide.[11]

So we must supplement the analogy of the seed with another. A man is not merely a seed developing out of a pattern, but also a gardener. We can create our own character through conscious intent, even to the extent that we can greatly alter ourselves.[12] This is what Tolkien defines as freedom. The Men of Middle-earth, for instance, can shape their life beyond the Music of the Ainur, an ability no other being possesses.[13] Yet humans rarely appreciate their gift, since their perspective is so limited.[14] All God's gifts contain an element of danger, since lack of danger means lack of power, and the gift would be meaningless. So it is with God's "Great Tale" and the free will of the actors within it.[15] The abuse of the gift of freedom, even to reject God himself, is a foreseen and acceptable byproduct.[16] Such a mystery is one into which angels long to look, but the patience of God in putting up with such disobedience is beyond their comprehension.[17]

This does not mean that every moment of our lives is the setting for an epic instance of self-determination. We make many decisions that do not qualify for this robust definition of freedom. Tolkien speaks here only of fully aware and conscious decisions. We constantly make other decisions on intuition or instinct, but praise and blame only accrue to those decisions based in considered reflection. The actively willed purpose can be either helped or hindered by chance, but a person remains morally accountable and cannot blame fate for their situation.[18]

CREATIVITY

Creativity is Tolkien's other great emphasis. Human beings create in our own derivative measure because we are patterned after a Creator.[19] Made in the image of the true God, even lost humans in turn make gods in their own image.[20] Estranged from God and disgraced we might be, but our creativity is still like the refracted rays of the single unified light of God, shining from mind to mind as we share our sub-creative activity with one another.[21] The reduction of reality onto the plane of scientific materialism is a violation of our essence. Tolkien decries it in his poem "Mythopoeia." He pictures the "progressive" element as so many erect apes, walking a flat and dusty path into the abyss, having forsaken artistry for immutable scientific determinism.[22] Indeed, Tolkien goes on to say that the suppression of creativity is akin to satanic tyranny.

Human beings create meaning not through observation alone but through imagination, gleaning the spirit of insight from the letter of sense experience. The truth of things resides just as much in this imaginative element as in the bare physical description. Stars are not mere balls of gas but really are, in a sense, bursting flowers of living silver. The heavens are not a void but a jeweled tent. The earth is not an expanse of dirt but the womb of the great mother. We are meaning-making animals, and the importance we bestow on things actually comes to reside in those things, for our creativity, especially in the realm of fantasy, is a natural activity in accord with our design.[23] Speech and language are direct gifts from God.[24] Creativity neither denigrates reason nor obscures scientific truth.[25] Rather than lead us to escape from the created world, it accents it. Art is simply an inescapable facet of our existence.

MORTALITY

There is also a privative aspect to the image of God. Children are like but not identical to their parents. Namely, human beings are limited and mortal compared to God's infinity and immortality. We are created and derived rather than Creator and Originator. Finitude and the mistakes and barriers inherent to it are not sinful but are inevitable byproducts of our creatureliness.[26] Mortality is also a part of the biological and spiritual nature of man as creature.[27] God the creator is spirit and totally simple. But embodied creatures are non-simple, composed of body and spirit, and so the separation of these two elements is always logically possible.[28] For a more extensive discussion of death, see chapter 12. Here we simply note the basic outlines.

All human beings desire to escape from death, but Tolkien's legendarium characteristically views death as a sort of gift.[29] Within the mythology, Men have a unique form of mortality different than the Elves. Whereas Elves can be killed and their spirits leave their bodies, they always return to them eventually in a form of reincarnation. Elvish death is impermanent, since they are bound to the life of the physical world.[30] But Men face a true death, an absolute departure from the circles of the world.[31] As such, this sort of death is in fact a return to the direct presence of God, a great gift enviable even by the Valar.[32] Death is ultimately the avenue of homecoming and should be seen as such rather than feared. This is as one with the next aspect of the image below.

Unlike the gift of freedom, however, the gift of death is not present in the earliest drafts of the story.[33] It is only during his middle period that Tolkien begins to conceive of death as an escape from the world into eternity. Tolkien's mature position is that death is a curse which can be transformed into a gift if accepted with faith. Regardless, Tolkien never departs from the belief that man as an individual and as a race will die, but that our spirits endure beyond death.[34] He is clear that the immortality of the soul is for him a logical necessity, though it is not certain why he takes this to be the case.[35]

HOMESICKNESS

All man's works are laden with a certain sadness, usually the sadness of exile.[36] The eyes of man always seek for something they cannot find and are therefore easily bored with the world and its contents. This is because the earth is not our home.[37] We are homesick for our eternal city. Humans are ultimately meant to escape the world and its bounds into eternity in the direct presence of God.[38] This discontented homesickness is bound up with both freedom and death.[39] God has willed that our hearts should seek beyond the world and find no rest within it, so that we are drawn fully toward him.[40] Here Tolkien echoes Augustine's famous dictum that our hearts are restless until they find their rest in God. Temporal things by nature can never satisfy the human soul, which is designed for eternity and the beatific vision.[41]

ASPECTS OF THE IMAGE: THE RACES OF MIDDLE-EARTH

Perhaps no element of Tolkien's fiction is better known than are his creations of separate sentient races of beings alongside the human. And although not human in the biological sense, all of Tolkien's mythical races participate in the idea of humanity. Indeed, each of his created beings serve to accentuate and expostulate on a certain facet of human nature.[42] "The ancient English ... would have felt no hesitation in using 'man' of elf, dwarf, goblin, troll, wizard or what not, since they were inclined to make Adam the father of them all," Tolkien writes.[43] Aragorn's comments on the universal nature of morality imply a continuity of experience between all of Tolkien's races.[44] By exploring the essential elements in each of Tolkien's fictional races, we are in fact exploring his evaluation of the human condition in its various modes.

It should here be noted that the two most important kindreds, Elves and Men, come about as a result of God's introduction of two new themes into the music of creation. Importantly, God creates Elves and Men alone, without contribution from the angels. This is why they are called the Children of God and specially loved or hated by the Valar, since they too proceed from God directly.[45] The Children are an incalculable element of mystery: free and rational creatures like the angels but of smaller status and power.[46]

It is important to flesh out whether, in Tolkien's cosmology, Elves and Men are introduced separately or at once. God inserts two new themes into the Music in response to Melkor's intrusions upon the first theme. Since the description of these themes is literally a tonal description of the nature of that aspect of creation, it is important to be clear on which theme represents Elves and which Men in Tolkien's mind. The second gathers power and has new beauty, while the third theme, beginning softly and delicately, nevertheless grows in strength and profundity.[47] Do both Children begin in weakness and grow in power, or is this a uniquely human or Elven characteristic? Christopher Tolkien has posited, and it has largely been an established point, that Elves come in the second theme and Men come in the third.[48] This is in keeping with the point of view of *The Silmarillion*, an Elf-centric work. Humans in this Elvish conception are a sort of back-up plan, a further fallback thought of God in response to Morgoth's interference.

But we have already seen that Men, not Elves, are the true focal point of creation, despite being the second-comers. Might it not be the case that the Elves are actually the third theme rather than the second? The scheme would look like this: God delivers a first theme, an unfallen creation with no blemish which needs no redemption. Due to Morgoth's malice (not, however, unforeseen by the Creator), this theme is corrupted, and God responds with a second theme. He introduces humanity (and the incarnation of the God-Man, the true

Adam) into world history in order to redeem the creation. But the Men of the second theme are also victims of sin, for Satan's counter-music continues. God thus introduces the third theme, the Elves, in order to aid mankind in its redemptive process.

We find good evidence for this view. "The fairies came to teach Men song *and holiness*," writes Tolkien in one of the earliest entries in his Elvish lexicon.[49] Humans are destined to replace Elves *from the beginning*, Tolkien states elsewhere.[50] Again, in *Tolkien On Fairy-stories*, Tolkien asserts that human beings *need* fairy stories in order to recover their vision for the mission they must undertake as sub-creators. The gospel is itself a fairy-story; it participates in the world of the Elves, to follow the logic of the essay. In short, human beings are not the afterthought but the essential. The Elves are the helpmates of humanity, inspiring art and creativity, teaching sensitivity to beauty and light, and exalting humanity to its proper place through this aspect of recovery.

Elves

The Elves are both fundamentally similar and different to Men.[51] They are both aspects of the "Humane," that adjective Tolkien uses to describe human nature without limiting it specifically to the Men of his mythology.[52] Elves represent certain elements of the talents and desires of men, having some of the freedoms and powers we wish we could possess, such as immortality and artistic prowess, along with the beauty and sorrow that comes with them.[53] Outside of his mythology, Tolkien continues to affirm that the Elves are made in the image and likeness of Men, freed from our most pressing limitations. Tolkien names these as mortality and the inability directly to achieve the objects of our imagination and desire.[54] Phrased in a positive way, Elves embody the artistic, aesthetic, and purely scientific aspects of humanity raised to a higher pitch than we actually observe, added to greater beauty, longer life, and nobility.[55]

The central characteristic of Elven nature is beauty.[56] Eru declares that they are the fairest of all earthly creatures, possessors and creators of more beauty than any other beings.[57] The Elven sensitivity to beauty means they are enraptured with creation in every sense. They love the physical world, seeking to contemplate and understand it for its own sake as other than themselves, especially in the sense of a reality proceeding from God in the same sense as themselves.[58] The Elves demonstrate Tolkien's distinction between art and technology. They do not use nature as a simple material for production or power. What we call their magic is simply art freed from its human limitations and made more effortless, complete, and correspondent to the vision of the artist.[59] They are specially talented in the construction of beautiful languages.[60] In short, they are the ideal sub-creators.[61]

This sensitivity to beauty causes both joy and sadness. A heart filled with beautiful and glorious visions is also one filled in large part with unsatisfied desire.[62] The Elves begin as "grown-up children" whose sight and delight are never dulled by familiarity or repetition.[63] But likewise their love of the world is poignant and increasingly sorrowful as the years lengthen, and they see its end approach. They become burdened with the memory of things they have loved which will never return.[64] Thus, by the end of the Third Age, the Elves are withdrawn from the world due to their own sorrows and concerns drawn from their long and tragic history.[65] They teach us that deathlessness is as much a burden as death, if not spent in the presence of God.[66] Each race has a natural life-span embedded in its biological and spiritual nature, which cannot be increased. Seeking to do so is a torment, Tolkien believes.[67] The history of the Elves teaches us to accept the span of time God gives us.

But the Elves are also filled with another sadness. Their doom is to love and beautify the world, never leaving it, and yet to make way for Men, fading as Men increase and come to enjoy the world that the Elves have prepared.[68] There is a sadness intrinsic to the Elves, who are destined to live only by the mingling of their bloodline with that of Men, as with Aragorn and Arwen.[69] In the final perspective, might we even conclude that in God's plan the Elves exist *only* to ennoble the human race?[70]

Men

While the primary focus of Tolkien's history is the Elves, Men must inevitably enter into it. Both the author and the audience are human, after all, and will desire that humans should be represented in themselves and not merely as transfigured or partially represented by other fantastic races. Nevertheless, while growing in importance by the Third Age of Middle-earth, Men are not yet the main actors.[71] This does not negate the thesis about the centrality of humans above; it merely states the perspective from which a certain tale is told. Because Tolkien writes his myths from an Elvish perspective, his description of humanity proper usually focuses on the way in which Men differ from Elves. It is a sort of description of humanity from outside, as if an alien species were performing an anthropological study. Tolkien's races reflect elements of human nature. When Tolkien comes to write about Men themselves, therefore, his observations must relate to what he conceives as specially central to the human condition. In other words, if other elements are represented by other races, then whatever is left for Men as such will be of prime importance. It is only Men, for example, who receive from God the ability to direct their own fates in the world, as noted above. In this section we will focus on the fictional interaction between Men and Elves, and the way this reflects back upon human nature in itself.

Besides freedom, the other chief characteristic of Man, according to the Elves, is world-weariness or a longing to depart from the world for somewhere else.[72] They are guests and strangers.[73] This is because the gift of Men is mortality, freedom not only from fate but from being bound to the world.[74]

Men are more readily manipulated than Elves, who can easily read the thoughts of Men—at least, those thoughts they wish to communicate.[75] They are shown to be easily swayed from the good, often using their singular gift of free will to the grief of God.[76] Partially this is because God has made the Elves too similar to the angels to become easy prey to wickedness. As such, Morgoth and his followers have chiefly focused on cozening and corrupting Men.[77] But the Elves observe a tension between failures and fizzles on the one hand and unexpected flowerings on the other.[78]

The Elves have a special power over the hearts of Men, which is both good and ill. We see the Elves as fair and wondrous, but we suffer by comparison, and our mortality becomes a heavier burden.[79] The Elven aspect of the humane—intense focus on art and beauty—ought to be only one strand in the web of humanity, which also includes freedom to action and a rootedness in simple pleasures. The Elves are an ideal to be striven for in one aspect of life, not a model to be copied *tout court*. Mythologically, Tolkien clarifies this through his various Elven intermarriages.

In general, Elves and Men should not intermarry.[80] This meeting of the kindreds only occurs as a result of God's own intervention and decree, for that which God has made different may not become alike while the world exists.[81] Through Beren and Lúthien, and the few others, there is an infusion of an angelic and Elvish strain into the human race—a link between ourselves and the older world.[82] Because of God's plan, human nature becomes more Elven. Human art and poetry are dependent upon the presence of this strain.[83]

This is because Men are destined to supersede the Elves. We do not love the world in itself as the Elves do, but we are paradoxically also the source of the world's ultimate healing. God's plan of redemption counters the destruction of creation by the wickedness of Men with its healing through the goodness of Men.[84] The Elves serve to offset the possessive domination of human nature and to train Men to achieve their ultimate destiny. Men, too, serve to fill up a lack in Elven nature. Men have the special inclination to love God above and before God's creation. The Elves prioritize the creation, which results in sadness since the creation is not eternal and can be corrupted and lost. But, Tolkien says, the Elves will be delivered from their sadness through the example of holy Men who teach them to love God first and foremost.[85]

Hobbits

Hobbits are a branch of the race of Men. Like Men, they lack the preternatural powers of Elves or Dwarves, but unlike the Big Folk, they are more connected to the natural world and free from ambition and greed.[86] *The Lord of the Rings* is told mostly from the perspective of hobbits and is thus the only anthropocentric legend of the Elder Days. The tale rises from hobbits rather than Men because Tolkien meant to emphasize the place of unforeseeable choices on world affairs and the oft-overlooked virtues of the small and forgotten.[87] This is why hobbits are short: partly to symbolize the pettiness of the unimaginative man but mostly to demonstrate the amazing unexpected heroism of the weak and ordinary.[88] They represent pity and a sort of uncomplaining courage in impossible situations.[89] They are able to cope with any conceivable amount of horror; their own nature and reasoning powers, combined with the grace they receive along the way, mean they refuse to compromise or submit to evil.[90] Hobbits are, in short, simple ordinary people, lacking in apparent artistry or heroism, but with the potential to see such things develop.[91]

But hobbits are by no means idealizations. They represent both the positive and negative aspects of a certain segment of human experience. We sometimes see in Sam (the most hobbit-like of the hobbits) a sort of vulgar closed-mindedness, proud of its own smug judgments based on a limited perspective.[92] However, many hobbits, like Sam, are transformed and elevated through contact with higher things. In an early draft of *The Lord of the Rings*, Frodo claims to be an ordinary hobbit bowed down by an un-hobbitlike fate. The Elf Gildor retorts that he must not then be an ordinary hobbit. But the hobbit half will suffer from following the other half of him worthy of so strange a fate, until it too (without ceasing to be hobbit) also becomes worthy. Indeed, says Gildor, that may be the purpose of Frodo's fate to begin with.[93] Here Tolkien implies a sort of synthesis between the simple hobbit aspect of humanity and the higher Elvish aspect. A fully-orbed humanity involves both. Our hobbit element should not be despised but trained to rediscover a higher beauty.[94]

We can see this transformation in all four of the hobbit characters by the end of *The Lord of the Rings*. Hobbits aren't fitted for high and noble things, says Pippin toward the end of their adventure. Perhaps not, Merry replies, but they can at least now see and honor them. The hobbits may never be the same sort of heroes as Aragorn or Faramir, but they can leave their insularity behind and cultivate an appreciation for the noble things of life. Begin with what you are fitted to love, but recognize the deeper and higher things and appreciate their impact on your own context, he recommends. He ends with a very hobbit-like dismissal, and a return to the practical: "But I don't know why I am talking like this. Where is that leaf? And get my pipe out of my pack, if it isn't broken."[95]

Dwarves

Because the Dwarves were made by Aulë alone and not in concert with the other Valar in the Music, they are more limited and alienated than other races. They have great skill but little beauty except when they imitate the Elves.[96] Though, like the Orcs, they came from the trespass of one of the Valar, they are not evil since they were not made from malice or mockery but from the desire to imitate God.[97] God adds females to the male Dwarves Aulë created, presumably because male and female complementarity is essential to life, whether in reproduction or in culture. But because God does not wish to alter Aulë's work, female Dwarves largely resemble their male counterparts.[98] Gimli's desire to leave Middle-earth and voyage into the West with Legolas is totally unique from every angle. But it is one of those exceptions that always seem to crop up in any history.[99]

For the major length of Tolkien's writing, the Dwarves are not numbered among the Children of God. Tolkien's Elvish annalist writes that they have no soul and therefore a skill in craft but no art or poetry.[100] Besides the idea of Dwarves as soulless creatures, shocking to anyone who has encountered the warmth and loyalty of Thorin's company in *The Hobbit*, we see here that Tolkien clearly associates art and poetry with spiritual activity. For Tolkien, art is impossible without a soul.

Tolkien revises this passage to make it clear that this is only an Elvish perspective, and that Eru will accept the Dwarves into eternal life.[101] They will be elevated to the place of Children at the end of time, and their destiny will be to serve Aulë and remake the world after the final battle.[102] There is also a very late note, postdating the manuscripts from which *The Silmarillion* is derived, stating that from the beginning the Dwarves are "the third children."[103]

Other Races

There are other races and creatures to whom Eru grants life. The Eagles and Ents are prime examples.[104] Whether creatures such as Orcs, trolls, or dragons have souls or spirits is a debated question. Tolkien does not include the creation of souls in the proper work of a sub-creator.[105] As such, if God grants souls to such creatures, this entails that they are not irremediably evil and must be granted basic rights as creatures of God.[106] In later writings, Tolkien struggles mightily to come up with a theological rationale for the existence of Orcs.[107] See the discussion on this subject in chapter 7.

Real Fairies?

Tolkien's musings on fairies in his drafts of *Tolkien On Fairy-stories* make it clear that his theories about the nature of Elves and Ainur in Middle-earth derive from his theories about the possible existence of fairies in the real world.[108] Here he remarks that on the one hand, fairies are near in stature to humanity, capable of sin and fall, taking or able to take human shape, and doomed to immortality while the world lasts, and afterwards perhaps nothing. On the other hand, they are non-incarnate minds or souls, appearing as human only because that is the impression they make on our own souls, minor daemons or spirits who aided God in making effective his divine idea for some particular element of the world. Regardless of their nature, they derive from the creating will of God and are subject to the same moral law as the rest of the universe.[109]

BODY AND SOUL

The image of God is not the only element in a theology of humanity. The body-soul relation, gender, and human society must also be considered. As is frequently the case with Tolkien, he freely discusses practical matters like gender and politics in nonfictional context, but when it comes to metaphysical issues such as the soul, he more frequently couches his views within his fiction. Nevertheless, as has been stressed before, the metaphysics of Middle-earth are by and large also the metaphysics of primary reality, so while this section draws largely from Tolkien's fiction, it is also in every point consistent with traditional Christian theology.

In "The Debate of Finrod and Andreth," Tolkien discusses the three standard views on the body/soul relation. In addressing this subject we encounter the two prominent Elvish words *fëa* and *hröa*, signifying roughly "soul" and "body" respectively.[110] *Fëa* is associated with breath, as it is in Hebrew and Greek, and also related to the word "radiance," for light is the most appropriate symbol of the indwelling spirit. The spirit is the light of the bodily house.[111] The body is the house of the spirit's inner fire. It indwells and permeates it and gives it life.[112] In strong souls, the fire of the spirit can consume one's earthly body.[113]

Finrod and Andreth discuss two deficient views first. Some say that Man is simply one of the beasts, although the newest and most cunning, and there is no such thing as spirit. For Tolkien, this stance has unwanted ethical consequences. In a draft passage of *Tolkien On Fairy-stories*, he writes that the expansion of evolutionary theory beyond the biological has tended to produce both arrogance and servility. We have dominated other animals by mere force and cleverness and are in the end tyrants rather than kings.[114] Others advocate for a bipartite distinction between body and spirit, referring to them metaphorically. The body is the house, and within it is the fire or breath of life. But this fire is more like a life force and is shared with all living things. Such a position may be the result of natural theology, but it is superseded by revelation.

The most correct position is a tripartite one, which distinguishes between "earth," "fire," and "Dweller." The body is the earth of which the house of the spirit is built. It is inanimate and inert. The fire is the life force, the principle of growth, commonly referred to as "spirit" in tripartite systems. But the "Dweller" or "Indweller" (always capitalized) is the master of both body and spirit. This is what tripartite systems call the "soul," the source of personal identity and agency. It is the soul that holds moral accountability, although its actions affect all three elements.

Why Tolkien most often speaks only of spirit/mind and body, rather than of all three, is unknown. Perhaps his tripartite views only develop later. After Augustine, the standard Catholic view is the bipartite one, so here in Tolkien's late thought we see him side with the early church fathers like Irenaeus and the Cappadocians against Augustine and Thomas. Likely this is merely a result of Tolkien's reading of Bible verses such as 1 Thessalonians 5:23 and Hebrews 4:12. As far as can be discerned, he uses the words "soul" and "spirit" interchangeably, and we will follow his usage.

All human beings consist of a soul-body structure.[115] Human souls come direct from God.[116] Only God can create spirits, and each spirit is unique by nature. But God has delegated the production of bodies to his creatures by natural processes. This is the particular trait of human beings, that they combine physical and spiritual elements in a single nature.[117] Our spirits are akin to those of angels, and our bodies to animals.[118] Each human soul is as strong and immovable as that of the mightiest angel, but as limited and little as the tiniest child.[119]

Personal identity resides in the spirit, although the concept of self includes the body.[120] Each spirit is integral and unique, like the Divine Spirit from which it derives, though finite.[121] Personhood derives from God.[122] It is a unique identity that cannot be disintegrated or absorbed by any other.[123] Each spirit is created directly by God and sent into the world.[124] The union of spirit and body, and the provision of body for spirit, occur in the act of childbirth.[125] At that point, spirit and body are intimately connected. Body and soul are totally distinct from each other but are designed for harmonious union of mutual love, essential to the true nature of incarnate beings.[126] Both are incomplete without the other.[127] It seems just as true that the soul is fitted to the body as the body is to the soul. Otherwise, there is a disharmony between the parts, and the body becomes a chain rather than a home.[128] The body is not some impersonal temporary dwelling place; it is a house made for a single dweller. In this way it is not only a house but a raiment.[129] Death is the separation of spirit and body.[130] It is not merely the body but the spirit which is designed for a short or long span on the earth.[131] Once separated from its body, the human spirit leaves time.[132]

Souls are non-spatial and can be united across any distance but can only fully commune with one another when their bodies are near.[133] This works itself out in the construction of language, one of the chief characteristics of incarnate beings.[134] Language is the principle of rational creativity, or *logos* as the New Testament has it. It possesses both a material and an immaterial element. When separated from the body, souls are more easily impressionable by other souls.[135] Tolkien does not shut out the possibility of disembodied wandering souls.[136] One can commune with these ghosts if one's mind is receptive, but it is a wicked and unlawful thing.[137]

Mind and spirit are separate concepts with substantial overlap.[138] Spirit is basically synonymous with soul, and with mind when we speak of rationality in itself (rather than the thinking process that also involves the brain).[139] The concept of mind is akin to that of spirit in its drive toward thought, inquiry, and reflection, in consciousness and self-awareness.[140] It does not occupy space, and perhaps not even time, though it is conditioned by both.[141] We cannot really speak of the mind as being anywhere; the closest we can come is to specify where its attention is.[142] So while it might be possible for a mind to be in more than one place, it is usually in only one.[143] This singular place of attention is centered on the body. Each affects the other. We can never really free ourselves from the body completely—possibly not even in death, since our bodies will be resurrected.[144] Mind always inhabits body, insofar as it is anywhere at all.[145]

The mind is anchored to the body, but there is another immaterial anchorage as well, distinct from the mind. Tolkien does not spell out what this other, non-bodily anchorage might be, but given the religious connotations of the passage, it might be the soul or even God himself.[146] Tolkien's comment here is representative, for the relation between body and soul will doubtless remain mysterious no matter how much we learn.[147] Nevertheless, humans have an intrinsic and instinctual understanding that their existence is contingent, relying on some Other for their continued being.

Tolkien proffers differing views on the nature of the body/soul relation in eternity but affirms that human nature will continue to be embodied in some sense. He speaks of ultimately spiritualized bodies constructed by souls.[148] Alternatively, the spirit takes its body with it, assuming it up into heaven.[149] Regardless, the soul is immortal and indestructible even by God.[150]

GENDER

From the beginning, God made Man male and female.[151] Both share in the image of God equally but play different roles. Despite complex depictions of female virtue such as Éowyn's "manly" stand against the Witch-king or Galadriel's prominence over her husband Celeborn, Tolkien has long been accused of misogyny for his dearth of female characters and outdated views.[152] In general, this is because Tolkien abides by gender roles out of fashion in modern society but hardly objectionable to previous generations. He is a traditionalist and complementarian overall. But Tolkien also offers a refreshing dose of realism by insisting that woman is neither passive and unrealistic object of affection nor merely identical to man. She is another fallen human with a soul in peril, just like a man, and should be treated with respect and concern as such.[153] This section addresses gender and male/female interactions in general, while chapter 10, on ecclesiology, deals more fully with Tolkien's views on the sacrament of marriage.

Gender is part of the soul and not of the body only.[154] It is an element of the whole person.[155] Relations between genders can fall into one of three categories: either purely physical, purely friendly, or that mixture and transcendence of the two which we call romantic love.[156] Souls are both gendered and familially related.[157] Brothers and sisters are spiritually related in a way that husbands and wives are not, for instance.[158] Like marriage, the family relation involves both body and spirit.[159]

All love in fact possesses both a spiritual and a physical component.[160] Married love begins and endures in the will (or the "motions") of the spirit but relates chiefly to bodily activity: closeness of presence, shared activity, and the ordering of daily life.[161] Romantic love cannot always be satisfied; the love between male and female does not always match up. Whether this is a result of the fall or a necessary element in human freedom is unknown.[162] Regardless, the spiritual mastery of the body entails the control of the sexual drive.[163] Tolkien's view of an idealized interaction between body and soul is probably evident in his depiction of the Elven version of this relation, as it is akin to those of Augustine against the Pelagians. Because their spirits are masters of their bodies, they are chaste by nature.[164] Like Plato's microcosm, the rational soul rules the passions of the animal nature. Human spirits are not now fully in control of their bodies.[165] Tolkien agrees with Lewis that a looser sexual ethic has only harmed things and made it harder to raise Christian youth in proper morals. And since these sexual morals are by definition universally correct, they will be lost but for their being passed down.[166]

Women are naturally monogamous. Men are not, at least according to their animal nature.[167] In general, real friendship between men and women is very rare and is usually only possible later in life when the sexual impulse cools down. Otherwise, one side or the other nearly always falls in love with the other. And as a rule, young men do not really want friendship alone, even if they say they do.[168] A male's desire for a female can be purely physical, but a woman's desire for a male means that she wants to bear the male's children. This is true whether the woman realizes it or not.[169] Conversely, women may sometimes enjoy sexual promiscuity, but this is rare. Modern conditions may have changed circumstances and cultural expectations, but they cannot change natural instinct.[170] God's design cannot be thwarted.

Femininity refines, warms, and colors the grossness of masculine nature and emotions.[171] This is our divinely-ordained way of complementing each other. Women are naturally less selfish than men.[172] They are in general more practical and less romantic, despite their verbal sentimentality. They are more inclined to accept bad men in an effort to reform them, and they do not worship the man in the sense in which a young man might adore an idealized woman.[173] They are more realistic about sex and don't find sexual jokes funny.[174] This is not to say women are not sexually driven. But God has given their sexual instinct a different form than the male.

Furthermore, this form makes women quite sympathetic and understanding.[175] The instinct to serve and help can drive a woman to achieve things otherwise outside her natural giftings. The female is receptive, stimulated, and fertilized by the male, and not just in a sexual sense. Tolkien uses female students as examples. An intelligent woman can quickly grasp the male teacher's point but can rarely go any further on her own, he opines. A man can think of his work, his friends, and so forth, but even career-focused women are almost immediately domestically minded.[176] While the first thing the Elven males see is the starlight and the world, the first sight for the Elven females is their spouse. Thus, her first love is for her husband, while her love for the world comes later.[177] Tolkien takes this idea from Genesis 3:16, God's decree toward Eve for her disobedience: "thou shalt be under thy husband's power, and he shall have dominion over thee." The male is outwardly oriented toward the world while the female is inwardly oriented toward marriage, family, and the home. In this Tolkien agrees with Lewis.[178] Children are not, however, a particularly female domain. Both male and female ought to partake of child-rearing and the life of the family.[179] Tolkien certainly did.

SOCIETY

A discussion of the nature of humanity necessarily also involves a discussion of human society. Despite the variegated picture of human nature Tolkien paints with each of his sentient races, he affirms that morality is universal and constant across cultures and even species.[180] The war between the heroes and the monsters still goes on.[181]

Our chief purpose is the glorification of God and the increase of our knowledge of him, and our knowledge of one another aids us in accomplishing this.[182] When the Valar, for instance, first behold the Children of God, they are delighted to see things other than themselves in which new aspects of God's mind and wisdom are reflected, which otherwise would have been hidden even from the angels.[183]

Tolkien echoes traditional Catholic social teaching in holding that all social bonds begin with the family. God's command to be fruitful and multiply means that marriage and the rearing of children are not mere social constructs. Parents and children are bound by more than just biology; there is an eternal aspect to this element of society.[184] Children themselves are part of society and not a different kind of creature. Both the idealization and the dismissal of children are errors. Growing older does not necessarily mean losing innocence. We are not meant to be eternal children. We should not lose innocence or wonder but mature in them on our appointed journey.[185]

Social cohesion does not require absolute conformity or agreement.[186] But it does need a certain commonality of vision. Usually this has involved a unity of religious sentiment. The agenda for the great meeting of Tolkien's youthful group of friends, the TCBS, included religion, human love, patriotic duty, and nationalism.[187] These four principles, we may imagine, are the foundational principles upon which social identity stands. As a young man he was much taken with the dangers of social degeneration.[188] He and the other members of the T.C.B.S. sought to combat this state, as instruments in God's hands.[189]

Tolkien believes that after the Middle Ages, society fractured because there was no unified religious understanding.[190] We are alienated from one another because we are no longer united in our metaphysics.[191] This is not merely a sociological observation. Human society requires a religious element because happiness comes from fellowship with God.[192] If this is accomplished, human destiny can be fulfilled. We can use all that we find in the world with gratitude and respect and act as the just stewards we were meant to be.[193]

In terms of culture, Tolkien supports Christopher Dawson's views in *Progress and Religion*.[194] Social and cultural similarities and solidarities can endure for many generations.[195] There are characteristic ideas and personalities to different cultures, and these are differences to be celebrated rather than sources of smugness or superiority. He does not accept prevalent colonialist views on non-Western or pre-industrial tribal peoples. More careful and sympathetic studies of these folklores reveal much more sophisticated thought patterns than are immediately evident to Western observers.[196] He is fascinated by the mythology of the American Indian, at least for a time.[197] His professional interest in ancient pre-Christian tales and myths demonstrates that he can see value in many cultures. Whether Christian or pagan, whether civilized or primitive, human cultures convey beauty and truth.

The idea of a race or nation which is inherently evil is heretical, violating the idea that all human beings are made in God's image.[198] In a draft passage reflecting on eugenics, Tolkien writes that evolutionary naturalism has undesirable social consequences.[199] Instead, without necessarily opposing evolution, he affirms a single descent of all human beings from Adam and Eve. He adamantly opposes racism as a result. His response to Nazi enquiries as to any Jewish heritage demonstrates an admiration for Jewish culture and achievement.[200] Regarding the problems between blacks and whites in South Africa, he writes to his son that he knew of them as a boy, and he says he has always taken a special interest in the question of *apartheid*. The treatment of black people almost always horrifies British travelers, but few retain such a generous sentiment for long.[201]

Importantly, though, even many of those who appear least redeemable can be remediated. There are no real Orcs, no people made evil by the intent of their maker, and few even who are so corrupt that they can be written off completely.[202] Social reform is not hopeless. Even many of Sharkey's men turn out alright.[203] Nevertheless, such people do exist and seem irredeemable short of a special miracle. While it seems at the time that there are more of these in Japan and Germany, they also exist in England.[204]

Tolkien's experiences in the Great War influence his depiction of violence and battle. He is no war eagle. When Sam sees a dead Southron, he does not immediately see an enemy. Instead, he sees a person. Sam wonders what the man's name is, where he came from, and whether he is really evil or simply a victim who would rather have stayed home in peace.[205] Tolkien bemoans a horrid pleasure in violence even when administered by the state. We might still have a need to execute a criminal, but not to make a gloating spectacle of his death.[206] Having also lived through the Second World War, he is especially keen on ideological violence. He opposes populism because humility and equality are spiritual principles corrupted by any attempt to formalize and mass-produce them. If we try, we get pride instead, and eventually slavery.[207] Individual ethics cannot be forced and still retain their merit. Such principles must be genuinely felt and internally motivated.

Tolkien has many other opinions about society, not all of which have immediately obvious theological bearing.[208] But even these comments reveal a deep commitment to the sinfulness of man and the corrupting nature of domination. By 1943 Tolkien classifies himself as an anarchist or an absolute monarchist. The idealization of government bureaucracy, and especially of the faceless and impersonal state, troubles him. The fewer people in power, the better, since bossing other men is the worst job a man can have. Almost nobody is fit for it, and especially not those who seek after it. Thus, as he remarks, the medievals were right in holding a man's desire to avoid a bishopric as his best qualification for the position.[209] But as Tolkien observes, this strategy only works if the one man in power remains relatively inefficient and limited. A single madman with an atom bomb is still a fearful prospect.

FURTHER READING

Covering as it does so much of relevant cultural discourse, this locus of theology has no shortage of engagement, especially those seeking to defend Tolkien against charges of bigotry or to bring him up to date with modern ideas. Along with some helpful theological resources, this list also includes some important non-theological texts which nevertheless have direct bearing.

Chance, Jane. *Tolkien, Self, and Other: "This Queer Creature."* New York: Springer, 2016.

Coutras, Lisa. "Part II: On Creation" and "Part VI: On Women." In *Tolkien's Theology of Beauty: Majesty, Splendour, and Transcendence in Middle-earth,* 45–88 and 185–254. New York: Palgrave Macmillan, 2016.

Croft, Janet Brennan, and Leslie Donovan, eds. *Perilous and Fair: Women in the Works and Life of J. R. R. Tolkien.* Altadena, CA: Mythopoeic Press, 2015.

Curry, Patrick. "The Shire: Culture, Society, and Politics." Chapter 2 in *Defending Middle-earth: Tolkien: Myth and Modernity.* New York: Houghton Mifflin, 2004.

Evans, Jonathan. "The Anthropology of Arda: Creation, Theology, and the Race of Men." In *Tolkien the Medievalist*, edited by Jane Chance, 194–224. New York: Routledge, 2003.

Fimi, Dimitra. "A Hierarchical World." In *Tolkien, Race, and Cultural History: From Fairies to Hobbits*, 131–59. London: Palgrave, 2010.

Fornet-Ponse, Thomas. "'Strange and free'—On Some Aspects of the Nature of Elves and Men." *Tolkien Studies* 7 (2010): 67–89.

Kreeft, Peter. "Anthropology." In *The Philosophy of Tolkien: The Worldview behind "The Lord of the Rings,"* 94–118. San Francisco: Ignatius, 2005.

Vaccaro, Christopher. *The Body in Tolkien's Legendarium: Essays on Middle-earth Corporeality.* Jefferson, NC: McFarland, 2013.

V

ANGELS

It is an angel which we must credit for giving us Middle-earth. *Éalá Éarendel engla beorhtast*, Tolkien read in a poem by Cynewulf in 1914—"Hail Earendel, brightest of angels." Tolkien's fascination with the name Earendel was the spark to a very great flame, and it led him to write what Christopher Tolkien calls the first work of his mythology.[1]

Tolkien has definite beliefs about angelic natures. He reminds his son to remember his guardian angel, who is certainly *not* a plump lady with wings.[2] Nor, he might add, are angels chubby children lounging on wisps of cloud. They are powerful beings, easily mistaken for gods by the uninformed, whose constant greeting in Scripture is "Fear not!" All angels, even fallen ones, are indestructible and immortal by right and nature.[3]

There are many kinds of angels, but the most familiar is the guardian angel, an individual spirit tasked with shepherding a single human soul. This is the sort of angel about which Tolkien reports having a mystical experience in 1944 while preparing to receive the Eucharist. In a letter, Tolkien relates a vision or mental image of the "Light of God" and one of millions of glittering motes suspended within it.[4]

The relation between the light and the mote creates a line of light, and it is this line which, Tolkien realizes, represents his guardian angel.[5]

An angel, he says, is not a thing standing between God and the creature; instead, the angel is God's attention itself personalized. Tolkien is clear that this is not a figure of speech but a real person. Tolkien goes on to reason from the Trinity to angelology. In a finite parallel to the infinite, the angel is the finite but divine love and attention of God manifesting as a person, as the love of the Father and Son is a person.[6] Our angel is a spiritual umbilical cord, a lifeline facing two directions: toward us, and behind us toward God. A guardian angel is a sentient mode of connection to God, which sustains us even when we are not attending to God directly. This does not mean that our angels somehow circumvent our own need to seek God. All humans, as souls with free will, are yet dependent upon and connected to God as creatures. We ought not to grow weary of facing God under our own strength, even though provided from behind.[7] Angels merely assist. They are, though, specially equipped to defend us from threats both material and immaterial.[8] Tolkien recognizes that guardian angels partake in spiritual war on behalf of God's creatures, such that there are times of more or less activity.[9]

Angels are not the same sort of creatures as we are. According to Thomistic metaphysics, angels are pure spirits—"they shall neither marry nor be married" (Matt 22:30). When Tolkien writes of his son's angel that "he" is specially needed, he places the masculine pronoun in quotations because he knows angels do not have gender in the way we do.[10] Angels, as pure minds, also do not have the same relation to place as do human beings. Minds can be in more than one place at a time but are more properly located wherever their attention is directed. For humans, this is probably in one place only, but angels might have the capability of directing their attention to multiple concurrent events and thus occupying more than one place, metaphorically speaking.[11] Despite being pure spirits, however, angels are not of the same nature as God. They are not eternal in the sense that God is, for instance; they change through time, though slowly.[12]

While Tolkien does make several statements about angels in his nonfiction writing, he has much more to say through his fiction. The remainder of this chapter will therefore focus on the role of angels in Middle-earth. Before we embark on such an extensive analysis of Tolkien's conception of the angelic beings who rule the world, we must meet with a serious objection. What is the point? Is this chapter not speculative? Does it not fallaciously blur the line between fiction and fact? An analysis of Tolkien's characterizations of Manwë, Aulë, and others must have little bearing on angelology in the primary world. To look to the roles and activities of the Valar in order to inform study on angelology in the primary world seems like a category mistake. But this is not the case. Tolkien's views (whether purely fictional or intended to reflect an actual belief) are in fact much more consonant with the biblical picture than our more modern, pared down picture. Our angelology is actually deficient. No, Tolkien's picture of the angelic kingdom is consonant to a remarkable degree with biblical theology's picture of what is termed the "divine council."[13]

THE VALAR AND
THE DIVINE COUNCIL

Many passages of Scripture speak of an assembly of powerful beings who serve as God's court. They are often called the "sons of God" (*bene' Elohim*). They can even be called gods themselves ("God hath stood in the congregation of gods: and being in the midst of them he judgeth gods," Ps 82:1). We see the angels present themselves before God in Job 1–2, and in God's reply to Job, he asks, "Who laid the corner stone [of the Earth], when the morning stars praised me together, and all the sons of God made a joyful melody?" (Job 38:6–7). Here the angelic court sings a song at the dawn of creation, praising God for his work. In 1 Kings 22:19–23, we glimpse the host of heaven standing before God and volunteering to go down and guide mortals into accomplishing God's divine decree. These angelic beings are called "Powers" and "Authorities," names which Tolkien also uses (e.g., Eph 6:12). Such passages could be multiplied.

But did Tolkien himself knowingly model his Valar on such a divine council, and did he intend for us to take them as representative of real-world angels? He surely knew the concept, as a divine assembly of beings appears in myths from Sumer to Egypt to Iceland. We recall that Tolkien self-consciously styles his Valar as a mode of low-ercase-g gods such as are found in these mythologies but which are amenable to Christian theology. He acknowledges that he believes in something akin to the Valar in a BBC interview with Denys Gueroult. At Guerolt's prompting, Tolkien speaks of the Valar as a "theocratic hierarchy" similar (but literarily superior) to the sort of angelic governance displayed in Lewis's Space Trilogy, and which fulfills the role of the gods of traditional mythology. Gueroult then asks Tolkien, "Do you in fact believe, yourself, not in the context of this book, believe in the sense of straightforward strict belief, in … some form of governing spirits?" Tolkien replies, "I don't know about *Angelology*. But yes, I should've thought almost certainly … Yes. Certainly."[14] We recall again Tolkien's claim that Middle-earth is theologically less "dissonant" from the real world than many assume.[15]

This argument finds further strength from the way fellow Inkling C. S. Lewis speaks of angels: "*The gods* are strange to mortal eyes, and yet they are not strange," he writes, using the same term Tolkien does.[16] And, like Tolkien, he affirms that they play various roles in the life of the Christian: "When he saw them he knew that he had always known them and realised what part each one of them had played at many an hour in his life when he had supposed himself alone, so that now he could say to them, one by one, not 'Who are you?' but 'So it was you all the time.' "[17] Lewis even associates the angelic "gods" with music: "The dim consciousness of friends about him which had haunted his solitudes from infancy was now at last explained; that central music in every pure experience which had always just evaded memory was now at last recovered."[18] And of course Lewis provides planetary angelic governors in his Ransom trilogy, to which (as we have seen) Tolkien compares his own creations.[19] Tolkien and Lewis are after the same thing: a way of enfolding the classical gods (in Lewis's case, the deities of the medieval planets) into Christian orthodoxy.[20]

None of this is sufficient in itself for us to conclude that Tolkien would apply characterizations of his Valar to angels in the primary world, but it is not outside the realm of possibility. Further, Tolkien here provides an example of a worked-out angelology consonant with biblical depictions of the divine council, which may well be of benefit in a constructive fashion. I therefore provide this chapter not only because it is unclear how much of it reflects aspects of Tolkien's primary belief and where he would draw such lines, but also because his fictional thought may serve as a nonfictional guide to others.

VALAR AND MAIAR

We cannot exhaustively present all that Tolkien has to say about particular angelic figures such as Gandalf or Elbereth, since these are major characters in his writing. Much more character study might be done, but, when dealing with Tolkien's fiction, this chapter will confine itself to direct metaphysical statements. As before, when it seems likely that Tolkien believes a fictional statement applies also to the primary world, I use the terms "angel" and so forth. But where it is less clear, I retain the terms Valar, Maiar, and the like.

ANGELIC HIERARCHIES

Ever since Pseudo-Dionysius elaborated his *Celestial Hierarchy* and the nine ranks of angels, no discussion of angelology can avoid a discussion of hierarchy. Tolkien's division of angels between Valar and Maiar is well-known and will be discussed below, but here we will first address the notion of hierarchy as such.

It must be said that Tolkien does not adopt a consistent vocabulary on this subject. *Usually* he speaks of orders of creatures as something synonymous with species, but sometimes his usage is explicitly contradictory.[21] We should not therefore read too much into the specific terminology because, once this is discarded, a relatively coherent picture emerges which paradoxically adopts hierarchy to accentuate the glory of difference, rather than denigrate it.

There is no chain of being in Tolkien's theology. While Tolkien affirms hierarchy, he also insists that all rational spirits proceeding directly from God are equal in order and status but not in power.[22] All creation has the same level of being, whether tree, Man, or angel.[23] The difference lies in each creature's natural capacities (here Tolkien clearly differentiates, using terms such as "power," "majesty," "stature," or other such ideas). The Children are created directly by God, just as the angels are. Therefore, humans are of the same historical rank as the Valar but of smaller spiritual and intellectual status and power.[24] The Elves are, in the present, more similar in nature to the angels but less in might and stature.[25] But while the Elves have an uncertain destiny, Men will, perhaps, *become* Valar—that is, they will become Powers and governors of the created world, not necessarily transform into angels.[26] Thus, compared to humans, the angels are more like elders and chiefs than masters, since they had no part in their making.[27]

Furthermore, there is, among beings of the same level of power, a differentiation in authority. The various angelic spirits have spheres of rule delegated by God.[28] So, for example, Manwë is equal to Frodo in the hierarchy of being, but higher in the hierarchies of power. He is equal to Ulmo in the hierarchies of power, but higher in the hierarchy of authority.

These hierarchies are not posted on a notice-board. They are real but sometimes unknown. Gandalf expresses uncertainty about his place in the hierarchy of power in Middle-earth. He admits that some powers of evil are greater than he, and that he has not yet been measured against others.[29] The chain of power is not sharply divided, and sometimes different orders overlap. Gandalf worries that he, a Maia, may not be powerful enough to defeat the Witch-king, a mere Man, though undead and energized by Sauron's will. Glorfindel, a resurrected Elf, is virtually equal to the Maiar.[30] We learn that Gandalf was coeval and equal to Sauron when they were first created.[31] Both are Maiar, but by the end of the Third Age, Sauron is far stronger than Gandalf alone.[32]

Tolkien also highlights that hierarchy does not destroy mutual interdependence. Lower beings may still adorn the glory of God in ways that higher beings cannot. Each is unique and plays its own irreplaceable role. All orders of creatures have a special talent that even higher orders can admire and love. Tolkien sees his angels as delighting in the work of lower orders of creatures and actually adopting their appearances and languages.[33] So this hierarchy is less that of some Byzantine or totalitarian system of control but much closer to that of a choir or symphony, which is of course Tolkien's opening metaphor. He compares different voices to different instruments or voices.[34] Each plays a greater or lesser role in the music, but the piccolo adds something to the symphony that the trumpet cannot. The Music of the Ainur finds its harmony when all occupy their unique place. We now turn to examining each of these categories individually.

Ainur

Ainu means "holy one" or "angelic spirit."[35] It is Tolkien's broadest term for angel and refers to the class as a whole, irrespective of their involvement with earth and its history. They have the greatest power and glory of any creature, he writes.[36] These angels have a definite hierarchy even before entering into creation, with multiple ranks and offices.[37] They are, at first, isolated and unable to understand one another, but can grow through cooperation and community.[38] They attain a harmony and become, quite literally, an angelic choir. It is interesting that Tolkien does not grant the angels community from the first, but casts it as something they must gain through effort. We note that, according to Thomas Aquinas, each angel is a different species, since it is pure mind and does not share a bodily form. This may be a motive for Tolkien's initial angelic isolation.

Each Ainu is powerful but created and limited, and their powers and limitations derive both from their nature as it arose in the mind of God, and from the parts of the Music to which they attended. Certain of the Ainur take more interest in creation than others. Those who enter into the story of earth and the Children of God become Valar and Maiar. But there are legions of angels who still dwell in the Timeless Halls with God, beyond the created universe.[39] They are likely the vast majority, unassociated with the world of time and instead devoted to contemplation and fellowship with God directly.

There are also Ainur who enter into creation but not into the drama of the Children of God. These far outweigh the number of Valar, virtually infinite to us but all personally known by God.[40] Tolkien offers the possibility that there are other sentient creatures to whom these Ainur may relate, such that there may be other dramas of redemption playing out throughout the universe in which these other angels function as Powers.[41] The other Ainur might labor elsewhere in other histories of the Great Tale, far beyond the limits of our thought in unknown worlds of which we can know nothing.[42] Tolkien does not reckon other life in the universe as likely, but if it exists, it will have angelic supervision.

What of the relations between Ainur and Valar? It appears that the Valar occupied high ranks among the heavenly host and were the chief musicians in the creation.[43] However, out of love, they voluntarily limited themselves in power. They profoundly love the beauty of creation and its history and wish to enter into their own artwork. God gives them leave to do this. But they must accept the condition that they will thence be bounded and contained within the world so that they are linked to its life.[44]

Valar

"Vala" means one having divine power or authority.[45] This is their prime function. They are the vice-regents of God and serve him in governing the world.[46] Etymologically, then, the Valar are distinct from the Ainur in that they have been given authority over the world and its inhabitants. The Valar do not have permanent ownership; they play a certain function in the history of God's tale and retreat into the background as new acts of the drama emerge.[47] As history progresses, they become less important because their role is to shape and prepare the world for the emergence of the Children of God. In this, we see Tolkien's rationalization for the prevalence of supernatural interactions in mythic or ancient tales and their relative rarity today.

In exchange for their authority over creation, the Valar undergo a process of self-limitation which is a necessary consequence of their new position as spatiotemporal beings. Having entered creation of their own free will, they now exist within time and can perceive nothing outside of it except through memory.[48] They are likewise now cut off from the direct mind-to-mind communion with God that the other Ainur still enjoy. While open to God, they cannot see any part of his mind by their own power; they appeal to him in prayer, and he may choose to respond.[49] This does not mean God cannot speak to *them*. He appears to Aulë, for instance, and he makes himself known to the first Men.

There are distinctions in rank within the Valar themselves. If the chief Valar lived in Valinor, this implies an ordering.[50] These chief Valar are more exalted than any other beings, whether of the Valar or of any other order.[51] The greatest of the Valar seem to be on a level ontologically, but there is further differentiation due to assigned roles, as based in their knowledge and interest in the act of creation. The Valar and Maiar differ in power in part due to the concern they take in the larger or smaller elements of the Song. For instance, Manwë the Elder King has a roughly complete knowledge of God's mind for creation, while the lesser spirits may have focused on some smaller matter such as trees or birds.[52] The Valar were the "major artists" or "masters" of the Music.[53] We read that though Manwë is their king, they are equal in majesty, and the feminine Valier are no less powerful or glorious than their masculine peers.[54] Rather than jostle one another for control, however, all the Valar defend Manwë's authority.[55]

In Manwë's role we have a small insight into Tolkien's concept of angelic hierarchy. Manwë, most exalted and holy of the Valar, is the vice-regent of God and chief defense against Satan.[56] He is dearest to God, most perceptive of all of his purposes, first and eldest of kings, lord of the world and ruler of all who dwell there.[57] This is, partially, because he is the wisest and most prudent. Having greater knowledge of the Music as a whole than any other finite being, he is thus best able to direct the course of events and govern the world under God.[58] But he is also the only being who can beseech and communicate with God directly.[59] All others—even, we presume, the other angels—must approach God by moving up the hierarchy of authority.

Maiar

The Valar are of a high angelic order but are attended in turn by many lesser angels, the Maiar.[60] These are the people of the Valar, serving and helping them.[61] Each is attached to one of the Valar as a lord or lady. They are of an unknown number, and few even have names among mortals, for most remain spiritual and invisible.[62] Both are members of the first order of created beings, the Ainur, made before the world.[63] Maiar have the same inherent powers as Valar, but in greater or lesser degree.[64]

There are rankings too among the Maiar, such that Tolkien can speak of Gandalf as equal to Sauron.[65] We also hear of greater Maiar, presumably in contrast to the lesser.[66] Gandalf is called a lesser angelic spirit but noted still to be mighty. Melian too is particularly noted as possessing great power and wisdom.[67] Other seemingly supernatural embodied beings in Middle-earth, such as Ents and Eagles, are lower Maiar who have clothed themselves in bodies.[68]

There may be other angelic spirits lower than the Maiar, or at least functionally distinct. In the earliest tales (but not later) we hear of brownies, pixies, leprechauns, and many others. These are precursors to the Maiar (they are older than the world and had a hand in its making) but seemingly of lesser stature, since they are playful and, if the names are to be believed, very minor spirits indeed.[69] Since they are not attached as servants to the Valar, they cannot technically be Maiar, though they may be of the same nature. Here Tolkien does for the nature spirits of myth and folklore what he did with the classical gods by creating the Valar. He adopts or interprets such beings as minor angels and thus as coherent with a Christian worldview.

In early versions, time is personified as the oldest of the Ainur, with children who personify subsidiary concepts. This entails a very different conception of the angelic powers and is much more closely in line with ancient mythologies of personified aspects of existence or society rather than distinct individuals with governance over such aspects. Or perhaps here Tolkien means to imply that Time is simply the Ainu with authority over time. We cannot tell.[70]

PURPOSE AND FUNCTION

The angels, like humankind, have a *telos,* a purpose in the overarching plan of God. Some reside outside the world and live in eternal fellowship and praise of God. The chief actors in the creation story dwell by love and choice within the world.[71] They exercise a divinely delegated authority within their individual spheres. This authority must follow that of God, and it thus concerns itself with rule or government rather than creation or recreation as such.[72] The many governing Powers each have their ranks and offices—specialized assignments and roles, with Manwë as preeminent ruler and direct vice-regent of God much as the pope functions as the vicar of Christ.[73] In a strange phrase, Tolkien says of the angels in the cosmos that they are its life and it is theirs.[74] This may mean that each of the ruling angels expresses and invigorates a unique facet of the creation or of God's character. Each Vala is particularly concerned with some special part of God's design, acting as his agent and sub-creator in that area.[75] So Tolkien can say directly that Tulkas represents the positive side of violence: warring against evil, refusing to compromise, willing to face any hardship rather than surrender to it, fully subservient to the power of God in history.[76] Ulmo glorifies God through the music of the waters, and Nienna exemplifies God's attribute of mercy and compassion.

Although the angels are powerful sub-creators, they cannot alter any fundamental element of the creation.[77] Here again Tolkien distinguishes between the ability to shape preexisting material and the creation ex nihilo of that material in the first place. The angels do not bring the world into being but accent God's blueprint, which he then gives reality. Nor can they change that blueprint into something essentially different from what God intends it to be. They share in the making of the world in the sense that we make a story or piece of art, but the bestowal of reality on the same level as their own is God's act alone. God also retains the freedom to intervene at any moment.[78]

But God also grants his servants the Valar a measure of freedom in their sub-creative acts. Prior to the creation, he tells his angels to display their powers in adorning the Music with their own contributions.[79] God sets out a general plan yet gives the angels freedom not only to choose whether they will participate but how they might add to it. God rejoices in the angels' wakening of beauty.[80] Their free acts in his service cause him joy, and he delights in showing them the outcome of their work, which they themselves could not have imagined. They recognize within the Music made real all their own unique contributions to God's design.[81]

After God gives reality to the creation, the angels continue to act as sub-creators, but in a different sense. The cosmos is bare and needs filling out. They are now to enact the Vision of history God has shown them, completing his blueprint.[82] In this sense Tolkien speaks of their work being "fore-ordained" by God.[83] While God grants the angelic powers the ability to shape the substance of the world, they remain obedient to God's purposes.[84] His design governs all their operations.[85] They are not the owners of the world, or its masters. They are ministers of God, with only enough control to serve their function. Their power is equivalent to their authority. They have only the power needed to fulfill their functions—namely, godlike control over the physical universe and an understanding of God's design for it.[86]

This is the time in which the angels exercise the most raw power, here at its very beginning. They undertake a "demiurgic" labor to prepare the universe for human habitation.[87] They work for long ages throughout space until the formation of Arda, the earth.[88] The vast cosmological timescales of solar and planetary formations, the imperceptible but dramatic geological upheavals of the early earth, the long eons of evolutionary development leading to an ecosystem suitable for the emergence of humankind—all of these, for Tolkien, were the primary realms of angelic activity, nurturing and guiding all things toward an anthropocentric future.

Tolkien depicts this age of angels laconically, for by the time the Elves awaken and the history recounted in *The Silmarillion* begins, the Valar are already nearing the end of their direct engagement with the world. They diminish as the mythological age gives way to history. For Tolkien, there is only ever one dominant force on earth at once. First, it was the angels, who gradually gave way to the Elves, who eventually give way to Men. Men, too, may give way to something entirely new. But the angels do not now govern the world in the same way they once did. The angels rule for the sake of the Children of Ilúvatar, ensuring that Men find a place prepared for them.[89] But for all their power to set the stage, they have no jurisdiction over them.[90] As Mandos says, it is for the Valar to rule the world, counsel the Children, and to command only when within their authority. They may advise a higher road, but not compel any to walk it.[91] Even Manwë cannot force obedience. He is to keep his subjects loyal to God, or bring them back into that loyalty, but to leave them free within it.[92]

As such, after their demiurgic mission, these mighty beings move into the roles of wise counsellors rather than executors.[93] Their experience has grown them, but the project is now virtually complete.[94] Once the past is set, only God can alter it. As the past grows in length and the future grows in definition, there is less room for radical unrestricted change.[95] They cannot change the work now, but they can advise and instruct on other projects. They are like government-contracted architects, whose importance diminishes as the plan is more nearly achieved.[96]

Once Men have grown into a sufficient maturity as a people, the Valar step aside and allow the true Children of God to shape history.[97] This is why the Valar do not directly solve the problem of the Ring, as noted in the Council of Elrond.[98] Their task is to make it possible for humans and Elves to live in the world securely, and they cease to be the active rulers when their task is done.[99] This agrees with Tolkien's statement elsewhere that Manwë's "prime function" ends with the defeat of Morgoth.[100] The angels clear the way for the time of Men, who find in the war with Morgoth's lieutenant Sauron their *Bildungsroman*.

Another major function of Tolkien's angels is to listen to the prayers of the people of Middle-earth.[101] Before the advent of Christ, God must be approached through the Valar who serve as intermediaries.[102] The Powers hear the prayers of mortals and intervene to aid them or bring their requests before God. Men view the angels as children view their parents or as adults view their supervisors. They know that ultimately there is a King above them, but he dwells far away.[103] They also act as priests and ministers and gather up other peoples and creatures into the praise and service of God, leading worship services and teaching about Eru.[104] We are not told what these events entail. Tolkien as an artist likely does not feel up to the task of picturing the voices that shaped the song of creation leading it in worship and the minds that know God intimately instructing the faithful about his glory.

Just as the Elves leave Middle-earth at the end of the Third Age, the angelic powers also recede when their time is done. They leave earth but somehow also dwell there secretly as mere shadows.[105] We are not told how they can do both, or perhaps Tolkien never decided which was ultimately true. Since the Valar cannot leave creation, they must either dwell physically somewhere else in the cosmos or maintain a purely spiritual existence.

POWERS

As stated above, an angel's power is limited and derives from God.[106] Unlike God, who is powerful in himself, angels only have what they have received from him. As the primary actors in God's drama of redemption, Men must remain free to play the parts God sets for them. They are too great for the Valar to govern directly.[107] The Valar cannot make Men immortal or otherwise change the fundamental nature of creatures.[108] They cannot alter the primary design of God and must plead to him directly when the Númenoreans attempt to invade paradise, as they are forbidden from destroying or even coercing them.[109] In some versions, the Valar lay down their power, and God bends the world into a globe.[110] In other versions, God empowers the angels themselves to do this.[111]

But this does not mean their power is not stupendous. We hear of Valar creating stars and holding perfect memory and knowledge of all certain future states.[112] Because they have taken part in the Music of creation, they know much of the future, and little surprises them.[113] But they are not omniscient. Their knowledge of creation is incomplete. None but God actually knows the future directly.[114] Not even all the angels together would possess a complete portrait of God's design.[115] They know nothing at all about the actions of creatures with free wills (though they can of course make educated guesses based on their vast intelligence and wisdom).[116] While they have prodigious senses, they cannot perceive everything. Manwë and Morgoth both need messengers and scouts.[117]

They control the weather, the seasons, and the passage of time, though they cannot stop time completely.[118] Their relation to time and space, however, is fluid. They can live at any speed of thought and travel backward or forward within time so swiftly that observers do not notice any movement.[119] As non-spatial spiritual beings, angels are also not bound by concepts of size or distance.[120] They have no size at all, strictly speaking, and so can operate at any scale. We make the mistake of considering angels only for their great majesty, and not also for their terrible sharpness, says Tolkien. We consider only the incalculable immensity of the cosmos and not its minute precision, but the angels shape both.[121] They operate on both the astronomical and subatomic levels, as it were. As to distance, any spirit moves by a simple act of will, so angels travel instantaneously.[122] By extension, an angel can transfer creatures across otherwise impassable distances or, by contrast, prevent creatures from going to certain places (whether through creating physical barriers, fogs of confusion, or other means).[123]

When they exist in their natural immaterial state, they are totally imperceptible, but Tolkien's angels can take bodies and self-incarnate at will.[124] They use bodies because they love the creation and want to participate in it. But they do not, for the most part, actually incarnate themselves in any permanent way. Rather, they clothe themselves in their own thought, in whatever way they choose.[125] Angelic bodies are far more under the control of the will, since their thought is far stronger and more penetrant.[126] Their shape is not material and acts more as a garment than a body. It can change radically, and if they are "unclothed" they suffer no loss of being. More than our clothes, however, an angel's body is an expression of its personality, desires, and role.[127] These shapes are not necessarily humanlike. Yavanna may, for instance, take the form of a great tree, so beautiful and majestic that it could only be described by all green and growing things singing together in one hymn of love for their queen that could be laid as an offering at the throne of God.[128] Unclad, they may be manifest as light or as fragrance.[129] Yet even this merely masks the inner spiritual glory of the angelic nature.[130]

Some shapes could be more than mere appearances, and the Valar have the capability, as part of their demiurgic power, to construct a physical body for themselves out of the stuff of Middle-earth.[131] Of the good angels, only Melian and the Wizards take on physical bodies as a permanent habitation, with all the limitations thereof.[132] The destruction of such a body does not harm the angel nor remove it from the world, but it does have a cost.[133] Constructing the body takes both time and spiritual energy, which Tolkien equates to will-power.[134] This energy is lost when the body is destroyed. If the will is shrunken too badly, the angel loses the ability to manifest physically and becomes practically impotent.[135] By contrast, Tolkien reasons, in any story where angelic spirits can take a physical and destructible form, they should be more powerful when bodily present.[136]

While clothed in material forms, they can eat and drink and receive nourishment, but this is of pleasure and not necessity.[137] The Valar do not produce children, nor do they eat and drink except at times of festival as a symbolic gesture of blessing.[138] Tolkien writes, though, that long or frequent use of the same body creates a habit (in both senses of the word): the spirit is more closely bound to the body, does not want to leave it, and approaches a state of true incarnation. Either by divine decree or logical consequence of divine order of creation, the enjoyment of a body as a true body (eating, drinking, or, most importantly, reproduction) results in the spirit becoming truly embodied.[139] Many of the lesser angels, who take the role of nature spirits in Tolkien's Christianized form of myth, are much more apt to do all these things.

Having no natural physical bodies, the angels have no physical sex, and they cannot truly be said to marry, since the institution of marriage requires reproduction. Thus, with the Valar, "spouse" means merely "associate,"[140] and unlike human relationships where Tolkien believes the male ought to lead, angelic spouses are fully egalitarian. There is no indication that Aulë leads or directs Yavanna, for instance. Manwë leads Varda not because he is her spouse, but because he is the King. But here Tolkien differs from Thomas, for though he denies angelic sex in the strict sense, he affirms a distinction between masculine and feminine. Embodied angelic forms are gendered, resulting from a difference in temper. Their bodily form shows their spiritual form, as our own garments also reflect our gender.[141] There is surely something significant in the fact that the prime mediator between Eru and the world, Manwë, is masculine, as all priests must be.

Finally, we ought to say something about angelic speech. Making language is, for Tolkien, the chief characteristic of an embodied creature, so, as a result of their delight in creation, the angels also create a language for themselves, though it is not strictly necessary.

They communicate directly from mind to mind when disembodied, though the habitual use of bodies and language reduces mind-to-mind communication and other purely spiritual powers.[142] This language changes little over time, but it does change, since nothing within creation remains the same forever.[143] This also means that no angel has a true name, only an irreducible identity referred to by varying nicknames which serve to pick out some notable feature of that identity.[144]

Tolkien's "Notion Club Papers" articulate another method of angelic speech. He reiterates that as spiritual beings, angels can communicate directly from mind to mind.[145] Here, though, he speaks of angel-to-human communication. Here they do not, when disembodied, communicate with sound, but produce direct impressions on the mind of the recipient.[146] They might direct your mind to specific words or shapes, but one could also be left to translate direct impressions into words on one's own. Tolkien the philologist notes that this process would be the reverse of normal speech practices: instead of moving from symbol to meaning, one would move from meaning to symbol. He says that the end result would seem like normal speech, save for some inner emotion attached to it and (sometimes) a noticeable difference in sequence. He does not elaborate on what these two exceptions mean.[147]

Tolkien describes the experience of meaning as immediate and direct, while the symbolic element (the words) follow audibly after a perceptible gap. He directly compares this to hallucination: something is affecting the mind and making it translate into sense experience. The difference is that the cause of strict hallucination is internal, while the cause of spiritual communication is external.[148] In a lexical note, Tolkien explains that the Elves believe the heart or conscience can sometimes be influenced by angels and thus indirectly by God.[149]

ANGELIC FREEDOM AND SIN

All of God's free gifts have their own dangers, as we have noted.[150] The gift of freedom to the angels is no exception. Tolkien asserts that within his mythology, angels are capable of various degrees of error and failure, from the satanic defiance of Morgoth to the idleness of some of the Valar.[151] When angels do rebel, being of higher metaphysical stature than Men, they also go further in sin.[152] Setting aside the discussion of demons and the angelic fall to their proper places, we here concern ourselves with the issue of apparent error or venial sin in Tolkien's good angels. This is a difference from standard Catholic angelology, which holds that at the time of Satan's rebellion angels were confirmed in either their obedience or disobedience. As such, obedient angels can no longer sin or fall away. Here, however, at least in Tolkien's earlier writings, the angels' incomplete knowledge of the future causes a constant temptation toward sin—namely, to force the free wills of other creatures in order to secure God's purposes.[153]

None of Tolkien's Valar, save Morgoth, consciously choose to disobey God, though all are capable of doing so.[154] Instead, they commit various errors which have moral implications. While all the angels yearn for God's will, the Valar can disagree among themselves as to the best course of action and can be corrected by others of their company, as we see in "The Statute of Finwë and Míriel."[155] They even take these concerns over their own limitations or errors to Eru himself. Manwë worries about the policy of Elvish reincarnation, stating that forming bodies seems to be beyond both their skill and authority. God tells the archangel that they already possess the skills and grants them the authority to provide the Elves with new bodies.[156]

As here, sometimes God directly communicates his will to his angelic vice-regents. Manwë, for instance, declares that he has been visited by the mind of Eru and warned against taking Men from the earth while alive.[157] The nature of the wording of this warning implies that such a removal is logically possible but immoral. We know from other statements that this is because humans cannot survive the strain of Valinor's differing relation to time. So when we read that the Valar "cannot" change the fate of Men, we should read this as not only a statement of impossibility but a moral warning against any attempt to do so.[158]

But God also allows the Valar to make mistakes. Tolkien speaks of Manwë having an inherent non-sinful fault which misleads him. He becomes virtually obsessed with maintaining the status quo, losing in the process all creative power and strength in facing difficult or dangerous situations.[159] Manwë also errs in allowing Morgoth the opportunity of repentance. He believes Morgoth's oaths of reform because he is himself free from evil and does not understand such deceptions.[160] He believes that were Melkor to repent and persevere, he might regain his original power and help to restore the world. He cannot comprehend jealousy or countenance the idea that all love has departed from Morgoth forever.[161] This is clearly a personal fault of Manwë's, as Ulmo and Tulkas are not deceived.[162] Aulë not only errs, but falls, in a sense, becoming victim to his impatience and preempting the Creator's will. He makes the Dwarves illicitly. God confronts him in anger, but also in pity. Aulë has no evil desire for slaves, only impatient love for God's Children.[163] Aulë suffers no apparent punishment, and, in fact, God grants the Dwarves true being.

The Valar's withdrawal from the world they ought to be governing is perhaps their most serious fault. The Valar raise a mountain range to block Valinor from the rest of Middle-earth and shut themselves away from its troubles. This might not actually be a bad action, but it may well be a mistake. While arising from a good motive, it seems also to be selfish and despairing. It counters Morgoth's possessiveness over

Middle-earth with another possessiveness over Valinor.[164] When they refuse to fight Morgoth, they lose their greatest chance for honor and glory, and may in fact have removed their option of saving the world themselves.[165] Further, removing the Elves to Valinor was also not in accord with Eru's design, arising from anxiety and a lack of trust in Eru's sovereignty.[166] This act has vast consequences. The stubbornness and self-inflicted harm that Men bring upon themselves, other creatures, and the world is partly due to this choice of the Valar to separate them from Elvish influence, Tolkien asseverates. But here he again distinguishes between sins and mistakes. To wit, such evils are due not to revolt or pride, but to mistakes arising from a failure to understand God's purposes or to place proper confidence in him.[167] Though deadly serious, they lack the intentional desire for departure from God's design which makes them sins in the proper sense.

All of these reflections on angelic faults drop away in later versions of the legendarium, where even the idea of angelic error is explicitly rejected, and Tolkien goes to great pains to explain how such seeming missteps and selfishnesses are in fact illusory.[168] They are lies of the Accuser that we accept as truth because of our own innate sinfulness.[169] Tolkien cautions us, as if from within the mythology, against blaspheming the glorious ones. If we dare to make assumptions about what goes on within the mind of the Elder King Manwë, we ought to remember certain important factors.[170] The Valar are more limited than Morgoth in their power because they devote themselves to obedience to the commands and laws of God.[171] They cannot enslave any being or imprison them forever, save at the express command of God, nor can they compel speech, and they must take even Morgoth at his word, giving him every opportunity to fulfill a promise.[172] The righteous angels are freely bound to do or not do by God's command, even with the full knowledge that Morgoth would use this to his advantage and betray them.[173] So while it may look as if the holy angels are naive and unwise compared to their fallen brothers, this is only because they will not meet lies with lies, or hate with hate. Rather than Manwë exhibiting foolish ignorance and being hoodwinked by Morgoth, Manwë shows something more than wisdom, being always open to the will of God and trusting in his ultimate sovereignty.[174] Tolkien goes on to offer a reframing of the narrative in which the Valar's final intervention is neither delayed nor unwilling, but precisely timed.[175] In the final case, Tolkien decides that those who hold that the Valar erred and disobeyed Eru have in fact adopted the lies of Morgoth.[176] Here Tolkien has consciously brought his mythology back into line with traditional angelology.

INCARNATE ANGELS

While most Maiar may be nameless, Tolkien's best-known angel is not one of the Valar but the great Wizard Gandalf.[177] This equation is not speculative—Tolkien refers to the Wizards as angels, and specifically guardian angels, using the Greek term *angelos*.[178] Though the Wizards present a unique case and cannot be directly mapped onto any theological situation in the primary world (that we know of), we can nevertheless glean some insight into Tolkien's conception of the role that angels play in history.

Tolkien's descriptions of the Istari in their pre-incarnate forms are limited, since they are in fact no different from the other Maiar. An Istar is not a metaphysical designation but a statement of function. Nevertheless, their personalities remain the same. We hear of Olórin (Gandalf in his pre-incarnate state) that he was a servant of Irmo, Vala of dreams. He was humble and sought no personal glory, but instead found joy in renewing hope and raising the fallen.[179]

We are told that Saruman and Gandalf are the first and second of their order, respectively.[180] The angels seem, then, to observe hierarchy even in a class as small as five. Gandalf, of course, eventually supplants Saruman as the highest of the Wizards when Saruman falls.[181] He assumes Saruman's function, for he is what Saruman should have been.[182] In fact, Gandalf has always been above Saruman in the hierarchy of power. Círdan the Shipwright is able to see that Gandalf rather than Saruman has the greatest power and wisdom of the Wizards but conducts himself with the most humility. Tolkien writes of his arrival that he came last and seemed the least, echoing Luke 9:48. [183]

The primary meaning of *angelos* is "messenger," and Tolkien ties this directly to the Wizards' functions as emissaries of the Valar.[184] But their arrival in Middle-earth is in fact a twofold sending. Besides the Valar, they are also mediately sent by God himself.[185] In other words, God is the ultimate sender, with the angelic powers as his regents, so that Tolkien can speak of the purpose of the Valar as being under the purpose of the One.[186] This situation also holds in reverse. As we have seen, the Valar and especially Eru must be approached through intermediaries, and the primary such intermediary in *The Lord of the Rings* is Gandalf. He is the "plenipotentiary" of the ruling angels.[187] Gandalf is the authority that accepts Arwen's request to allow Frodo to go over the sea, for instance.

Aside from acting as heavenly representatives and intermediaries, the Wizards' central function, the task for which they are sent, is to encourage and bring out the inherent powers of God's creation against the diabolical encroachments of Sauron, inspiring them to use their own inborn gifts to come together and overcome this evil.[188] Though mighty, these angels eschew might so as to engage equally with the Children of God. In order to respect creaturely free will and the responsibilities of Elves and Men, the Wizards are forbidden from matching Sauron's power with power or dominating creatures through fear or force.[189] They are not to do their job for them, but to advise and instruct, and so they take the form of old sages.[190] Each of the five seems to have a different part in the overall mission, since Gandalf is specially tasked to watch over Men (and by extension hobbits).[191]

The most interesting aspect of Tolkien's Wizards is of course their incarnate nature. Tolkien writes that, with Eru's consent, the Valar send members of their own order in the bodies of Men, truly incarnate.[192] Unlike the other Valar and Maiar, they do not wear a body as a set of clothes, to be changed or removed at will. In biblical terms, this is a genuine incarnation, and not a mere angelophany. They are not invulnerable and are subject to fear, pain, weariness, hunger, thirst, and even death—all the limitations of a true mortal existence.[193] While all the Wizards appear in the bodies of old men even from the beginning, they are real bodies and age even further (though slowly) before the end, as is the nature of all things on earth.[194]

They can also be tempted. Their embodiment is a danger which limits them, diminishing their knowledge and confusing them with the weaknesses of the flesh.[195] This is due to what Tolkien calls the peril of the incarnate, the increased possibility of falling into sin which having a body in a fallen world brings.[196] Clearly, having a body is no precondition of sinfulness, else Melkor could never have fallen, but for Tolkien the exigencies of physical existence and its inherent limitations create more dangerous opportunities to choose evil. So while all angels can fall, the incarnate Wizards are more likely both to sin and to make mistakes. The Ring exerts a corrupting influence even over these heavenly beings.[197] Besides Saruman, who becomes truly evil, Radagast and the two blue Wizards simply neglect their tasks or become distracted. While even Gandalf makes mistakes of judgment, he is the only Wizard to fully pass the moral test.[198]

This temptation also partially arises because there is a disconnect between their pre-incarnate and embodied natures, which affects their mental processes. They need to slowly relearn many things, and their pre-incarnate existence in Valinor seems like a far-off, much-desired vision.[199] Tolkien compares Gandalf's incarnate knowledge of spiritual realities to that of a human theologian, with no more or less certainties or liberties.[200] Surely this refers not to any unclarity as to the factual existence or nature of God or the Valar, but to the details of their plan and how it might unfold.

Even here, a Wizard is not without guidance—Tolkien hints that Gandalf's "heart" might have known more than his "waking thought" or "waking mind."[201] He does what seems best to him at the time, with no hint as to how any overarching divine plan might work out. His conscious mind used whatever laid at hand and seemed best, but what his heart might have known and how it may have guided his choices is another issue.[202] Gandalf himself surmises that his angelic mind (subconsciously?) directed his conscious decisions in ways even he cannot define.[203] He seems to draw upon christological dogma here, giving Gandalf a sort of two-nature composition.[204] As such, when Tolkien twice mentions that Gandalf has a deep premonition somehow outside of his conscious awareness, he seems to imply that, just as Jesus did when *he* became truly incarnate, so too does Gandalf's angelic mind also reside at a deeper level beneath his more limited Man-like one.

This mix between differing levels of weakness and power is part of a larger pattern. Wizards can (and usually do) veil their true power.[205] Though possessed of a high authority and dignity, they avoid manifesting their glory fully, but instead incarnate themselves under weak and humble appearances.[206] Here we hear a form of the Christ-hymn of Philippians 2, though in a lesser register. The word "veil" follows

Gandalf in particular like a leitmotif. Gandalf the White's veil is both physical (he flings away his grey rags) and spiritual. Aragorn speaks of a veil over his sight which kept him from recognizing him.[207] With a spiritual sense, Pippin realizes that Gandalf has great power, deep wisdom, and a veiled majesty.[208] Even before they see Gandalf, the three companions feel a strange expectancy, as of something with a "hidden power."[209]

He prefers to inspire and act through others.[210] But while Gandalf may hide his power, it is nevertheless always present. He is allowed, when physical opposition is too great, to act supernaturally—but no more than did the angel who released Peter from prison.[211] We see one of these instances when Gandalf moves to rescue the men of Gondor from the Ringwraiths. From the walls, Pippin sees a flash of white and silver light. He realizes it is Gandalf. The Wizard moves to drive away the Nazgûl. He is "unveiled," and a light shines from his hand. They will not face the white fire he wields.[212] Later, when Gandalf rushes to save Faramir from being immolated, men fall away and cover their eyes because he comes like a white light into a dark place, and in great anger. He lifts his hand, and Denethor's sword flies from his grasp. This is nothing natural, for Denethor steps backward amazed.[213] As Gandalf the White, he cannot be harmed by mortal weapons.[214] Physical objects break at his command. He can look into the minds of others and communicate from afar.[215] The Wizard is able to urge Frodo to remove the Ring while he is on Amon Hen.[216] Gandalf provides his own commentary on the event, stating that he sat in a high place and strove with Sauron.[217]

But the most significant power of these incarnate spirits is not really their power at all. It is their function as a channel through which greater power works. Saruman knows as well as Gandalf that what mortals call "fortune" is the providential direction of heaven. As such,

Saruman is fully aware that he is resisting the finger of God.[218] Gandalf indeed says that his purpose in being sent to Middle-earth is to act as the enemy of Sauron, the adversary of the Adversary.[219] As Manwë and Morgoth did in the First Age, Gandalf and Sauron thus represent the Michael/Satan opposition present in Scripture.[220] But, says Tolkien, that would have meant more at the end than at the beginning. God sees more and further than his angels see. Gandalf was sent by the Valar as a prudent plan, but God took this plan and enlarged it when it failed at the Bridge of Khazad-dûm.[221] God supervenes over and above the plans of the higher order of angels and fulfills his own purposes through the Grey Pilgrim, and particularly in his death.

While this is an unexpected setback to both Gandalf and the Valar, it is exactly what God intends. Tolkien writes that God intended to offset the failure of the other Wizards (especially Saruman). Things had become too dire and needed increased power, so God uses Gandalf's righteous death in order to provide it.[222] Gandalf undertakes a self-abnegation in order to follow the natural and moral order instituted by God.[223] For all Gandalf knew, he was the only one capable of successfully directing the war against Sauron, and he chose to fail in his mission through self-sacrifice rather than succeed by any means necessary. But this is not a mere principled stand. Gandalf displays the faith of Abraham, who is willing to sacrifice the only child of promise because he trusts that God can raise him from the dead. By the same token, Gandalf gave up hope of personal success and handed the situation over to the Authority that ordained the rules in the first place.[224] He trusts God in the face of apparent failure and sacrifices himself.

He says he strays outside of thought and time and is sent back. By whom? Tolkien answers for us. The Valar only deal with this world and its time, so the sender must be God himself. He returns naked, like a child, symbolically undergoing a new birth, receiving the white robes of the "highest."[225] Are these the white robes of the highest Wizard, or the white robes of the Most High, which are given to his martyrs (Rev 6:10–11; 7:13)? Likewise, in *Unfinished Tales*, Gandalf looks into the West, toward Valinor, and we are told that his face glows. It is only the setting sun's light, but it is also the shining face of those who have seen God.[226] Tolkien equates Gandalf's enhancement of power with enhancement of "sanctity."[227] Such a remark is telling: Tolkien's use of power, at least as it relates to the angels, is a synonym for holiness. So while his personality remains, his power and authority are much greater.[228] He now possesses a good form of the awe and terrible power of the Nazgûl.[229]

He is no longer as restricted by the burden of the world as he previously was. His transformation has reopened to him knowledge he had previously given up.[230] He forgets many things he knew and relearns many things he had forgotten.[231] He seems not even to remember his own previous incarnation until he reconnects with his friends. He can easily see things from afar but not close by.[232] Tolkien says the Wizards reveal their true names to few, but Gandalf seems to have forgotten his entirely—or at least his earthly one.[233] When the three companions ask Gandalf the White for his name, the Wizard laughs, echoing the angel's reticence in Judges 13:18.[234]

The laughter of Gandalf the White is always significant within the novel. It is one of the ways in which Gandalf's attitude changes after his death. Perhaps on his return to the West, Gandalf is able to recall and observe the ways in which God's servants have the matter of the war well in hand—God's plans can never be derailed. He is more open and laughs more than he talks.[235] Aragorn hears his laughter and feels a thrill like the bite of cold air.[236] Moments later, his laughter is warm as sunshine.[237] We read that, when Pippin observes Gandalf in Minas

Tirith, he sees at first only care and sorrow, but underneath a great hidden fountain of joy that could set a whole kingdom laughing.[238] To Sam, Gandalf's laughter is like music or water in a dry land and acts like an echo of all the joys he has ever felt.[239] Here we have a glimpse into that divine mirth of which Chesterton speaks—something that must be veiled because of its overwhelming power.

FURTHER READING

Kreeft, Peter. "Angelology." In *The Philosophy of Tolkien: The Worldview behind "The Lord of the Rings,"* 71–81. San Francisco: Ignatius, 2005.

McBride, Sam. *Tolkien's Cosmology: Divine Beings and Middle-earth.* Kent, OH: Kent State University Press, 2020.

McIntosh, Jonathan S. "The Metaphysics of the Valar." In *The Flame Imperishable: Tolkien, St. Thomas, and the Metaphysics of Faërie,* 157–202. Kettering, OH: Angelico, 2017.

Trimm, Charlie. "Gandalf, Sauron, Melian, and the Balrogs as Angels? A Study of J. R. R. Tolkien's Maiar in the Context of Biblical Angelology." In *Tolkien and Theology*, edited by Douglas Estes. Lanham, MD: Lexington Books, 2022.

Whittingham, Elizabeth A. "Tolkien's Mythology of Divine Beings." In *The Evolution of Tolkien's Mythology: A Study of the History of Middle-earth,* 64–99. London: McFarland, 2007.

VI

THE FALL

Any legend that purports to tell of the mythical history of our own world must accept that men have fallen, Tolkien boldly asserts.[1] For him, *the fall*—that event in which the human race (and the world) lost the original innocence with which it was created by God—is inescapable.[2] It casts its shadow even over our stories.[3] At least for our own human minds as we know them, all stories are ultimately about the fall, and no story can occur without it.[4] The fall is the primeval disruption of equilibrium that precipitates the plot of history. But this does not mean that the fall is merely an existential or psychological paradigm. Tolkien believes that myths are made largely of truth and can present aspects of the truth that can only be received in such a way. These aspects were discovered long ago and are bound always to reappear, similar in many ways to Jung's archetypes. So while Tolkien believes in a historical Adam and Eve in a historical Eden, our reports of them in Genesis take mythical forms, and the paradigms that Adam and Eve first embody continue to recur throughout history.

Tolkien's fiction thus presents the fall in cycles. It is not simply a single isolated event but a recurring pattern—the essential mode of history in Middle-earth.[5] Men fall in the First Age, and fall again in the Second: the Akallabêth is explicitly named as the second fall of

Man, consequent on the first fall.[6] The Elves have multiple falls as well. The rebellion of the Noldor occurs through Fëanor's possessiveness; the construction of the Rings of Power is due to a desire for power to resist Time.[7] The Doom of Mandos is the Elvish equivalent to God's curse in Genesis 3. Even angels fall more than once. Melkor falls continually, further and further into nihilistic self-destruction. After the first fall of angels, Sauron repents but falls again.[8] Sauron's later actions inevitably resemble those of his master, such that his temptation of the Númenoreans echoes Melkor's primal temptation of the first Men.[9] For Tolkien, all stories at root echo the *typus* of the fall.[10] This is especially true in his own tales. Evil reincarnates and reiterates the fall.[11] While the destruction of Sauron at the end of the Third Age is the last time evil will be physically embodied, it will continue to rise again and bring down the peace that has grown up in its absence.

But Tolkien does point out an explicit difference between his legendarium and Christian mythology. The fall of men depends (though not in a necessary sense) on the fall of Satan and on other free wills higher than humans. But it is debatable whether the fall corrupts the nature of the creation itself. Instead, evil comes in from outside, introduced by Satan, and acts as a subsequent corruption of a preexisting good. In Middle-earth, however, the rebellion of Satan is interwoven with the very stuff of existence, such that evil enters the world simultaneously with the "Let it Be" of the original creation.[12] His fictional Satan's influence over the material world introduces what Tolkien calls the "peril" of the incarnate: the possibility of sin.[13] Because of this influence, fall is not merely a corollary of free will, but of material existence in itself. This difference must occupy a prominent place in our evaluation of Tolkien's *fictional* statements on the fall, but such statements need not therefore be discarded. For Tolkien gives us his reason for such a portrayal: he has deliberately concretized genuine theological concerns through a *visible and physical* sub-creative lens in order specially to illustrate the effects of sin and the misuse of freedom on a much larger scale.[14] In other words, the principles remain the same, only magnified and made more explicitly evident.

Tolkien is correct in thinking his idea of a pre-creational corruption is novel. But despite his protestations, the idea of a *cosmic fall*—of a consequent wounding of the universe itself—is widespread since well before Augustine, supported by such passages as Romans 8. And Tolkien here (unknowingly) agrees with major twentieth-century theologians such as Barth and Niebuhr that there was never a golden age in which the universe enjoyed a *iustitia originalis*. For them, things are as they always were. Tolkien's universe was already imperfect when the primal sin of humanity occurred (something Middle-earth still holds in contradistinction to the moderns).

In this chapter, as in the previous one, we therefore find grounds to focus mostly on Tolkien's fiction, though his nonfictional remarks will appear when relevant. This chapter proceeds in roughly chronological sequence. First, we will treat the fall of angels and of Satan in particular. This fall is necessary to make sense of the events that occur in the garden, where Adam and Eve transgress God's ban and become corrupted through the serpent's deceit.[15] We will then examine fallenness as a state of corruption, noting its universal scope and its effect on human nature.

THE FALL OF SATAN

Tolkien believes in the fall of Satan in the primary world and adopts the same idea for Middle-earth.[16] Indeed, it seems almost necessary. All mythologies that begin with a transcendent and unique Creator God include an inevitable rebel bent toward worship of the self.[17]

He names his Satan figure Melkor, and we can be confident that Melkor's depiction hews fairly closely, at least in characterization, to Tolkien's views on the devil in the primary world. Tolkien himself frequently and directly labels Melkor as Satan in his private letters, and Melkor is genuinely meant to *be* Satan in the distant mythic past of Middle-earth, in the same sense that Eru *is* the Christian God.[18] As such, while Melkor may be somewhat mythologized, his motives and manner overlap to a large degree with the Christian depiction of Satan, including in his fall.

Created the most powerful of all the angels (and in one instance named as Alkar "the radiant," echoing Lucifer, "light-bearer"), Melkor is a bright and glorious being.[19] Though beginning with an ostensibly good desire, he is unsatisfied with the place assigned to him and seeks to rule over all things, becoming first jealous and then hateful of all other light or existence other than his own.[20] Tolkien's Melkor wants aseity: to exist without a dependence on God and to have no limit to his will or desire. He wants to be God himself. So while the music of creation as composed contains no flaws, Melkor decides to insert new ideas, in disobedience to the guidance of God, in order to increase his own glory.[21]

Nevertheless, things have no existence in themselves; they receive it constantly from God. For evil is "fissiparous," while being is inherently good and will revert to a good state unless continually dominated.[22] In order for Melkor to bring other beings under his control, he has to diffuse his own being into them, diminishing himself in the process. Note that Melkor does not immediately reach the nadir of depravity, but falls in stages, from an unassailable cosmic power to a petty tyrant king able to be collared and executed. This is because he is increasingly separated from the Prime Source of goodness and light, and actually suffers a *lessened existence*.[23] Thus,

Melkor falls from splendor to contempt, from understanding to perverse craftiness and lies, from desire of light to destructive flames and darkness.[24] Though he begins by wishing to alter creation to his own whims, he becomes so enraged at his failure that he craves instead creation's utter destruction. However, things once brought into being by God cannot be annihilated, only deformed.[25] He cannot succeed in his rebellion.

While the idea of a spiraling fall further and further into non-being is not entirely unique to Tolkien, he goes much further than most in illustrating and meditating on it. Just as we do not know the true name of the fallen angel we call Satan ("Adversary"), so too after his rebellion does the Satan figure Melkor ("he who arises in might") lose his proper name, and henceforth he is instead called only by the title Morgoth ("the black foe").

Eventually, Morgoth/Satan conceives a plan to ruin the most precious creation of all and turns to the destruction of humanity. This leads to Tolkien's own reimagining of the narrative of Genesis 3 and of the act and state of original sin. But this is not the only such story in Middle-earth. Tolkien freely admits that several of his fall narratives resemble each other. This is not authorial laziness but a commentary on the way evil functions. It reincarnates itself throughout history, reiterating the fall.[26] Evil counselors in later tales repeat the same tropes as their primeval archetype, Satan.[27] Such a situation stands for the primary world as well. Satan has his standard tools of sex, greed, and power, and yet generation upon generation continue to fall prey to the same lures. We need only modify Tolkien's words slightly to make the point. That any community in possession of the story of the garden could still find themselves cheated by Satan may be sad, but it is not incredible.[28] Evil is repetitious, but its tricks still work.[29]

ORIGINAL SIN

Original sin (i.e., the sin of origin) differs from *actual sins* (i.e., sins of action). Original sin may be further distinguished as an event (the sin of Adam and Eve in the garden of Eden) and as a state inherited as a result of this event. As noted above, Tolkien is not ashamed or doubtful of the Eden "myth," even as history. It cannot, for him, be historical in the same sense as contemporary New Testament documents, as its subject must have happened so long ago. But at its root it refers to an actual event. Genesis as a text is separated by an unknown number of sad and exiled generations from the events it relates, but we can be certain that Eden existed somewhere on this unhappy globe.[30] So many of our common desires for peace, home, and purity have their source there. So while we cannot perhaps nail down all the details of that original transgression, we can ascertain some basic facts.

All accounts of the fall deal inevitably with some sort of prohibition, writes Tolkien.[31] For example, in Genesis, God tells Adam and Eve that they are free to eat of anything in the garden except the tree of the knowledge of good and evil. He places a rule—slight, easy, even trivial—upon his creatures as a way for them to demonstrate their obedience to him in a world full of sinless freedom. But an act of obedience implies the possibility of disobedience, and thus of a temptation toward destruction. Tolkien notes that this is a widespread mythological motif. The "Thou shalt not" extends from tribal taboos to Victorian nursery rhymes. Transgressing past the "Locked Door" brings endless regret, but it still stands as an eternal temptation.[32]

Humans unfortunately succumb to this temptation and do not remain in their primitive innocence.[33] As long as we have a record of human thought, it is therefore concerned with joy and its loss.[34] We all have a desire or intense longing for something lost and half-remembered, a thirst in our hearts for a flawless loveliness we will never find.[35] This is because we have been exiled from our true homeland due to disobedience of God's commands. Due to the loss of Eden, unsatisfied desire is a basic fact of existence.[36] One may exchange one desire for another, but the longing remains.[37] This longing, half-understood and unfulfilled, yet constantly glimpsed, is actually the desire for a return to paradise. Our entire human nature at its best and purest is still soaked in the sense of exile.[38]

But the way is guarded, and we cannot go back.[39] Eden is gone, and we will never recover it. That is not God's way with repentance, which works in a spiral rather than a circle, expanding rather than simply repeating. We will recover something like it, but on a higher level.[40] We cannot return, but we can move forward. A thing recovered is often more precious than the thing never lost, just as grace recovered by repentance is different (but not worse) than original innocence.[41]

THE FALL(S) OF MAN IN MIDDLE-EARTH

Tolkien frequently draws on Edenic images in his writing.[42] Paradise, for example, contains two special trees, the access to which is lost until the end of the world.[43] The word *aman* is simultaneously the land of the Valar and a word meaning "blessed," "peaceful," and "free from evil" but also in harmony with God.[44] In many ways it corresponds to the Hebrew *shalom*.[45] The light of the two trees symbolizes the purity of unstained creation, while the light of the sun is, in contrast, a synecdoche for the fallen world and a disrupted vision.[46] While God allows Elves to return to this earthly paradise even after the fall, for Men it is now utterly removed and inaccessible.[47] This sense of loss permeates *The Lord of the Rings*. Faramir describes the long slow fading of the glory of the Men of the West. Their only hope, he believes, is the return of the king.[48] The springtime and summer of the Elves have passed forever.[49] Legolas recounts tales from a time before the world was "grey."[50] This image returns again as they leave enchanted Lorien to the grey leafless world of winter.[51] In Tolkien's earlier conceptions, even the gods suffer an irreparably diminishing loss by removing themselves from Middle-earth to Aman.[52]

More specifically, Tolkien is at first hesitant to present any fictional account of the fall itself for fear of making his work into a parody of Christianity.[53] Until the publication of *Morgoth's Ring* in 1993, the fall of Man was an off-stage event in Middle-earth.[54] Tolkien's Men would only say that a darkness lay behind them and that some turned their backs on the darkness and sought the Light.[55] They refuse to discuss this darkness even among themselves. We are again reminded, as in chapter 2, of the Old English attempt to write their ancestors into Old Testament history while remaining respectful of its structure.[56] Tolkien offers a picture intentionally consonant with biblical history but occurring outside its main narrative. Whatever the Bible describes is true, but there is space at the edges to fill out the story. In *Morgoth's Ring*, then, we are provided with Tolkien's own Middle-earth version of the events in the garden. Just as in Scripture, the original human beings (here a group rather than an initial pair) disobey God and heed the devil, and this results in the curse of death, exile, and bondage, along with a change in nature.

His short story "The Conversation of Finrod and Andreth" is not presented as an *argument*, but as a thought experiment, he claims.[57] Likewise, our use of the text ought not involve the assumption of a one-to-one correspondence between Tolkien's fictional fall and his beliefs about the primary world, but it can act as a spotlight to illuminate what Tolkien considers to be thematically important.

In this tale, we hear a human woman, Andreth, tell Galadriel's brother Finrod the legend of the primal sin. In the very first generation of humankind, the voice of the One speaks to them and tells them they are his children. Tolkien leaves the nature of this speech vague: either a messenger angel, or an audible voice, or an internal and inborn knowledge.[58] God says that he has sent them to live in the earth and in time to inherit and rule it. But first they must pass through a stage of childhood and learning, and they should call upon him for help since he is watching over them. Soon humans develop language and seek to explore the world and increase in knowledge. While they frequently call on God, he encourages them to find the answers for themselves in order to grow naturally into maturity (here Tolkien echoes an Irenaean account of a humanity created in a state of spiritual infancy).[59]

However, the human impatience to order things to their own will leads to an increasing distance from God, and, eventually, a beautiful human-like figure (later revealed to be the devil figure Morgoth) appears, claiming to have come out of pity.[60] He tells them they may have riches, splendor, and ease through the things they can make—if they take him as a teacher. Here Tolkien's concern with creation and creativity makes its mark on his picture of the first temptation. Satan comes as a craftsman. He awakens new desires but is slow to aid in their fulfillment. He gives great gifts but also slowly begins to lie about the Creator, portraying God as an enemy seeking their destruction. He calls God the "Dark" and himself the master and giver of light. He is here portrayed already as prince of lies, echoing Isaiah 5:20 and perversely inverting the natural order.

Suddenly, at a time of eclipse and unnatural darkness, Satan appears again and says that the light has gone because Men still listen to the "Voice of the Dark" (God). It is not said in the story whether Satan himself has manufactured the darkness, but this is possible. He plays upon their fear and forces a choice between himself and the

Dark. The people obey, vowing to reject the Voice and take Morgoth as lord and master.[61] They construct a great temple and continue to worship and sacrifice to this angel of light, though his requirements become more evil and his rewards more sparse.

God never speaks again, except once in the quiet of the night, where he declares that though they have rejected him, they remain his. Now their lifespan will be shortened and they will come before him to see who is the lord in truth.[62] Men now fear the Voice of God because they have believed the lies of Satan, and they begin to dread their deaths. They beg the fair-seeming Satan to save them, but he answers finally that he cares not whether they live or die, and he reminds them of his ownership. They are assailed by grief, hunger, weariness, disease; the natural world becomes hostile and dangerous. They wish to go back to their old life but now fear and hate both their master Satan and the God whom Satan has deceived them into forsaking.

Those who are most eager to follow their new diabolical despot in wickedness are rewarded with power and domination. Eventually, some realize Satan has lied and is himself the darkness and the source of their pain, and they reject his service. Many are slain, but some manage to flee, seeking the Light. But as they had already built Satan's temple and worshiped in it, they do not escape the curse of God. In fact, they find Satan waiting for them in Beleriand. This first exile, though, includes its own *protoevangelium* in the form of a rumor that Eru shall enter the world to heal its marring.[63]

At the end of the First Age, in reward for their alliance with the Elves, these repentant Men are given mercy: the island paradise of Númenor and a greatly extended lifespan. But, as Tolkien writes, earthly reward is often more dangerous than punishment. It is by exploiting this increase in lifespan alongside their original weakness that Sauron is able to achieve a second fall.[64] Just as in Eden, the blessed inhabitants are free in all other respects except for the injunction that they may not sail any further west. The Númenoreans have the whole wide world for their explorations, and at first they are content. But their fall from grace moves them first toward unwilling obedience and then toward outright disobedience.[65]

This time, however, the demon Sauron plays an instrumental role as the new *diabolus*. He adopts a false appearance of beauty and new names meant to signify his generosity and helpfulness.[66] To the king of Númenor, who desires absolute power and an unlimited sway for his own will, he declares that God is a lie devised by the Valar to hold onto power.[67] He puts Morgoth in the place of the true God and tantalizes the imperialistic Númenoreans with the possibility of new worlds to conquer.[68] If only they would break the ban and sail to the Undying Lands, they would be as gods.[69] He uses deception and beauty to keep separate his two roles as enemy and tempter.[70] Just as the serpent does in Genesis, Tolkien's fictional devils inveigle against the goodness and trustworthiness of God. Such a denial is the root of all evil.[71] This second fall ends the same as the first, with the denial of Eru, Satan-worship, exile, and the repentance of a righteous remnant.[72]

Outside of this major fall narrative, Tolkien's descriptions of Satan are full of botanical and arboreal metaphors that still hearken back to the serpent and the tree in the garden: the devil's temptations and lies are seeds which are sown, rooted, spread like rank weeds, and are reaped and harvested.[73] Tolkien also explicitly refers to a tree of evil that cannot be uprooted and bears fruit of humiliation and dismay.[74] And yet this harmful horticulture can continue to produce evil even after it has been exposed as falsehood.

But far more frequently Tolkien portrays his Satan figures as serpents or dragons. Tolkien consistently harps upon the patience, subtlety, and artfulness of the tempter's work. Within *The Lord of the Rings* itself, Saruman and his lackey Wormtongue fulfill the function of the tempter from the garden. Tolkien deploys heavy snake imagery for both Wormtongue and Saruman.[75] The word *Saruman* in fact means "cunning, crafty," just like the serpent of Genesis 3:1. He is called "an old liar with honey on his forked tongue … dealer in treachery and murder."[76] He can make words stand on their heads.[77] Théoden calls Saruman a liar and a corrupter of hearts.[78] To this Saruman responds in anger. They seem to see a snake coiling to strike.[79] After Saruman's defeat, Treebeard and Gandalf again refer to Saruman as a snake left with only one tooth, the poison of his voice.[80] Saruman's voice is delightful and enthralling.[81] But its power lies in persuasion, not hypnotism. Agency is not removed in some sort of trance, but directed to an evil end through argument. One could always exercise free will and reason to reject this corruption of the reason, however.[82]

Saruman's servant Wormtongue echoes the same serpent-tempter imagery. Gandalf sees through Wormtongue's deceptive words, which have only the appearance of wisdom. Instead he has become a witless worm in truth, and Gandalf orders him to keep his forked tongue behind his teeth.[83] Wormtongue's response only confirms Gandalf's evaluation. They hear his voice hiss in the darkness, and we later catch a glimpse of his long pale tongue flashing from his lips.[84] Gandalf directly calls him a snake twice and commands him down onto his belly.[85] In response, Wormtongue's eyes glitter with malice; he bares his teeth and hisses again.[86]

Like Saruman and Wormtongue in their temptations and twistings, Tolkien's primary version of Satan, Morgoth, likewise never begins with an outright rejection of the truth. Instead, he seeks out a receptive audience, plays upon their good desires, and feeds them gradually on half-truths. It rarely matters whether his hearers even believe what he says—it is enough that the thought has been introduced. It will return on its own accord later and will prepare the mental soil for further obfuscations and slanted views. He allows his brief and casual deception to multiply and spread like a rumor, veiling its source so that hearers are further duped: those who would never trust the fallen angel will give credence to their own friends. Even more, he creates implications and allows his victims to draw the untrue conclusions themselves, believing them to have arisen from their own hearts.[87] Eventually, he seeks to supplant God in the minds of his audience. In a remarkable early passage illustrating the results of fallen wisdom, Morgoth impugns the Valar with the same selfish desire that he himself seeks to satisfy.[88] He dangles promises of greater freedom and hidden knowledge before the Elves, working upon the half-hearted desires of his hearers, granting gifts that were better never to be received. The Elves begin to know more and sing less, forsaking true knowledge for cunning lies.[89] Satan deploys an admixture of context-less truth with the hearer's own desires or fears and (in increasing doses) actual falsehood.

INHERITED SIN

The condition of *original sin* is an inherited corruption passed down to all humans as a consequence of the actions of our first parents. While Tolkien never directly addresses the issue of inherited *sin*, as is fitting for a philologist, he often speaks of our inheritance from Adam in linguistic terms, and of a cross-generational inheritance in general.[90] He bemoans the curse of Babel just as much as the curse of Eden.[91] In fact, he toys with the controversial idea of a native language—that is, a linguistic aesthetic or aptitude passed on through generations. His affinity for Anglo-Saxon and Western Middle English are due to his ancestry as much as academics.[92] Extrapolating backward to the origin of humanity, he can thus muse that there might be a primitive

Adamic tongue, though he stops short of arguing that all languages derive from it. Our only certain inheritance from Adam is the propensity for making words itself.[93] He can perhaps suggest that certain basic assumptions or paradigms might remain constant through many centuries and vast separation.[94] For example, Bilbo and Gollum understood one another better than hobbits have ever understood other races because of a shared background.[95]

Indeed, while we may be quick to condemn Adam for his mistake, we can see a possible Tolkienian response to Adam's sin in Gandalf's account of Gollum's fall. Frodo writes it off as "loathsome." Gandalf is not so sure. He calls it a sad story that could have happened to many hobbits he knows.[96] Adam is the source of certain of our own tendencies, and any of us could have been Adam under the circumstances.

THE NATURE OF FALLEN REALITY

GOOD IN ORIGIN

Tolkien repeatedly affirms the goodness of existence as such and the belief that evil only arises at a later stage. All things are created good and fall away from this goodness. But, since goodness and being are ultimately unified in God, a fall from goodness is also a fall away from being itself. This has a twofold implication: on the one hand, the more evil something is, the more being it loses; on the other, as long as something exists at all, it possesses goodness on some level. This is one of the most important principles of Tolkien's theology of evil: it cannot create but can only corrupt and distort.[97] Its power to do so may be immense, but it must always work on preexisting materials.[98] There is no such thing as evil being. Being is good, a gift from God, so that even to exist entails a modicum of goodness. Absolute evil would deny even this most basic quality.[99] As a corollary, the more evil attempts to extend its power contrary to the design of God, the more it is continually diminished.[100]

Nothing is *intended* as evil (though the world itself, intended as good, is actualized with the possibility of evil due to Morgoth's pre-creational interference at the time of its coming into being).[101] Evil in Middle-earth is not a creation of Morgoth's thought. He is neither desirous nor capable of bringing forth any offspring. He wants only to destroy, stain, and corrupt things in their generation. Evil beings come from a marring of the biological paradigm, from the discords and dissonances, the lack of accord between Eru's themes and Morgoth's.[102]

Tolkien describes exhaustively how every evil being in his mythology has either chosen corruption or had corruption thrust upon it.[103] As such, every evil retains vestiges of its good origin. Elrond states forthrightly that nothing is evil in the beginning, not even Sauron.[104] His former Morgoth-worship is a residue of good: the love of something greater than oneself. Likewise, his ability to coerce and deploy others springs from his original desire for ordering things toward the good of his subjects.[105] Orcs, as we have seen, were not made as evil, and they retain the goods of sociality.[106] Conversely, Manwë, free from evil, does not understand Morgoth's loveless heart, thinking only of his good beginning and his return to it.[107] It seems that virtually the only goodness Morgoth retains is the goodness of existence itself.

Despite recognizing the terrible effects of the fall, Tolkien holds the goodness and corruption of the world in tension and deliberately emphasizes not only that all things are created as good, but that the creation remains good after the fall.[108] Even in the midst of a global war and a world darkened by fear, laden with sorrow, and full of dread, he quotes Chesterton to the effect that we ought to keep the flag of this world flying—that is, to believe in and fight for the inherent goodness of the universe God has created.[109] At any moment one can be taken aback by the startling beauty of the world and can learn to cultivate this response.[110] Much worth can often lurk under a dreadful appearance, for, again, there is no completely evil thing; existence itself is a good. Large tracts of Tolkien's "Mythopoeia" are devoted to the insistence that, while Man is now distant and estranged from his original estate, he retains his inherent dignity, recalling and imaging God through his sub-creative activity.[111] We are disgraced but not dethroned.[112]

Indeed, the world may look very different from the heavenly perspective. Evil labors in vain only to prepare the way for good to arise.[113] Materially futile deeds are still good in themselves, regardless of outcome. One small act of charity may outweigh a mountain of wrong, for it is heavy with the weight of glory. Good is always present, though frequently hidden and humble. Even genuine sanctity is often invisible, despite being so much more powerful than wickedness, which is usually much more visible.[114] Tolkien remarks that people's hearts are not as bad as their acts, and rarely as bad as their words; we claim to be worse than we really are.[115] On the one hand, evil is rampant and staggering. On the other, goodness is humble but indomitable. God will not allow his creation to cease reflecting his splendor.[116] For all its ineluctable evil, the world retains the fundamental goodness with which it was made.[117] And, in the end, it is God's work rather than ours that shall turn the tide of history.

UNIVERSALLY CORRUPTED

Tolkien's insistence on the persistent goodness of creation must sit alongside his equally stringent insistence upon the universal scope of the effects of the fall upon the world and its inhabitants. While there are several hints that Tolkien does not believe sin to have affected the whole world immediately, but rather to have spread gradually, it is abundantly clear that the fall is a universal condition.[118] The darkness of the Great War was not an exception to the history of the world—it was the rule.[119] The Christian cannot expect history to be anything other than a "long defeat" (though not without hints of final victory).[120] While it will not remain so forever and, as noted above, continues to partake of much good, the fall has introduced a humanly irrevocable alteration.

Even a cursory knowledge of human history presses down the head with the unending repetitive weight of evil. Every culture, every city, every house sinks under the weight of the awful power of original sin.[121] Tolkien writes honestly that he can at times feel appalled by all the misery in the world and that, if it were made visible, it would immediately shroud the globe in an impenetrable black cloak.[122] We both pursue evil and neglect righteousness. Though we may avoid active evil, we do very little of active good, and most of our accounts are in the debit.[123] Tolkien's common use of quotations and qualifiers when speaking of human goodness remind us that this can only be understood in relative terms.[124] While humans and their world are often much better than they appear, they are never as good as they are meant to be.

In Tolkien's fiction, too, existence is tragic, passing from the high and beautiful into darkness.[125] Even "Farmer Giles" speaks of the wide and wicked world.[126] The fall, as universal, is contrasted with bondage to Morgoth, something not all Men endure.[127] Being fallen is not necessarily identical to being enslaved to sin or to the devil, and those who remain under the ownership of the ruler of this world may resent their bondage.[128] Lotho, for instance, begins as a willing co-conspirator but soon discovers he is unable to escape his own destruction.[129] Saruman finds the same fate.[130] But even the Men who repent of Morgoth's lies descend from those under the curse, remain under it, and may revert to evil.[131]

Tolkien distinguishes between the curse of death and the corruption of nature. Christians, of course, are still fallen though no longer enslaved to the devil. Their bodies and minds are still subject to corruption, but death is now transformed from a curse into a passageway to new life.[132] Mary is the only unfallen person.[133] As the mother of God, she could not have been allowed to see bodily disintegration, corruption, decrepitude, or other marks of extreme age as we know them. If Mary is preserved from them, this means that such things as we experience them must be a result of the fall and must affect all other humans universally. While Men may be corrupted to greater or lesser degrees, it remains the case that each and every person and their works will perish.[134] But even Mary is affected by the fall in a sense, since it gives her an elevated destiny.[135]

The fall is not confined to rational beings alone. It corrupts the goodness of nature as well, bringing forth decay, fear, and animal violence.[136] Because of Melkor's work, everything has an inclination to evil and to being perverted from its natural course. All things that partake of matter are more or less prone to grief and unnatural suffering, and the Valar can see no cure.[137] After the Blessed Realm is removed from the physical world, there is no place on earth that preserves an image of a time without sin.[138] The taint touches all matter whatsoever.[139] Destroying Morgoth's power would require the destruction of the world itself.[140] Even Morgoth himself, had he repented, could not heal the hurt, since his power cannot be recalled and continues to operate in the chain of cause and effect that has already been initiated.[141] Likewise, Sauron's own evil can outlast his destruction.[142] In this way the Valar were correct: the power of evil cannot finally be resisted by any creature.[143] No matter how often one chops down evil, its roots run deep, and it will grow back immediately, never to be slain.[144]

We return to the key difference between Tolkien's own cosmology and that of the primary world: Melkor/Satan introduces corruption into the *blueprint* of creation, so that it is already actualized as fallen. Even apart from the metaphysical inevitability of fall due to human freedom, his involvement creates an inescapable possibility of corruption for all inhabitants and things in the world.[145] Furthermore, at a later stage, Melkor/Satan attempts to incarnate himself within the world, much as ancient thinkers believed angels indwelt and moved the celestial bodies as their proper forms.[146] Though he does not wholly succeed, all matter contains, to a greater or lesser extent, a tendency toward Satan. None are wholly pure of this tendency outside Aman. While Sauron attempts the same with the Ring, there is a difference. While Sauron's power existed in a particular piece of gold, Morgoth's power exists to some degree in gold itself.[147] It is anyone's guess how this can be reconciled with Tolkien's statement that matter is neither intrinsically evil nor opposed to spirit, that it is good in origin and remains still largely good and self-healing.[148]

FALLEN HUMANITY

The fall clearly creates a universal problem, but what does this problem look like in human life? Catholic theology speaks both of an incurred *guilt* of original sin and a *fallenness* from our original station. This fallenness consists furthermore in a loss of original righteousness and a corruption of nature: we both lost the special gifts we once possessed and altered our natural capacities.[149] We are now weakened against the temptation of sin and incline toward it and away from the good. There is no aspect of our nature unaffected by these wounds, and while human freedom is not extinguished, it does not choose the good apart from the grace of God.

Sin affects both body (the physical aspect of creation) and mind (the non-physical aspect). Even the exiled Elves, returning to a Middle-earth that Morgoth has poisoned, soon face weariness, sickness, and weakness, if not death.[150] There is, though, an ordering to things. When Finrod asks whether it is the soul that has received the wound of the curse, Andreth denies this. It is the whole human being: body, soul, and spirit. But it must have been the soul that sinned, reasons Finrod; a house might suffer for its owner's faults, but not the owner for the house's.[151] Ideally, the mind is meant to rule the body easily and easily to concern itself with spiritual matters, but the fall's change of plan means that such goals now require effort.[152] The evil present in the world can "cloud" the mind—a symbol of occlusion and hampering, the opposite of the pure clear light of reason.[153] Our spirits themselves are weakened by the fall.[154]

While Tolkien therefore thinks it much more common that corruption starts at the moral or theological level, a creature that calls Satan "Lord," "Father," or "Creator" is quickly twisted in body as well as mind, the mind dragging the body down into hate and destruction.[155] Corruption thus begins in the will but proceeds until the creature is affected entirely.[156] The mind and body are intimately and holistically united; one always has an effect on the other.[157] But in the same instance, those whose bodies partake of the corruption of Arda find that this corruption can seep into the mind as well.[158] Theologically, we might say that a being thrown into a sinful world-system will also be infected by that system. While fallenness per se began with mind, mind and body now influence each other in a vicious circle. While Tolkien does not deny the possibility of progress, he remains skeptical about it.[159] He can describe the present world as a prison from which fantasy can help us escape, or a miserable Reich against which one must rebel.[160]

Tolkien contrasts the eucatastrophic redemption with the "caco-catastrophic" (evil catastrophic) fallen world.[161] He can describe its state with words like "shadow," "blemish," "sickness," "deformity," and "stain."[162] Our nature suffers an unnatural weakening or debility, characterized as a tendency to aberrate from God's design.[163] The fall is an "estrangement" resulting from a "seduction" away from God.[164] The noble pagans were cut off from God by the fall.[165]

The Fall and Sub-creation

For Tolkien, this also affects our relation to the rest of the world. We feel not simply a separation from the rest of the world but a sever-ance—a sense of guilt. We have broken off relations with the rest of creation; we see things now from the outside looking in, living in some sort of uneasy armistice.[166] We need recovery, return, renewal of health, and the regaining of a clear view. We do not now see things as we are meant to see them, but inevitably view them through the lens of possessiveness.[167] Tolkien believes fairy tales and fantasy can aid us in this.

He notes that Christians were at first doubtful of the seemingly deceptive world of Faerie due to theological suspicion. But eventually our longing for beauty won out over our fear of demons and gave rise to the wistful, half-glimpsed dreamlike quality of Faerie which, we might theorize, is really a longing to return to paradise. For while we reject evil, we are also sick of ugliness and aimless false beauty. We use Faerie as an escape from the world of the fall, from its mechanism and ugliness.[168]

But mythology itself may become diseased, like all human works.[169] The echoes of the original fall continue to be felt throughout subsequent situations and accentuate the likelihood of further disobedience. After the primal fall, in which the wound of death is inflicted, our sub-creative desire finds itself simultaneously in love with and unsatisfied by the real world.[170] Such dissatisfaction can lead the intrinsically good sub-creative impulse astray. It may then fall in various ways, such as through possessiveness, which is really an exaltation of the self into the God of one's private world. Or it may choose to rebel against the laws of God, such as mortality.[171]

Both the sub-creative impulse and rebellion against mortality, whether combined or isolated, lead to the desire for power in order to accomplish one's desire's—which Tolkien notes often plays out in either magic or the machine.[172] No longer content with the limits set upon it, or with the ban that measures obedience to God, the human being seeks to supplant God. Fallen man creates fallen myths: false religions and false gods.[173] Fantasy has created both ideals and idols—but then humanity makes idols of everything anyway. It can do great harm because *free will* can do great harm.[174] The sub-creative spirit can fall and destroy the primary creation along with it.[175] But abuse does not negate proper use. Fantasy, and the freedom of the will that enables it, is an irremovable right of the human being as in the image of God.[176]

Dislocation of Desire

There is a proper order to the world and a right use for all things in it. We have departed from this order. The proper use of fruit is to be ripe; to misuse it unripe (as Augustine did) is not merely injustice and robbery toward the fruit tree's owner, but robs the world by hindering a good thing from fulfillment.[177] The world should be engaged with reverence and respect. To rejoice in wanton destruction is to pervert the course of creation. Beings that do so may be likened to cankers—they live, but their life is death.[178]

A chief example might be the dislocation of sexual desire to great damage of soul and body for all involved.[179] As Tolkien says, the world has always been going bad; social forms may change, but concupiscence has been omnipresent since Adam fell.[180] Concupiscence is an appetitive desire contrary to holy reason, though it may simply be used as a synonym for "lust." Before the fall, Adam and Eve were given a special gift by God to resist concupiscence, which they subsequently lost. Concupiscence is not a wound of sin but a side-effect of creatureliness. As Tolkien has it, finitude necessarily entails an inability to deal with certain states of affairs, but this failure is not moral as long as the creature does his best with the conscious intent of serving God—even if he is mistaken as to what this might be.[181]

It is clear that Tolkien does not mean to equate concupiscence with sexual lust, but rather with this richer theological sense. In a fallen world, our bodies, minds, and souls do not always sync up; the essence of the fall lies here in the fact that the best must be attained through denial and suffering rather than self-indulgence.[182] We cannot follow our desires because they are disordered; we seek goods other than the Highest Good. These desires, while they are a result of imperfection, are neither sinful nor corrupt in themselves unless the will assents.[183] For Tolkien, then, there are actions which are not necessarily evil but may be foolish and dangerous.[184] An Elf who decides to resign her bodily life has some sort of fault implying a defect or taint in her soul but is not considered wicked.[185] Aulë erred in making the Dwarves, trying (unintentionally) to usurp God's own unique power, so that while he "fell," he did so out of love.[186]

Many of our fallen works are thus mixtures of both good and evil, and many evils arise from good motives.[187] Tolkien provides no shortage of fictional examples. Melkor falls through a misuse of his *good* sub-creative power, and the Elves, interestingly, do the same. They fall into possessiveness and a desire for power out of an initial drive toward creativity, craft, and preservation.[188] For the Wizards, temptation takes the form of impatience toward the good, first desiring to force others toward this end and then merely to force others toward their own will in general, and by any means.[189] The Númenoreans fall through a love of beauty into cupidity, one of the seven deadly sins.[190] Gandalf is tempted to wrestle with Sauron in the *palantír* and use it to view the beauties of the vanished past.[191] Boromir sees himself as a great captain in a just cause.[192] Frodo too thinks of mighty deeds and rulership over the whole world. He would exalt his friends and the other hobbits to a ruling race. He fancies renowned poems and songs, generous feasts, and a blossoming earth.[193] Sam sees himself as a captain and a gardener, turning ash to beauty.[194] Sam also says that if Galadriel wore the Ring, she would make the bad pay for their deeds. She agrees but warns that it would not stop there.[195] Note that none of these temptations begin with a desire for evil in itself, but for good things wrongly gotten, because they were gotten through evil. Evil will eventually corrupt any vestige of good intentions.[196]

An Evil Race? The Problem of Orcs

One final element of fallen humanity must detain us here. In addressing sub-creation and the fall, we must also address what is ostensibly the creation of an intrinsically evil race in Middle-earth: the Orcs. If Tolkien truly believes that Morgoth can corrupt a race to such an extent that they are fit for nothing other than destruction, this obviously has major implications not only for the extent of the damage the fall can inflict on human nature, but also for Tolkien's doctrine of humanity. Are there such evil races in the primary world, and what should good folk do about them? Such a hypothetical question has added poignancy in a writing published after the World Wars.

Within Tolkien's myth, creatures are given the power to make (not create) things of their own, subject to certain limits and prohibitions.

But if they fell as Satan did and begin to make things in order to act as God to them, such creations would still be granted existence in order to uphold the consequential necessity of freedom—even if Morgoth breaks the ultimate prohibition and makes his own sentient creatures in mockery of those made in the image of God.[197] They are his greatest sins because they come from the abuse of his highest privilege and would be begotten of sin.[198]

Could God allow this? Tolkien speculates that this seems no worse theologically than God allowing the torture, brainwashing, and tyranny that we see every day.[199] Perhaps the primary world does not appear completely coherent because God allows for such sub-creational counterfeits on our plane as well.[200] By bestowing the gift of being on such creatures, God is actually sharing himself: being itself is a good. Melkor's attempt to mock God, to be a self-existent creator in complete opposition to God, is nonsensical. For his creatures to exist, they must receive being, and being comes only from the God against whom Melkor is attempting to rebel. He thus depends on God in the exact moment he is attempting to be the most independent of him.

Nevertheless, Tolkien still seems uncomfortable with the idea of God permitting the creation of an "evil race" *de novo*. Instead, he concludes that rather than God granting the Orcs being directly, they must be corruptions of previously existing good creations. A permanent alteration to an entire species is beyond the power of Satan, who instead can only corrupt or destroy *individuals*.[201] Only God can change (or permit to be changed) the nature of an existing form, and he would not allow a sub-creator to bring a wicked counterfeit into being unless it could ultimately be saved.[202] As such, though the Orcs may be naturally bad, they are *not irredeemably* bad, and they must be given mercy if it is begged, and even at personal cost.[203]

Tolkien sees this line of reasoning about the Orcs to be a direct result of his doctrine of humanity. He can call human beings "Orcs" in his letters, but always with the distinction that such a name is a metaphor; nobody is made bad by God's intention, and very few are irredeemable even after persistent wickedness.[204] Furthermore, those that appear to be so may still be brought around by a special miracle of God. Frodo denies the absolute wickedness of both Lotho and Gollum, and he is prepared to pay such a cost in order to offer them a chance at redemption.[205] King Tar-Palantir, much like Josiah of Judah (2 Kgs 22), offers a last gasp of righteousness in the otherwise satanic Númenorean culture, though he too is too late to save his nation.[206] The whole history of those Men recounted in the legendarium follows the line of those who repent of Morgothism and seek to return to the service of God.[207] Morgoth boasts to the imprisoned hero Húrin that all the world bends slowly to his will. But Húrin rejects Morgoth's claim to have such power over the world. He will not fool him as he fooled the fathers of Men. Now Men have seen the Light and know that the world was made good and shall be good once more.[208] There is no such thing, for Tolkien, as an evil race, at least in the sense that it is good for nothing more than extermination. He acknowledges that cultures can be more or less wicked, but not that we can write them off into damnation without also turning the judgment upon ourselves first.[209]

CONCLUSION

Men were made mighty under God, and their fall was a calamity more dreadful than all others. Their stature is now shrunken and their power removed.[210] In this chapter we have seen that Tolkien closely follows a traditional account of the fall of Satan yet has his fiend exert a pre-creational influence on matter in order to more visibly depict the effect of evil free choice in this sub-created world. While he does not treat extensively of Adam, he hints at an Adamic inheritance and is greatly preoccupied with the garden of Eden and the loss of paradise. He offers a typological and cyclical version of the ban, temptation, and fall without denying an original historical event. This occurrence results in the vitiation of human nature and the corruption of the original goodness with which all things (even Satan) were made. Yet despite an apparent pessimism, Tolkien consistently affirms the continuing goodness of creation and of creatures. Evil is everywhere but is always mixed with good. Nevertheless, human beings as they now exist are weakened, wounded, and out of sync with the created order. In the next chapter we will continue our examination of the dark subjects of theology: evil and the devil.

FURTHER READING

While good and evil are a well-worn trope in Tolkien studies, the doctrine of the fall specifically has received fewer treatments. Many of the materials listed in the next chapter apply to the doctrine of the fall in a more limited way.

Fisher, Jason. "Tolkien's Fortunate Fall and the Third Theme of Ilúvatar." In *Truths Breathed through Silver: The Inklings' Moral and Mythopoeic Legacy*, edited by Jonathan B. Himes, Salwa Khoddam, and Joe R. Christopher, 93–109. Newcastle: Cambridge Scholars Publishing, 2008.

Gallant, Richard Z. "Original Sin in Heorot and Valinor." *Tolkien Studies* 11 (2014): 109–29.

Schweicher, Eric. "Aspects of the Fall in the Silmarillion." *Mythlore* 21, no. 2 (1995): 167–71.

Wood, Ralph C. "The Calamity of Evil: The Marring of the Divine Harmony." In *The Gospel according to Tolkien: Visions of the Kingdom in Middle-earth,* 48–74. Louisville: Westminster John Knox, 2003.

VII

EVIL AND SIN

G ood and evil are perhaps the most extensively retrodden tropes in Tolkien's corpus. Any attempt to treat half of this intersection must be limited by two factors: First, there is simply too much material to cover exhaustively. Second, any good author shows rather than tells. Tolkien describes many instances of sin and evil which can only be analyzed literarily rather than as isolated propositions. Morgoth's seizure of the sacred jewels, Sauron's monstrous breeding experiments, Saruman's pathetic bitterness toward the hobbits—our author has made these figures into major characters in his story who cannot therefore be fully treated in a summary fashion. Whereas, for example, we could examine virtually every instance of Tolkien's reference to revelation, this is not the case here. Representative samples will instead illustrate the major elements in Tolkien's doctrine of evil and some of the more prominent facets of sin in his thought.

EVIL

Evil is a tendency to aberration from the design, asserts Tolkien.[1] It is fundamentally negative, an absence of what ought to be rather than a substance in itself.[2] Tolkien follows a profoundly Augustinian course in his understanding of evil, both in its nature, in its manifestations, and in its effects.[3]

Tolkien makes several remarks on the nature of evil in itself. All evil hates, he says, for instance.[4] But what is hate? Even God hates (sin and evil). As Lewis reminds us, there is a certain sort of hatred entailed by love. Loving justice requires hating injustice. There is a lawful and just hatred of evil, which we in a fallen world may never experience without some admixture of error.[5] This is because the fundamental meaning of hatred is not necessarily malice but rejection. When God says, "I have loved Jacob, but have hated Esau" (Mal 1:2–3; Rom 9:13), he does not mean he wishes Esau's harm, but that he has rejected Esau from inheriting the blessing. All of this is to say that, for Tolkien, the reason that all evil hates is because all evil stems from a rejection of the good.

Recall that in Christian theology, God is identical to the transcendentals: absolute truth, goodness, beauty, and being. Any rejection of God is also in itself a rejection of all good things, which have their source in God. Life, light, reason, fellowship, joy—all of these flow from a participation in God's eternal abundance. And, we reason, if God is one, and God is perfect life and perfect light and perfect fellowship and perfect joy, then all of these concepts must, in the end, be identical to one another, different facets of the single divine Being. Furthermore, as Augustine has taught us, evil is no substance but a negation of proper substance.[6] Evil is loss, shadow, absence, cancer, deformity. Absolute evil can possess no good thing, and in the end that includes even the good of existence. He denies dealing in any such thing as "Absolute Evil," since that would be pure absence. No rational being, not even Satan, is wholly evil.[7] This is because any rational being by definition still possesses at least two great goods: rationality and being! But certain beings can approach absolute evil more closely than others, and there is a direct correlation between one's choice for evil and the loss of more and more inherently good things.

As such, the nature of evil for Tolkien must be that of decline and loss.[8] It constantly divides rather than multiplies because unity, cooperation, creation, and being are goods.[9] So evil is also banal and repetitive, lacking the creativity and endless variation of the works of God.[10] Morgoth's music is loud, inharmonious noise.[11] Evil leads to loss of identity, the God-given uniqueness of each creature.[12] It also leads to a loss of power, which Tolkien, in accord with Thomas, equates with being, act, and potency. This is a metaphysical law of creaturehood. Power has to pass out of one's own hands in order to shift from potential to actual effects in the world. But because of this, the being exercising such power then depends upon the objects of that power.[13] Furthermore, the act of domination itself shrinks and lessens the being who dominates as well as its victims.[14]

We see this in the diminishment of Morgoth. As his hatred grows, his courage fails, and he retreats into his iron fortress, fighting only the weak and trusting his slaves to take on any real danger.[15] Full of self-imposed pain and weariness from his iron crown, which he never removes, Morgoth's misery is in large part of his own devising. He diminishes from demiurge to despot, unable anymore to overcome the Valar when they arrive to chain him.[16] He has squandered his power and become a shrunken shell of himself, fallen so low that even beings of far smaller natural power may overcome him.[17] Sauron, too, progresses downward into virtual nothingness. When he is defeated, his spirit is so weak that it is left with only impotent desire, unable anymore to achieve the malice that it wills.[18] He reduces to a vanishing point, a shadow, a memory.[19]

The Wizards, becoming incarnate, also take upon themselves the possibility of falling away from the good.[20] This brings with it a fall away from power and wisdom, both of which find their source in God. We see that after Saruman's turn to evil, the power of his voice decreases.[21] He relies on machines and slaves and becomes cowardly.[22] Saruman loses his native wisdom and is no longer able to understand Gandalf.[23] His power of persuasion, once his spell is broken, is reminiscent only of a court jester. Saruman's diminishment is visually symbolized by the breaking of his staff. It falls at Gandalf's feet, demonstrating that whereas once Gandalf submitted to Saruman, the situation is now reversed.

Aragorn affirms that Saruman truly was, at one point, the friend of Rohan.[24] His fame was well earned, his skill and wisdom deep.[25] But now, Saruman has degraded from a dragon to a jackdaw, a small bird that hoards glittering garbage instead of gold.[26] Saruman begins to be described not as a man but as a starved animal. His face is shrunken and his hand looks like a claw. And, like a hunted animal, he falls into the trap of trying to play both tyrant and advisor. Now, instead of acting the predator, he will be devoured like prey.[27] Gandalf remarks that if Saruman chooses to stay and gnaw the ends of his plots like a beast with an old bone, then he shall be cast from the order of Wizards and from the White Council.[28] Saruman's servant Wormtongue, too, seeks to reduce Théoden from a man to an irrational animal. Théoden cries that he would soon have been walking on all fours like a beast.[29] In truth, however, Wormtongue is the one reduced to beastliness. Gandalf says that he was once a man, but now he calls him a snake instead.[30] Saruman implies that Wormtongue may even have resorted to cannibalism.[31]

Gandalf laments that nothing more can be done with Saruman and that he has "withered" totally.[32] This is borne out at the end of the story. When he dies, Saruman's shrouded ghost "dissolves" into "nothing" with a sigh.[33] All of these words are deliberately chosen. He sighs, a symbol of the ejection of the breath/spirit/life within him, and then dissolves. The word "dissolve," an uncommon Latinate, contains no less than three etymological elements signifying negation. The prefix *dis-* attaches to *solvere*, which is a combination of *se* ("away") and *luo* ("loose, untie"). Saruman is reduced to utter formlessness, aging and shriveling into a skeleton at once.[34]

THE THREE ENEMIES OF THE SOUL

In categorizing Tolkien's depictions of evil, we might rely on a well-established medieval distinction as a guide. Peter Abelard, the medieval theologian, writes, "There are three things which tempt us: the flesh, the world, and the Devil. The flesh tempts us through the belly and luxury. The world tempts us through prosperity and adversity; through prosperity in order to deceive us, through adversity in order to break us. The Devil attacks us in all modes, and tries to lead us toward everything worthless."[35] These three things—the flesh, the world, and the devil—are often referred to as the three enemies of the soul.[36]

The Flesh

Sins of the flesh are internally motivated personal acts. They rely on the weaknesses or faults of the creature. Most of these sins are obvious. Ungoliant is such an avatar of gluttony that she ultimately devours herself.[37] Gollum cannot restrain his appetite for the Ring. The traditional interpretation has focused on carnal sins such as these, but sins of the flesh can also be understood as sins of the individual arising from that individual's fallen nature. Thus, the higher sins like pride or greed may also be included among sins of the flesh.[38]

Such sins do not have to manifest in such profound ways. Many hobbits have a tendency toward gluttony and sloth which does not reach the level of Ungoliant.[39] Outside the legendarium, the Father and the Son discuss Niggle's everyday faults at length. His heart was in the right place but did not function properly. He did not think productively, wasting time and never preparing for his journey.[40] In other words, Niggle has not disciplined his soul for eternity. He neglects his moral obligations—not in a flamboyant but in a humdrum sort of way, viewing them as interruptions.[41]

The World

The material world, is of course a good creation of God, though distorted and defiled by the fall.[42] But if the human soul struggles against its own nature, it also finds itself within a network of evils that also set themselves against God. The "world" in the relevant sense here is the collective noun for those external evils which oppose and threaten the human soul.[43] *This* world is full of fear, sorrow, and dread.[44] Tolkien can refer to the world as equivalent to an evil spirit, a sort of *Zeitgeist* toward certain forms of wickedness, which he equates in contemporary times to scientific materialism, fascism, and communism.[45] So much of public policy involves trying to conquer Sauron with the Ring.[46] Our battles against evil still participate in the same broken systems that bred the evil in the first place.

Resultantly, the flesh and the world influence one another, and not for good. Tolkien tells Lewis that people who divorce, for instance, hurt not only themselves and their family, but all of society.[47] How? Individual sins of the flesh such as divorce or drunkenness create social expectations and customs which spread and exert pressure on all members of society. They shift from personal sins into external social forces which influence individuals toward wickedness. Thus, ordinary people are actually being encouraged toward evil.[48] Individual internal temptations now become external communal forces. And these forces compound upon each other. So Tolkien asserts that wrong behavior (if truly wrong based on universal Christian principles) never remains static: it is either healed or continues downward into total depravity.[49] The "spirits of wickedness in the high places" (a reference to Eph 6:12) can be so powerful and prevalent that often an individual Christian must think not of overcoming it but only with personally avoiding worship of it.[50]

This sounds harsh already, but Tolkien admits that he casts the world in an even harsher light in his fiction. Due to Morgoth's maleficence, Tolkien's world includes evil and discordant elements even at the very instant the "Let it Be" is spoken.[51] As a result, sin is always a possibility and perhaps even inevitable. From trees to Elves, all things may do evil deeds as a result of their corruption. Even the Valar can make mistakes. Wizards may become self-seeking.[52] But Tolkien's radicalization of the felt reality of universal temptation finds echoes in primary reality.

The Devil

As for the third enemy of the soul, the devil, Tolkien seems to cohere with Abelard. The devil uses any means at his disposal to attack the human being. This third category, universalized to supernatural and/or spiritual evils in general, blends elements of both of the other two. Like the world, the devil is an external foe. But like the flesh, he dangles internal temptations. As a spiritual being who does not need to communicate by means of a body, the devil transgresses the boundary between internal and external in his direct mind-to-mind contact with his prey. Tolkien's supernatural, demonic, or otherwise spiritual evils include Morgoth, Sauron, Saruman, balrogs, Ringwraiths, and the Ring itself, for which see the following chapter.

THE NOETIC EFFECTS OF EVIL

These three sources of evil—the flesh, the world, and the devil—are relatively uniform in their effects, since they all follow the metaphysical paradigm of evil as absence and corruption. They lead to decline, loss, decay, destruction, darkness, and damage. In keeping with this conception of the gravity of evil, Tolkien harbors no illusions that the traumas of demonic acts and other great evils can be swept away. Frodo's knife-wound will never completely heal.[53] He carries a painful reminder of the reality of wickedness in his own body. Gandalf tells Théoden that Sauron's evil cannot simply be erased as if it had never existed.[54] While Tolkien has the liberty of personifying Satan's will as a force in Middle-earth, in the primary world it still remains true that evil acts, once done, exhibit permanent consequences. Their effects can even be felt long after their perpetrators are judged and destroyed. Surely two global wars exhibit this plainly to Tolkien's moral consciousness. But why, if such effects are so evident, does anyone choose to continue in evil at all? This is because evil not only corrupts the world and the body, but the mind as well.

As a departure from the good, which is also the Logos, the principle of reason, evil creates irrationality and stupidity. Tolkien also makes reference to a time when Morgoth is still capable of rational thought, prior to his further descent into evil and therefore into nihilistic madness.[55] Evil cannot understand good, but good can understand evil.[56] This is why Tolkien can comment that Sauron does not understand Gandalf. He has become too evil, and therefore too stupid, to comprehend his behavior.[57] To Sauron, Gandalf is just a smarter version of Radagast: interested in people rather than animals, but ultimately naive and foolish. To a heart estranged from pity, only pure self-interest is a comprehensible motive. Altruism is an opaque concept.[58] Evil sees good as naive, hypocritical, and weak, and therefore frequently underestimates its true power. Again, rationality is a good and thus an aspect of prime goodness which the evil creature rejects. We have seen that evil is inherently self-destructive, but it is also unintentionally self-destructive by reason of its folly and cognitive distortion. To a mind which assumes everyone else will follow the same crooked path as itself, the straight and narrow line between two points comes as a shock.

SIN

Sin is a particular type of evil committed by moral agents. As a descendant of Adam, Man falls under the curse of God, called *original sin*. But each particular man is not only under an inherited curse; he also sins in his own personal ways.[59] The individual sins we commit, over and above the inherited state of sin, are called *actual sins*. These do not have to involve actually carrying out specific actions in the world; a choice of will, even if it remains merely internal, is still sinful.[60] For these and for original sin, Man is estranged from God, and our spirits will be punished after the death of the body.[61]

Sin relates not to courtesy or manners but to the higher moral law and is an intrinsically religious concept.[62] Our ethical life takes place on two planes: one the real and enduring world of the eternal moral law, the other a relative and fleeting world of cultural custom. Most people blend these two, so that it is hard to distinguish between the moral and the merely mannerly.[63] As such, not all things a society deems unacceptable are actually sinful, and many sins are perhaps even socially admirable. We might think of the Underground Railroad as an example of the former, and the idealization of greed in capitalism an example of the latter. Tolkien does not focus on all sins equally in his writing, and here we will analyze only the three most characteristic of those with which he deals: deceit, domination, and idolatry. But first, we must discuss the experience of encountering sin. While sin partakes of all the characteristics of evil discussed above, Tolkien also knows that, unlike natural or external evils, which one must simply endure, sin and its attraction are something each human soul must fight. Thus, we must face and overcome temptation.[64]

TEMPTATION

It is likely that there are some forms of prohibitions in all possible worlds.[65] And with a command comes the impulse to break that command.[66] Some of these impulses arise from a tempter—demons exert spiritual pressure toward wickedness upon unwary souls. This sort of spiritual warfare is discussed in the next chapter. But temptation also arises from the weakness of our own wills and characters. The Wraiths tempt Frodo with lordship and power, but he recognizes this as an external attack and rejects it.[67] Tolkien, however, deliberately juxtaposes the external temptation with the temptation within Frodo's own soul. He will keep the Ring and rule as "King of Kings," and the earth will flourish and songs will be sung.[68]

Tolkien identifies the two points of attack by which temptation assaults us. Tolkien describes the Ring's temptation as "gnawing" at Frodo's will and reason.[69] Temptation distorts our moral vision and clouds our sight toward the truth. Thus, Frodo briefly sees Sam as an Orc when the Ring is threatened.[70] Who knows which of Wormtongue's lies Éowyn whispered to herself late at night, which she would have seen as lies in the light of day?[71] Our self-justification of sin can also occur after the fact, not just beforehand. If Frodo were to claim the Ring, his acts would seem good and beneficial to himself for a long time.[72] Temptation makes the reason follow the will—we seek to justify morally whatever transgression we desire: "Were I to claim the Ring, as my heart desires, it would not *really* be wrong after all." Alternatively, one may plead ignorance, as when Pippin takes the *palantír*, and Gandalf's intervention saves them from being discovered by Sauron. Pippin is remorseful, claiming not to have known what he was doing. But Gandalf is a keen psychologist. He understands that Pippin had even told himself not to take the orb but rejected his own advice. Nevertheless, the burned hand teaches best, and experience teaches in a way that argument cannot.[73] Here Tolkien is aware that there are actually several voices struggling within us for mastery and that we can both want and not want to sin. Furthermore, no amount of warnings about the dangers of sin and evil will penetrate a clouded heart until one experiences their damage for oneself.

We can see the interplay between desire and rationalization in the temptation of Boromir. Echoing the reasoning of his father Denethor later in the novel, Boromir rejects the words of the wise. He wants only to defend his land, not to dominate, or so he says. He cloaks his evil desires with self-justification until his eagerness overcomes him and he ceases to beat around the bush, speaking directly of his delusions of grandeur as a great captain.[74] Tolkien's use of language is telling. Folly "possesses" him, and evil "comes into" his heart.[75] Frodo refuses Boromir's pleas with solid wisdom, reminding him that none can use it and that all its effects turn toward evil.[76] Any way which seems too good to be true and which blithely rejects the road of actual moral effort—any way which does not fully reckon with the human heart, which is deceitful above all things—is likely to be temptation to sin rather than wisdom.[77] Of course, Boromir eventually breaks out of his rotten reverie. While he sees the errors he has committed, the impulse still lingers. In his draft text, Tolkien allows for some ambiguity in whether Boromir genuinely wants Frodo to return for his own safety or so that Boromir can be near the Ring. His is a halfhearted repentance, not yet fully wanting to put desire for the Ring away completely.[78]

Frodo, too, suffers from residual effects of a temptation which has taken root. After Mordor, he is troubled by irrational self-condemnation, seeing all he has done as a failure. But Tolkien parses this as an evil temptation, a form of pride. Frodo was discontented with being an instrument of good and wanted instead to be seen as a hero. Alongside it, Frodo faces another deeper, and perhaps more merited, temptation—still to desire the Ring. For in the end, he had not given it up of his own free will.[79]

But as Tolkien says, much of the danger of temptation can be avoided through moral deliberation and constancy. The Ring's deceit fills the imagination with enticements toward power. The wise consider and reject these enticements beforehand, and they found their right decision in the moment of temptation on previous resolve.[80] Frodo and Sam offer Galadriel the Ring in Lorien, again with the assumption that it would not be a sin to take it. Galadriel would fix things, Sam insists. But while she does not deny this, she also understands that her rule would not stop there.[81] Gandalf, too, rejects the offer to justify the means by the end. The Ring would work upon his pity and his desire for power to do good, but eventually it would overcome him. Gandalf has, like Elrond and Galadriel, already considered his own weakness and planned his counterattack with truth.[82]

One should not, however, investigate the deep things of Satan too extensively, even in order to oppose them, unless one wants to be bent inward oneself.[83] Such a preoccupation is unhealthy; getting inside the mind of the enemy cannot but leave a taint behind. Evil ought to be approached with all the caution of a viper ready to strike. One ought to bear the blame for such behavior, since we should know evil's power is deeper than our own.[84] Tolkien is here likely thinking of the New Testament's warning against not giving angelic majesties their proper dignity and underestimating one's enemy (2 Pet 2:10–11; Jude 1:8). Studying the arts of the enemy is not *necessarily* wicked or foolish, but it certainly puts one in a sort of moral peril.[85] It is deadly serious. It destroys souls and should not be laughed at or made light of.[86] Some things are not fit for joking. This is perhaps why Tolkien was so mortified when C. S. Lewis dedicated *The Screwtape Letters* to him; they both place the reader into a demonic mindset *and* take the matter too lightly.

DECEIT

Deceit is a characteristic sin of Tolkien's villains. The will to obtain power inevitably turns toward lies as yet another tool in making its desires effective.[87] In turn, ourselves deceived and deceiving, we are all more or less likely to accept or practice untruths out of suspicion or our own selfish desires.[88] Such acts include both lying, manipulation, and treachery. We will discuss Satan's role as deceiver in the following chapter but can make some general comments on these three concepts here.

Tolkien recognizes that the most nefarious *lies* are those which have a basis in truth, or slant the truth to insinuate or imply.[89] Thus there exist both lies and half-lies, instances in which the truth is withheld or the plain meaning is distorted.[90] The liar projects a false vision of the world. Looks can be misleading, and evil often wears a beautiful face. As Tolkien explains, our own consciousness of the evil and ugliness of our works leads us to think that the two must always go together, and we can no longer conceive of evil and beauty together.[91] Frodo knows it, however. He recognizes that, were Aragorn one of Sauron's spies, he would seem fairer and feel fouler.[92] With spiritual sight, the true hideousness of evil can be revealed.[93]

Deceit can flourish through *manipulation* as well. Any liar with enough intelligence can find words that sound reasonable and persuade the crowd.[94] This is what Tolkien frequently calls "subtlety."[95] Saruman can turn language on its head, and only the very wise can detect his falsehoods, so insidious are they.[96] One is not controlled but convinced; such sophistry corrupts the reasoning powers.[97] The power of the lying voice and the false word must consequently be met with free will and reason.[98] Penetrating false rhetoric and lies is an active endeavor, as Tolkien frequently suggests, and needs refreshment through constant reminders of the truth.[99]

Deceit also includes *betrayal* and treason, and failure to keep faith reappears several times throughout the corpus.[100] The Dead Men of Dunharrow are cursed to undeath for breaking their vows, and the Orcs as a people are so untrustworthy that even their master Saruman does not allow them to guard his gates.[101] Those who practice treachery know that the same might be done to them, and so they frequently distrust even those who seek to do them good.[102] Since evil is fractious and fissiparous, the ultimate betrayal of the good always betokens other subsequent betrayals, such that any evil alliance ultimately fragments into smaller and smaller factions, until the evil soul is left alone and isolated.[103] All unions are temporary and self-serving, with ulterior motives lurking under the surface.[104] Thus the Orcs in the guard tower actually all slay each other and allow Frodo and Sam to escape with the Ring, so that a traitor may in fact betray himself and end up achieving an unexpected good.[105]

In Tolkien's earliest writings, he sometimes allows that lying might be permissible under certain circumstances. No one blames Lúthien for her deception of Morgoth, since she lied to a liar and under mitigating circumstances.[106] Even the Valar deceive Morgoth, to the extent that Manwë pretends almost to kneel at his feet.[107] But in his developed thought, Tolkien rejects an ends-justify-the-means approach toward deception. Any seeming good in such a circumstance is swiftly corrupted.[108] We can presume that other such instances of lying for good purposes would also fall under this purview.

DOMINATION

Perhaps the single most characteristic sin upon which Tolkien reflects is that of domination. According to Tolkien, the Ring primarily symbolizes a will to power, setting the sin of domination squarely in the center (and the title) of the narrative as the supremely bad motive.[109] As Tolkien writes, power is evil when it seeks to dominate other wills or minds—that is, to make other people do what you want.[110] Governing or constraining the will of another creature is insurmountably evil, and any good motives one may have are quickly destroyed.[111]

Exerting power toward domination is in effect exercising the status of lord (*dominus*) over a creation to which one has no right. Sauron seeks to subdue others to his will, envying their divinely-bestowed gifts, wanting himself to be God and master.[112] But only God is Lord. And since free and rational beings are the greatest reflection of God in creation, seeking to be an illegitimate lord over such beings is the greatest evil. Domination usurps the prerogative that should be God's alone.

Humans are sub-creators and vice-regents and can never rule over free beings as God can, for only God can give the faculty of love and independent existence.[113] Even when we sub-create, we make only puppets with no free life of their own. The impulse is a subtle one, but Tolkien warns that a possessive ownership of one's work is actually an avenue toward sin. We do not possess anything we have made, except secondarily. But it can happen that the sub-creator actually desires to rebel against her subsidiary status and become the god of her own private world, going against the laws of the true Creator.[114] The desire to create and rule (which both have as their root the desire to effect one's own will) inevitably lead to a desire for power as such, for making the will immediately effective. And this in turn leads to whatever best instrumentalizes such power: machinery and magic.[115]

The basic motive for magic is immediacy—reducing the gap between an idea and its realization.[116] Magic is ultimately the impulse to mimic God's own *creatio ex nihilo*, a creaturely arrogation of the divine fiat. Tolkien defines magic as the use of external means in place of the development of internal capacities. Alternatively, one could use these capacities with the motive of bulldozing over the real world.[117] Magic is a shortcut which denies otherness—either the otherness of the world or the otherness of other people. But magic is not the only form of domination. The machine is much more closely related to magic than we usually admit.[118] Tolkien decries the space-destroying and tranquility-shattering effect of modern modes of transport, as is well-known. This is because "Americo-cosmopolitanism" also denies difference and introduces monotony. Culture becomes flattened and interchangeable.[119]

Tolkien's predictions came true—in many parts of the world one city is very much like any other, with the same shops, the same shows, the same songs, and the same sentiments. The global village is actually decreasing culture rather than broadening it. Tolkien even bemoans the spread of his beloved English, calling down the curse of Babel and joking that he will only speak his own regional Old English dialect.[120] This commercial and cultural domination is insidious precisely because it does not explicitly intend any evil. While the dominator always veers into magic and machinery, he does not always do so from bad motives. Often, he wants simply to benefit the world—but according to his own vision.[121] It is sin nevertheless because it denies the otherness and freedom of the persons so "benefited." Even a benign tyranny leads to an impatient desire to force others into doing what is best for them, and so inevitably into a simple impulse for absolute control by any means.[122]

From the smallest impulse toward possessiveness we come, without caution, to absolute tyranny. The tragic despair of machinery is that it attempts to raise sub-creative artistic power into a power exertable upon the primary world, and this cannot ultimately be done satisfactorily.[123] Once the process is begun, we must also factor into the fundamental creaturely limitation the corruption of the fall; to failure must be added evil.[124] Thus there is another moral or pathological factor following on the first, where the object no longer really matters and the destruction and pain begin to be pleasing for their own sake.[125]

Tolkien offers two slightly different accounts of the sin of domination in his fiction, embodied in his two Satan figures. On the one hand, there is Morgoth, who in his titanic lust for control is so self-absorbed that he hates even the existence of the other and uses physical force (the only power he believes matters) to destroy them, body and soul.[126] But Morgoth actually wastes his own power of being in seeking control over others.[127] Inevitably the tides turn, and the tyrant realizes that more power lies in his teeming hordes of slaves than in his own two hands—as the Egyptians realized in Moses' day. He becomes isolated even from his slaves. The natural end of this sort of domination by force is fear, paranoia, and, eventually, destruction.

Sauron embodies an alternate impulse toward domination. He wants not destruction but control.[128] He thus dominates through manipulation, deceit, and reward rather than through sheer power. He is the corrupter rather than the destroyer because his form of subjugation is a holdover from his original desire to order the lives of his subjects toward good.[129] This has now been perverted into a demand for worship and absolute rulership over the world.[130] This same impulse would overtake any who claimed the Ring, standing as it does for the will to power itself.[131]

Unlike Morgoth, Sauron is thus more willing to pretend humility if it gets him the control he wants. He deviously succumbs to the mastery of Númenor, utilizing their desire for secret power beyond their proper limits.[132] He pretends servitude in order to bind his erstwhile masters into servitude themselves. He succeeds where Morgoth failed, stoking the fires of ambition in the heart of the king, infecting him with lust for unbounded control.[133] Sauron is now the master and his master the slave, worshiping Morgoth and exalting Sauron so high that he might have claimed the throne had he wanted it. But Sauron is content to see Ar-Pharazôn destroy himself.

The Ringwraiths are perhaps Tolkien's most iconic picture of domination. Sauron uses their rings to devour and enthrall them.[134] Now, they have no wills of their own, acting only as extensions of Sauron himself.[135] Their voices speak only his will and his hatred.[136] They exist in a sense only for him, invisible to all other eyes.[137] Even their very life force is tied to Sauron rather than to themselves. They can only be destroyed if Sauron is destroyed.[138] They seek to entrap others in this same mindless slavery; the Morgul-blade is meant to subdue Frodo to the will of the Wraiths, and thus to Sauron himself.[139]

If Sauron lusts after complete power, then Saruman is in the process of following the same path.[140] Treebeard describes him as a mind of metal and wheels, caring only for what serves him at the moment.[141] The only things Saruman cares about are the things that get him what he wants. But in seeking service to a lord who promises to fulfill Saruman's desire for power, he has in fact enslaved himself. Gandalf remarks on the irony. Trapped, held, persuaded, daunted, the predator has become the prey of a bigger beast.[142] Gandalf offers freedom, but Saruman cannot let go of his desire for power over others.[143] Saruman refuses to serve. He wants only to command.[144] Cast out from his tower, Saruman in turn does to Lotho what Sauron did to him. Lotho wants to boss everyone around and own everything.[145] Saruman offers him the ability to do so, as Sauron did to Ar-Pharazôn, but it too costs Lotho his life in the end. Saruman takes pleasure in using petty thugs to dominate Frodo's home, destroying merely for the sake of destruction.[146] This is an impulse he shares with Sauron, who would also enslave hobbits merely for malicious pleasure in revenge.[147] When he is defeated by the humble once again, Saruman is left with nothing. From a second Sauron, Saruman is left only with his pathetic domination of Wormtongue, like the master of an abused dog. Wormtongue himself, once the de facto ruler of Rohan, is now merely Worm, crawling in the dust. But this slave too gets his revenge.

IDOLATRY

While many other readers have noticed Tolkien's particular emphasis on domination and power, there is another sin which Tolkien considers to be at least as important, but which is rarely if ever discussed: idolatry.[148] *Idolatry* is the corruption of a good and natural impulse to worship God, instead directed toward an improper object.[149] The root of idolatry lies in created beings desiring to be their own masters and to have all things their own way.[150] The worship of a false god is always, in the end, worship of self, as we shall see below. As such, idolatry is an element of the human heart that may never be expunged in this life.[151] For example, Tolkien equates this same sort of blasphemous worship with the totalitarianisms of his own day and their worship of the "State-God."[152]

The primal idolatry, historically speaking, is the rejection of God in Eden and the acceptance of Satan as god in his place.[153] This causes huge metaphysical damage. Our spirits, weakened by denying their true nature, lose mastery of their bodies, which themselves turn toward corruption.[154] Nevertheless, people still seek to reject God and set something else in his place. Tolkien writes that men fell under Satan's domination quickly and indeed still feel a pull toward his kingdom.[155] Ultimately, this is because they see worship and service of idols as the best way to achieve their own desires. The devil knows this and uses it. In order to seduce a mortal away from their allegiance to God, it is easiest to offer another object of allegiance, another opportunity for benefit—but from a god who will sanction rather than forbid their illicit desires.[156] People, with their wicked and self-interested hearts, will eagerly hear what confirms their own beliefs, rather than attend to a truth which might demand change and difficult sacrifice.

But Tolkien also describes idolatrous worship as akin to seeking favor from a tyrant.[157] He might grant power to some, but he punishes others and often acts arbitrarily. This is at once a theological statement about Satan and a phenomenological statement of the way the gods must have seemed to peoples such as the Greeks or Danes.

Tolkien paints a picture of a *sensus divinitatis*, a natural knowledge of the true God inherent in all beings. He likely shares the views of Anglo-Saxon authors such as Aelfric of Eynsham, Wulfstan, and the *Beowulf* poet here.[158] The noble pagans knew that God exists and is the giver of all good gifts, despite never having heard the gospel. But the fall cut humanity off from God so that in desperate and doubtful times they were increasingly vulnerable to the devil's snares and thus prayed to false gods for help.[159] It is no surprise that people might desert the true God for false ones, for quick and easy answers to temporal problems. God has never guaranteed his people immunity from trials, even after prayer.[160]

But if there is only one God, how could these idols be expected to answer prayers? Again, Tolkien frames the origin of idolatry in the human decision to worship Satan as god and king.[161] The fallen men are deceived, taking Satan and his servants to be gods; this is the true origin of other religions.[162] Tolkien explains that the Christian theory is that such gods do not actually exist, being inventions of the devil— they are masks behind which demons hide.[163] Tolkien clarifies that the Danes were not deliberate Satanists, but they were indeed praying to the devil when they prayed to their idols.[164] These are just the facts, regardless of what the worshipers themselves might feel about the situation. This is clear from a reading of the Old Testament itself, from Caedmon and other versifiers, and from actual reports of contemporary pagans, he argues.

Tolkien notices that the *Beowulf* poet is interested in the good elements of pagan culture but removes the names of their idols because he believed that they were lies of the evil one. Even people like Hrothgar were aware of this at the time, since they only trafficked with such heathen gods when specially tempted by Satan.[165] Tolkien's Anglo-Saxon characters in *The Homecoming of Beorhtnoth* call their pagan enemies the devil's offspring, who drink to Thor to drown their sorrows as children of hell.[166] This is perhaps the reason why Tolkien refused to syncretize any of his angelic Powers with their classical or Northern counterparts (Mandos with Hades, for instance). He seeks to retain the narrative benefit of such figures without capitulating to idolatrous worship himself.[167]

Idolatry in Middle-earth

A resistance to idolatry is perhaps the fundamental theological theme in *The Lord of the Rings*, even more than the nature of domination and power. Tolkien states that the conflict of the book is not about freedom but about God and his sole right to worship.[168] His Satan figures, Sauron and Morgoth, demand divine honor from all thinking creatures.[169] Sauron's will to power and desire to set himself up as a false god are the driving motivations for the War of the Ring.

While Tolkien famously removes virtually all organized religion from Middle-earth, he retains the refusal to worship any created being and especially any satanic demon.[170] He explains that, in such a mythical state when evil is physically incarnate, and when physical resistance to that evil is a major act of loyalty to God, it seems quite reasonable that the good and faithful folk would concentrate their belief systems on the negative, on resistance to evil, rather than on the positive development of doctrine.[171] In other words, a concern for proper worship and a resistance to idolatry are the hallmark of Middle-earth's religion. We see it explicitly in Húrin's defiance of Morgoth, for instance.[172] Tolkien is clear that proper worship comes before all other concerns. As Elendil, Aragorn's ancestor, says, all objects of loyalty, even the royal house of Númenor, must take second place in a decision between Sauron and Manwë.[173] Resisting such horrid idolatries is indubitably the right thing to do.[174]

There are only three references to idolatry in *The Lord of the Rings* itself, both of which associate it with Satanism. First, Gollum worships Shelob when he first encounters her in the mountains.[175] Second, Gandalf tells the suicidal Denethor that only the heathen kings who worshiped Sauron would kill themselves, frequently taking their relative along with them into the grave.[176] Third, the Mouth of Sauron, we are told, worshiped Sauron along with the other Black Númenoreans.[177]

We later learn the full story of these Black Númenorean idolaters, whose false worship destroyed a kingdom and reshaped the world. In order to destroy the Númenoreans, Sauron takes the role of a high priest, treating Morgoth as God himself and claiming that he will fulfill the Númenoreans' deepest desires: immortality and an equal status with the gods.[178] He tells them that the One (and his ban on traveling to Valinor) is an invention of the Valar meant to hold onto power and that the true ruler of the gods is Morgoth, who dwells now in the Void and who will make unlimited realms there for his subjects to rule.[179] Projecting their own selfishness and power politics onto those who are in fact acting in their best interest, the Númenoreans in turn accuse the Valar of seeking to control and dominate them.

Sauron plays up their desires, promising them eternal life and dominion over the world in exchange for allegiance to Morgoth.[180] This new god is the "Giver of Freedom." *This god* will let you do whatever you want, unlike the old God who demands so much. The consequence is perhaps inevitable. Ar-Pharazôn the King turns to Satanism, first in secret and then publicly, and his people follow his example.[181] This leads to institutionalized idolatry: a Satanist religion, including a large temple, priests, and dark sacrifices.[182] Religious plurality does not last long. The idolaters now persecute the faithful and forbid the true worship. And soon they go further, executing and even sacrificing the remnant of the faithful on false pretenses.[183] They inaugurate the new temple with a fire kindled from the wood of the sacred tree Nimloth.[184]

Tolkien's description of the Númenorean idolatry draws from actual practices, though framed in such a way as to reveal the truth behind idolatrous religious philosophies. The temple is stained with spilt blood and shadowed with torment as Men sacrifice to Morgoth, begging him to rescue them from death.[185] We hear of cannibalism and human sacrifice upon black stones in order to absorb the life force of the victims.[186] But while they may receive material wealth, they get cold spiritual comfort. They still fear death and the dark realm of their self-selected lord, and their agony only leads them to curse themselves.[187] In the end, his false faith provides no salvation.

The true divine council of God holds the idolatry of Men to be a grievous sin, and there is no easy absolution for their treason.[188] God sends plagues and punishments, like the judgments on the Israelites of the Old Testament, in order to turn the people back to truth, but instead they rebel even more. Some repent for a time, while others harden their hearts and shake their fists at heaven, accusing the Valar of violence against them. The Valar symbolically judge the wicked religion of Númenor by cleaving the roof of the great temple with lightning, but like the evil magicians of Pharaoh's court, Sauron meets this miracle with his own pseudo-miracle, showing himself unharmed. From this point on he receives worship as a god himself.[189] Sauron sets himself up in the inner circle of the temple and receives human sacrifices.[190] Númenor's decline ends only with its absolute destruction.

Elsewhere, we also find a few fleeting references to a place called Nan Dumgorthin, the land of the dark idols. Here evil renegade humans sacrifice to hidden unspeakable idols (the meaning of *dumgort*).[191] Túrin and his companion wander there after he slays Beleg, trapped in unholy twilight mazes where "nameless gods have shrouded shrines in shadows secret, more old than Morgoth or the ancient lords the golden Gods of the guarded West."[192] Who or what might these elder gods be? We are not told. Tolkien provides only a hint when he writes, "The ghostly dwellers of that grey valley hindered nor hurt them," though they fancy they hear the "distant mockery of demon voices."[193] Ultimately, the power behind such idols remains that of evil spirits, fallen angels, as the author of *Beowulf* preaches.

Atheism

Tolkien's attitude toward atheism in large part follows the contours of his response to idolatry. His comments on totalitarian state-gods reveal that the ideologies of Marxism or other atheistic systems simply substitute one God for another of human making. It is probably the spirit of atheistic totalitarianism or political materialism to which Tolkien refers when he writes of the spirit of wickedness in high places, visualizing it as a many-headed hydra and urging us not to worship any of its heads.[194] He indicates that while atheists might deny the existence of any god, their own denial has itself a supernatural cause, being inspired by demonic forces to further their own agenda. As Baudelaire says, the greatest trick the devil ever pulled was convincing the world he didn't exist.

At one point Tolkien considers having his Satan figure convince many that the downfall of Númenor was a natural event.[195] In other words, Sauron provides an atheistic explanation that denies God's judgment on sin. This is because, though Sauron of course cannot doubt God's existence, he can preach atheism in order to weaken the resistance of his hearers, and because he himself no longer fears God's judgment.[196] On the human side, perhaps because of their experience with the false gods of Morgoth, many in Middle-earth believe the gods to be cruel and wicked.[197] As a result, many abandon them, excising them from their legends and even their dreams.[198] In either regard, then, for Tolkien atheism arises not from logical reasoning but from a principled refusal of worship.

THEODICY

When Tolkien claims that evil is timeless and wins out as often as the good does, he is not being cynical but realistic.[199] The greatest objection to Christianity is the problem of the existence of evil in a universe ruled by an omnibenevolent and omnipotent God. Why some children die in infancy is an inexplicable problem, for example.[200] But Tolkien provides several responses to this objection. For instance, he can illustrate how humanity itself is God's theodicy: they enter the Music only after Melkor's initial disruption. Tolkien argues that, in his fiction at least, God allows evil in order that he may heal its breach through Men, who elevate his creation to new heights. Men are the heirs and fulfillers of creation.[201]

The idea that certain goods may only come into being because of evil is known as the *felix culpa* theodicy, and it was broached by Augustine and Aquinas.[202] It argues that God allowed the fall in order to bring about the greater good of redemption. Tolkien makes a similar argument in the "Statute of Finwë and Míriel": Eru does not specially desire an evil thing as an instrument of his goodness, but he does indeed use all things whatsoever instrumentally to achieve his final purposes.[203] And, as Tolkien points out, God allows for truly monstrous actions and consequences in the primary world as well. But he is clear to affirm that evil does not in this mode become good, nor does God actively will evil or author sin, but that God can and does work *all things* to the good.[204]

Tolkien illustrates this in his stories. He sees in Morgoth's evil a limited music that always finds itself being subsumed into a greater harmony.[205] The eucatastrophic subversion of evil into good is the essential way that God has designed Middle-earth to function.[206] This implies that some goods require at least the possibility of evil. The melancholy of loss is one of the chief attractions of the music of Ilúvatar.[207] As the Elf Haldir comments, it is perhaps the peril and darkness of the world that serves to increase our love for it.[208] All the tales of Middle-earth are sad but fair, and they can still be uplifting for their beauty.[209] In the same way, Tolkien believes the tragic element elevates the medieval poem *Pearl* from a theological treatise to art.[210] Meditation on sadness can teach the theological virtues of pity and endurance in hope.[211] While Gimli resignedly notes a pattern of human failure after early promise, Legolas points out the unexpected good that springs up from the dust.[212]

Alternatively, evil may in certain circumstances accentuate a goodness not otherwise achievable. Allowing Morgoth to shape Orcs, for example, actually introduces goods that would otherwise have been lacking.[213] As Frodo reminds Sam of Gollum, despite his betrayals, they could never have gotten to the end of their quest without him; Gollum and his evil must therefore be a part of the divine plan.[214] Several times in *The Book of Lost Tales* Tolkien states that specific evils have come about in accord with God's sovereign will.[215] This will includes a certain sort of loss even apart from Melkor's intrusions, since Men were from the beginning meant to replace the Elves, who would fade from the world.[216] In the ultimate view, evil is a part of the whole and serves to supplement its beauty.[217]

Tolkien also offers a version of the other major theodicy on offer—the free will defense. Here, God allows creatures to perpetrate great evils in order to uphold the greater good of creaturely freedom. Freedom makes men most like the gods, but its corollary is disobedience. God knows this when he gifts it to our first forebears, though he grants it nonetheless because it serves to accentuate his own glory.[218]

As we learned in chapter 4, the gift of freedom is what makes us human, though we are set amid the troubles of the world and often stray from God's design.[219] The risk and reward of free will extends even into our sub-creative faculties, as humans, which is why false religions and distorted myths exist, even though they ultimately lead away from the True Myth. Myth and legend can do great harm, especially when deliberately used to combat the truth. It is a right that can be abused as much as can free will.[220] Indeed the root impulse of such making is still the remnant of a good motive, though distorted: a desire for and love of creation. Such a trespass beyond the bounds of our rightful freedom, though, as with Aulë's creation of the Dwarves, pulls its object down from love into slavery, even if done unintentionally.[221]

Free will exists only as God allows it, but in order for it to exist at all, God must guarantee it even when it goes against his will.[222] He does not simply cancel out or reverse sinful acts and consequences.[223] But Tolkien reminds us that God's will has multiple senses. For, of course, in another sense, our current sinful state is willed (or at least permitted) by God. Consequently, men were *designed and intended* to inhabit a fallen world, for nothing happens apart from God's intention.[224] The fall did not catch God by surprise or derail his plan, as every world is under God's will.[225]

In any event, we do not know all the good reasons God may have for allowing this or that evil, or the measures he might put in place for meeting it. He keeps his providence secret.[226] But we can sometimes make educated guesses. In Tolkien's abandoned story of the Fourth Age, Borlas wonders whether God has preserved him to old age so that he can recognize the old evil on the rise again. Borlas's speculation seems to be confirmed in the repetition of the same phrase later in the story, where he does indeed recognize the presence of evil.[227] We too are within our rights to speculate as to possible purposes, but in the end, we must leave the answer behind a veil of mystery. We are ignorant of the reason behind the danger in our path, but there it is.[228] In fact, Tolkien debates whether grief and disorder arise solely as a result of the fall or whether this possibility is an inherent mystery of this great gift of free will.[229]

FURTHER READING

This field is well-researched and is in fact too abundant to list representatively here. Virtually any treatment of Tolkien will hit upon his notions of good and evil. Furthermore, most scholars, no matter their own ideological leanings, are willing to discuss the ways in which Tolkien's theology comes into play here, so even less specifically theological readings will often have something of import.

Birzer, Bradley J. "The Nature of Evil." In *J. R. R. Tolkien's Sanctifying Myth: Understanding Middle-earth,* 89–108. Wilmington, DE: Intercollegiate Studies Institute, 2002.

Chance, Jane. "*The Lord of the Rings*: Tolkien's Epic." In *Tolkien's Art: A Mythology for England,* 141–83. Revised edition. Lexington, KY: University of Kentucky Press, 2001.

Clark, Craig. "Problems of Good and Evil in Tolkien's *The Lord of the Rings.*" *Mallorn* 35 (1997): 15–19.

Duriez, Colin. *Bedeviled: Lewis, Tolkien and the Shadow of Evil.* Downers Grove, IL: IVP Books, 2015.

Ellison, John. "Images of Evil in Tolkien's World." *Mallorn* 38 (2001): 21–29.

Freeman, Austin M. "Flesh, World, Devil: Evil in J. R. R. Tolkien." *Journal of Inklings Studies* 10, no. 2 (2020): 139–71.

Garbowski, Christopher. "Evil." In *A Companion to J. R. R. Tolkien,* edited by Stuart D. Lee, 418–30. Chichester: Wiley, 2014.

Hibbs, Pierce Taylor. "Meddling in the Mind of Melkor: The Silmarillion and the Nature of Sin." *VII: Journal of the Marion E. Wade Center* 33 (2016): 41–56.

Houghton, John William, and Neal K. Keesee. "Tolkien, King Alfred, and Boethius: Platonist Views of Evil in *The Lord of the Rings.*" *Tolkien Studies* 2 (2005): 131–59.

Kreeft, Peter. "Ethics: The War of Good and Evil." In *The Philosophy of Tolkien: The Worldview behind "The Lord of the Rings,"* 173–91. San Francisco: Ignatius, 2005.

McBride, Sam. *Tolkien's Cosmology: Divine Beings and Middle-earth.* Kent, OH: Kent State University Press, 2020.

McIntosh, Jonathan S. "The Metaphysics of Melkor." In *The Flame Imperishable: Tolkien, St. Thomas, and the Metaphysics of Faërie,* 203–60. Kettering, OH: Angelico, 2017.

Milbank, Alison. "The Grotesque." In *Chesterton and Tolkien as Theologians: The Fantasy of the Real,* 56–86. London: T&T Clark, 2007.

Nelson, Charles W. "The Sins of Middle-earth: Tolkien's Use of Medieval Allegory." In *J. R. R. Tolkien and His Literary Resonances: Views of Middle-earth,* edited by George Clark and Daniel Timmons, 83–94. London: Greenwood Press, 2000.

Shippey, Tom. "Orcs, Wraiths, Wights: Tolkien's Images of Evil." In *J. R. R. Tolkien and his Literary Resonances: Views of Middle-earth,* edited by George Clark and Daniel Timmons, 183–98. London: Greenwood Press, 2000.

———.*The Road to Middle-earth.* 3rd edition. New York: HarperCollins, 1993, 159–197.

VIII

SATAN AND DEMONS

T his chapter, by its nature, will have many commonalities of theme
with the previous chapter. It differentiates itself in that we here
address specific evil agents and their activities rather than, for example, temptation in general.[1]

SATAN

Most of Tolkien's theology of Satan must be discerned from his fiction,
but this should not give us too much pause.[2] He deliberately identifies Morgoth with the Christian Satan.[3] But Tolkien's writings also
present a unique problem: it is clear that Morgoth, and *not Sauron*,
is the devil of Christian theology. Sauron, therefore, though the most
powerful and most wicked of Satan's servants, is, strictly speaking,
a demon and not a depiction of Satan himself.[4] Once Tolkien refers
to him as a "satanic demon," a peculiar combined expression.[5] And
yet, with Morgoth shut outside of the universe until the end of time,
Sauron fulfills the role of archfiend in Middle-earth in a way that
Morgoth cannot. Since Tolkien did not believe that Satan is ban-
ished from the world, we can therefore assume that this particular
element of his fiction—of a secondary demon taking the rulership
in the absence of Satan—is not transferable. Consequently, in tales

of the Second and Third Ages of Middle-earth, we can *functionally* equate Sauron and Satan, in the sense that theological statements made about Sauron's role and work at this point would equally apply to Satan in primary reality. He represents something as close to complete evil as is metaphysically possible.[6] Ultimately, then, Tolkien's complex of characters represent different facets of a single, nonfictional demonology. As such, I will use the name Satan when I wish to bring out certain points Tolkien would believe apply to the primary world, and retain the name Morgoth or Sauron when referring strictly to the fictional characters.

THE FALL OF SATAN IN MIDDLE-EARTH

All stories that begin as does the primary world, with a transcendent single God, inevitably involve some rebel who seeks worship for himself instead.[7] Eldest and mightiest of all the angelic host, the most shining and radiant of all created beings, Tolkien's Melkor shares in all the gifts of his fellow angels and himself possesses the greatest portion of knowledge and power. His sin, unsurprisingly, has its roots in pride.[8] He desires not merely to shape and finish but to make and bestow being, the prerogative of God alone. He lacks patience to wait for the fulfillment of God's design.[9] But Tolkien says that Melkor only becomes evil after the completion of the Music and the creation of the world.[10]

For Tolkien, we recall, nothing begins by desiring evil for itself. Satan too begins his rebellion by seeking not darkness but light. Melkor's strange thoughts have come from the outer darkness to which God has not yet turned the light of his face.[11] This isolation from the community of the other angels, this dwelling in darkness rather than the light of God, betokens Melkor's eventual fate. In his self-exalting pride, he takes a form of overwhelming brightness, but he still stands dim before God's brilliance. This provokes jealousy in him, and he seeks to seize the brightness of other creatures and add it to his own, owning all light for himself.[12] But his attempt to rise to the light of God results instead in a descent into darkness and nothingness.[13] We are told that he now gathers the strength of darkness into himself as he plots evil.[14] And so he becomes the supreme spirit of pride and rebellion.[15] Evil can be said, in an informal sense, to be incarnate in Melkor.[16]

Tolkien characterizes Melkor (and later Sauron) as having descended in his rebellion at last into absolute satanic evil.[17] Despite the measureless size of the universe, and the many spirits who would have followed him into it to create his own empire, Morgoth instead resents the rulership of the one planet he cannot have. He is jealous of his brother Manwë, the steward of earth, because he knows his is the highest position. To these lesser beings, Men and Elves, he can be an absolute master in a way that he could never be among other angels. His fellow spirits of course know that God exists and must agree to his rebellion freely, but Melkor intends to hold even the knowledge of God from the Children, imposing his own worship instead—a sort of intellectual bondage.[18] This is the point at which Melkor becomes truly evil and even insane.[19]

What, though, of the other Satan-figure, Sauron? Like his master, he is not evil from the beginning, but falls.[20] Indeed, he falls more than once. He is originally corrupted by Morgoth, but he is given an opportunity to repent at Morgoth's defeat.[21] For a time he seems to have reformed, perhaps even to himself.[22] He wants merely to hurry the reconstruction of Middle-earth along, but through this exertion of the will to control he falls back into pride and lust for absolute power.[23]

And then he goes the way of all tyrants: he begins with a desire to order well the lives of those under his charge, but his own conception of that order becomes its own end.[24] He is unable to humble himself and ask for ultimate pardon, and his temporary turn back to good ends in an even greater relapse, so that he begins to represent himself as Melkor's chief servant and high priest, and later as Morgoth returned—as himself the one god and king of the world.[25] Very slowly, and from a good beginning, Sauron descends into a reincarnation of evil, lusting for total power and therefore hating all who might oppose him, especially Elves and the Valar.[26]

This raises an interesting theological question: could Satan, if he repented, receive forgiveness from God? Tolkien seems to believe that Satan's repentance is (or was) at least logically possible, as he toys with this for Melkor as well. [27] For Tolkien, even contemplating real repentance is either a special grace from God or the very last vestige of his original good nature.[28] There is a fragile moment in which Melkor nearly repents, but fails to do so.[29] But he snuffs out this last dying ember by his refusal to humble himself. The jealousy and rancor of Melkor's heart block out the possibility of repentance.[30] Instead, he falls deeper into wickedness and therefore foolishness.[31] It is as if he has amputated a part of his soul, such that goodness is no longer even a possibility for him.[32] He makes a mockery of repentance, receiving perverted pleasure in desecrating the holy.[33] We can surmise from this that Tolkien believes Satan at some point in the past had the choice to humble himself and receive forgiveness or to confirm himself in inveterate wickedness, and that he chose the latter through pride. The habits of the soul to which he has set himself are too deeply entrenched. It is not that God will reject Satan's bid for pardon, but that Satan himself has freely closed off the possibility of his ever asking for it.[34]

THE DECLINE FROM MELKOR TO MORGOTH

As we have seen, for Tolkien, "power" is always a foreboding word.[35] Tolkien's Satan is obsessed with power. Melkor is the greatest created being, meant to begin what Manwë completes and refines. He is in fact so strong that he cannot be defeated by all the forces of the Valar combined.[36] As a being concerned with material creation, he is mightiest at the beginning of cosmic history, possessing a demiurgic drive to exert his will upon the universe at a vast scale.[37]

Melkor's self-centeredness even from the beginning of creation means that he pays little heed to things not directly related to himself.[38] He becomes so curved inward upon himself that he is simply unaware of the smaller and less momentous aspects of creation. His will has distorted his very perception of reality. If forced to acknowledge other creatures, he is angry and hates them, since they are not his.[39] But he has no love even for his own imitations or mockeries of the works of others.[40] Tolkien describes Melkor's music as a storm raging against itself.[41] It has a sort of unity of repetitive noise, but little harmony, and refuses to allow other voices to participate.[42] He imposes his will on others by drowning out their own unique contributions.[43]

Again, Melkor's God-given power focuses on the material world.[44] So when this power is corrupted, it means that he disregards anything but direct force. He despises anything weaker than himself. He seeks always to break and master other wills, or to absorb them into himself, before destroying their physical form. In fact, their physical form becomes the only thing he finds worth considering.[45] His disdain for otherness leads him to misunderstanding and thus to misrule. But he blames even these mistakes on God.[46]

Melkor has no evil plan save the reduction of the world into non-existence.[47] He wreaks evil in wrath and malice—that is, in a deliberate intent to harm brought about by overwhelming anger. He acts for the defilement of the Children of God and the blasphemous mockery of the designs of Eru.[48] Tolkien calls this sheer nihilism, since negation is its sole object.[49] Tolkien means this quite literally. If Melkor cannot be god of creation, then he will destroy it utterly. But even Melkor is aware, as long as he is capable of rational thought, that he cannot actually annihilate other creatures.[50] His goal is futile. Neither matter nor spirit can be destroyed as if they had never been, only ruined.[51] While God's servants can still love the earth as stained by evil, Melkor cannot so compromise. The world does not proceed from himself alone, even if he has influenced every part of it, and so he can only try to reduce it to oblivion. But even this formless matter would be a world outside of his solipsistic self-idolatry.[52] His defeat is inevitable.

His disregard for spiritual power in the interest of fast and direct physical power has, ironically, lost him both. Valuing only the material, he is inextricably tied to his physical body, and for this reason he fears for its safety, waging his war almost completely through his dominated pawns.[53] His lust for domination has become habitual and even necessary. He begins to need his slaves.[54] He cannot think otherwise. He is trapped not only physically but mentally.[55] He is only potent insofar as he still commands his armies through fear.

At this stage, Tolkien distinguishes between Melkor, as supreme power on earth, and that to which he eventually diminishes: the Morgoth, a central tyrant will plus its teeming hordes of agents.[56] His dispersion of power has led to a decrease in personhood.[57] Though possessed of vast power, Morgoth is still a finite being. Part of his native (and God-given) power has been given over into making independent evils such as Orcs, able to grow and act outside of his direct control.[58] His constant expenditure of will to dominate the teeming legions of Orcs and monsters under his service so diminishes his power that he shrinks into a petty tyrant king shut inside his fortress.[59]

Utumno is a synthesis of biblical and medieval images. It is his kingdom, with a throne and servants, but it is also a prison, as it is under
siege and Satan is shut in by his own fear.[60]

In the end, Morgoth's nigh-demiurgic potency, vestige of his original angelic might, is frittered away. He is weakened in power, prestige,
and mind.[61] Though he is a monstrously powerful despot, this is a
far cry from even his hate-fueled nihilism. He has fallen so low as to
like being a warlord with vast obedient armies of conquered slaves,
something any mortal could achieve.[62] This is a point often ignored:
Morgoth's furious all-destroying malice, his drive to annihilate all
things which are not himself, is too great a goal for the petty warlord
he has become. His desires, formerly so wicked and yet so prodigious,
are now also stunted.

While Morgoth desires to dominate or negate creation *as such*,
Sauron is only interested in the minds and wills of creatures. Even
though lesser in angelic rank and power, he does not yet fall so low
as his master. Having no need to expend as much of his being upon
evil, Sauron still retains more of the wisdom of being than Morgoth.[63]
He in fact leverages the power Morgoth has already expended for his
own purposes. Sauron eventually grows to be more powerful than
Morgoth, at least at his bitter end. But as Tolkien reminds us, he
too eventually disperses his power in attempting to control others.[64]
Sauron's power works through particulars, Morgoth's through gen-
era.[65] But both focus on the perversion and domination of other souls.

LIAR AND TEMPTER

Tolkien divides Satan's activity into two roles: enemy and tempter.[66]
Temptation includes all forms of deception and manipulation toward
destruction. In John 8:44 Jesus says, "Ye are of your father the devil,
and the lusts of your father ye will do. He was a murderer from the

beginning, and abode not in the truth, because there is no truth in him. When he speaketh a lie, he speaketh of his own: for he is a liar, and the father of it" (KJV). Tolkien's Satan figure is thus also master of lies, shamelessly turning understanding to subtlety and perverting everything to his own will.[67] He may appear as an angel of light in order to lead souls astray (2 Cor 11:14), deceiving all but the most cautious.[68] The devil is infinitely ingenious and uses sex as his favorite tool. He can catch us in his trap just as easily through seemingly romantic or tender motives as through animal instinct and lust.[69] As a good hunter, he adapts his method depending on his prey and often approaches indirectly.[70] He does not, at least at first, simply *tell* us what he wants us to believe. The serpent in Genesis does not begin with, "You will not surely die." Instead, he offers a question, a doubt. "Did God actually say?" (Gen 3:1 ESV). Thus we internalize twisted beliefs without ever hearing them directly from the evil one. All evil counselors may indeed derive from this primeval model, says Tolkien.[71]

He describes the process of Morgoth's deception in the same way. At opportune moments he sows seeds of lies and hints of evil, but cunningly, so that they propagate as source-less rumors and prized gossip.[72] They soon rue their open ears. The lie that Satan has planted in our hearts is a deep seed, and it will sprout up and bear fruit until the end of time.[73] Among his praises, sweet as honey, are always mingled poisoned words, so subtly that the listeners believe them to arise from their own thoughts.[74] Moreover, the most powerful lies are always partly true. For this reason Morgoth rarely lies without any mixture of truth. The exception may be his lies against God himself, which Tolkien suggests are ultimately the reason why Morgoth is cut off from the possibility of repentance.[75]

Sauron more subtly manipulates events and perceptions in order to distort the truth and divert right action. He guilefully leads God's chosen people, the Númenoreans, to manufacture a diabolical religion based in a delusion or satanic lie.[76] The lie is satanic because it is deliberate, malicious, and blasphemous. In one draft Satan's temple stands on God's holy mountain itself, echoing the defilement of the Temple Mount and the abomination of desolation of Daniel.[77] He employs a devious denial of the true God, who he says is merely a tool used by those in power to manipulate their followers.[78] The truth, ironically, is that this is exactly what Sauron is doing. But such is Sauron's craft and cunning that, led astray by subtle arguments, the devil-worshiping people of Númenor seem to prosper materially, all while becoming spiritually bankrupt.[79] He works not only through outright lies but through more subtle deceits such as the confusion of loves.[80] For example, the men of Gondor would never heed the words of Sauron but can still accomplish his desire. When Gandalf finds the porter slain by Beregond, he calls it the work of the enemy, who loves to pit friend against friend, confusing hearts and dividing loyalties.[81]

Satan's temptation is not an overpowering force; it does not negate the will of the listener. It is more akin to seduction than compulsion.[82] Thus Saruman, the quintessential Tolkienian tempter, is a sophist rather than a hypnotist. He corrupts the listener's reasoning powers with his seemingly persuasive words.[83] Every soul is affected in a different way and to a different extent, but no soul is unmoved or rejects Saruman's command without mental effort and willpower.[84] His audience cannot afterward recall the exact words, and when they can the words are robbed of their force. It is the sound of Saruman's voice itself that enchants and that makes hearers want to appear wise by agreeing with it.[85] Saruman's speech has little intrinsic meaning or power, having abandoned the Logos; it remains at the level of appearances.

But when one lives in a world of phantoms and illusions, one loses touch with reality. As is always the case with evil, Satan's deceptions harm him just as much as his victims. They lead to self-delusion and uncertainty. Tolkien broaches the possibility that Satan, having practiced deception for so long, is no longer able to distinguish truth from falsehood even if he wishes. For example, just like Satan in the primary world, Morgoth and Sauron cannot genuinely deny God's existence—they have known him face to face.[86] So why does Satan continue his rebellion against God if he knows that God must ultimately triumph? Perhaps because he has submerged himself in lies for so long that he lies even to himself.[87] He convinces himself that his lie is truth, and he loses all grip on the distinction between truth and fiction. He is such a habitual and skillful liar that he no longer knows whether to believe anything he hears, and resultantly he disbelieves anything except what he wants to be true. Paradoxically, honest and simple statements deceive him the most.[88] Innocence wields the greatest power.

SATANIC SYMBOLS: MONSTER, DRAGON, SHADOW

Tolkien's depiction of Satan owes much to his studies of early Christian contact with native English mythologies. Any humanoid monster was especially prone to develop in new directions upon contact with Christian ideas of sin and demonic spirits. They could present these new theological ideas in visible form. This is why both monsters and demons are hideous. Their parody of humanity is an explicit symbol of sin, that twisting, corrupting force which violates the good which has been created and shaped by God.[89] Thus, folkloric depictions of Satan as hideous and hiding in dark forsaken places, though symbolic, are nevertheless revealing.[90] For the same reason, Tolkien highlights the biblical link between the devil and dragons: overwhelming forces of power, pride, greed, and cunning malice.[91]

The Morgoth of Tolkien's mythology is only the first of many such concentrations of evil into definite power-points that must be fought and overcome.[92] But Sauron is the last of such enemies to take a mythological mode—that is, as a monster: a bodily, personal, non-human form.[93] Note, however, that even Sauron is much less physical and much more of a spiritual threat than Morgoth. Even here the transition into the realm of the will and the soul has already begun. While Satan certainly stands behind the evil forces of the world today, good cannot triumph simply by having a stronger sword arm and killing the right enemy. Evil is primarily spiritual, not physical. It is much more like a hydra than a dragon, constantly cropping up again when defeated.[94]

This physicalizing of the spiritual is one reason why, in mythological or symbolic terms, evil also manifests as darkness and shadow. As Shippey observes, a shadow is at the same time physical and intangible, a fitting representation of evil as absence.[95] Morgoth, apart from his physical avatar which could at times still deceive, was revealed only by a great dread and darkness.[96] Sauron too is a "shadow" of Morgoth, a "ghost" on the way toward the emptiness of the "Void."[97] He is a shadow of a shadow. And when he loses his body, he broods like a shadow, "dark" and "silent" until he can create a visible image of his hatred, the Eye of Sauron.[98] Sauron's will is described as psychological darkness, a menacing presence like a black wall of night at the end of the world.[99] The literal shadows surrounding Morgoth and Sauron are, we are told, the physical representation of their desire for spiritual solitude and secrecy.[100]

THE DEFEAT OF SATAN

Ultimately, Tolkien believes that, while mere mortals may not be able to triumph over the power of Satan, Satan is nevertheless doomed to destruction by God, as we shall see in chapter 12. In the meantime, God uses his instruments to stave off Satan's victories. Frequently, in addition, we see that due to Tolkien's theology of evil as decline and absence, Satan ends more with a whimper than a bang. The insubstantiality of shadow also governs his depictions here. We read that, when the One Ring is destroyed, Sauron fails and, utterly vanquished, he passes away like a shadow.[101] The verb "fail" here is significant. Failure connotes deficiency, missing the mark, falling short of a standard. Sauron is both *vanquished*—that is, defeated—and *fails*. He simply stops being in the way he was before. His deprivation of being—his sin-warped lessening of existence—is finally completed. His reaching hand, though immense, is impotent. Like a guttering candle flame, he simply goes out. This is not to say that, as an immortal soul, he ceases to exist altogether. Rather, he is rendered powerless to such an extent that he cannot rise again. He has lost all that power of being available to him at his first good creation, and he is reduced to a maimed spirit of malice gnawing itself in the shadows, unable any longer to access the created goods of shape or form or power.[102] Saruman, likewise, ends as a pathetic shadow blown away by the wind.

DEMONS

Satan, the chief spirit of rebellion, brings a third of the angels of heaven with him in his fall. The fall of angels, a rebellion of created wills higher than ours, occurs when Satan promises his angels power and earthly kingdoms in exchange for swearing allegiance to him rather than to God, much as he will later do with Christ himself.[103] Satan perverts them to his own service.[104] These fallen angels are now known as demons. To Tolkien, they are less corrupt than their master for the very reason that they do not seek their own supremacy but instead serve another, who at some point they had loved.[105] As such, Tolkien characterizes lesser demons as more capable of rational thought and deliberation than Satan himself, who is too engrossed in his own hatred.[106] His powerful will moves his demonic servitors to seek the overthrow of God and the injury of his servants.[107] Satan wields others as his weapons, the ultimate in means-versus-ends thinking, and his servants follow suit.[108]

The central qualities of a demon are not horns and pitchforks but deception and destruction of the soul.[109] A demon is an accursed spirit targeting the soul for eternal death, even though it may take a visible and horrible form that can both bring and suffer physical pain.[110] As an immortal spirit, a demon cannot be permanently destroyed. But it can be defeated, reduced to impotence.[111] Scripture states that demons will be imprisoned in hell for eternity and offers no hint at the possibility of demonic repentance. A demon is irretrievably damned.[112] There is no hope for its redemption. And since God holds out redemption to all for whom it is possible to repent, we conclude that demons are evil to such an extent that they can no longer desire the good in any coherent and effective way.

In a departure from most earlier demonology, Tolkien believes demons to be more active in waking life than in the liminal spaces of sleep. We are more easily distracted by waking life, and demons work more often by deceit than direct attack. The body is an easy mode of influence over the mind, and in deep slumber we are very remote from our bodies.[113] Tolkien describes a demonic encounter as a frightening "knock" at the door of one's consciousness. It inspires great fear and a sort of "dream-concussion."[114] Tolkien provides an analogy: the uneasy prickling on the back of your neck while you work alone late at night draws your attention to your isolation there in the dark. You are suddenly conscious that there is an outside trying to get in. But in this spiritual sense, there are no walls. Your soul is terribly naked, unarmored.[115] Only your guardian angel is there, commanding a swift retreat.[116] You might disobey or deny your guardian angel, if you are foolish. You might even begin to become attracted to the fear and fascinated by its numinous power.[117] This rejection of angelic protection puts one in a terrible state of danger.

Some people do indeed develop a fascination with the demonic, and this can lead in certain cases to *demonic influence* and, in the worst cases, to complete *demonic possession*. Tolkien places Hitler in the former category. Without losing complete control of one's faculties, one can be guided and even infernally inspired toward evil. Demonic inspiration does not enhance the actual intellect, only the will.[118] Hitler's demonic influence led to his perversion of the Northern spirit which Tolkien so much admired in its nobler sense.[119] The Orcs that attacked Isildur are under demonic influence when they are filled with an added ferocity and desire due to the influence of the Ring and its will to return to its maker.[120] This influence may be masked, as in many versions of occultism. Some of the experiences of mystics or other supernaturalists might be lies—that is, manufactured in order to deceive and harm human souls.[121]

Demonic *possession* involves the loss of one's agency altogether. One becomes a puppet or slave of the demon. Frodo's clear, powerful, booming voice as the demonic Ring finally overtakes him indicates a well-known effect of possession—speaking in a voice or language not one's own.[122] The Nazgûl, absolute slaves of the Ring, have an almost diabolical presence. It is as if the demonic Ring has taken full possession of these former Men. Their voices speak only Sauron's will and are resultantly filled with evil. The Ringwraiths are so malefic that they frighten even other creatures of evil. One Orc complains that they frighten him, as they can skin your body off and leave you cold in the dark on the "other side."[123] What exactly this other side might be is left to the reader's imagination, but we can safely assume it is the afterlife. Compare the Witch-king's threat to Éowyn, in which he will take her to the "houses of lamentation," beyond darkness, where her flesh will be devoured and her mind left exposed to Sauron's gaze.[124] Indeed, Tolkien portrays the effect of these possessed creatures as akin to that of ghosts.[125] The Witch-king receives additional demonic force in order to accomplish his task.[126]

THE DEMONIC IN TOLKIEN'S FICTION

We can see, aside from these examples, that throughout the various draftings of the legendarium Tolkien moves his own stories ever closer toward primary theological reality. Makar and Meássë of the earliest *Lost Tales*, though part of the discords of Melkor, do not seem to be demons but vestiges of mythological figures such as Ares or Eris.[127] In the earlier, more mythological drafts, Morgoth also has a Balrog son, for instance.[128] Tolkien distinguishes between the strange, gloomy, and secret spirits of the peaceful darkness and the servants of Morgoth. These latter unwholesome spirits turn the dark into a fearful thing, which it was not before. In a nod to Northern myths, Tolkien highlights pine forests as special haunts of evil spirits.[129] All of these figures drop away quite soon in the revisions—presumably at the same time that the Valar cease to have children. Notably, in the earliest conceptions, it is a demon and not Satan himself who tempts Men to the first sin, though of course at Satan's bidding.[130] By the end of Tolkien's life, Satan tempts Men directly.

And yet Tolkien does not merely abandon the mythic conception of a physical battle between good and evil. As we have seen above, he instead uses this imaginative scenario in which evil is incarnate to visibly illustrate spiritual truths.[131] As he writes of the *Beowulf* poet, the Christian battle against the devils, though admittedly on a different plane of imagination, is nevertheless quite similar to the conflicts between the heroes and monsters of legend.[132] The reverse is also true: slaying a very real dragon is akin to the triumph of the soul over its enemies.

The *Beowulf* poet allows his monsters, as adversaries of God, to symbolize and even to equate to the powers of evil and yet remain mortal and physical foes.[133] Tolkien provides his own approach to this problem in many of the monstrous creatures of his fiction, a twilight conception between fiend and mortal foe similar to that of Grendel. Morgoth's corrupted Maiar manifest in stench and darkness.[134] A warg is a demonic wolf and yet has a physical body.[135] Likewise, the word "Orc" derives from the Anglo-Saxon word for "demon."[136] This link between Orcs and demons lasts into the very latest stages of the legendarium. In *Morgoth's Ring*, we read that they were named Orcs because they were as strong and deadly as demons. The narrator, however, denies that Orcs *actually were* demons, since they could be killed.[137] Just like the Anglo-Saxon monsters, Orcs remain physical flesh-and-blood monsters, but they are already beginning to be described with terms most applicable to evil spirits.[138] Tolkien muses on a half-theological idea that the monstrous damned carry hell with them in their hearts—a very Miltonian conception.[139]

His depiction of Shelob gives us a further glimpse into his notion of demonic psychology. Her eyes reveal an intelligence yet mingled with bestial delight, gloating over her hopeless prey. She releases them from her holding spell only so she can relish their panicked flight.[140] And yet Shelob is never satisfied, hungering eternally. She herself cannot escape her own wickedness. Likewise, Ungoliant desires light but spins such webs of darkness that she chokes and starves herself of it.

When Frodo and Sam attempt to pierce Shelob's darkness with the star-glass, Tolkien reminds us that other "potencies" exist in Middle-earth, ancient and mighty powers of the night.[141] Potencies perhaps echoes the *principes et potestates* against which the Christian wrestles according to the Vulgate translation of Ephesians 6:12. Middle-earth is full of these demons.[142] Since Morgoth cannot *make* anything of his own, many of the forces of evil he deploys are preexisting demonic spirits inhabiting a physical form. Glaurung the dragon is a demon in worm form, made to indwell a destructive body at the behest of Morgoth.[143] Certain minor spirits become special servants of evil and leaders of Orcs, taking physical shape, though terrifying and demonic.[144] We also find evil spirits in the Watchers at the gates of the tower of Cirith Ungol.[145] The demon inhabits the stone bodies, like a heathen idol, and guards its domain. It is able to exert physical pressure upon Sam's head and chest, stopping him from moving forward.[146] The glitter of pure malice in the stone eyes of the Watchers makes Sam tremble with its power.[147] The sense of malice that emanates from Shelob also affects Frodo physically.[148] The spirits whose eerie voices the company hears in the winds of Caradhras originally serve Satan directly.[149] In an early draft, where Gandalf reminds the fellowship about bodiless servants of the enemy, they are directly called demons of the mountains.[150]

But Tolkien does not believe that Satan or his slaves are now incarnate, nor that spiritual warfare can correspond with physical war in the clear-cut way in which it occurs in mythology. There will be no more demon incarnate as a physical enemy, except perhaps at the end of time. Instead, Satan will use men as his pawns. We must deal instead with the half-evils, defective goods, and twilights of doubt which leave the right side much harder to discern.[151]

SPIRITUAL WARFARE

How, then, do humans experience the malice of Satan and his demons today? This is the realm of *spiritual warfare*, in which humans find themselves party to the great ongoing conflict between God's angels and the powers of darkness. While Tolkien thinks it dangerous to study the arts of the enemy too closely, any Christian ought to be aware of the realities of the devil and his minions, who roam about like roaring lions, seeking souls to devour.

Demonic attacks most frequently take the form of compulsions or influences upon the will.[152] On Weathertop, for instance, Frodo feels an overwhelming temptation to wear the Ring, which Tolkien describes in physical terms as laying hold of him. He can no longer control his own thoughts. Frodo does not himself desire this—the desire seizes him, as if from outside. Despite his cognizance of its danger, he is compelled to yield to the temptation and ignore all the warnings he has been given. Afterward, he realizes that his own foolish and weak will has obeyed the commands of his enemies rather than his own desire.[153]

Later, in the Morgul Vale, compelled by some external force once more, Frodo totters toward Minas Morgul.[154] As he fights the temptation, it seems almost to physically attack him, dragging and blinding him.[155] The Ring calls to the Witch-king, and Frodo feels more urgently than ever the mental command to put on the Ring. But he no longer feels a desire to yield. The demonic pressure beats upon him from the outside, but his will remains firm. Frodo has grown spiritually; he is able to discern the difference between demonic temptation and his own will. But the impulse remains, dominating him. As if from outside himself, the Ring takes control of his body and moves his hand toward the Ring. Frodo must exert his own will consciously to resist it. Frodo moves instead to touch the sacramental star-glass of the blessed lady, Galadriel. This gives him relief from his temptation, and the crisis passes.

Not all spiritual warfare is conducted so pointedly. It can often be more subtle and gradual. Once, Tolkien writes of Frodo that the Ring *may* have aided Frodo's choice to go toward Mordor.[156] Here the spiritual warfare is subtle; one cannot tell where one's own will ends and where temptation begins. Atop Amon Hen, as Sauron's will leaps toward him, Frodo hears two voices within him crying out at once: "Never, never! Or was it: Verily I come, I come to you? He could not tell."[157] Tolkien's draft text concludes it is probably both.[158] Faramir slowly becomes a victim of spiritual oppression by way of the Black Breath.[159]

Sam watches helplessly as Frodo is increasingly oppressed by the demonic Ring, both in body and mind. We see Frodo struggling to maintain control of his own mind and body. His struggle with the Ring begins imperceptibly, except for moments of crisis such as Weathertop, but by the end of his journey the Ring's spiritual attacks dominate his every thought.[160] Frodo can feel the Eye as a physical pressure. The "veils" between himself and Sauron have grown thin and frail.[161] These veils must refer to some sort of spiritual barriers in place between Frodo and Sauron—barriers that disappear when Frodo more fully enters the spiritual world, such as when he wears the Ring.[162] At once able to perceive the spiritual world, he sees the true shapes of the Wraiths, and they see him more clearly as well. Frodo's invocation of Varda (both angelic protector and Marian figure) saves his life from direct demonic attack, though he is permanently injured.[163] Later, Gandalf will assert that God's providence was at work alongside Frodo's own courage. He survived because he resisted to the end.

Periodically, many characters may see into this otherwise invisible spiritual realm. When Frodo wears the Ring, he does not merely see the Ringwraiths; Glorfindel also appears as a shining figure. The unseen realm is not merely a creation of the Ring—it is a spiritual reality always present in Tolkien's world but not always visible.[164] High Elves like Glorfindel and Galadriel always live in both the seen and unseen realms and so have power over both. But once even Sam is granted spiritual vision, seeing Frodo and Gollum anew at Mount Doom. One, a mere ruined shadow of life; the other, robed in white, untouchable by pity and holding a wheel of fire. It is no longer Frodo that speaks, but the Ring. The voice that commands Gollum to be gone comes *out of the fire*, that is, out of the Ring.[165] Gollum, himself demonically oppressed, cannot decide between terror and desire.

Certain actions open one up to being influenced by evil spiritual forces and make one visible to the forces at play in the unseen realm. In a draft text, Frodo remarks that it is a pity Bilbo did not stab Gollum from behind. Gandalf responds not just with the extant speech on the importance of pity but with a further clarification on Bilbo's danger. Slaying Gollum would have been wrong, against the "Rules" (thus capitalized). The Ring would have instantly conquered him, and he might have become a wraith at that very moment.[166] Additionally, an object might be a source of spiritual influence, for good or ill. Evil things are written on the Morgul-blade, though they may be invisible to mortal eyes. Glorfindel cautions Aragorn not to handle it any more than necessary, lest, we presume, he become tainted by it.[167] The Orcs' trampling on the *lembas* bread, symbolically akin to trampling on the eucharistic host, is a clear sign of satanic presence.[168] He is the cause of revulsion toward holy things.[169] Other objects, like Galadriel's phial, possess a spiritual sacredness. As mentioned above, Sam uses the sacred phial to fend off the demonic Watchers in the Orc tower.[170]

For spiritual warfare is not only conducted upon the side of darkness. God, too, works to defeat the forces of evil and empowers his servants to resist, though in a markedly different way than the devil empowers his minions. At the Ford of Bruinen, Frodo feels commanded by the Nazgûl not to cross, and, again, with his last remaining strength, he rebukes the Riders and speaks the names of Varda and Lúthien. It is notable that Frodo here wields no evident spiritual power. The Wraiths laugh at his declarations and strike him mute. His sword breaks in his hand. But the power in this confrontation does not lie with Frodo. At this very moment, unknown to all, providence has guided Gandalf and Elrond to let loose the torrent of the river, sweeping the Nazgûl away.[171]

Much later, at the gates of Minas Tirith, the demonically empowered Witch-king meets his only opposition in Gandalf. Once more, as he did with the balrog on the bridge of Khazad-dûm, Gandalf rebukes the demon with words modeled after an exorcism, commanding him back to the abyss and to nothingness. The Witch-king laughs in scorn: this is his hour. But while Gandalf does not best him in battle, God nevertheless empowers Gandalf's command. The Witch-king does not enter the city; he is forced to return to the field to deal with Rohan, and there he meets his doom. For Tolkien reminds us that no incarnate creature, however good, can ultimately defeat evil. Only God can do that. But even evil is under his rule.[172]

FURTHER READING

As with the doctrine of the fall, most of the treatments of satanic or demonic characters occur in passing during an overarching discussion on sin or evil, which subsumes most of the subcategories in this chapter. Aside from any particular examination of one of Tolkien's supernatural evil characters, such as Sauron, there is very little dedicated material here.

Devaux, Michaël. "Les anges de l'Ombre chez Tolkien: chair, corps, et corruption." In *Les Racines du Légendaire (La Feuille de la Compagnie no. 2)*, edited by Michaël Deveaux, 191–245. Geneva: Ad Solem, 2003.

Freeman, Austin M. "Flesh, World, Devil: Evil in J. R. R. Tolkien." *Journal of Inklings Studies* 10, no. 2 (2020): 139–71.

IX

CHRIST AND SALVATION

T he dual themes of Christ's beneficent and powerful kingship and his eucatastrophic triumph over Satan through a seemingly hopeless death dominate Tolkien's doctrines of Christ and salvation. Here, perhaps more than anyplace else, Tolkien's Anglo-Saxon spirit shines through and shapes a distinct contribution to twentieth-century theology. It is a theology of retrieval in the fullest sense. Tolkien's adoption of Anglo-Saxon modes of thought will thus be especially noted.[1] In this chapter, we will outline Tolkien's position on the person and office of Jesus Christ (*Christology*), noting particularly the ways in which Christ does and does not appear in Tolkien's fiction and the mode in which Jesus is depicted as the ideal king. We then turn to the two elements of *soteriology* (the doctrine of salvation)—namely, what Jesus did in his death and resurrection (salvation accomplished) and how the benefits of this are applied to the individual believer (salvation applied).

CHRISTOLOGY

Tolkien absolutely rejects any implication that Christ appears in Middle-earth. The fullness of time is still far in the future.[2] The Creator is not embodied anywhere in his mythology, since the incarnation of God is infinitely greater than any subject he would dare to write.[3] He continually stresses the disanalogy between his own alleged Christ-figures and Christ himself. Though Gandalf may have died and returned, he is a created person; one may be reminded of the Gospels, but it is not the same thing.[4] Again, speaking of Eärendil, the first savior of Middle-earth, Tolkien says its original use in Anglo-Saxon symbolism as herald of the rise of the true sun is not at all related to Tolkien's own use.[5] The incarnation is a singular event, not a recurring motif, and therefore the Son of God can find only echoes in Middle-earth.

THE INCARNATION

If Tolkien deliberately avoided setting his pen to the prodigious subject of the incarnation of God, we must understand him to mean that he would never take it upon himself to write a *fictional account* of such. He does in fact provide several comments on the manner and metaphysics of the incarnation. In Tolkien's notes on fate and free will, he equates the incarnation in a limited way with the presence of an author in his story.[6] Under normal circumstances, a human author is both present and not present at every point in the world of the story. Here, there is an asterisk pointing to a puzzling comment that ends the original document. Tolkien states that if the author writes himself into the story as a character, the character is always only a lesser and partial picture of the real author.[7] While Tolkien eventually picks the document back up and continues writing, he leaves this thought as it stands. What is its intent? Does this mean that Christ becomes only a lesser and partial picture of God? No. Christ's human nature *is* finite and circumscribed, both revealing and concealing. This particular human body is not all of God, though the person encountered *through* the body is very God of very God. This is precisely where

Tolkien senses the analogy to break down, as evidenced by his generous hedging immediately beforehand.

The inverse of the statement is equally telling. Christ is God, the Author of the story, who enters into his own tale without diminishment or alteration, to write not an imagined tale but a real history of redemption. He cannot be contained or limited by creation, not because he is dimensionally greater than the world but because he is altogether measureless. Just like the human author, God the Son is indeed within creation already, though not in the same manner in which he exists apart from it. But to imagine the Creator himself actually entering creation in bodily form is qualitatively distinct from his meta-authorial presence. How this is possible without shattering the fabric of reality is beyond the comprehension even of the angels. Nevertheless, God is omnipotent; if he desires it, it will come to pass.

And as Tolkien writes elsewhere, even if God were to enter within, he would remain also the Author without.[8] Christ does not lay aside his divine nature in the incarnation; instead, he assumes a human nature alongside the divine nature for the sake of saving humanity.[9] This is Tolkien's way of affirming the *hypostatic union*, the belief that Jesus is both truly God and truly man, without confusion or separation. The divine Son ultimately overflows his human nature, much like an idea inhabits but is not encompassed by a word. Tolkien stresses that language confronts us with endless tiny parallels to the mystery of the incarnation.[10] He takes seriously the idea presented in the Gospel of John, that Christ is the *Logos*, the principle of reason, of the whole creation, the paradigm in which and by which things come to exist.

When we move from the metaphysics of the incarnation to incarnation as historical event, Tolkien grows more reticent. While there are numerous Anglo-Saxon poems addressing the nativity, Tolkien's remarks on the religious nature of Christmas are sparse. Perhaps unexpectedly, there is no reference to Jesus or his birth in *The Father Christmas Letters*. Though Father Christmas says he was born around 1930 years ago, he does not make it any clearer than this.[11] Recently, however, an unpublished poem called "Noel" was discovered in a school annual from 1936.[12] The poem begins by setting a harsh and hostile winterscape, ruled by a cruel lord of cold.[13] Into this blind and wild world comes the Christ-child. The star of Bethlehem shines in the night, and the bells of the towns ring in jubilation. Mary (mother of the King of heaven) sings at Christ's birth and also causes heavenly bells to ring in echo. The poem ends with an inversion of the first stanza, where in place of darkness and cold there is gladness, laughter, light, and crackling fires. The image evokes a mead-hall feast. Heaven rings with bells of Christendom, while Christians sing *"gloria"* because God has come to earth.

With the important caveat that Tolkien would never accept a one-to-one correspondence, we can hazard a guess as to his beliefs on Christ's experience of the world in his incarnate person after Christmas. The Wizards, previously spiritual beings, take on true bodies as part of their mission to heal Middle-earth. As such, we can *cautiously* read Tolkien's comments on the nature of this embodiment as also applying to Christ's human nature. For instance, the Wizards are clad in real bodies able to feel pain, fear, weariness, and hunger.[14] This is a true incarnation, not merely a sort of avatar as the Valar can assume. Though mighty peers of Sauron, they must choose to set power aside so as to interact on a level with Elves and Men, winning their trust and persuading their free wills toward the good.[15] But this condescension puts the Wizards in real danger. There even arises the possibility that the Istari, having taken bodies formed of matter corrupted by Morgoth, could fall away from their mission into evil.[16]

Their native wisdom is dimmed, and they must relearn much that they once knew, only remembering the Blessed Realm as a distant vision for which they constantly long.[17] It is no great stretch to apply such a situation to Christ. Jesus in his human nature experiences all the limitations and loves appropriate to other embodied creatures.[18] He is no docetic image. Nor is the incarnate Christ so elevated by his divine nature that he refuses to experience the dangers of pain and suffering, even on the everyday scale. He knowingly limits his omniscience while on earth (see, for example, Luke 2:52; 8:45; etc.).

CHRIST FIGURES IN TOLKIEN'S FICTION

Tolkien famously flouts allegorical readings of his fiction. In a radio interview, Denys Gueroult asserts that Frodo, through his trials, becomes a Christ figure. "Why," he asks Tolkien, "did you choose a halfling, a hobbit for this role?" The answer is quite blunt. "I didn't ... all I was trying to do was carry on from the point where *The Hobbit* left off." Both agree that Bilbo at least is not very Christ-like, but Gueroult pushes the comparison: Frodo suffers through terrible danger and wins out. Again, Tolkien rebuffs the comparison: "[T]hat seems I suppose more like an allegory of the human race. I've always been impressed that we're here surviving because of the indomitable courage of quite small people against impossible odds: jungles, volcanoes, wild beasts ... they struggle on, almost blindly in a way." He seems insistent that Frodo is not a stand-in for Jesus Christ.[19] Christ was not the only person to die in order to save something.[20]

However, Tolkien acknowledges as "true enough" the interpretation of Barry Gordon which finds Christ's *threefold office* of priest, prophet, and king in the roles of the book's three main characters.[21] Frodo is the suffering priest who offers himself up as a sacrifice; Gandalf is the wise prophet and counselor who speaks to and for the divine; Aragorn is the returning king of justice.[22] This reading works, says Tolkien, but it was not consciously intended. This is part of a larger pattern of thought in which Tolkien gradually came to accept others' theological readings as valid.[23] Similarities emerge from the leaf-mold of Tolkien's mind. There is, furthermore, a difference in finding a "Christ-figure"—that is, a fictional stand-in for the Redeemer such as Aslan—and finding christological types, or partial echoes that point forward to a full realization. This is the sense in which we will draw upon Tolkien's fiction to illuminate a doctrine of Christ, of which the image of king is most prominent.[24]

If Jesus embodies the ideal divine king of Anglo-Saxon theology, we ought to be able to look at the more elevated of Tolkien's kingly heroes and see christological echoes. Indeed, this is what we find when we read of King Arthur: "Never had Arthur need or danger / tamed or daunted, turned from purpose / or his path hindered. Now pity whelmed him / and love of his land and his loyal people, / for the low misled and the long-tempted, / the weak that wavered, for the wicked grieving." Arthur's mercy on the weak and wicked subjects parallels Christ's mercy on rebellious sinners, as does his determination to rescue them. "With woe and weariness and war sated, / kingship owning crowned and righteous / he would pass in peace pardon granting, / the hurt healing and the whole guiding, / to Britain the blessed bliss recalling." Arthur, like Christ, wages war on sin and death in order to bring peace on earth and restore the world. However, just as Christ must face the cross before his triumph, so too, for Arthur, "Death lay between dark before him / ere the way were won or the world conquered."[25] Given the incomplete status of "The Fall of Arthur" as a poem, we can speculate that Tolkien might have laid stress on Arthur's removal to Avalon and eventual return in order to strengthen this parallel further.

Again, in Tolkien's adaptation of the Völsung myth, he slightly alters the prophecy about Sigurd's fate to make him into an echo of Christ. Of royal and divine lineage, yet raised as a commoner, Sigurd is the world's chosen who will slay the Serpent. "If in day of Doom / one deathless stands, / who death hath tasted / and dies no more, / the serpent-slayer, / seed of Óðin, / then all shall not end, / nor Earth perish. / On his head shall be helm, / in his hand lightning, / afire his spirit, / in his face splendour. / The Serpent shall shiver / and Surt waver, / the Wolf be vanquished / and the world rescued."[26] Sigurd slays the dragon Fafnir during his first advent, and will slay the World Serpent at his second.

With Arthur and Sigurd, however, Tolkien is constrained by the beats of a preexisting plot. There are many discontinuities between Arthur, Sigurd, and Jesus. Within Tolkien's own freely developed legendarium, we can examine the Christ-like kingly hero Aragorn for further insight into Tolkien's views on Jesus' own kingship.[27] Again, this is not to deny other Christ echoes such as prophet or priest, nor to claim Aragorn as a stand-in for Jesus, but instead to illuminate the most relevant facet of Tolkien's real-world Christology through these fictional parallels.

The state of the kingship before Aragorn's return coincides with the apparent post-exilic loss of the royal line in Judah. Like Saul and the other disobedient kings of the Old Testament, the kingdom is lost for lack of trust in divine providence. Malbeth the Seer, like the prophets, encourages the Dúnedain to make the choice that seems less hopeful, but they reject the Seer's words and the last king, Arvedui, perishes.[28] The return of the king and the restoration of the monarchy seem to most a far-off dream—when any remember the king at all.[29]

Unlike the Peter Jackson adaptations, when Aragorn returns, he boldly proclaims his right to kingship and pronounces a litany of titles. When Aragorn reveals himself in full majesty to Éomer, a white flame flickers on his brow, visible to those like Legolas who can see into the unseen world, and aptly attesting his spiritual power. His companions look on him in amazement as he challenges Éomer with a version of Matthew 12:30/Luke 11:23.[30] Those who do choose to follow Aragorn endure death only out of submission to his will and personal love.[31] Faramir, despite never having seen Aragorn before, is summoned back to the land of the living by the voice of his king. He immediately looks on him with love and eagerly submits in humble obedience.[32] Aragorn's thanes love him, the primary bond of loyalty in Old English culture. Notably, *thegn* is the word used to translate "disciple" in the Anglo-Saxon Bible translations. Thus, Jesus' commanding call to obedience is not to fearful servitude but the loyalty of a sword-brother to his captain.

Aragorn's ministry of healing is also part of his christological echo. We have already seen that Tolkien adopts the Old English word *Haelend* to speak of Christ.[33] *Haelend* is a standard title for Jesus in Old English poetry, normally translated as "Savior" but obviously encompassing the sense of "Healer" as well. In Tolkien's mind, the healer, savior, and king are inextricably linked. This dual aspect coalesces in the old Gondorian proverb that the hands of the king are the hands of a healer.[34] After the battle of the Pelennor, Aragorn takes on the mantle of "the Renewer."[35] The word spreads through the city that the king has come back, bringing healing.[36] The people "pray" to Aragorn to heal their family members of hurts and wounds, so he travels through the city performing a ministry of healing. In this way he gains the love of his subjects, and the name foretold at his birth is given him by his own subjects.[37]

An interesting complication of Tolkien's kingly archetype occurs when Aragorn first meets the resurrected Gandalf. Aragorn, tall and strong, like a legendary king of old, faces Gandalf, old and stooped, yet shining with an inner light. Gandalf holds the greater power, having returned from death.[38] Aragorn recognizes this and regards the Wizard as the true captain of the West, much as the good kings of Judah took their counsel from the prophets. The evil one may have nine dark servants, but the champions of light have one, mightier than they. He has come through fire and abyss, and all the servants of evil will fear him.[39] This sort of language is also reminiscent of Anglo-Saxon narrative poems, contrasting the warrior Prince of the radiant realms of heaven with the fearful and fleeing demons. Here we are reminded that no single character directly represents Christ; rather, the Christic echo emerges from the story soup in various ways.

For example, both Aragorn and Gandalf appear first full of care, sorrow, and sternness, but joy can eventually be glimpsed underneath.[40] Tolkien uses the same metaphor to describe them both. Their joy is a hidden fountain that gushes forth like a spring from the depths of the rock, enough to set a kingdom laughing.[41] This joy comes out into the open after Sauron's defeat.[42] This perhaps subconsciously relates to a vision of Jesus as "man of sorrows" (Isa 53:3) who "sets [his] face like flint" (Isa 50:7 NIV). Many critics have remarked on the fact that Christ is never recorded as smiling or laughing. But here, Tolkien's solemnest characters, which happen to be two of his most Christ-like characters, hide a secret joy which seems lifted directly from the final pages of G. K. Chesterton's *Orthodoxy*: "There was some one thing that was too great for God to show us when He walked upon our earth; and I have sometimes fancied that it was His mirth."[43]

At Aragorn's coronation (for which see also chapter 10), Gandalf proclaims that "the days of the King" have come, and blesses them as long as the throne of the Valar should endure. When Aragorn rises, it seems to all that he is revealed for the first time, "ancient of days" and yet in his prime, full of wisdom, strength, and healing, and surrounded by light.[44] Of course, the title "ancient of days" is a clear allusion to Daniel 7:9, where it serves as a divine epithet. This passage in particular sees God, the Ancient of Days, taking his seat on his throne in heaven. This description of Aragorn in his majesty applies equally well to Christ.

Afterward, when Gandalf leads Aragorn to a sapling from the White Tree preserved from destruction, we see symbolically the reminder that Aragorn is only a type of the One to come. Nimloth, says Gandalf, was a descendant of the Eldest of Trees, placed in the Garden of the Gods at the dawn of time. Here we have a reminder of Adam, primal king, steward of his own tree. Down through the ages the endurance of the trees can represent the endurance of God's promise to Abraham, finally fulfilled in the Christ to come. The tree is synonymous with royalty and also with priesthood.[45] Though its fruit seldom ripens, it may lie dormant through the ages, and none know when it will awaken again.[46] The stump of Jesse seemed desolate for many years as well, only to spring up to new life. Yet Gandalf reminds us that Aragorn is only a small part of a much larger story, for the line of Nimloth is far older than that of Aragorn.[47] Here is a hint of expectation, foregrounding Aragorn's finitude and inspiring thoughts of kings yet to be born. We recall that Aragorn's name *Estel* means "faith," a looking ahead, while Jesus' name *Emmanuel* means "God-with-us," an expectation fulfilled.[48]

The self-condescension of Christ for the good of his people, the ultimate kingly generosity, causes us to bow down with Prince Aldarion and give praise.[49] But of course this is the central facet of Christology as a whole: Jesus' obedient death and resurrection. Tolkien accepts Lewis's trilemma: If Jesus' claims to divinity are false, he is nothing but a demented megalomaniac.[50] But if his claims are true, and he is the God who humbles himself in order to exalt the humble, then Tolkien's epigram for Gandalf also applies to Christ: humble and seeking no renown, but triumphing instead in raising the fallen and renewing hope.[51]

THE RESURRECTION

Tolkien recognizes the distinctiveness of the resurrection. It is not like that of Lazarus, since God raises himself.[52] The resurrection is the central piece of the central story of humanity, the eucatastrophe of all eucatastrophes.[53] It is the foundation of all our hope in the face of the monstrous and overwhelming evils of the world.[54]

If Aragorn draws on the Ancient of Days reigning from the throne, Gandalf in his resurrection echoes the risen Jesus in a glorified state. We recall again that Tolkien stresses the disanalogy between Gandalf's resurrection and Christ's. We must remember that Tolkien does not *intend* Gandalf to represent Jesus here. But there is nothing to prevent us from also observing the relevant similarities. It is not so much that Tolkien is depicting Gandalf as Jesus, but that when Tolkien's mind conjures up an image of a resurrected being, Jesus is what he sees. For example, John the Revelator, in his vision of the resurrected Christ, sees "one like a son of man, clothed with a long robe … The hairs of his head were white, like white wool, like snow. His eyes were like a flame of fire … In his right hand he held seven stars … his face was like the sun shining in full strength. When I saw him, I fell at his feet as though dead" (Rev 1:13–17 ESV). Tolkien reproduces this description identically in our first sight of Gandalf the White.[55]

Gandalf's resurrection is also eucatastrophic. He returns beyond all hope.[56] And, like the disciples on the road to Emmaus, his closest friends are at first unable to recognize his resurrected form.[57] Though he is still the same person, he has surpassed many of his previous limitations. His spiritual power is greatly increased. He cannot be hurt by physical weapons. Gandalf declares that, with his return, the tide of war against the evil one has turned, and he exhorts his friends to be merry.[58]

SALVATION ACCOMPLISHED

Salvation is an infinitely rich truth which we as finite beings can only partially grasp.[59] Salvation is not an adjustment to God's story; it *is* the story, meant that way from the beginning. The study of the way in which Christ saves human beings is called soteriology, and the method by which Christ does this is called the atonement.

EUCATASTROPHIC SOTERIOLOGY

The single final act of salvation occurred on the cross. But like a refrain that echoes throughout a symphony, this singular act of salvation, written into the fabric of reality, reappears again and again, especially in fairy stories. This is their special attraction: a resolution achieved through a sudden and miraculous grace which can perhaps never occur again.[60] Happiness or victory arrives when all seems lost.[61] The highest function of a fairy tale is the "Consolation of the Happy Ending," this sudden joyous turn which echoes the salvation that God actually bestows in the real world.[62] Tolkien calls this *eucatastrophe*, a good catastrophe.[63] In essence, eucatastrophe is a sudden revelation of the truth behind the universe. Tolkien compares it to a limb being popped back into joint. This sort of salvation does not deny the existence of real disaster and damage—far from it. It is the preponderance of evidence for perdition that causes such a joy in deliverance in the first place. Salvation, *evangelium*, the good news, proclaims a universal final victory and a glimpse of joy beyond the limits of the created world.[64]

This sense of overwhelming joy is the central element in Tolkien's doctrine of salvation. The Christian joy that provokes us to give glory to God is something like the emotion one might feel if a favorite fairy story had been found to be true. But this story is infinitely high and joyous, or would be if our capacity were not finite.[65] It is the tale above all that we would wish were true, and the only tale which so many skeptics have accepted on its own merits.[66] The happy ending is no longer a mere narrative convention. It is a reflection of the metaphysical structure of reality.[67]

The joy of eucatastrophe is the realization that the most wonderful reversals of fiction are actually echoes of the way things work in the real world. This is why our nature finds such a resonance with the sudden joyous turn—because we are made for it.[68] As storytellers, we are redeemed in accord with our nature by a moving story. But the Author of this story is also the Author of reality, and so this story is not only true but real.[69] The gospel is fairy story that has come true without evacuating its mythical or allegorical significance.[70] But despite being their supreme fulfillment and archetype, this gospel is not the end of stories and legends, for in God's kingdom both small and great find their place. Man after redemption is still the storyteller, and so man's stories as well ought to go on. God's gospel has not done away with legends but hallowed them.[71]

Just as all the tales of Middle-earth are wrapped into a single strand to begin the story of Eärendil, so too all of myth and history have met and fused in the central story of Jesus, which begins and ends in joy.[72] His birth is the eucatastrophe of the story of human history, and the resurrection is the eucatastrophe of the story that begins with his birth.[73] It is the greatest eucatastrophe in the greatest story of all (Tolkien also calls it the "Primary Miracle"[74]), and, as such, it brings forth the greatest joy—a joy full of tears, almost indistinguishable from sorrow because it comes from a place in which joy and sorrow are united and reconciled, just as selfishness and altruism find their union in love.[75]

HINTS OF SALVATION IN MIDDLE-EARTH

Since Tolkien sets his stories in a mythical version of our own history prior to the advent of Christ, there can be no direct analogy to Christian salvation in his fiction.[76] But, for the same reason that it *will* occur in the future of Middle-earth, his writing is replete with hints of such an event. Even in *The Book of Lost Tales*, the Music of Ilúvatar reveals that the Valar will not save the world or free Mankind; instead, hope dwells in a far land of Men—namely, in Bethlehem.[77] In the first design of God, Men were destined to govern the earth and ultimately become Valar to enrich heaven.[78] This destiny is not lost. Even after the fall, Finrod sees Men as the agents of the "unmarring" of the world, the means by which God not only undoes the fall but raises creation up into a newer and richer existence.[79] This in fact is God's ultimate plan, since in his infinite knowledge the fall does not take him by surprise, nor does it derail his story. For example, both Arwen and Frodo's self-denial and suffering were parts of God's strategy to regenerate the human race.[80]

Just as he did with the stumblings and exiles of the children of Israel, God supervises and directs history to accomplish his purposes. Satan cannot crush the lineage out of which God will raise the savior. Sauron is right to fear Aragorn; he is indeed very mighty. He comes from the line of Lúthien, which, like the Davidic covenant, will never fail.[81] Are we meant to understand Jesus to be not only the seed of David, but of Eärendil and Lúthien? Regardless, though the world's salvation is ordained from the beginning to come from Men, the "Old Hope" is ultimately grounded not in the might of Men but

in God himself. God himself will enter the world and heal the marring of both the world and the human race, from beginning to end.[82]
And God himself has given this promise from the moment of the fall.

THEORIES OF ATONEMENT IN
TOLKIEN'S LEGENDARIUM

There are several theological models of the atonement—the precise
way in which Christ reunites human beings with God. During the
high Middle Ages, Anselm's *satisfaction* theory addressed the way in
which God the feudal lord reclaimed his besmirched honor. After the
Middle Ages, most theologians have tended toward a *substitutionary*
theory in which Jesus exchanges places with sinners and pays the penalty in their place. There is no word of substitutionary atonement in
Tolkien's published writings.[83] In fact, apart from Tolkien's assertion
that the slightest escape from our own sin and error is an extravagant
generosity fitting of the divine king, Tolkien rarely speaks of salvation
as forgiveness at all.[84]

He instead retrieves an earlier model. At the time of the Anglo-
Saxons, and indeed for the first thousand years of the church, the most
widespread and influential theory was that of *Christus Victor*, Christ's
victory over the devil. Significantly, Tolkien speaks of salvation virtually exclusively in this manner. The eucatastrophe of salvation comes
from victory over a seemingly insurmountable foe.[85] Tolkien describes
the incarnation as God's reentry into the world *to defeat the devil.*[86]

The only usage of atonement language in *The Lord of the Rings*
or *The Hobbit* is itself couched in the context of *Christus Victor.*[87]
When the host of the West announce themselves at the Black Gate,
they declare that Sauron should *atone* for his evils and depart.[88] But
Aragorn is not the only Christ-type to participate in the *Christus Victor*
motif, and many of Tolkien's examples are less explicit. In one notable

draft (in which Sharkey has not yet become Saruman), Frodo reenacts the battle of Fingon and Morgoth from the Silmarillion. Not even half the size of the brutish Man, Frodo draws Sting and casts his cloak aside. "Suddenly he shone, a small gallant figure clad in mithril like an elf-prince."[89] The striking image of a bright knight standing firm against the massive devil is here replayed by the hobbit reclaiming his homeland. Even Tom Bombadil drives out the evil spirits of the barrow-downs.[90] Likewise, When Frodo puts on the Ring at Amon Hen, Gandalf sits in a high place and strives with the enemy, and "the Shadow" passes from seizing upon Frodo.[91] Indeed, Gandalf has a reputation for showing up just when things are darkest.[92] Sometimes people actually cry out for Gandalf to save them from the forces of darkness.[93] Aside from his final stand against the balrog, Gandalf also pronounces judgment against the captain of the Ringwraiths at the gate of Minas Tirith.[94] The Witch-king is nonplussed; this is his time. He prepares to strike the Wizard down. But this is not a defeat as many suppose. Providence gives the victory. For at that moment, a rooster crows the dawn. Rohan arrives and sounds its horns. The Witch-king flies to his death at the hands of Éowyn and is destroyed, surpassing all hopes.[95]

Finally, there is at least one instance in Tolkien's writing that exemplifies the "fish-hook" view of salvation, a version of the ancient *ransom* theory.[96] Gandalf, in "The Last Debate," advocates that they must make themselves the bait and let Sauron's jaw's close on them, and thus Frodo will slip past Sauron's watch.[97] They will let this apparent folly be a cloak and a veil to Sauron, who mismeasures any motive that is not based in a desire for power. The evil one would never conceive that any would willingly lay down power or act in such a self-effacing way.[98] Thus their salvation comes through apparent folly, at least as measured by those who count worldly wisdom without regard to the power of God.[99] Thus, though the enemy is immeasur-ably strong, the faithful have a hope at which he cannot guess.[100] Help comes, by God's power, from the hands of the weak rather than the wise.[101]

Gandalf therefore does not counsel prudence, since victory cannot be achieved by force. But there are other means of victory.[102] At the brink of desperation, hope and despair are closely related.[103] Despair is only for those who see failure as a certainty. Taking the Ring to Mordor is at once the path of greatest hope and greatest fear.[104] There is no mundane reason why the plan should work, but Gandalf coun-sels trust in the apparent folly of the Ring-bearer's mission, one he knows to be ordained by God. Giving up on the hope of life and plac-ing it instead in the divine plan, as Aragorn and the lords of the West do when they march in their sacrificial mission to the Black Gates in order to give Frodo and Sam a chance at Mount Doom, seems utter foolishness, but one must accept the impossibility of salvation by one's own hand in order to hope in the deliverance of God.

THE HARROWING OF HELL

Perhaps no other culture has made as much hay out of the three days between Christ's crucifixion and resurrection as the Anglo-Saxons. The *harrowing of hell*, when Jesus descends into hell to rescue the saints born before his incarnation, is in fact the first instance of the use of the word "harrow" in English. Old English sources are rich with meditations on Christ's military raid on the underworld.[105] One of Tolkien's translation projects, *Sir Orfeo*, dealing as it does with a descent into the underworld, has also been read as an allegorical descent by Christ into hell.[106]

Tolkien mentions the harrowing of hell directly when he muses alongside the *Beowulf* poet whether Christ's redemption might work backward, with the harrowing also a hallowing of all those righteous pagans who lived before the appointed time.[107] But he also provides an excellent fictional representation in Aragorn's return from the Paths of the Dead.[108] For a long time, Aragorn has known that he will face a dark fate, not least since receiving a prophecy to that effect from Galadriel.[109] Following her advice at the hour of desperation, to save his kingdom, Aragorn commits to take the Paths of the Dead, descending beneath the earth to the place where the damned wait. He will go alone if he must.[110] His choice to take the mountain path is a death sentence in the eyes of many. But he succeeds. The Dead obey his commands. Here, at the time foretold, Aragorn offers the damned and forsaken dead men an opportunity for redemption, and they take it. [111] Legolas sees shapes of men with pale banners and spears like winter thickets following behind. The Dead have been summoned.[112] Thus, in March, the month of Easter, the king emerges from the grave and from the hell where the cursed dead reside, out under the bright sky again. He blows a horn and unfurls his royal banner. Some flock to him, but others shrink away in fear and amazement. According to an early draft, the people in fact acclaim him as a king risen from the dead.[113] Later, Tolkien softens this. They cry instead that "the King of the Dead" is upon them.[114] But Aragorn still leads captivity captive in a royal procession.[115] Finally, on the ships of Umbar, which he seizes with the help of the army of the Dead, Aragorn sends his servants to set the captives free and comfort them.[116]

Each of the elements in this account can also be found in artistic representations of the harrowing of hell. For example, Jesus is frequently depicted holding a banner while leading the dead forth from hell, as he is in the carving above the chapel at All Souls College in Oxford. In most images, he extends his hand to lead a group of dead souls out of the mouth of hell. Frequently, Roman guards and onlookers flee or shrink away in fear and awe, while angels blow trumpets to announce victory over death. We can also compare the elements of this scene to those which occur in the tale of Beren and Lúthien to see that Tolkien is working from a stock set of imagery. Tolkien writes that, when the host of the Valar at last throw down Morgoth's fortress of Angband (the hells of iron) and the Satan-figure has been defeated, a multitude come out of the deep prisons into a changed world.[117]

SALVATION APPLIED

While salvation was accomplished at the cross, it is applied to each believer through a process known as the *order of salvation*. Among the elements in the order of salvation, Tolkien dwells most commonly on election and faith.[118]

ELECTION

Election by God for some specific purpose is a common theme in Tolkien's writing, though the word is never used. Certain figures are chosen (by God, but only implicitly) to play special roles.[119] Frodo is *meant* to find the Ring, and Aragorn is *meant* to restore the kingdom. Faramir's life is charmed, or spared by fate for some other purpose.[120] Faramir recognizes this. Both he and Frodo must go on the ways appointed to each of them.[121] Galadriel teasingly suggests that each companion's path is already laid before his feet, though he cannot see it.[122] God elects Frodo to the Ring,[123] Sam to Frodo,[124] Gandalf to the hobbits,[125] Aragorn to many things. His birth is the subject of prophecy,[126] his time of appearing a summons through dreams,[127] and his journey to victory through the world of the Dead is "appointed."[128] This is the sense in which we can locate the doctrine of election in Tolkien's thought.

This sort of election is not only confined to *The Lord of the Rings*. In *Unfinished Tales*, the Vala Ulmo himself comments on his election of Tuor as emissary to Gondolin. Here, Ulmo combines a sort of merit on Tuor's part with an instrumental use beyond Tuor's control. If Ulmo chooses to send him, then he should assume the sending to be worthwhile. And he is sent not only for his bravery but in order to bring into the world a hope beyond his own mortal sight.[129] Here, Ulmo is speaking of Tuor's son Eärendil, perhaps the first Christic echo in Tolkien's corpus.

"Doom" and "fate" are two other terms in the orbit of divine election. Apart from Mount Doom, Tolkien can also speak of doom in a favorable sense.[130] Now only associated with a judgment of destruction, the word originally meant a legal decree or ordinance, though it was heavily associated with God's justice from the beginning.[131] Doom can thus be equated to the divine decree. God has decided the fates of Men and even of the great Powers.[132]

This is the way in which it is used of Frodo and his quest. If any character in Middle-earth is the subject of God's election, it is Frodo.[133] He is explicitly ordained to be the Ring-bearer.[134] When Frodo ponders why he has been chosen as Ring-bearer, Gandalf bluntly replies that such questions cannot be answered, but that Frodo may be certain it was not based on merit. He has, nevertheless, been chosen, and ought therefore to use what abilities he does have to the fullest.[135] Similarly, in a draft passage, he states that Frodo's importance is non-necessary but real; someone else may equally have been chosen, but the job is up to Frodo now.[136]

And yet Tolkien can write that while Frodo was fated to go on his mission, he was not fated to destroy the Ring. His falling into the role of Ring-bearer was an accidental chance, as it were, not subject to deliberate thought on Frodo's part. But Frodo was always free to deliberately reject his task. Tolkien is no Calvinist. Fate is fully resistible. God can provide an opportunity for salvation, but it is up to the individual to grasp it. This does not, though, mean that God's design can be thwarted. If it were truly part of God's plan, then some other method would have arisen. In the end, of course, this is what happens. "When Frodo's will proved in the end inadequate, a means for the Ring's destruction immediately appeared—being kept in reserve by Eru as it were."[137]

FAITH

Tolkien writes that faith is an act of will inspired by love.[138] It is a decision to be made and stuck to. God demands belief and, proceeding from that, a trust in him.[139] Tolkien equates hope and trust here, and in the context of belief as something demanded by God, we can understand him to be uniting belief, faith, trust, and hope into a single multifaceted complex of ideas. Tolkien most commonly uses the word "faith" to refer to this sort of act of loyalty (faithfulness). But this is no innovation; instead, it shows a firm grasp of the original meaning of the New Testament word *pistis*, translated as "faith." Tolkien may have been ahead of the curve here, as several recent New Testament studies have focused on the "allegiance" aspect of faith in contrast to mere intellectual assent.[140]

Throughout *The Fall of Arthur*, faith in the Christian sense and faith in the chivalric sense are frequently interchangeable. Mordred and Lancelot are false to their faith both to Arthur and to God. Tolkien brings both together explicitly in his description of Mordred's men: "their king betraying, Christ forsaking, / to heathen might their hope turning."[141] This sense is also present in a more limited way in Middle-earth, such as when the captive hero Húrin rejects Morgoth's lies and remains loyal to the Valar, trusting that they will defeat him.[142]

Righteous Númenorean lord Amandil places loyalty to the Valar above loyalty to any earthly king, including his own.[143]

While Christian faith as trust and loyalty do play a role in Tolkien's writing, there is no real engagement with faith as a means of entry into salvation. It seems likely that, for Tolkien, the application of salvation is less a matter of a personal encounter with Jesus as it is an issue of being on the right side. This allegiance extends outward to the body of Christ as well. The lengthiest discussion of the person of Christ in the *Letters* occurs with regard to the church and its authority.[144] Here Tolkien directly refers to Christianity as the "allegiance" of the Lord.[145] He also says of one couple that he fears they have left their allegiance to "our Mother [the Church]."[146] This is because trust in Christ, not calling him a fraud, means maintaining membership in the Roman Catholic Church which he founded. In short, allegiance to God *is* allegiance to the church of Christ. He believes, for instance, that Jesus likely regards offenses against his incarnate person to be less culpable than sins against other members of his mystical body.[147] This is at least how Tolkien conceives it in his own earthly mother's case; he believes her death to have been hastened by a martyr-like loyalty to the Roman Catholic Church, which many take to have influenced Tolkien's faith profoundly. Would Mabel have thought in these terms? It might instead be the case that the reverse is true: Tolkien's faith profoundly influenced how he thought about the death of his mother.[148]

Though less explicit in *The Hobbit* and *The Lord of the Rings*, faith still plays a pivotal role as a sort of trust which, when exercised, is rewarded. When Bilbo thinks of Gollum's sad lot in life and decides to pity the creature, he is lifted by new strength and resolve to leap over Gollum and escape rather than kill him.[149] We know too well that this act of pity rules the fate of many. Tolkien comments that the leap itself was not physically remarkable, but that it *was* "a leap in the dark."[150] Why this particular phrase? Surely Tolkien is not *merely* commenting upon the ambient light in the tunnel. Given the fact that this idiom is so heavily associated with the idea of faith (correctly or incorrectly), and given that we have seen Bilbo's pity and pity in general reflect religious connotations, is Tolkien implying that Bilbo's pity prompts an exercise of faith? How might this work? Given our observations in chapter 2, Bilbo's pity likely prompted a divine bestowal of grace here, such that Bilbo actually was buoyed up from outside, so to speak.

Taking it on luck, or an inchoate trust in some beneficent power guiding the universe, may be all that is required, at least prior to Christ. The hobbits trust to a wise governance of the universe, and they are judged according to the light that they have. While not even Frodo may have consciously understood himself to be guided by God or the Valar, for example, the highest concentration of the word "luck" (twice as many occurrences as in any other passage) lies in Frodo and Sam's journey across the plains of Mordor. They chance their luck in heading toward the Orc-tower.[151] After imaginatively entreating Galadriel to find water, Sam trusts to luck, and luck does not let him down—they find a miraculous pool of clean water.[152] Later, he feels his trust in luck *has* let him down when they encounter marching Orcs, but in fact their following the Orc party is the only safe way to continue their journey.[153] And again, it "chanced" that in the confusion of several companies meeting at a dark crossroads unwatched, the hobbits are able to escape safely.[154] Sam trusts to luck again in returning to the road, and because of Aragorn's provocation and Sauron's own paranoia, their luck holds, and the roads are deserted.[155] By "fortune," the road is not blocked.[156] Sauron's own road and door into the Sammath Naur provides Sam and Frodo the only entrance into the mountain they are able to reach.[157] Sam feels a sense of urgency pressing upon him which he does not understand. He is being prompted to act while Sauron's gaze is drawn toward the Black Gate.[158] God here works upon the chances of the world to guide and save those who trust to providence.[159] This sort of guessing faith would perhaps be insufficient after Christ's incarnation.

FURTHER READING

Most works dealing with this locus revolve around finding types of Christ in Tolkien's fiction. If we expand the concept of salvation to include eucatastrophe in general, this list grows substantially. "Eucatastrophe" is one of the core terms in Tolkien studies, both as an element of Tolkien's literary theory and as a manifestation of his theology. It crops up in virtually any discussion on Tolkien's larger themes.

Chance, Jane. "The Christian King: Tolkien's Fairy-Stories." In *Tolkien's Art: A Mythology for England,* 74–110. Revised edition. Lexington, KY: University of Kentucky Press, 2001.

Dickerson, Matthew. "Frodo and the Passion in J. R. R. Tolkien's *The Lord of the Rings.*" In *Engaging the Passion: Perspectives on the Death of Jesus,* edited by Oliver Larry Yarbrough, 211–24. Minneapolis: Fortress Press, 2015.

Flieger, Verlyn. "Eucatastrophe." In *Splintered Light: Logos and Language in Tolkien's World,* 21–32. Revised edition. Kent, OH: Kent State University Press, 2002.

Gunton, Colin. "A Far-off Gleam of the Gospel: Salvation in Tolkien's *The Lord of the Rings.*" In *Tolkien: A Celebration,* edited by Joseph Pearce, 124–40. New York: HarperCollins, 1999.

Pearce, Joseph. "Christ." In *Tolkien Encyclopedia,* 97–98.

Ryken, Philip. *The Messiah Comes to Middle-Earth: Images of Christ's Threefold Office in "The Lord of the Rings."* Downer's Grove, IL: IVP Academic, 2017.

Spirito, Guglielmo. "Eucatastrophe and Tolkien's World Building: 'A ray of light through the very chinks of the universe about us'; A Theological Reading." *Hither Shore* 14 (2017): 158–70.

X

THE CHURCH

As a Roman Catholic, Tolkien believes that the life of the church is an extension of Christology. Christ continues to be present and minister to his people through his bodily presence in the Mass. Likewise, the church functions as Christ to the rest of the world and in a sense continues his incarnation. We should therefore be mindful that any discussion of Christ and salvation in Tolkien must also deal with Tolkien's doctrine of the church and the sacraments.

ECCLESIOLOGY

Tolkien describes the "True Church" as the temple of the Holy Spirit, on the one hand corrupt and dying, on the other holy and eternal, always reforming and rising again after struggle and seeming defeat.[1] The church, however, is not centered upon its members but upon its Head and Founder.[2] Christianity, sustained by the life of God, will persevere and will more than likely save what is noble in any society out of which it emerges. Just as it preserved and transformed the best of the classical civilization after its fall, so too will the church outlast its current culture, unless driven down once more into the catacombs.[3] Indeed, both may be true. For Tolkien notes that whatever is really important and lasting seems always hidden from its contemporaries, whose eyes are usually on much more mundane matters while the seed of the future quietly grows in an inconspicuous corner.[4] The frail, moldering community of believers in one age may, in the next, blossom into glorious life. But there is no guarantee that any particular Christian will live to see it. The individual Christian, or even wide swathes of Christendom, may have little hope of surviving the onslaught of the enemies of the faith but can possess an intrinsic nobility borne from dedication to the renewal God will eventually bring.[5]

The presence of the Holy Spirit ensures that participation in the life of the church bears fruit, as we can see in a few of Tolkien's reflections on the experience of church attendance. He outlines the marks of a good sermon: the combination of native talent with practice, delivered with sincerity and truth and devoid of moral defects or vices. At rare times the Holy Spirit provides a special grace of inspiration, speaking through a human mouth with an art, virtue, and insight the speaker himself does not possess.[6] Tolkien mentions a particular example of a good sermon in Letter 89. It involves a vivid illustration of a healing passage in the Gospels, and more vivid illustrations of contemporary miracle healings that bring the biblical passage into bearing on our contemporary life. In one of these good sermons, Tolkien experiences that effect after which he strives in his own fiction: the eucatastrophic, joyous resolution when all hope seems lost.[7] Even bad sermons, though, ought to be heard with the intention to apply the truth they contain to oneself and not in order to judge others.[8] He attempts to write something like his own sermon in Letter 310, writing to Camilla Unwin on the meaning of life as praise to God.[9]

ROMAN CATHOLICISM

Tolkien is not a mere Christian, but self-consciously and possessively Catholic.[10] He is not a cradle Catholic but a convert.[11] He describes himself as one who, like the Israelites, came out of Egypt and the desert into the promised land of the church. While those who were born in Jerusalem may behave badly, it always retains a special aura of sanctity for those who came in from outside.[12]

As for the concrete fact of organized religion—what theology calls the visible or institutional church—Tolkien has rather a more complex view. One simply cannot maintain an organized religion without its organizational trappings: professionals such as priests, bishops, and monks. It may be a degradation, but it is an unavoidable one.[13] The precious wine of truth must have a bottle, and dust and cobweb are no sure indication of spoiled contents. The church always seems to be succumbing to Mammon and the world, but it is never finally overwhelmed.[14] Obviously, any congregation is full of sinful people, even among its ordained ministers. All Christians and not simply its professional members degrade and sometimes do outrage upon their confession.[15] Love may cool and the will may flag because of the sins and scandals of the visible church. But God remains present, ruling over his body on earth, and the cause of the true God is *always* the right one, even if its allies do not act nobly. Tolkien therefore does not expressly dissent from the teaching of the church on any issue, as, for Roman Catholics, faith includes "saving obedience" to the magisterial teachings of the church.[16]

The tumultuous changes in the Catholic Church of Tolkien's later years become a source of anxiety and a cause of prayer. The Catholic modernist heresy often pitched out the deposit of faith in an attempt to appeal to the masses.[17] He lauds Pius X's fight against modernism and emphasis on eucharistic Communion.[18] On the other hand, his daughter-in-law reports that he felt an increasing worry about the changes to the liturgy instituted by the Second Vatican Council, especially the loss of the Latin Mass. He found the changes to the liturgy

disturbing and felt a sense of betrayal by Rome.[19] Instead of acquiesc-
ing to the English liturgy, he continued to make his responses (loudly)
in Latin.[20] There may be several reasons for Tolkien's rejection of the
English Mass. Sayer records that Tolkien thought the English translations to be quite bad.[21] It is also likely that Tolkien felt the Tridentine
Mass to be an organic growth from the liturgy of antiquity, in contrast
to an artificial sort of return to antiquity attempted by Vatican II.[22]
Finally, the Latin Mass united Catholics across the globe in a single
tongue, a unity of worship otherwise unparalleled in Christian history.
Regardless of the reasons for Tolkien's displeasure, he continued to
remain faithful to the Roman Church to the end of his life. One must
pray, he writes, for the church, the pope, and oneself, all the while
exercising that virtue of loyalty which can only truly exist when one
is pressured to desert.[23]

Regardless of the behavior of Christians, the heart of the church
is the Eucharist, not its ministers.[24] Tolkien is in no doubt that the
Church of Rome is the true church on earth, due to its reverence for
the sacraments. It is the established and authorized altar founded by
God himself.[25] Ultimately the only reason to leave the Roman Church
is because of unbelief—a denial of the Eucharist, tantamount to calling
Jesus Christ a fraud to his face.[26] The ministration of the sacrament
is the essential practice of the visible church, and we turn to this in
the next section.

Tolkien also makes several comments on particular Catholic
Christian practices both within and outside of his fiction.[27] In his
early Elvish lexicon there are, alongside universal Christian terms
for saints and martyrs, gospels and crucifixions and missionaries,
words for Catholic institutions such as "monasticism" and "Holy
Orders."[28] The parish church plays a vital role in both "Aotrou and
Itroun" and "Farmer Giles," in keeping with their medieval setting

(and their author's medievalist philosophy).[29] In the latter, we see liturgical feast days (especially of saints), church buildings and services, and good-natured and educated parsons. The king (with a saintly name) even uses religious curses. These stories combine with Tolkien's daily attendance at Mass to paint a picture of the church as a central institution in society.[30]

The Virgin Mary

Aside from the Real Presence and the papacy itself, there is perhaps no more distinctive marker of Roman Catholic devotion than the role of the Virgin Mary. It is therefore no surprise (especially given the prominent women in his life) that Tolkien has much to say about her. The mother of God is, for Tolkien, the foundation of his perception of the beauty of majesty and of simplicity.[31] Tolkien condemns a lack of youth education about Mary, known only as an object of worship by sinful papists.[32] Mariological devotion is God's way of refining manly nature, but also of adding warmth and color to what can often be a hard and bitter faith.[33]

Tolkien ascribes to the immaculate conception of Mary, her birth without the stain of original sin, calling her the only unfallen person.[34] While sinless, Mary nonetheless chooses to participate in the story of sin's destruction, and thus achieves a destiny far higher than any unfallen man would have had. She is also the immediate source of the body of Christ, without any other physical intermediary. As such, her departure from the earth is as unique as her birth. Mary's assumption seems to follow logically for Tolkien. It is unthinkable that the vessel of honor would have suffered disintegration or corruption. Mary of course aged at a normal rate but was assumed before this process reached decrepitude or loss of beauty. She desired to be with her Son after his ascension, so at some point after this she asked to be received into heaven, having no further purpose on earth, and her request was granted. Like her immaculate birth, this too is a renewal of Edenic grace and liberty—the way in which unfallen man would have been bodily translated into heaven once his time on earth was done. It is important that Mary does not assume herself. This direct translation is still achieved by the power of God, much like the resurrection of Lazarus is distinct from the resurrection of Christ.[35]

Tolkien clearly admires Gawain's zealous piety and devotion to the "Blessed Virgin,"[36] the "Queen of Courtesy," as the *Pearl* author has it.[37] He adopts this attitude in his own writing. In "Aotrou and Itroun" we hear of the wish to enter the joy of heaven where the pure maiden Mary is queen.[38] Tolkien begins a Marian poem titled (in Latin) "Consoler of Afflictions" and "Evening Star" with the phrase, "O Lady Mother throned amid the stars," a poetic device for heaven.[39] Likewise, in the related Corrigan poems, Tolkien depicts Mary on a throne surrounded by joy, holding the holy child Jesus in her arms, while the protagonist appeals to her as the "Mother of pity."[40] Note here that heaven is singled out not as the domain of God or of Christ, but of Mary. This is because Mary is the supreme created exemplar of God's generosity and grace, or what the medieval would call "Heavenly Courtesy."[41] One can likewise hear Tolkien's note of judgment against his otherwise beloved *Kalevala* when he declares that the unrefined spirit of the story of the virgin Marjatta has nothing in common with its Christian source.[42]

When we consider Middle-earth itself, the abundance of Marian imagery became apparent even in Tolkien's own lifetime. When asked about one of the few prayers in the book, Tolkien tells Gueroult that "many people have notions that praying to the Lady or the Queen of the Stars are … like Roman Catholics in the invocation of Our Lady."[43] He accepts this analogy as valid but does not here claim it as his own view. The parallels are rich, all the same. Varda is the special friend of the Elves just as Mary is the special friend of Christians. Varda is called "Queen of the Blessed Realm" just as Mary is queen of heaven.[44] Satan fears her more than any other, since the light of God still shines in her face.[45] The Sun-maiden Arien is another Marian ectype, a very holy and powerful spirit who wishes to remain a perpetual virgin.[46] Her loss of virginity results in a loss of power, reflective of Tolkien's medieval Catholic valuation of virginity as a unique form of holiness.

Tolkien also accepts the assertion of another critic that his portrayal of Galadriel derives from latent Roman Catholic devotion.[47] Galadriel and her land contain no evil, but let those who bring evil into her presence beware.[48] She is perilous because she is strong in herself, such that a man could dash himself to pieces upon her as a ship against a rock.[49] Both Treebeard and Gimli are said to feel "reverence" toward her.[50] We know that Galadriel, like Varda and Mary, can hear and grant petitions. Gimli's love is so great that he is given the "grace" of special passage to Valinor, perhaps arranged by Galadriel herself as an intercession.[51] Later, deep within Mordor, Sam offers a simple prayer for light and water, wistfully wishing the Lady could respond. The request is granted, despite distance and even possible ignorance.[52] Sam's devotion to Galadriel is taken up and answered not by Galadriel herself but by the providential God.

The major difference between Galadriel and Mary, of course, is that Galadriel is not a virgin.[53] Her daughter Celebrían marries Elrond and bears Arwen. Furthermore, for most of the history of Tolkien's manuscripts, Galadriel is an exile from Valinor. For example, in 1967, Tolkien writes that she is one of the leaders in the rebellion of the Noldor. Because she believes her exile to be permanent, she prays that Frodo may be given a special grace to sail to Valinor in her place. This prayer, demonstrating true penitence—not to mention her service against Sauron and her final personal triumph over the temptation of the Ring—results in the lifting of her own ban.[54] One of Tolkien's final writings, however, recasts Galadriel's history to remove any hint of association with the rebellion of Fëanor.[55] She is "unstained," having committed no sin. She left for Middle-earth on legitimate grounds.[56]

Other Roman Catholic Markers: Relics and Pilgrimages

Tolkien's white Lady also gives out blessed relics such as the phial of Elbereth. Galadriel even appears to Sam in a vision, prompting him to use the star-glass. It gives not only light but hope, responding to Frodo's ebbing and growing will with corresponding power.[57] Touching the phial relieves Frodo of the mental weight of the Ring. It rewards Sam's courage as well, and the two hobbits speak in tongues twice while using it.[58] And the Lady's cloaks possess protective properties.[59]

These physical items function much like relics of the saints, imbued with a special holiness by dint of their origin. We know Tolkien himself venerates the saints (he takes St. John as a patron[60]) but realizes that they have only a limited and derivative power coming not from the saint but from God.[61] This is most evident in the treatment of such relics after the person's death. Fictionally, for example, Boromir's body is said to have achieved a sort of saintly beatitude thanks to his valiant efforts on behalf of Merry and Pippin.[62] Tolkien speaks elsewhere explicitly of the incorruptibility of bodies of saints in Middle-earth, those whose souls were always turned toward God in love and hope. God thus preserves their bodies from decay as a sign, to increase their hope.[63]

Tolkien also knows of holy sites of pilgrimage, places of special sanctity preserved from evil.[64] Numerous times he writes that, due to a heroic action or deed of purity, evil beings here shy away or flowers grow perpetually.[65] Examples include Túrin's grave, Snowmane's mound, and the "hallow" of Elendil's grave on the peak of Halifirien, the holy mountain.[66] Here the kings of Gondor visit annually the memorial of Elendil the Faithful, especially when they seek wisdom.[67] The "high place" remains in reverence even after Elendil's bones are removed.[68] Other fictional works also attest to medieval traditions about Christian death, such as prayers for the rest of the deceased.[69]

PROTESTANTISM

Tolkien's attitude toward Protestantism seems to soften with age. Early in life, he writes to Edith that the Anglican church is a "pathetic and shadowy medley of half-remembered traditions and mutilated beliefs."[70] Later, he is much more open to ecumenical concerns, and indeed apparently enough to be nominated as the secretary for an interdenominational Christian council in Oxford, though he declined this position.[71] John Tolkien attributed his own ecumenical efforts to his father's example.[72] The Inklings was of course an ecumenical group, and two of Tolkien's closest friends at different periods of life were Christopher Wiseman (a Methodist) and C. S. Lewis (an Anglican).

Tolkien comes to believe that outside the Roman Church there are true Christians, for God is not limited in his dispensation of grace.[73] Nevertheless, at an institutional level, everything must eventually return to its God-ordained course or perish.[74] While other groups may reflect a good deal of the light of truth, the church remains the source of that light. Without Rome, Christianity may become unrecognizable.[75] For Tolkien, there is little question where the major difference between Protestantism and Roman Catholicism lies. The Protestant "revolt" was mainly against the Mass, with the supremacy of the pope as a mere distraction.[76] Nevertheless, he mentions several other differences worth noting.

The Protestant impulse to reconstruct simple, primitive New Testament Christianity is well-meaning but misguided for three reasons. First, because much of it must remain largely unknown. Second, simply because something is early does not make it more valuable: many early practices were a result of ignorance! Here Tolkien cites the abuses of the Lord's Supper among the Corinthians as an early problem now remedied. Most importantly, though, Tolkien insists that the church was never intended by Christ to remain at the static point of early childhood, but to grow and develop like a plant.[77] It is meant to transform as a result of the mutual influence between its own principles and its divinely decreed place in history. There is no resemblance between seed and tree. Though the history of growth of this divine thing is sacred, for us now living, the tree and not the seed ought to be the subject of our care and attention. That is where all the power of the seed now resides.[78] What worse harm could the ecclesial tree's caretakers do than attempt to reverse its growth? No, they must instead look after the tree with wisdom and trepidation, ever conscious of their limitation.[79] In short, Protestantism seeks to reverse time and rejects allegiance to the church as it actually exists today.

This schism of the church has led to "the decay of faith, the breakup of that huge atmosphere or background of faith which was common to Europe in the Middle Ages."[80] This in turn leads to alienation and degradation of beauty.[81] Tolkien can write as a young man, "It is the tragedy of modern life that no one knows upon what the universe is built to the mind of the man next to him in the tram: it is this that makes it so tiring, so distracting; that produces its bewilderment, lack of beauty and design; its ugliness; its atmosphere antagonistic to supreme excellence."[82] He is sympathetic toward ecumenism and the healing of this schism but hesitant toward its practical realization.

He participated in plans for a United Christian Council of Oxford, for instance.[83] But he is saddened by the long-standing post-Reformation anti-Catholic sentiment in his home country. Neither of his closest friends, Christopher Wiseman or C. S. Lewis, shared his allegiance to the Roman pontiff. Sometimes this could be a matter of jest, sometimes of sharp dispute.[84]

He is keenly aware of the unique and sometimes unpleasant situation of English Catholicism. Tolkien's concern for the state of the church in England specifically manifests in an as-yet-unpublished manuscript present in the special collections of the Bodleian Library, in which Tolkien attempts to write a history of the church in England.[85] In this incomplete work, titled *Church in Ancient England*, he details how the Catholic missions were vital in redeeming the existing English culture. They were one of old England's foremost glories and chief contributions to Europe.[86]

While lauding an increase in Christian love, the growing fellowship between Anglicans and Catholics that marked Tolkien's time led to many minor absurdities, much resentment and patronization, much head-patting for those Catholic separatists who have now seen the error of their ways and want to play with the rest of the group. Very few Protestants, though, seemed to note the real historical reasons why English Catholics might hold such an attitude, or how even at that time Catholics faced very real persecutions.[87] During the Great War, for example, we find him attending Mass on the field with another battalion—Tolkien's own chaplain was hostile to Catholics.[88] But, says Tolkien, love covers a multitude of sins. Despite the dangers, the church militant cannot shut its soldiers away in a fortress.[89] This only leads to losing ground against the enemy.

CHURCH IN MIDDLE-EARTH

Alongside Tolkien's direct remarks on ecclesiology, there are numerous correspondences in his fiction. Within Middle-earth, organized religion plays a larger role in the First and Second Ages than the Third. Tolkien writes of a "heresy" in the earliest years of the Elves that doubts the existence of the Valar and holds instead that the Elves are themselves meant to conquer "the Dark" and rule the world.[90] This heresy reappears later in a new form, arguing that while the Valar do exist they have abandoned the world and simply want to use the Elves to retake control of it.[91] Finwë, the most prominent elf with heretical ideas, is converted and becomes especially faithful to the Powers when he arrives in Valinor.[92]

Both Valinor and Númenor have calendrical dates of worship atop a mountain, involving feasting, joy, prayer, song, praise, and thanksgiving.[93] The Valar have regular festivals on the height of the holy mountain Taniquetil. They robe themselves in white and blue and ascend to hear Manwë give a sort of sermon on creation and God's glory.[94] Likewise, the Númenoreans have a holy mountain, the Meneltarma, the only religious site on the island.[95] Echoing scriptural images of holy mountains and altars made without human hands, there is neither roof nor building nor altar, not even a pile of undressed stones.[96] Here the Númenoreans practice bloodless offerings of grain and fruit.[97] The people are free to visit, whether alone or as part of a procession in festal raiment, but remain completely silent. This is not a rule but a natural instinct; even a stranger knowing nothing of Númenorean customs would feel the same impulse.[98] Only the king is allowed to speak, and then only three times a year, to lead the people in public prayer to God.[99]

The Númenoreans practice a simple, monotheist religion focused on an imageless, non-localized God, and steadfastly opposed to the worship of any other being.[100] They create images of the Valar but not of God.[101] Tolkien deliberately compares Númenorean religion to Hebrew practices.[102] While the Edain attempt to teach true religion, they are revered as gods by the men of the darkness.[103] There is some evidence of natural religion apart from contact with the Elves, but it is never depicted positively. Dunharrow (another mountain) is said to have been a religious site before the influence of the Men of the West.[104] In fact, the door to the Paths of the Dead in *The Lord of the Rings* is an entrance to an evil temple.[105]

Tolkien consistently contrasts man-made places of worship with natural ones, and he heavily associates temples, fanes, and shrines with idolatry and evil.[106] The great temple of Middle-earth is not to God but Satan. Built in Númenor after it adopts Morgoth-worship, Sauron's temple receives human sacrifice and other horrific rites. Sauron as high priest also forbids the use of the true high place, though even he does not dare defile it.[107] The kings (who in Númenorean society also function as the only priests) neglect the holy mountain, the festivals, and the offerings.[108] Cultists afflict the Eagles sacred to Manwë who dwell at the mountain's peak. King Tar-Palantir is a last gasp of holiness before the fall. He reinstitutes public worship and gives safety to the faithful. He tends the holy tree and prophesies that it is bound up with the fate of the people. But his righteousness comes too late to assuage the Valar's wrath, and most of the people have not repented from their faithlessness anyway.[109] Only Elendil and his group of faithful retain the right to worship and supplicate God directly.[110]

By the Third Age, the good characters have practically no visible religious acts or practices, save for brief prayers at mealtimes among the descendants of Númenor.[111] This is a result of the true worship and the sole authorized holy ground being lost,[112] much like the destruction of the temple in Jerusalem.[113] Again, as was mentioned in our chapter on Christology, the role of priest and king are identical in Númenorean thought. When the kings disappear, this therefore also brings an end to the priesthood. Aragorn, the new priest-king, eventually reenters the forgotten hallow of Minas Tirith and reinitiates corporate worship of the true God, calling upon his name but still building no temples.[114]

Instead, pious Men focus on God as an element of moral philosophy and, most commonly, turn their religious attention toward combatting the darkness. Tolkien explains that in a mythical state where physical resistance to an incarnate evil is a major act of loyalty to God, the good people would likely focus on this resistance to the negative, leaving positive truth aside as more a historical or philosophical stance than an active devotional principle.[115] Besides, before the world is made round, there is no religion per se, since the Divine is physically present. Cults and religious practices only arise afterward.[116] Tolkien can speak of wars of faith on the international political scene of Middle-earth.[117] From this point onward, the true history of the Eldar and Valar are gradually forgotten, until a modern father can tell his son that they remain only insofar as they have been implicitly worked into Christendom.[118] In this way, Tolkien subtly implies that whatever remains of truth, goodness, and beauty from the ages long past find their way—sometimes under new guises—into the Christian theopolitical structure. Only here can we recapture what we have lost.

There are other less explicit echoes of the church in Middle-earth. The Bible speaks of the church as a people of promise. The two Testaments refer to the binding pledges that God makes toward the faithful. While Tolkien does not explicitly deal with the idea of the church as a covenant community constituted by God's own oath, he does affirm the necessity of keeping even harmful promises. Together with obeying any prohibitions, this is one of the key signatures of Faerie.[119] In other words, we know that Tolkien views promising as a weighty and even metaphysical activity, such that his thought is consonant with the biblical picture of covenant.

We might point out the two most solemn oaths recorded: the terrible oath of the sons of Fëanor, and the compact of Cirion and Eorl. The two rulers meet at a hallow watched over by the Valar so that their oaths may be of deepest solemnity. Everyone stands in silence with bowed heads.[120] It is even said that Cirion's oath was divinely inspired.[121] Here Tolkien's characters declare that their oath will stand in memory of Númenor and the faithfulness of Elendil, and it will be overseen by the ruling angels and God himself, above all thrones forever.[122] This oath between Gondor and Rohan is directly compared with the bond between the Edain and the Eldar in the Second Age.

Conversely, the sons of Fëanor swear a terrible oath in the name of God, calling hell down upon themselves for breaking it, naming Manwë, Varda, and the holy mountain in witness. They vow that none whatsoever—even one of the Valar—should take a Silmaril from them.[123] This oath inspires dread in its hearers, for once sworn, such an oath cannot be broken and will pursue its speaker to the end of the world.[124] In both instances the holy powers and even God himself are directly involved with the establishment of a covenant.

Alongside the picture of covenant community we must place the picture of a band of believers. We need each other. No one can be a Christian on their own. There must be a fellowship. The body of Christ helps us in our weakness, complements our own limited perspectives,[125] provides needed companionship,[126] and allows us each to reflect the light and love of God toward each other.[127] Note the tender moment we find toward the end of Frodo and Sam's journey. Frodo whispers for Sam to hold his hand; he can no longer make his own body obey him. Sam takes his hands, places them together in imitation of a gesture of prayer, kisses them, and holds them between his own. Sam supports Frodo when he is weak and keeps him faithful in the face of adversity.

Tolkien's image of the church under persecution might also be summarized by Aragorn's words at the Last Debate. They must walk knowingly into a deadly trap with courage but little likelihood of their own survival. This, he says, is their duty, and better to perish fighting for the dawn of a new age than to sit in temporary safety forsaking all hope.[128] It is not for us to control the tides of the world, only to do what we can, taking action against the evil at hand in order to ensure a good chance for those that come after us. But the future is in God's control.[129] A Christian does her small part and trusts God for the outcome.

God, too, can grant hope along the way, depicted for example in the brief vision of the statue of the fallen king re-crowned,[130] or the glimpse of the star Sam sees above the reek and cloud of Mordor.[131] Evil cannot conquer forever, despite present circumstances.

This is the point of Sam and Frodo's musings on their own story on the stairs of Cirith Ungol. Prompted by their evil situation, they note that many of the heroes of legend were simply people thrown into extraordinary circumstances who chose to persevere. Beren and Lúthien's story goes beyond both happiness and grief, passing the Silmaril on to Eärendil and then into the light of the star-glass in Frodo's very hand. Here Sam realizes they themselves are part of the same narrative still. The great stories never end, though their characters may come and go as their parts are completed.[132] The idea that the tale goes ever on does indeed give hope, such that Frodo can laugh in the very shadow of Mordor.[133]

SACRAMENTS

Roman Catholic theology recognized seven *sacraments*, or sacred signs which act as means of grace. These are the Eucharist, baptism, marriage, penance, confirmation, holy orders, and extreme unction or last rites. The sacraments are central to Tolkien's theology. While he was most impacted by the Eucharist, he is also noted to have been appreciative of Francis Thompson's depictions of "Catholic ritual writ large across the universe."[134] Here, then, Tolkien seems to partake in what has come to be called *sacramental ontology*—the reflection of sacramental power at every level of reality. This intuition can be trained through attention to the faerie element in life: "One must begin with the elfin and delicate and progress to the profound: listen first to the violin and the flute, and then learn to hearken to the organ of being's harmony."[135]

Other scholars have developed more extended treatments of Tolkien's sacramental thought.[136] These mostly take the forms of suggestive parallelisms between events in Middle-earth and ordinances of the church. One hears the tinkling of the baptismal font in Bilbo's esoteric, "I am he that buries his friends alive and drowns them and draws them alive again from the water."[137] Tom Bombadil also invokes the rebirth of baptism: "You've found yourselves again, out of the deep water." A newly warmed heart and a time of naked frolic symbolize a second infancy.[138] We might also note Boromir's confession and penitential practice,[139] or Thorin's desire to clear his conscience before his death.[140]

Rather than examine each of the seven sacraments, which would entail a large amount of inference, we will restrict ourselves to the three Tolkien discusses explicitly. We know Tolkien attended confession regularly and perhaps daily (at least once in Latin).[141] We know that he had his own children baptized and confirmed.[142] Alongside this, he offers several reflections on penance in his essay on *Gawain and the Green Knight*. But the two most significant sacraments in Tolkien's theological landscape are undoubtedly the Eucharist and holy matrimony.

EUCHARIST

Tolkien writes that he fell in love with "the Blessed Sacrament" from the beginning and by God's mercy has never fallen out of it. Francis Thompson's "Hound of Heaven" is not for him. Instead, there is the constant silent appeal and starving hunger of the tabernacle, the place where the holy wafer is kept.[143] Tolkien calls the Blessed Sacrament the supreme thing to love on earth, full of romance, glory, honor, fidelity—in fact, it is the truth behind all other loves.[144] It is itself a divine story in which we find the summation of every good and beautiful thing. And like the true fairy story, the Eucharist also provides the wondrous eucatastrophe that subverts death itself. In this divine paradox, life comes through death, and the realization of all love, faithfulness, joy, and desire comes through absolute surrender. All our worldly loves are transubstantiated into an eternal form.[145]

Frequency of Communion is important—Tolkien took Communion daily and encouraged others to do so.[146] He advises that Communion is the only cure for weakening faith. Though always perfect, complete, and inviolate, it does not operate in a once-for-all fashion. Much like faith itself, its effect grows through continuous exercise.[147] In fact, he actually recommends communicating in an unpleasant place, full of people who may offend one's sensibilities. In this way, and by praying for those partaking alongside, the communicant is drawn to focus more on the sacrament itself rather than its aesthetic experience.[148]

But what is the heart of the sacrament? It is, in short, the feeding on the real, literal body and blood of Jesus Christ, transformed through divine power and existing under the appearance of bread and wine. Jesus' charge to "feed my sheep" refers to the blessed sacrament, and the feeding of the five thousand and Jesus' words in John 5–6 look forward to it.[149] Again, denying the Real Presence in the Host is, for Tolkien, synonymous with calling Jesus a fraud to his face.[150] We can either believe him or reject him, but we must take the consequences either way.[151] Those who have even once been to Communion with the right intentions cannot escape the blame for such sacrilege.[152] Indeed, Tolkien views the division over the Real Presence to be the foremost cause of schism between Catholic and Protestant.[153] The chief marker of the truth of the Catholic claim to continue the tradition laid down by Christ is its defense and veneration of the Eucharist. Pope Pius XII's liturgical reforms (encouraging more meaningful participation in the Mass by the laity) are, for Tolkien, even more significant than the Second Vatican Council, of which he was not terribly fond.[154]

Such an important element cannot fail to find a parallel in Tolkien's fiction. Notably, while Tolkien did not seem to have intended most of these parallels, he does not deny them and in fact accepts them as valid.[155] His mental makeup—formed so fully by the rhythms of the faith—influences his mind even when it turns to lesser things.[156] The parallels with the Elvish *lembas*, at least, *was* a deliberate choice. Tolkien admits that the main significance of *lembas* is of a religious nature.[157] *Lembas*, which means "waybread" in Elvish, corresponds to the Host or *viaticum* ("supplies for a journey"), in Catholic practice given to Christians in preparation for the journey of death. Its power cannot be analyzed in a laboratory, yet it provides a virtue that preserves the will to life.[158] *Lembas* bestows an endurance not merely physical, for while it does not satisfy bodily desire, its potency increases as travelers rely upon it alone.[159] This finds parallel in lives of saints in which the holy figures sustain themselves solely with the Eucharist.

Lembas feeds not primarily the body but the will, giving strength to endure and to master the physical body.[160] The will is the source of moral choice and of the obedience of faith. Those who exercise their wills toward God find them further strengthened toward holiness. The contrary is also true. Tolkien directly ties Gollum's revulsion toward *lembas* with demonic influence and a lack of the divine presence. Likewise, *lembas* is especially effective against the poisons of Shelob.[161]

MARRIAGE

Marriage is a sacrament that sanctifies romantic love and creates the family. Tolkien's views on the importance of marriage are pronounced and arise no doubt from his own sometimes tumultuous personal experience with Edith.[162] This is perhaps one theological topic upon which Tolkien was prepared to sermonize. His copy of Thomas Aquinas's *Summa Theologica*, while unmarked in most other passages, shows evidence of deliberate engagement on this score, and Tolkien drafted a lengthy letter to C. S. Lewis taking him to task for his public endorsement of the two-marriage system.[163]

He believes that God's original design for marriage remains intact and profitable. Furthermore, it is actually the best and most satisfying way of getting sexual pleasure.[164] This is because Christian marriage is the truth of sexual behavior for all humanity. By the very nature of the faith, Christian sexual morals are correct for all.[165] This is how we were designed to function.[166] Monogamy is the only way to total health for men and women.[167]

But as we have seen, nothing escapes from the fall. Marriage too suffers the effects of the world of sin. The unmarred design of God is that each shall take only one spouse; having more than one marital partner is a result of sin—coming about either through divorce or death.[168] Having more than one *sexual* partner is also, though natural in a biological sense, in fact a corruption of nature in a theological sense. Monogamy is a revealed ethic arising from the faith and not the flesh. In a fallen world, our bodies, minds, and souls are not always aligned.[169] Christian marriage denies this self-indulgence, since self-indulgence is really the denial of the good of other selves.

Instead, marriage entails faithfulness in suffering and great mortification. Sexual desire, as disordered, may not be satisfied, but it *will* be sanctified. This involves great difficulty. No man has remained faithful to his wife without conscious self-denial and exercise of the will, regardless of how truly he loves her.[170] Tolkien continues that our guides in marriage are wisdom, a clean heart, and a faithful will.[171] There can be no doubt that a spouse might have made a better match, but the real soul mate is the one to whom you are actually married. There is little choosing involved; God uses life and circumstances to work his will.[172] Marriage, like all things, lies in his hand.

Marriage is for life and cannot be ended except by death.[173] The debasement of marriage by divorce, adultery, and lack of seriousness is a slippery slope, for fundamentally wrong behavior always progresses into deeper and deeper wrong.[174] To tolerate divorce is to tolerate the abuse of self, of other people, and of society as a whole. The evil of divorce can only be justified by extenuating circumstances, if even then.[175] In fact, Tolkien is so opposed to the practice that he acknowledges an impulse to save people from themselves by keeping divorce too expensive for many people (though he admits this is open to misunderstanding).[176]

In all this, Tolkien himself adopts the teachings of the church cheerfully. As he explains, he himself once felt them to be arbitrary until he perceived their wisdom. Eventually, however, he was freed from the "delusion" that the sacrament of marriage is simply a strange sectarian practice of his community.[177] He marvels at how often simply holding an opinion along with the church is a true guide.[178] As previously mentioned, Tolkien finds the practice of conducting both a religious and a civil marriage to be abominable, since the state marriage amounts to a piece of propaganda implying that a church marriage is somehow less real.[179] This religious element, by contrast, invests the marriage contract with awe and guards against any degradation of the sacrament.[180]

He took his own duties as a husband (and father) very seriously, keeping the religious element of the relationship quite central.[181] By 1913 he began to perform his religious obligations more actively in preparation to become a husband.[182] He did not become formally betrothed to Edith until she was received into the Catholic Church in 1914.[183] On this occasion, the betrothal was performed in church by the priest, and Tolkien likely marked the occasion with a poem to the "great glory of God" dedicated to Edith.[184] Later, though Tolkien was unable to celebrate his wedding service as part of a Mass, he and Edith afterward receive a prayer of nuptial blessing from their friend and parish priest Father Augustin Emery.[185] It worried him tremendously when Edith stopped attending church in the latter years of their marriage. Robert Murray (a close friend of the Tolkien family to whom many of the published letters are addressed) reported Tolkien feared going to hell because he had failed in his duty to impart the faith to Edith.[186]

Marriage in Tolkien's Fiction

Within his stories, Tolkien takes the opportunity to expound his views on marriage unfettered by practical social considerations. We can gather much from passages on Elvish marriage customs that would apply, were Tolkien to have his druthers, in normal theological discourse. Indeed he acknowledges that much of his discussion of Elvish marriage applies as it takes its proper course in an unfallen world.[187] For example, the Elves believe that sexual desire never occurs without love in an unfallen world and should never be separated from the procreative impulse.[188]

While Elven marriage customs must take into consideration their unique physiology and the fact of Elvish reincarnation, they otherwise embody traditional Christian practices, including parental permission and cohabitation.[189] The Elves, for instance, believe that while spiritual union is not broken by distance, yet for embodied creatures spirit can commune with spirit only when the bodies also dwell together.[190] Tolkien decrees this to be so because he works within the marital principles laid down in Genesis 2:24: "Therefore a man shall leave his father and his mother and hold fast to his wife, and they shall become one flesh" (ESV). Bodily activity here reinforces a spiritual connection. Finding and reintegrating with one's spouse and children is the very first purpose of a reincarnate Elf.[191]

Marriage is achieved not by ceremony but by sexual consummation, and no ceremony need be observed except the exchange of blessings and the invocation of God.[192] It chiefly relates to the body, as it is begun through sex and its primary purpose is the begetting of children.[193] We can see this even in biological design: God wills that his Children should have bodies capable of marriage and reproduction (including that between Elves and Men).[194] The pregnancy period is therefore one of deep joy and anticipation.[195] For the Elves, more spiritually elevated than Men, childbearing expends great physical and spiritual energy but also creates more lasting fulfillment.[196]

The act of sex differentiates married love from all other relationships; the closeness and permanence of the bond exceeds those of friendship.[197] The love between husband and wife is distinct from other kinds of love (such as between siblings), arising from correspondingly distinct motions in the soul.[198] As noted in chapter 4, souls are themselves gendered, such that male and female have specific gender roles that surpass the merely physical.[199]

Elsewhere, Tolkien transforms the medieval focus on *amour courtois*, with its romanticized conception of love, into a much more grounded focus on the glories of an everyday marital relationship. Courtly or chivalric love glamorizes adultery, unrealistically exalts the woman as a sort of idol, and distorts the nature of marriage. It is not wholly true, and not properly theocentric. Women are not lesser divinities but fellow sinners in need of grace.[200] Such idealized tales promote a false and genuinely harmful view of love as some sort of perpetual exaltation with no bearing on life, circumstances, or decisions.[201]

In his own work, he therefore promotes a purified version of the chivalric tradition. He takes the main point of *Gawain and the Green Knight* to be the sublimation of courtly or adulterous love into Christian (married) love. The true knight, in *Gawain*, upholds marital fidelity as the highest form of chivalry and escapes sexual temptation through prayer.[202] Tolkien himself tells his own version of the chivalric romance in the Breton *The Lay of Aotrou and Itroun*, where the knight steadfastly rejects the advances of the faerie antagonist, even in the face of death. God will decide when he dies; until then, he will be faithful to his bride.[203] Middle-earth is no different. While Aragorn and Arwen may have the noblest and more essential love story, the homey marriage of Sam and Rosie reveals Tolkien's unique conception of the relationship between heroic and ordinary life. Sam may foray into the epic, but he ends in contented domesticity.[204] Aragorn and Arwen are an "allegory of naked hope,"[205] while Sam and Rosie are rooted in reality. This is not to say that more exalted presentations of love have no place. They can provide models to strive after, and perhaps a vision of what love should have been in the garden.[206]

PENANCE

In Catholic sacramentology, "penance" can mean either the sacrament of confession or the acts enjoined to demonstrate true contrition. Tolkien's habitual practice was always to attend confession before taking the Eucharist at his daily morning Mass.[207] One must purify one's soul before encountering and feeding on Christ bodily. His thoughts on the sacrament of penance appear in his treatment of *Gawain and the Green Knight*. He considers Gawain's temptation and confession to be the heart of the poem, vitally important though often overlooked.[208] For Tolkien, the entirety of the interpretation and valuation of the poem lies in the confession.[209] This is foreshadowed earlier in the poem, when Gawain's act of contrition brings an answer to his prayer for shelter.[210] Though Tolkien is here only commenting on the work of another author, it is clear from his phrasing that he both affirms and adopts the same position as the poet.

He breaks down the steps of penitence in the standard way. First, there is a feeling of shame for a sin committed. The Christian must repent from this sin, turning from it with the intention never to repeat it. She should confess to God (through a priest) unreservedly, demonstrating her sorrow over her sin through an act of penance, making up for the wrong in some meaningful way. The priest, as mediator of God's forgiveness, grants absolution to the penitent, reconciling her to God again. But God grants not merely forgiveness but redemption, so that harm actually turns to glory.[211]

Tolkien repeatedly stresses that the efficacy of confession depends on the penitent and his or her intentions. The priest's pronouncements do nothing if the penitent is not in a proper spiritual state.[212] A confession in which one willfully conceals sin will not produce the proper effects: neither forgiveness nor the light heart that accompanies it.[213] Such joy remains independently of exterior circumstances, such as fear of death.[214] So Gawain's courage is exactly in line with the comfort offered by the faith and the joy that comes from confession and absolution.[215] Gawain feels morally clean, able to face death by thinking of God's ultimate protection of the righteous.[216]

FURTHER READING

Aside from various introductory or survey articles examining the role of Catholicism (or religion) in Tolkien, this field is well covered by two dedicated monographs, Bernthal's and Testi's. Those interested in Tolkien's own religious practices should consult Hammond and Scull's *Reader's Guide*, vol. II, under the heading "Religion."

Bernthal, Craig. *Tolkien's Sacramental Vision: Discerning the Holy in Middle-Earth*. Lechlade, UK: Second Spring, 2014.

Testi, Claudio A. *Pagan Saints in Middle-earth*. Zurich and Jena: Walking Tree Publishers, 2018.

Wood, Ralph C. "The Lasting Corrective: Tolkien's Vision of the Redeemed Life." In *The Gospel according to Tolkien: Visions of the Kingdom in Middle-earth*, 117–55. Louisville: Westminster John Knox, 2003.

XI

THE CHRISTIAN LIFE

The spiritual peaks of the holy sacraments are not the only land-scapes of the Christian life. Besides this, there are the everyday habits of holiness based in faith. These do not always come naturally, but as a decided and sustained choice. "Faith is an act of will, inspired by love," states Tolkien.[1] The right use of the will is a major theme in Tolkien's conception of the daily Christian life. Free will occurs in our responses to the states of affairs we encounter in the world. We may be fated to meet an enemy but not to respond to him in any particular way. Furthermore, the will is only fully free, and therefore morally accountable, when it is directed to a certain purpose with full awareness.[2] In this chapter, we will summarily examine some of the golden threads of daily life in the faith, those purposes to which our wills ought to be directed.[3]

DAILY LIFE

Tolkien harbors no illusions that the Christian life is an easy one. The whole world is a battleground between God and the devil, with Christians playing the part of soldiers pushing back the territory of the enemy.[4] His protagonist Frodo, the most saintly of halflings, endures more pain than any other and is without honor in his own country, where the adulation goes toward more puissant heroes.[5] But, writes Tolkien, "I do so dearly believe ... that no halfheartedness and no worldly fear must turn us aside from following the light unflinchingly."[6] Tolkien himself was scrupulous in his own spirituality.[7] Christian vocation requires dedicated, continuous perseverance in the face of temptation. This includes the temptation to despair at the very failure of the church and its ministers to live up to its calling as a holy institution. In the end, Tolkien believes that unless we view our lives as a journey to God, our efforts will be futile.[8]

GRACE

Tolkien holds closely to the classic distinction between nature (our inbuilt human capacities) and grace (the additional gift of God that allows us to surpass those capacities).[9] He seems to define "grace" as God's instrumental enhancement of natural human capacities.[10] This is not to say that nature and grace are mutually exclusive. Our creaturely capacities are also divine gifts. This includes mythopoeia, for instance. God, as the source from which all reality and art arise, empowers all fantasy through grace. It is a grace-filled activity from beginning to end.

We are infinitely and recessively derived from God. We need "Grace" to do the good, and "grace" to cooperate with "Grace."[11] Here, in Tolkien's terminological difference between "Grace" and "grace," we see the theological distinction between a *state* of "santifying Grace" — of fellowship and unity with God through Christ—and individual specific gifts bestowed by God—actual grace. God gives us both the ability itself and the motion of will needed to use it.[12] There is here a reliance on God as the foundation of being that far surpasses specific instances of divine favor. But God does not empower forever. Grace, in this sense of spiritual assistance toward a goal, is not infinite, and

God usually limits it to the accomplishment of whatever appointed task the person accomplishes in the network of providence.[13]

Tolkien illustrates this in *The Lord of the Rings*, where he says that grace does in fact appear, but under mythological forms.[14] He explicitly states that Frodo receives grace to take up the quest, to resist temptation, and to endure fear and suffering to a heightened degree.[15] The entire final trek into Mordor seems accomplished only by continuous infusions of grace and the will of providence. At each obstacle, the hobbits trust in luck, which always holds out, even when at first it appears to have deserted them. Grace impels Sam's song in the Orc tower, through which he is able to find Frodo.[16] Grace strengthens their endurance; the journey is full of a sense of crushing and suffocating exhaustion, but their wills remain firm.[17] When their provisions begin to run short, they decide to walk along the road to Mount Doom to quicken their journey, chancing their luck again. Only a few lines later, Sam trusts to luck to find water, and it does not let him down.[18] Soon, they run into a band of marching Orcs on the road. Frodo, dismayed, moans that their trust in luck has failed them.[19] Yet the Orcs take them for deserters and force them further along the road to their goal, where it "chances" that they run into another Orc party, and Sam and Frodo escape in the confusion.[20] What seems to them disastrous is grace in hidden form.

Eventually Frodo seems unable to do more than walk forward, so the point of view shifts completely to Samwise. He feels tired but unburdened and clear-minded, unhindered by doubt or despair. His will is set, and the desires of the body fall away from him.[21] After Frodo can walk no more, Sam lifts Frodo onto his back, expecting a dreadful burden. But instead, for reasons unknown to him, Frodo is as light as a child. Sam wonders whether he has been given some gift of strength for the ending of their mission and their lives.[22] The sentence is clearly a divine passive, phased as such because simple Sam is ignorant of the true Source of his empowerment, though he has noticed this strange gift of strength before.[23] The more knowledgeable Frodo has already speculated whether this is actually luck or "blessing."[24]

As Tolkien writes, grace operates toward some definite end, and this is not always perspicuous. Gollum's reappearance at the moment of Frodo's failure is another unexpected hidden grace that accomplishes a specific end. Here, grace follows not a person but a cause.[25] Frodo's personal failure is inevitable, his situation in fact impossible.[26] But his willingness to undertake the quest and his earlier exercise of mercy[27] bring him only to the point at which the Other Power takes control of the narrative.[28] Here, pity, mercy, humility, suffering, patience, and forgiveness create the circumstances in which Frodo's own insufficient power is raised up into a larger plan.[29] Gollum's life has been spared by many merciful souls before, and these prior acts of empowering grace providentially set the stage for a completely external grace: the intervention of Gollum and the destruction of the Ring against all odds.[30]

MERCY

In fact, failure is central to Tolkien's depiction of heroism. The hero fails, but mercy triumphs over judgment. Frodo spares the undeserving Gollum's life, and God rewards his deed by making Gollum Frodo's unwitting deliverer.[31] Frodo's patience and mercy toward Gollum gain him "Mercy."[32] The capitalization here is a clear indicator that this particular grace comes from God. The divine scales, tempered by mercy, save the world.[33] The day is saved not by strength or even will but by the absolute power of pity and forgiveness.[34]

Tolkien asserts that *The Lord of the Rings* is a moral work "founded on Pity; on the triumph and the defeat of Pity."[35] It "breathes Mercy

from start to finish," but this is especially notable in the final chapters.[36] The lavish dispensation of mercy in the conclusion of the novel
begins with the remarkable scene in which the party, returning to their
homes, encounter Wormtongue and Saruman on the road, shriveled
and beggarly.[37] Their consistent mercy and extensions of kindness
toward mortal enemies only infuriates Saruman. Wormtongue is too
terrified to accept it. Once they have returned to find the Shire under
the control of the ruffians, Frodo, now a master in mercy, forgives his
captors and stops the hobbits from condemning Lotho too quickly.
He has acted wickedly, yes, but he is a victim too.[38] Nor will he allow
deadly violence against even the most traitorous of hobbits, and nobody
is to be slain at all if possible.[39] Once the hobbits have unmasked
Saruman as the root of the ruin of the Shire, he too receives mercy.
Frodo declares that meeting revenge with revenge is useless and heals
nothing.[40] Saruman attempts to stab Frodo before fleeing, but Frodo
will not have Saruman killed even now. He chooses to leave the former
Wizard alive in the hope that he may find redemption. Saruman stares
at Frodo with a look of wonder, respect, and hate. Admitting Frodo's
great spiritual growth, he finally declares Frodo to be wise and cruel,
robbing his revenge of its sweetness, forcing him to leave in debt to the
hobbit's mercy. But he chooses to hate rather than accept such mercy.[41]
Saruman, shown overwhelming and undeserved mercy, refuses to be
reconciled because he refuses to repent of his pride.

Tolkien insists that mercy (or pity, which to him is synonymous) is
a necessary element in our moral judgment since it is present in God's
own nature.[42] Even God practices the self-abnegation of mercy, which
we ought to imitate. He may in fact be more pained by our injury to
one another than any offense we commit against his incarnate person.[43] We are likewise empowered, as members of the body of Christ,
to extend mercy on sinners ourselves—to retroactively transform

thievery into gift.[44] Jesus, remember, prays that the Father forgive those who revile him on the cross.[45] Here we see illustrated Tolkien's principle that mercy is not mercy when exercised for its usefulness; it is only really present when it goes against common sense, as Frodo's did. Pure pity is separate from any liking.[46] But at the same time, only such extravagant generosity ensures that we ourselves will be met with mercy toward our own failings.[47]

REPENTANCE

There is a sort of repentance which is really simple fear, the desire *only* to escape the consequences of one's sin. But true repentance also involves a real admission of one's wrongdoing and even an acceptance of judgment should it be deemed necessary.[48] Indeed, repentance is the only way to escape divine punishment for sin.[49] Neither is repentance identical to restoration.[50] The state of grace, which was the natural position of humankind before the fall, is only partially regained through repentance.[51] Human beings may repent of sin but are not fully cured of it until they enter the final state.

In the meantime, Tolkien is conscious of the way in which repentance is a real choice that confronts the sinner—a slim margin may be all that separates repentance from relapse.[52] In this case, such a failure is a great tragedy. Tolkien says that Gollum's near-repentance on the stairs of Cirith Ungol is one of the most impactful moments for him personally.[53] Frodo's mercy has stirred the goodness left dormant within Gollum, but because of Sam's misunderstanding and harsh words, his repentance is ruined and Frodo's hard-fought pity come to nothing (at least it seems so). All of us are sometimes guilty of spoiling an opportunity for salvation, since the instruments of justice are not often themselves just or holy. Good people are often the worst stumbling blocks to repentance.[54]

But, says Tolkien, Gollum's choice was all but inevitable in itself. "He'd been evil for too long. There's a point of no return in these things, and Gollum had passed it."[55] This point also occurs in Ar-Pharazôn himself, wavering on the very shores of Valinor. He too almost repents of his madness, but pride has become his master, and he goes forward to defy the Valar.[56] Human beings are the product of their choices. Facing evil requires a deliberate motion of the will, whether to yield or resist.[57]

Some hearts, like Gollum's or Ar-Pharazôn's, can be hardened in such a way as to close themselves off from further opportunity for divine mercy; a Christian will, empowered by grace, can receive a strengthening and a confirmation to do good.[58] Repentance then returns the generosity of mercy with love.[59] It works spirally and not in a closed circle—that is, it must be a continuous and ever-broadening activity rather than a reflexive and insular one.[60] Yet God uses this process in marvelous ways. After shame comes repentance, then confession and contrition and penance, and finally a forgiveness that is so redemptive that the healing of the wounds becomes a glory.[61]

HUMILITY

The movement between simplicity and nobility, or from ignobility to honor, are especially important to Tolkien.[62] All of us stand equal before the Great Author, who casts down the proud and exalts the humble.[63] He once recounts that many people at his parish church were edified by a visiting tramp, dressed in rags but visibly holy and devout. This man, says Tolkien, probably looked a great deal more like St. Joseph than the statue inside the church.[64] The tramp's holiness (and perhaps his acceptance by the churchgoers) pleases Tolkien greatly: an image of God's concern for the downtrodden and the surprising way in which godliness may be wrapped in a dingy package.

Tolkien remains humble about the runaway success of his own work and the great praise heaped upon it even for its palpable air of holiness.[65] He is quick to point out that whatever holiness inhabits his own work comes not from him but through him.[66] Likewise, at the end of *The Hobbit*, Gandalf reminds Bilbo that his adventures were providentially arranged for more than just his sole benefit. He is only a very little person in the wide scheme of the world. He is testing the hobbit's heart: Has his journey of growth grown his head? But Bilbo passes the test, responding in the beautifully ordinary and matter-of-fact way of all hobbit-folk: "Thank goodness!" he laughs, and passes Gandalf the pipe tobacco.[67]

The hobbits as a whole provide not only a way to ground the epic romance of the tale, but a prime subject for this ennoblement of the humble. They do not want to be heroes but answer the call and rise to the occasion.[68] In an earlier draft, Bingo (Frodo) protests that he is just an ordinary hobbit. The Elf Gildor corrects him. He may have a good deal of the ordinary (or commonplace) hobbit inside, but there is something else, something which will elevate and temper Bingo's everyday nature until it too becomes worthy of its high calling, while remaining hobbit. Gildor remarks that the Shire-loving hobbit nature needs to be trained, not despised.[69] We see this mature sort of hobbit virtue in Thorin's well-known evaluation of Bilbo: "There is more in you of good than you know, child of the kindly West. Some courage and some wisdom, blended in measure. If more of us valued food and cheer and song above hoarded gold, it would be a merrier world."[70]

Humility also casts the light of truth upon worldly standards of success. True wisdom recognizes necessity, even when it may appear foolish to all others. So Gandalf exposits 1 Corinthians 2–3, declaring that folly will be their cloak in the eyes of Sauron, who knows only the desire for power.[71] The very humility of the quest is its safety; the

Fellowship plays upon Sauron's worldly wisdom, his *Realpolitik,* which is actually foolishness. Their apparent foolishness is true wisdom, for when the humble recognize that neither strength nor wisdom create success, both weak and strong are free to become agents of providence. The task falls to Frodo of the Shire, afraid and ill-equipped. Elrond sees that behind the initial surprise, such an event almost smacks of inevitability. The wise know to expect that mysteries shall only be revealed at the proper hour.[72] Divine passives litter the chapter.[73] All recognize the hand of God at work in the most unlikely way. And it is often the case that such small hands do the great deeds of world history because they must, while the powerful are busy elsewhere.[74]

Yet, when it is all over, Frodo is eventually tempted to despair, through a last remnant of pride. He wishes to have returned a hero rather than as an instrument of the good. He is pulled toward condemnation of his own failure to destroy the Ring and a regret borne from not having actually done so.[75] He will struggle against this reverse sort of pride for the rest of his life, and he only finds final healing across the Sea. These sorts of struggles help Tolkien to ground humility as a real choice and not merely a quality with which some people are born. It is a habit that must be developed.

PRAYER

Tolkien believes in the efficacy of prayer and is confident that prayers *are* answered.[76] Hope and prayer are virtues.[77] For Tolkien, prayer seems to be mostly other-centered, whether in order to help other people or to praise God. Tolkien is almost certain that God (perhaps humorously) holds himself readiest to answer the prayers of the most unworthy if they are directed toward the good of others.[78] Sometimes, God prompts his people to answer one another's prayers. At one point he offers a friend some money, "Since

I guess it to be an answer to prayer, for on the way from church on Sunday I had a sudden clear intuition that you were worried and in difficulties."[79]

It is, however, downright bad theology, and empirically absurd, to assume that all prayers are immediately and straightforwardly answered. Often we must be content with no visible answer, or only a partial one.[80] One must grapple with long periods of silence, not to mention the problem of evil itself. Tolkien points out that many people in both history and Scripture turn away from God to the devils for just this reason: they seek rapid and magical answers to prayer. The God of Scripture never guarantees his servants immunity from pain and danger, either before or after prayer.[81] As mentioned, however, there is no doubt that God *does* answer many prayers.

Prayer was one of the issues on which Tolkien and Lewis fervently disagreed. Tolkien found Lewis's book *Letters to Malcolm: Chiefly on Prayer* theologically unacceptable, distressing, and sometimes horrifying. He began a commentary but abandoned it as it was too harsh.[82] This unpublished commentary, titled "The Ulsterior Motive," presumably details not only a response to Lewis's attacks on the Mass and purgatory but on liturgical prayers and the veneration of the saints.[83]

Much of Tolkien's prayer seems to have been liturgical. This does not mean the dry recitation of meaningless phrases, but traveling along long-beloved and proven tracks of meditation and devotion. Tolkien recommends that Christopher memorize the praises so that he always has "words of joy" ready at hand.[84] Tolkien himself frequently recited (in Latin) the *Gloria Patri*,[85] the *Gloria in Excelsis*,[86] the *Laudate Dominum*,[87] the Magnificat,[88] the Litany of Loretto,[89] the *Sub tuum praesidium*,[90] and, his favorite, the *Laudate Pueri Dominum*.[91] We can see some of these prayers (in Latin) jotted down in the midst of his lecture notes for *Tolkien On Fairy-stories*.[92] He advises that one should also try to memorize the canon of the Mass, in case anything prevents one from attending.[93] Tolkien also did some unpublished academic work on the form and history of the *Pater Noster* and translated several prayers into Elvish.[94] He seems to have had a fondness for variations of this prayer, as he was also able to pray it in Gothic when he humorously exorcised George Sayer's new tape recorder.[95]

Within Tolkien's fiction, prayer plays many roles. Elves believe direct contact with Eru is not allowed, or at least not appropriate unless in dire emergency.[96] They instead look for enlightenment or counsel from God via the delegated authority of the Valar.[97] They seek answers to these prayers in the inmost mind or heart where God provides guidance.[98] In Húrin's time the Men of the West invoke the names of the Valar to sanctify their meetings.[99] Later, the faithful Númenoreans do believe they are still permitted to address God through thought or prayer directly, given his special grace and relationship toward Númenor and their status as a remnant.[100] Their long life is a literal answer to prayer.[101] By the Third Age, Men no longer have any petitionary prayers to God, though they do still have a sort of prayer of thanks.[102] Gondorians face west in a time of silence (possibly of internal prayer), in which they look toward Númenor, the Lonely Isle, and finally Valinor, the eternal home of the gods.[103] Frodo's passage on the ship into the West comes about through a chain of petitions specifically called a prayer. Gandalf is here the authorized plenipotentiary of the Valar, able to accept prayers on their behalf.[104] The prayers of Middle-earth are transmitted in a mysterious way to Manwë, while Manwë himself seeks the counsel of God in his inmost thought (or heart), where God's will is revealed.[105] Unworthy souls, by contrast, ought not to expect their prayers will be answered.[106] The Valar can choose not to hear certain prayers from rebellious petitioners.[107] Elsewhere, Aotrou and Itroun pray fervently for their hearts' desire, a baby, and God hears their plea. Prayer is thus a spiritual practice involving both an outward movement and an inward attentiveness to God's response.

Aside from direct prayers to God, Tolkien's devotion to Mary leaves us with several Marian prayers, both liturgical (as outlined above) and fictional. Notably, of the recorded prayers Tolkien gives us, all of his prayers to God are praises, while all of his Marian prayers are petitionary.[108] This is true of his fiction as well. Sam indirectly invokes the "Lady" (Galadriel), only to have his request for clean water and light later answered.[109] The only directly addressed Valië in *The Lord of the Rings*, Elbereth, is also a Marian figure—literally the Queen of Heaven—and all invocations of her name meet with immediate results.

SANCTIFICATION

Sanctification, the lifelong move toward holiness as well as its final achievement, is the ultimate goal of the Christian life. Tolkien exhorts his son not to grow weary of facing God with the power provided "from behind" by God himself. And if he cannot achieve the rarely given inward peace, he can recall that the search for it is not useless, but a concrete decision with its own rewards.[110] The journey toward final sanctification is itself a sort of sanctification: a transformation from passivity to proper exercise of the will. The human being is like a seed, gradually growing up and out into something totally new, yet ever working out the innate pattern held within the seed itself. There is a continuity and a discontinuity to human identity through time, influenced no doubt by environment and heredity, but also a result of conscious effort toward pruning and improvement. Yet the human being is not only a seed; he is also a gardener. Sanctification is no solitary process.[111] Even in "Leaf by Niggle," as we have seen, other members of the church actively partake in helping to sanctify one another through service and even sometimes through being served (especially unworthily!).

While Tolkien says he consciously planned very little religious symbolism in *The Lord of the Rings*, the symbolism of sanctification is one of the more evident religious images in Tolkien's writing. This is the inevitable outworking of a faith that has nourished him and taught him all he knows, itself derived from the martyrial care of his mother.[112] Perhaps this is the impulse behind Tolkien's early Elvish aphorism, "We indeed endure things but the martyrs endured and to the end."[113] Already after Weathertop the martyr Frodo has become spiritually radiant, like a glass filled with clear light, visible to those with spiritual sight. The endurance of faith, the constant movement toward God despite the opposing pressure of evil, results in an ever-greater conformity to God himself—a sort of translucence through which the light of God shines. Gandalf says Frodo looks "splendid."[114] The choice of words seems significant; Tolkien himself considers the ongoing martyrdom of Frodo the most important element of the story.[115]

Glorfindel has this spiritual power of light in abundance, as does Gandalf the White.[116] But Tolkien also notes that there is a power of a different sort in the Shire, different indeed from that of Rivendell and the Elven rings or the hidden truths of the Unseen Realm.[117] This different sort of power lies in the hobbits' remarkable ability to buckle down and keep going in the face of difficulty.[118] They are, in a sense, favorably wired for progressive sanctification. "I think that there is no horror conceivable that such creatures cannot surmount, by grace (here appearing in mythological forms) combined with a refusal of their nature and reason at the last pinch to compromise or submit," Tolkien writes.[119]

Interestingly, Tolkien's earliest conception seems to have been that Elves play a role in the redemption, recovery, and sanctification of mankind, for he writes that "the fairies came to teach men song and holiness."[120] Much later, he writes that both Frodo's and Arwen's self-sacrifice were part of God's plan for the regeneration of human nature.[121] Recalling that Elves symbolize artistry, creativity, and a delight in the world, we might say that Tolkien sees a re-infusion of these traits as important to the sanctification process, which is not merely a painful endurance of suffering but a growth toward receptivity to the joy and holiness of God, which shines through all of creation. In this way, the Elves teach holiness not only *within* Tolkien's works, but, as exemplars, in the primary world as well.

CHRISTIAN ETHICS

The depictions of good and evil in Tolkien's universe are perhaps some of the best-rendered in Tolkien studies and offer many excellent resources.[122] This section will provide an overview of only the more explicit discussions of ethics to be found in Tolkien's writing.

All life centers on increasing the knowledge of God and moving from knowledge into praise. This is, in an important sense, then, an ethical imperative. Not only theology but all activity that rejoices in God's creation—science, for instance—may and should be a type of worship.[123] The moral sense in some way thus proceeds from natural law and should be our guide to conduct.[124] Morals are objective and real, equally binding on all regardless of belief. They are, in fact, an eternal law.[125]

As such, Christian morals are compulsory for all humans, not just Christians.[126] God is the designer and ruler of the whole world and has created it to run in a specific way. To disagree about the evil of divorce, for instance, is equivalent to disagreeing about the nature of auto repair. But this sense of objectivity does not imply naiveté, since a thing may be clear in theory but painful and complex in practice.[127]

Certainly Tolkien is no stranger to the ethical dilemma or to the hard work of discernment, as we shall see below.

For Tolkien, ethical decision-making always has two sides: the individual and the communal. We are irrevocably singular, and also uniquely connected to the world around us and to each other.[128] We must consider how to develop our own talents without interfering with those of others.[129] This is perhaps Tolkien's more philosophical gloss on Jesus' reduction of ethics into love of God and love of neighbor.

PERSONAL ETHICS

On the individual level, ethics are an impulse we are perhaps born with, but eventually forget. Children, correctly, are concerned with right and wrong, a question just as important in Faerie as in the real world.[130] The kingdom of heaven belongs to those who become like little children, after all. This sort of innocent insistence on the right soon meets the need to weigh deeds according to their contingencies. All absolute ideals are conditioned by their unique placement in time and cannot be judged in a vacuum.[131] One's own moral situation is made evident through one's allegiance to the cause of right over against evil, regardless of outcome. Morality inheres in specific acts and not in their approbation by others. Godly allegiance engenders a soul that resists evil to the end rather than compromise with it, yet admits that only God can truly right wrongs.[132] While evil seems to triumph, this faithful remnant still bring the blurred image of the divine king into the world. The timid hearts that hate evil, even those that fear it and yet resist it anyway, are blessed.[133] Like Noah, these have faith in a day on the other side of shadow.

Tolkien advocates a sort of binocular view, on the one hand charting a course according to the divine standard of perfection, and on the other realizing that other limiting factors come into play. We ought to hold ourselves to the ideal without compromise, not knowing our own limits or the additional capacities grace may bestow. And if we do not aim for perfection, we will certainly fall far short of what we might otherwise achieve.[134] Actually, all reasonably charitable people frequently use a double scale: judging themselves harshly under great strain and difficulty, while extending charity toward others in the same circumstances.[135] Indeed, the more charitable the person, the wider the divergence, as we see in the saints who reckon themselves moral failures.[136] Tolkien hints that this more objective external standard may be more weighty than one's own purely internal drive toward a sometimes unattainable perfection.[137] The outside judgment of natural finite limitation against the force of circumstance creates a scale of moral failure in which blame can increase or decrease depending on how closely an agent falls short of her moral limits.[138]

Furthermore, every ethical judgment involves a consideration of the history of both the individual and the world. That is, one must think not only of the actor's own opportunity for good, but of the good to the world that might come about through her success or failure. Certain situations might even be sacrificial—entailing doom and failure on the personal level but great success on the world scene.[139] Sometimes even saints can be overcome by a stronger power, broken against their will.[140] This is the meaning of the petition of the Lord's Prayer, "Lead us not into temptation, but deliver us from evil." Clearly such a situation can occur; there is no point praying against an impossibility.

How then to make sense of 1 Corinthians 10:12–13, where Paul writes, "Wherefore he that thinketh himself to stand, let him take heed lest he fall. Let no temptation take hold on you, but such as is human. And God is faithful, who will not suffer you to be tempted above that which you are able: but will make also with temptation issue, that you may be able to bear it." Bearing temptation here must only apply to the period in which the agent is still in normal control of her will and fully able to resist.[141] Once the will has been ravaged, salvation from destruction devolves onto the general holiness of the person in such a sacrificial state.[142]

CHRISTIAN POLITICAL ETHICS AND CHRISTENDOM

On the corporate level, ethics cannot be legislated or enforced externally. They must be embraced from the heart. Humility and equality are spiritual principles which, when formalized, only turn to pride.[143] A government cannot take the place of an individual's own ethical decision-making, though it can help or hinder it. Indeed, there may be a difference between a social convention of rightness and the truly moral.[144] Tolkien recognizes the intersection of two different planes of consideration: the real, permanent world of morality on the one hand, and the changing, subjective game of honor on the other. In other words, we can suffer confusion between aesthetic distaste and hatred of sin.[145] Most people unreflectively operate with a blend of both, and both have a very similar emotional flavor. Usually only the rare crisis will be able to separate the two elements.[146]

In an ideal world, of course, earthly political structures align with and reinforce Christian ethical dictates. For example, Tolkien supports monarchy not so much because he values the obeisance but because he values the humility such hierarchical structures engender.[147] Monarchy reflects the "theocratic hierarchy" of the spiritual world, in the words offered by Gueroult.[148] It echoes in a limited way the ordering of the harmonious heavenly court. This is the true meaning of a code of honor: not the customs of earthly courts but of the court of heaven, of divine generosity, grace, humility, and charity.[149] Here, all are equal before the one true King and rule not for their own glory but for the good of others. Tolkien characterizes the ideal human king, Arthur, as "in kindly Christendom ... a king of peace kingdom wielding / in a holy realm beside Heaven's gateway."[150] By contrast, as Mordred seizes control of the land, "There was woe in Britain and the world faded; / [church] bells were silent, blades were ringing / hell's gate was wide and heaven distant."[151]

Likewise, the hostile, devious, and uncivilized Faerie in *Aotrou and Itroun* contrast sharply with the kind air, blessed waters, and brave wars of Christendom.[152] Early in life, Tolkien can bemoan the loss of unity that results from the breakup of this overarching Christian political structure, but he seems to soften his views later.[153] He notes, for example, that the chivalric tradition is a product of Christendom but not therefore identical with Christian ethics.[154] Tolkien prefers instead to see small local governments left to their own devices and the Christian ethic adopted uncompelled.[155] He sees himself as part of a minority party, always defeated but never destroyed, intensely loyal to a state while hating empire and expansion.[156] His opposition to the Boer War and to British control of Ireland likewise make it clear that for Tolkien there is no such thing as Christian imperialism.[157]

This is not to say that he resists all government as such. God has also decreed that the ruler should bear the sword.[158] In the world after the fall, there is indeed such a thing as *too much* mercy—mercy unmodulated by justice.[159] Evil structures and governments arise and must be resisted. Tolkien's attitude toward war is not as simplistic as some critics would have us believe. He understands both its necessity and its regrettable terror all too well. But he ultimately sides with the just war theorists such as Augustine and Thomas. Tolkien declares that he will not bow before the prince of this world and, just as the young men do in the book of Daniel, never allows obedience to temporal authorities to lead to rebellion against God.[160]

ETHICS IN NARRATIVE

Most of Tolkien's ethical reflection, of course, occurs in narrative form. For him, the fairy tale is the best medium for teaching morality.[161] This is because, in fantasy, the moral law is much more plainly revealed than in our own world. In the realm of fantasy, good and evil show forth with strong clarity because of their strange symbolic forms in new situations.[162]

His writings are full of both direct statements on morals and illustrations of ethics in action. The mantra for a Middle-earth ethic might be, "Have patience, do what is necessary, and hope."[163] Hope is perhaps the primary practical virtue for Tolkien, while love (in the form of pity) remains the chief theological virtue overall. This hope takes concrete form in loyalty to God and the ultimate victory of the right, even in the face of overwhelming present opposition. But such resistance must also be upheld even through the threat of ignominy. Frodo at one point concludes that he must do what is right whether anyone else ever finds out about it or not.[164] This sort of thinking would be unimaginable to a pre-Christian society, and Aragorn must correct the proxy for honor-based culture, Éowyn, who wishes for a merit that must be recognized.[165] When she defends her people, her deeds will be no less brave because unheralded.[166]

Regardless of specificity as to its source, Tolkien's characters clearly believe in an objective, constant standard of right and wrong, as Aragorn plainly says to Éomer.[167] To Tolkien, this objective morality, grounded in the hope of the victory of God, might best be labeled an ethic of *allegiance*.[168] Those who rebel against the angelic rulers or God himself are by definition evil and ought to be shunned.[169] Morality is universal, and universally binding.

One cannot thus plead ignorance or unbelief as an excuse to depart from Christian ethics. But this does not require an explicit knowledge of God as revealed in the Bible; the understanding of such a natural law might still be quite vague. Frodo may not explicitly understand himself to be trusting in *God*, but simply in whatever beneficent power rules the universe and from which the Valar derive their authority. In an earlier draft, he appeals to the "rules" to argue against killing Gollum.[170] These rules are also referenced in the riddle game between Bilbo and Gollum. Once, too, Sam asks for forgiveness from no one in particular.[171] For Tolkien, though, this appears sufficient. Both Frodo and Sam are blessed to go to the earthly paradise, after all.

Rather than an external text or code such as might be revealed in Scripture, the source of the moral sense for Tolkien seems to lie in the heart.[172] In a line of thought very similar to Lewis's argument from desire, Tolkien writes that, for the Elves, fundamental desires of the heart are indications of our true nature and lead us toward our true fulfillment. This does not mean that every wishful thought ought to be indulged. He speaks instead of a perception of the absence of something right or necessary, and the resulting hope or desire for it.[173] Souls are built with instincts just as much as bodies, and they respond to their desires in the same way. For the Elves, at least, the stirrings of joy in the heart upon hearing a proposition or argument is an indicator that the soul is on the path of truth.[174]

The created principles of human behavior, though obscured by the fall, are still present. Sam's heart always led him truer than his head.[175] His ultimate moment of charity toward Gollum comes about in this way. Slaying the treacherous Gollum would be just, but empathy for Gollum's long slavery to the Ring moves Sam's heart toward pity for the wretch lying forlorn and ruined in the dust.[176] In following an inwardly bestowed impulse, Frodo undertakes his quest from love and in complete humility, relying totally upon God.[177] It is perhaps Frodo's humility, in contrast to Gollum's self-serving behavior, that allows him to resist the lure of the Ring in the first place. In possession of a weapon with absolute power, Frodo instead looks to others to help him remain on the path of goodness. The ethic of humble trust does not just appear in Middle-earth. Its presence in "Leaf by Niggle" strongly suggests that these passages display Tolkien's own felt beliefs. Niggle (an allegorical stand-in for Tolkien) is a mostly humble fellow who does not pretend to be any better than he is. While he does not take pains toward piety, he does help his neighbor without expecting anything in return.[178] This is a true sacrifice, and his continued concern for Parish proves that he is ethically improving. He is truly other-centered.[179] Throughout the judgment scene in "Niggle," intention is contrasted with action, the heart with external action. The sort of menial or polite kindness that makes one uncomfortable more than it makes one act, the kindness that does not curtail grumbling when doing a good deed, does not proceed to the higher plane of self-sacrifice for love.[180] The highest ethical goal is to love the unlovable and to see in even the most corrupt the remnant of a damaged good.[181]

Tolkien is steadfastly against any ends-justify-the-means ethical thinking. Sometimes a harm might be permitted in order to achieve an otherwise unattainable good, such as allowing Boromir to redeem himself attempting to rescue the hobbits, but this sort of decision seems only to apply to God.[182] When Boromir appeals to Frodo for use of the Ring, Frodo's heart is uneasy despite the plan's appearance of wisdom. He does not put his trust in men, for there is a way that seems right, the end of which is death.[183]

By contrast, Faramir asserts he would not take the Ring if he found it on the side of the road and would not use a tool of Sauron to accomplish any amount of good.[184] He would not even lie to an Orc.[185] Faramir understands that good actions have value in themselves, regardless of their pragmatic outcome. An unseen power lies at work behind the world we see. He resists the use of dominating force even to accomplish noble purposes, such as the peace of his kingdom. An earthly ruler or state should be as a monarch among other monarchs, not a master of slaves, even if the master is kind and the slaves willing.[186] A good ruler is loved for virtue, not feared, unless in a sort of reverence for wisdom and dignity.[187]

At times, of course, wickedness must be actively punished. War is necessary, but we must love not war itself—only that which wars are fought to save.[188] One must always be ready to lay down one's arms, as Gimli does when faced with his professed enemy Galadriel. Rather than continue in his trenchant opposition to her, he is disarmed by love, seeing in his enemy's eyes instead only acceptance and understanding.[189] This twofold perspective on war and pacifism heightens Tolkien's narrative ethic since it recognizes the complexities of life and avoids naiveté. The heroes Aragorn and Gandalf are clearly martial figures. Simultaneously, though, the equally heroic Frodo eschews the use of all weapons and continues this abstinence during the scouring of the Shire.[190] This is in proportion to his clarity of vocation—Frodo is not an armsman but a more spiritual warrior. Like the monastics, he enforces pacifism upon himself but not upon others. He *does* guide and encourage peace to all who will listen.

Frodo himself utilizes the binocular moral judgment Tolkien elaborates in his letters, blaming himself for his failure at the end of the quest despite the practical and perhaps metaphysical impossibility of his success.[191] He judges himself according to the divine standard of perfection. Nor does he keep his self-assessment private. He confesses all.[192] None of the wise, such as Aragorn or Gandalf, attach any blame to Frodo for finally succumbing to the Ring, however.[193] They rely on this more measured judgment and take account of the very real and overwhelming exigencies of Frodo's situation, judging him highly morally praiseworthy overall.

We must remember, though, that we are all imperfect judges, and that there *is* an absolute Judge who is the final court of arbitration. While Tolkien is lenient in his ascriptions of implicit faith, it remains the case that our ethical acts, considered in themselves, are both limited and tainted. Salvation, even in Middle-earth, does not result from mere ethics but from a more fundamental trust or allegiance out of which ethics rises.[194]

FURTHER READING

Linked as it is to the bellwether "good and evil" topic in Tolkien studies, Tolkien's approach to ethics and to the good life of fellowship, beauty, and peace has generated no small amount of material. Aside from the devotional books mentioned above, the following works are good introductions to the discussion.

Dickerson, Matthew T. *A Hobbit Journey: Discovering the Enchantment of J. R. R. Tolkien's Middle-Earth.* Grand Rapids: Baker, 2012.

Kreeft, Peter. "Ethics: The Hard Virtues" and "Ethics: The Soft Virtues." In *The Philosophy of Tolkien: The Worldview behind "The Lord of the Rings,"* 192–220. San Francisco: Ignatius, 2005.

Smith, Mark Eddy. *Tolkien's Ordinary Virtues.* Downers Grove, IL: Inter Varsity Press, 2002.

Wood, Ralph C. "The Call to Companionship in J. R. R. Tolkien's *The Lord of the Rings.*" In *Literature and Theology,* 25–36. Nashville: Abingdon Press, 2008.

———. "The Counter-Action to Evil: Tolkien's Vision of the Moral Life." In *The Gospel according to Tolkien: Visions of the Kingdom in Middle-earth,* 75–116. Louisville: Westminster John Knox, 2003.

XII

LAST THINGS

This final chapter addresses *eschatology*, or last things, including death and the afterlife. Tolkien has much to say on these subjects, particularly on death and the desire for escape from death. We have already made mention of "Fíriel's Song" as a sort of creed for Middle-earth. Five of the thirteen lines in this short song deal with the end of the world and the judgment to follow. It reads: "But my heart resteth not here for ever, / for here is ending, and there will be an end and the Fading, / when all is counted, and all numbered at last, / but yet it will not be enough, not enough. / What will the Father, O Father, give me / in that day beyond the end when my Sun faileth?"[1] Here Fíriel acknowledges death and the human yearning to leave the world, then speaks of the end of all things and some sort of reckoning. Yet she is not satisfied with a mere accounting of things—she desires redemption. The song ends with a plaintive prayer to God the Father, expressing hope that he will have yet some gift to give beyond the end of all things, which will make right the brokenness of the world.

This chapter will therefore cover death, the mixture of ignorance and hope that characterizes Middle-earth, the end of the world, the last judgment, and the final states of Christian eschatology: heaven, hell, and purgatory. These subjects will entail analyses of the three most significant texts for Tolkien's view of eschatology: "The Debate of Finrod and Andreth," "The Statute of Finwë and Míriel," and "Leaf by Niggle."

DEATH

Tolkien's view of death is one of his most identifiable characteristics, and he in fact makes death a sort of defining trait of his fictional anthropology. *The Lord of the Rings*, he says, is only indirectly about power—really it is about death and a desire for immortality, what he calls the "Great Escape."[2] He writes that his whole legendarium is a vehicle to demonstrate his view that "Men are essentially mortal" and should not seek bodily immortality.[3] The message of *The Lord of the Rings* is, if anything, the danger of confusing eternity (freedom from time) with the clinging to time represented by limitless serial longevity.[4] Time and creation, whether fallen or unfallen, are not eternal.[5] Nothing stays unchanged, and attempts to make them so merely result in ruination.[6] Even in Tolkien's unstained paradise of Valinor, where he excludes decay, sickness, and other disorder, he still permits a sinless sort of corruption or weariness.[7] His unfallen history still includes the waning of the Elves.[8]

Humans as inhabitants of the world are thus also intrinsically temporal.[9] Our nature cannot in fact endure immortality within the world as it is.[10] We are destined to be transfigured into a new, eternal, bodily existence in a heavenly realm apart from time. Unfallen man would have been bodily assumed into heaven, just as Mary was.[11] Now, after the fall, death is the transition point into this new existence.[12] We cannot seek to seize that eternal existence within the present world. Attempting to lengthen life or capture immortality is unnatural and leads to wickedness, and it is one of the most common snares of the devil.[13] It is a denial of the actual transition point into eternity and a form of captivity within the world of the fall.

But in contrast to this calm acceptance of death as an inevitability of the natural order, and perhaps even as an escape from sin, Tolkien can also quote Simone de Beauvoir with approval: "There is no such thing as a natural death: nothing that happens to a man is ever natural, since his presence calls the world into question. All men must die: but for every man his death is an accident and, *even if he knows it and consents to it,* an unjustifiable violation."[14] This seriousness in approaching death, this conviction that death deeply matters to the human condition, no doubt arises from the many deaths Tolkien witnessed throughout his life. In remarking on Gandalf's return, he says that Gandalf's death necessitated a significant change in his nature, since to him representing death as making no real difference is unacceptable.[15]

One can read his disgust with modern clinical approaches to death in a brief exchange from "Niggle" that contrasts what we may call a spiritual and a materialist view. One villager opines that they should have put Niggle away. The other villager, puzzled, asks whether he means forcing Niggle to start his journey (death) before the proper time. The first villager is dismissive, calling the journey metaphor a meaningless expression. He denies that the journey exists and phrases it instead as pushing Niggle "through a tunnel into the great Rubbish Heap" beyond.[16] Such an undignified and reductive approach is repulsive to Tolkien, who sees the human person as destined not for dust but for divine fellowship.[17]

Regardless of its cause, all death is ultimately under the control of God, to permit or to prevent. He may take his servants' wishes into account but he cannot be gainsaid. It is the human's duty to accept what comes. In *The Lay of Aotrou and Itroun,* for example, the pagan Corrigan threatens the hero with the curse of death in three days;

Aotrou is dismissive since he knows God alone decides the time of his death.[18] Likewise, even after the curse is fulfilled, Aotrou's death still rests in the hands of God.[19]

As we have seen, death is a major theme in Tolkien's fiction, but his views on the subject develop substantially over time, and always toward a more orthodox understanding. The next sections will outline Tolkien's unfolding treatment of death, from the view that death is a good to the standard Christian view that death is a curse and the last enemy.

THE GIFT OF DEATH?

In the earliest writings, Tolkien names death the "Gift of Men," given directly by God and unable to be revoked by any other being. Specifically, the gift of death signifies (a) that our hearts will not find rest in the world but seek beyond it into eternity, (b) that we have the power to shape our lives beyond the strictures of fate or the Music, and (c) that in some way these free human actions will in fact complete the story of the world to the last detail. Men are free to leave the world; they are only "Guests" or "Strangers." This ability will, as time lengthens, be the envy even of the Valar. Death as originally intended partakes of good and even of hope.[20] It is not an evil but part of our biology and therefore also of our spiritual nature, since these are integrated.[21] Death is inevitable, but, in an unfallen world, its occurrence is voluntary, painless, and late.[22]

The fall then acts only as an overlay of negativity upon a good substrate. As Men continue in rebellion, life is shortened, dotage accompanies old age, and the end comes forcefully and involuntarily.[23] This is the only time human free will is denied.[24] Tolkien allows Frodo and Bilbo the chance to die according to the original plan for unfallen humanity: voluntarily, desiring in faith to move into eternity.[25]

Aragorn does in fact accomplish this.[26] But even these cannot now escape some of the effects of the fall on death itself; they leave their bodies behind. Sometimes a body fails prematurely; sometimes a spirit wearies of the world too soon. This failure of body and soul to sync with one another comes from the taint of Melkor and the fall.[27] Whereas death was once painless, Morgoth has cast his shadow on it, bringing evil from good and fear from hope.[28] The penalty of the fall is not death itself but a change in *attitude* resulting in pain, fear, and reluctance.[29] The uncertainty about what happens after death only increases this fear.[30] Even for the Elves, whose bodily resurrection within the world is certain, death involves bereavement.[31] Conversely, dwelling on death can still give dignity and sometimes wisdom.[32]

There is evidence that this approach to death is based on some form of Tolkien's primary belief, for, as we noted above, he writes that the legendarium is based on his own view that humans are essentially mortal and should not try to become immortal in the flesh.[33] Death here is in some sense proper to the nature of Mankind and not a result of sin, but rather of creaturely finitude. The emphasis here on the gift of death lies in its transitioning us from creation into eternity.

Tolkien later seems to backtrack on his view of death as gift. While he feels artistically bound to his earlier position (formulated at the first composition of the "Ainulindalë" (1918–1920), he becomes increasingly uncomfortable with it and seeks to render it theologically acceptable. He struggles to reconcile this with what he himself declares to be the Christian view: that death is not part of human nature but punishment for sin and a result of the fall.[34] In Middle-earth, for example, Tolkien declares that death is "certainly" not an enemy.[35] It is explicitly *not* a punishment for the fall. It might be bad theology in the primary world, he writes defensively, but it is an imaginary idea capable of revealing truth and able to be legitimately used in fantasy.[36] Such a metaphysic might be heretical if such fantasy were regarded as true statements about the nature of humanity—then again, it might not. But the "view of the myth" is still that a finite lifespan is not a punishment for the fall.[37] Here, we note, it is not *his* view but the view of the *myth*.[38] He has become aware of the dissonance. This forces him toward an incoherency, since in his late fiction, he defines death as the severance of soul and body, something intrinsically unnatural.[39] This is in direct conflict with the idea of death as a gift from the Creator of nature.

"THE STATUTE OF FINWË AND MÍRIEL":
GRAPPLING WITH THE PROBLEM

This struggle between these two perspectives on death is given narrative form in the short tales "The Statute of Finwë and Míriel" and "The Debate of Finrod and Andreth."[40] In the former, which can be read as a transitional piece, Fëanor's mother refuses to be reborn in accord with Elvish nature and marriage, and his father wishes to remarry. The Valar permit this, but only after a lengthy debate over whether Míriel's death-without-rebirth comes as a result of the fall or a special permission of God. In discussing this ruling, Manwë distinguishes between justice and healing. The former works within the state of affairs as it is found, and though it is not evil, it accepts evil as a part of the world. He decides the ruling is just—that is, it accepts death although death is actually unnatural.

Aulë wonders whether Míriel's death did not come from sin but from the strain of birthing one so great as Fëanor—perhaps a development unforeseen by the Valar. Ulmo denies this; death is evil, and though God may bring good from evil, it is not his "prime motion" to grieve his children. If this death came from God, it would not contain grief or doubt. Yavanna points out that while the wills of Finwë and Míriel may not have fallen to Morgoth and thus brought corruption into untainted Aman, nevertheless they *are* embodied beings and their bodies participate in the matter tainted by him. Nienna agrees that death is intrinsically evil but says that God can have good purposes for *specific* deaths. Whether this purpose bears evil fruit is the result of hope or its denial. Ulmo says it may be both: God may have willed it, but Finwë and Míriel still lacked hope.

Manwë responds that the Children were meant to enter a fallen world and to endure it. In a very Thomistic moment, he argues that in their original unfallen state, human beings are a holistic soul-body structure. But, because they are two things and not one, separation is at least logically possible, and this severance we call death. He denies that there can be a distinction between an evil death and a death meant for good, since separation is the characteristic of both, and this breach of nature is always a grief. He affirms a tension as well: while God would not desire to use an evil thing as an instrument of benevolence, he is Lord of all and uses *all things* to his ultimate good purposes. Nevertheless, he wills that his creatures ought not to despair but through hope should grow into daughters and sons of God.

This passage can be taken as very close to what Tolkien would consider a theologically correct reading of the situation, since at this point in the mythology the Valar are said to be free from sin.[41] Each of their arguments should be read as valid and reasonable, though Manwë's position would be closest to Tolkien's own, since Manwë is portrayed as the wisest of the Valar and the most in accord with God's own knowledge. Here, in this work, the characters themselves slowly arrive at the view that any sort of death is a grief and cannot therefore be natural, in the sense that it is God's original design.

"THE DEBATE OF FINROD AND ANDRETH": TOLKIEN'S MATURE VIEW

In the second narrative essay, "The Debate of Finrod and Andreth," Tolkien approaches a more coherent and traditional view. Finrod, the Elf, takes what we may call the "Gift" view, while Andreth, the woman, takes the "Curse" view closer to that given in the "Statute" passage. While the essay unfolds dialectically, the views can also be compared side by side.

For Finrod, who details the earlier "Gift" view, body and mind are united like a "House" and its "Dweller." Death is the severance of these two; deathlessness is their eternal unity. Even the Elves do not possess this. For at the end of time the Elves will cease to exist, and they have no rumor of hope as Men do. Death remains ultimate, merely more distant. He is skeptical that Morgoth/Satan, by some special malice, was able to inflict mortality on an immortal nature in itself, rather than on individual beings.[42] Only God could have done such a thing. Finrod argues that death is therefore a part of nature, and though Men are Children of God and their death therefore more tragic, it still seems natural. He points out that *all* things in the world are now tainted, even Elves, and distinguishes between death and the shadow of the devil. Otherwise there would be no death of any sort in this world, which was designed by God and not Morgoth. Instead, death must be our name for something Morgoth has tainted but which in itself was meant for good.[43]

Finrod continues: Men may love the world as guests but are dissatisfied with it, longing for another world. He observes that harmony is essential to the unfallen nature of the Children of God.[44] How could soul and body thus exist out of harmony with one another? How can a mind or soul be a mere guest destined for eternity if its ordained habitation (the body) is inextricably tied to a perishable world? He concludes that the body, too, must be immortal—but how could Men have had imperishable bodies unbounded by earthly limitations, yet composed of and sustained by earthly elements? The soul must then at some point choose to release itself from its body and go home to a higher realm. This then would be death, the simple transition from one to the other.

Not so, answers Andreth. She outlines the "Curse" position. Men's short lives are the result of Satan's malice, though there are legends that God is the one who inflicted the curse. There was at one time no difference of mortality between Men and Elves. Andreth in fact asserts that Men were meant, not merely for a longeval life such as the Elves possess, but for true everlasting life.[45] Indeed, many Men hold that no living things suffer death in their original nature. All death is a result of the fall. Furthermore, each soul is perfectly fitted to its body. To imagine a gnostic escape from the body as from a set of chains is a notion of Satan, since true unfallen incarnate life is a union of mutual love between its parts.[46] Here she agrees with Finrod but draws the opposite conclusion. The severance of soul and body cannot accord with the true nature of Man, for such would be a disharmony, and the parts would not be united by love.[47] As such, Andreth claims, humans were not made for death; instead, it was imposed upon us, and we therefore attempt to escape from it.[48] She believes this flight to be futile—death is now inescapable for Men, even in the Blessed Realm. Echoing Ecclesiastes, she says that no skill or strength may forfend death and the ineluctable transformation of a living being into carrion fit only for disposal. It does not matter whether one is wise or wicked, death comes for all alike.

For this reason, before Finrod's correction, Andreth is doubtful that, even if the Elves can be slain, they can truly understand the human experience of mortality. For the Elves never leave the world and can return to life. Whereas, now in an echo of the Hebrew of Genesis 2:17, Andreth declares that dying we die, and there is no return. Death is the ultimate end and an incurable loss and wrong.[49] They both agree that death involves harm, loss, and (for Men) grave injustice. Living in mythological pre-Christian times, they can only speculate on its remedy.

At this point the dialogue moves toward a final solution. Finrod surmises that if death is unnatural and the body an innate part of the human being, then this must entail that the soul has the power to uplift the body into a new mode of existence in eternity. Such goes beyond anything glimpsed in the Music. If this is true, Finrod exclaims, then Men were indeed mighty in their design, and their fall is more terrible than any other disaster.[50] Men must look toward an Arda made complete, indestructible, and eternally beautiful. Or, Finrod asks, is there another world of which all that we see and know are only reminders or reflections?[51] If such does exist, it lies in the mind of God, replies Andreth. We cannot find the answers in a marred world in any case. But they each take comfort from the hope that God will not abandon them.

Tolkien's rather brilliant theological retcon amounts to this: death is only called a "Gift" by the Elves, as a sort of imaginative literary device. It is a mystery into which they long to look.[52] These stories, after all, are Elf-centered, he reasons. If humans invent Elves and fountains of youth to escape from death, then Elves may invent the idea of the "Gift" as an escape from deathlessness.[53] The Númenoreans then inherit this perspective. It does not necessarily apply to the Christian view of death as punishment. It is an Elvish idea of what death (as freedom from the world) should now *become* for Men, regardless of how it arose.[54] Earlier Men and their Elf friends now indeed view death as a punishment, but one meant for the ultimate healing of the punished.[55] The conclusion: whether death is a penalty or gift may depend on whether such a gift is accepted. Submission to the will of God transforms the curse of death into an opportunity for hope, while clinging to life in rebellion against God ends in despair.[56] This, we can guess, is likely close to Tolkien's own mature view of death.

HOPE

Hope is Tolkien's other great theme, and its end is future blessedness and God's redemption of the world.[57] Since hope is a virtue, however, it cannot be commanded. Tolkien invariably ties hope to faith in God and its opposite to unbelief. He resists the comparison of hope with a dream and belief with waking reality. This is a smokescreen to make the former seem less substantial. Such is not the case.[58] Belief and hope are bound together. On our appointed journey through time, we must travel hopefully if we are ever to arrive at all.[59] Hope is a necessary condition for future blessedness, but such hope is in something which will *actually occur*, or else it is empty.

While history may be nothing but a long defeat, it nevertheless contains such foreshadowings of final victory. These glimpses form the basis of the Christian's hope in the face of apparent hopelessness.[60] Such a victory will not be accomplished through human effort, but only as a direct intervention by God in which he establishes an "unmarred" creation anew. Hope, then, is not an end in itself. Rather, it is specifically the *hope of restoration* in this new creation.[61] Healing comes only through suffering and faithful endurance. In fact, a steadfast and hopeful endurance of the ills of our marred world demonstrates that such a person belongs in the world to come.[62]

But before Christ, death is the reason why Tolkien's characters may only operate in a realm of "Hope without guarantees."[63] In his reconstruction of the *Beowulf*-poet's moral, he draws a contrast between the people of Beowulf's day, who had never heard of Christ, and his Christian audience. God is distant, the evil is near at hand, and hope is absent. Beowulf thus dies full of sorrow and fear of God's wrath, although in Tolkien's view the poet extends a flicker of hope for Beowulf after death. Conversely, the youths in the poet's audience shall also die, but with hope of heaven if they use their gifts well.[64] Heaven is a privilege only realized after Christ.

HOPE WITHOUT GUARANTEES: PRE-CHRISTIAN FAITH IN MIDDLE-EARTH

Tolkien's fictional version of God, Eru, demands both belief and a hope or trust in him.[65] The soul ought ever to hold the thought of the unfallen world in its heart, waiting with patience until the day of renewal. This hope is the most beautiful of all the virtues of God's Children, says Manwë.[66]

Tolkien distinguishes between the casual sense of hope as the uncertain but possible expectation of some particular good and this deeper sense of hope.[67] The Elvish word *estel* is specifically hope or trust in God—that is, religious faith.[68] This faith-hope cannot be overcome by the world, arising as it does not from experience but from our nature and essence.[69] If we are Children of God, then God will not allow himself to be deprived of us by any enemy or even by ourselves. The final foundation of *estel*, enduring even in the face of final ending, is that God always ensures his Children's joy.[70] Some dim hope lies at the end of the Music of the Ainur, though we are not told what.[71] The Elves cannot abide the possibility of annihilation and are forced to rest on naked *estel*, trusting that whatever God has in store for them will be recognized as not only wholly satisfying but unimaginably joyful beyond expectation.[72]

Thus, even a natural theology rooted in a good Creator condemns a lack of hope in the face of death.[73] The fate of Men is a point of ignorance for the Elves and even for Melkor,[74] but they know at least that God the Father will not let those who love him and his creation perish forever. The failure to wait upon hope is a grave fault.[75] For example, Denethor's final hopeless suicide attempt is at the same time a rejection of the theology he knows. Gandalf explicitly ties such despair to heathenism and satanic domination.[76] Denethor ends as virtually a nihilistic Morgoth-figure himself, proudly proclaiming that if doom (a circumlocution for the divine) denies him his wish, he would rather have nothing at all—neither life, nor love, nor honor.[77] His erstwhile liege-man Pippin, however, when he falls at the battle before the Black Gates, accepts death with a laugh. For him, it is an escape from doubt, care, and fear.[78] Denethor opposes himself to Gandalf as emissary of the Powers and ends in heathen hopelessness, while Pippin, trusting Gandalf and thus Eru—without consciously knowing it—finds death a gift. Tolkien likewise contrasts Sam's self-centered defiance with the hope that he attains once he accepts that all shall ultimately be well. When he sees a star high above the clouds of Mordor, he is pierced with the realization that the shadow is a small, temporary thing while light and beauty remain forever. This frees him, too, from the fear of death.[79]

The good Man dies in this sort of faith, for "Death" can also be equated with "Escape" from the world of the fall.[80] Tolkien cites Aragorn as the prime example of this—indeed his childhood name is Estel, and this name reappears at the moment of his death. Aragorn has the grace to depart life at a time of his choosing, to give back its gift. He still acknowledges death as a gift, though neither he nor Arwen minimize its tragedy; Arwen says it is a bitter gift indeed. But Aragorn is swift to correct her. So it *seems*, he answers. But though they must part in sorrow, they ought not part in despair, since they are not bound forever to the physical world, and beyond it lies more than memory.[81] At his death he then manifests a sort of saintly incorruptibility.

Tolkien also allows his pre-Christian characters knowledge of a good original creation and a fallen state. But in the "Debate of Finrod and Andreth," for example, he also shows how dwellers in Middle-earth might move from hopelessness to a very explicit form of pre-incarnational belief. Andreth, at first, can see little but despair. Far from the original immortality with which humans were created, it now seems as if Satan is the lord of the world and God perhaps a distant dream. This lack of *estel* is a result of the wound of the fall. She believes whatever hope humans have is a mere wishful desire, and not true *estel*. Perhaps, answers Finrod, but desire may be the last flicker of faith.[82] By dint of their conversations, touched on above, Andreth eventually asks whether there may not be some greater thing after the end of the Music, into which both the created and fallen world might be taken up. The "Great Hope" of Men lies in their speculation that God himself will enter the world, defeat Satan/Melkor, and heal past, present, and future.[83] But, asks Andreth, how and when will such healing occur? Into what sort of creature will these souls be remade? And what of those who have already died before then?[84]

Here Andreth distinguishes between the *final state*—that is, the situation at the end of time—and the *intermediate state*—the fate of a soul after death here and now. Before Christ, such a state would have been an open question. In an attempt to combine an explicit after-life with the obscurity of pre-gospel hope, Tolkien's Elves are certain that they go to the halls of Mandos in Aman (an intermediate state), though they do not know what will become of them at the end (the final state). In contrast, though the Elves do not know where Men go in the intermediate state, they are certain Men have an eternal life as their final state.[85] This, to the Elves, seems a better fate (though not all Men agree).[86] Tolkien seems also to leave space for interaction with the spirits of the dead who roam the earth, but to seek to do so is unwise and wicked.[87]

Tolkien pictures the intermediate state in Middle-earth as a time of reflection, in which souls are corrected, comforted, instructed, or strengthened, as is fitting to each.[88] But the Elvish soul retains its freedom even after death and can refuse instruction and calcify in rebellion. Tolkien seems to have subtly divided the unrepentant into two camps: those with the hope of healing and those who have done such great evil that they seem beyond healing. This latter camp, a very small one, would from a Christian perspective correspond to those who die in mortal sin.[89] Such people are bound for hell, while the former camp seem clearly to dwell in purgatory, where, depending on the extent of their evil, they will eventually reach blessedness.

While pre-Christians might be familiar with a judgment after death and even with a place of punishment, references to a blessed reward in heaven within the legendarium are rare.[90] Correspondingly, while Tolkien pictures a more or less felicitous life after death in the *intermediate state*, the hope of heaven in the *final state* is vague. The "Great Hope" having been accomplished in primary reality, however, we may now turn to Tolkien's thoughts on explicitly Christian eschatology and seek a more well-defined picture.

THE END OF THE WORLD

Creatures are not the only things to suffer the pangs of death. The universe is finite and impermanent by nature; Tolkien describes time as the "life" of the universe, flowing from its first to last moment.[91] The world itself will also come to an end. He divides Middle-earth history into three phases, which we will also adopt in speaking of the primary world. First comes Arda Unmarred, the pristine and wholly good creation envisioned by God. In theological terms this is the world before the fall. Next comes Arda Marred—that is, the world as we currently experience it, subject to the fall, corruption, and decay. But after the end of Arda Marred there comes Arda Healed—the redemption of the new creation.

The original creation, Arda Unmarred, lives now only in thought and memory. It actually exists in the mind of God, just as an author can revisit previous chapters of her book, but is inaccessible to the characters within the tale. It remains, however, the paradigm from which the standards of order and perfection are traced. We live now in Arda Marred, though, as stated above, Tolkien suggests that humans, even before the fall, might have been destined to leave the world and enjoy a bodily existence outside of time.[92] The end of Arda Marred will be catastrophic, involving the dissolution of its material components and not merely a gradual decline into heat death.[93] This end, however, the Elves cannot predict, since it rests wholly within the freedom of God.[94] The "Ainulindalë" describes the end of the world as a single chord played by God, deeper than the abyss, higher than heaven, more glorious than the sun, piercing as the light of God's eyes.[95]

There is a miniature apocalypse at the climax of *The Lord of the Rings*, when the Ring is destroyed. Images of a mighty wave whose crest comes crashing down upon the land tie this cataclysm directly to Númenor, itself directly stated to be a foretaste of the final end.[96] "This is the end," says Frodo, as he surveys the "ruin" of the world which is the destruction of Mordor. But in the midst of "the end of all things," he is free and joyful.[97] Galadriel later says that the lands of Beleriand destroyed many ages before will be lifted up above the waves again. This implies that the passages in which the world is "changed" may not mean simple change but also remaking, Arda Healed.[98] Both characters' attitudes signal their faith in different ways, as we will see below.

However, Tolkien's views on the appropriateness of a more detailed Middle-earth eschatology seem to have shifted. Christopher Tolkien points out a tripartite division of purgatory, hell, and heaven in the early *The Book of Lost Tales*.[99] Other writings move away from this explicit theology and speak only of the Elves, deliberately excluding the fate of Men in order to provide an open place for a specifically Christian eschatology only to be revealed later.[100] In this version there is an Armageddon, excised from the published *The Silmarillion*. When the Valar grow tired and the world is old, Morgoth will return from his banishment and destroy the sun and moon. Eärendil will fight him with the holy light of the Silmaril, and the last battle will begin. Tulkas, Fiönwë, and Túrin will defeat Morgoth. Túrin himself will kill Morgoth and avenge all Men.[101] The earth will be broken and recreated. Fëanor will offer up the regathered Silmarils, and, with their light, the Two Trees will be rekindled.[102] The mountains of Valinor will be leveled and the holy light pour over the whole world. In this restored light the Valar will grow young, the dead will rise, and the purpose of God will be fulfilled.[103]

Elsewhere, Tolkien is more reticent about the ultimate end. In the latest writings, neither the Elves nor the Valar have a certain fate beyond the end of the world, while humans have a surety of immortality.[104] The apocalypse at the end of *The Silmarillion* is now said to be Númenorean and not Elvish.[105] Even so, the hope of healing Arda Marred is only feebly asserted at the close of *The Silmarillion*.[106] In keeping with a pre-gospel world which can rely only on a shadowy *protoevangelium*, Tolkien removes even the slight remark that Sauron's final doom at the end is far away and known only to the wise.[107] In some late writings, Tolkien *does* speak of an Elvish eschatology, in which both Elves and Men grow in bonds of friendship, and in which the unique Elvish contribution will be the memory of the past.[108] They will participate with the Powers in a "Second Music,"[109] greater in every way than that which shaped the world at its beginning. In this Music every player will know fully the mind of God for their part.[110]

There is a restorative balance here. The Elves are always specially attached to creation and thus inescapably sad because of its impermanence. Sadness is the inevitable result even of *pure* love for anything impermanent—which, ultimately, is anything other than God himself.[111] Men, who care little for the world the Elves love so much, have a unique capacity to love God for himself, apart from a love of the world, although they also have a capacity for great evil. The world will be destroyed by wicked and loveless Men but healed through good and holy Men. And through Men the world will be remade and the Elves delivered from their sadness.[112]

In these shifting conceptions, we see Tolkien pondering what is appropriate to a sub-creator in dealing with a theological future. At some points, he adopts Christian eschatology; at others, Christian eschatology is inappropriate for a pre-gospel world. Sometimes he gives a destiny only to his fictional races while leaving actual humanity aside in an attempt at deference; sometimes, in the interest of consistency with revealed theology, he gestures toward the fate of humanity given in Scripture while moving his own creations into a subsidiary role.

But he consistently places human history at the center of world history; our end will be the end of Arda Marred and the achievement of Arda Healed.[113] This will not simply be a restoration of the world before the fall, but something new and greater.[114] And if Men are at the center of the world's cure, then Jesus Christ is the center of that center. Andreth speaks of a secret handed down by God from before the fall.

In fictional parlance, we read of the "Great Hope" that God will enter the world to heal Men and all the "Marring" of the world. God would never abandon his work to Melkor, but since only Eru is stronger than Melkor, Eru himself must enter the world to conquer him.[115]

Such a logic likely holds for Tolkien's own beliefs as well. In short, and in the language of primary reality, the victory of Jesus Christ heals humanity and, in so doing, the world, since humans were made to exercise dominion over the world. But the consummation must await his return. In the meantime, the world is still a hostile place, and the war against the monsters of the previous age continues, under a new aspect, into the new. The tragedy that characterizes the pre-Christian end is still poignant but subsumed under ultimate hope. Now, after Christ, even the end of all mortal things cannot be merely a defeat, as it is part of the design of the Judge above the world, who has revealed the possibility of an *eternal* victory or defeat for the soul. Therefore we still deeply feel the worth of bravery defeated.[116] Some griefs may never be healed within the walls of the world,[117] though in fact sorrow and the wisdom arising from it serve to enrich the joy of what is to come.[118]

Tolkien also believes in a sort of "Ragnarök" or final battle[119] and alludes to the antichrist and the beast of the book of Revelation in referencing a physically tangible demonic enemy appearing before the end.[120] This battle between the forces of God and Satan will be the end of the world as we know it—the world of the fall, that is.[121] For the end will not merely be the breaking, but also the remaking or mending, of the world.[122] After the apocalypse comes the millennium, the rule of the saints over the pacified earth.[123]

And, last of all, there is the new creation. Tolkien speculates whether this new creation will be similar to our own world, enjoyed within time and space in a succession of moments continuous with the old world,[124] or, more interestingly, whether the recreated world might be more like a timeless state of fulfillment only able to be enjoyed from the outside.[125] A reader of *The Lord of the Rings* might read through the story in a succession of moments, from beginning to end, and thus be inside the tale and experiencing it in a similar linear sense to the characters within it. But only at the end, from the outside, can the reader mentally survey the complete story, including its climax and resolution, and either admire or criticize it as a whole.

Furthermore, the resolution of the tale might exert a backward influence on the earlier parts, casting them in a new light. Gollum's final intervention, for instance, causes the reader to reevaluate many other scenes. The good which is the eucatastrophic arrival of the Rohirrim at the Pelennor fields can only exist because of the apparent hopelessness of the situation beforehand. In the same way, the "Marring" will be either completely undone, healed, or absorbed into goodness, beauty, and joy.[126] Arda Healed might be the completion of Arda's history, *including all its evil*, which at the end will be seen to have contributed to the world's ultimate goodness in accordance with God's promise. But this final state also makes right all the wrongs of the marred world that were not so utilized.[127] Perhaps God will even heal not only the living but those who have already died and those yet to be born.[128] This final assize and remediation is our next topic.

FINAL JUDGMENT

God judges both particular individuals at discrete times and, eventually, the whole of creation. Here he assigns souls a place in one of three realms: heaven, hell, or purgatory.[129] After death, God reviews the deeds and motives of each person and provides an appropriate outcome, though God's standard of merit may not be perspicuous.[130] It will involve consideration of selfishness against self-sacrifice,

Christian discipline, and, of course, whether the soul has chosen to bow to God or to the evil spirit of the world. No soul, however, even one destined for heaven, will be free of all imperfection.[131] In fact, Tolkien accepts the possibility that God may permit the majority of humanity to choose damnation.[132]

God is merciful, though, and reckons good deeds as well as bad. Tolkien's remark about literary criticism might hold equally true of the record of one's life in general: Christ is the greatest admirer of the gifts he himself gives, even more than their recipient.[133] No human being is evil in origin, and therefore no human being is in principle unredeemable—unless they choose damnation for themselves.[134] There are objective standards of right and wrong, and people can fall onto one side or the other,[135] but to seek to assign any particular individual to a specific eternal fate is to overreach and usurp the role of divine Judge.[136]

Tolkien believes that our fellow human beings also play a role in the final judgment of our deeds. If a victim forgives his wrongdoer and chooses not to press charges, as it were, God may freely accept and abide by that decision. The wrongdoer should be repentant and the victim desirous of mercy, but how surprising it would be at the bar of final judgment to find that so many of your offenses against your brothers and sisters had already been waived, he dreams. What if one even had a share in the good brought forth out of that offense, now transformed?[137] This sparks an eternal relationship of relief and gratitude.[138]

In Tolkien's fiction, the Anglo-Saxon concepts of the great judgment and the grim hall of the dead exercise great influence on Middle-earth.[139] Tolkien feels free to use such ideas since they are already present in pre-Christian mythology. Here the hall is overseen by Mandos, the doomsman of the Valar, ordained by God to judge right and wrong and the deeds done in the body. He sentences each Elvish soul to a time of waiting (before rebirth) proportionate to their deeds.[140] Men he also judges, but after a time in the dark halls of waiting they depart, none know whence. Tolkien, though, still distinguishes between Mandos's delegated judgment and the final judgment of God, which none can escape.[141] There are only a few glimpses of judgment at the time of *The Lord of the Rings*. When Saruman dies, his spirit is denied entrance into the West and dissolves into nothing.[142] But Tolkien's Valar refuse to remit only the most rebellious of the Noldor. Galadriel gains admission to the Undying Lands as a reward for her resistance to Sauron and her victory in temptation.[143] She is healed by hope.

HELL

Nobody enjoys thinking about the eternal punishment of the wicked, but one cannot get around it. If the words of Jesus are true—that the way to heaven is narrow and few find it—then one could struggle with believing in the goodness of God in a universe where the majority of human beings are damned to hell.[144] But the fact is that some people *do* give in to temptation, reject the chance of salvation, and appear to be damned.[145] The terrible realms of doom full of agonizing fire await those who refuse to repent.[146] In Christian theology, contrary to popular misconceptions, hell is the place of God's judgment, not the kingdom of Satan's power. Hell is God's prison-house for those who will not accept his clemency.

Tolkien's idea of final judgment toward damnation is not concerned with good deeds or with whether the ends justify the means. A wicked soul may exhibit admirable traits—may even bring about good in the world—but this gains it no credit. Repentance or rigidity in wickedness are ultimately matters of the heart. Tolkien is concerned only with the orientation of the individual soul toward evil or God.[147] This orientation becomes fixed through deliberate choice of will, although persistent wickedness can weaken the will's ability to resist evil to such an extent that it loses the choice completely. Gollum, for instance, could not have resisted the Ring at the end, but this was only because he had not strengthened his will to do so at the beginning, so many years ago. Now, having succumbed to temptation so many times, he falls over the horizon, so to speak, and is lost.[148]

This *akrasia* (weakness of will) is the final state of the wicked. A soul in hell may undergo a sort of fixity of desire, which, without repentance, transforms a person from a grumbler into a mere "grumble" (or some other sin), going on forever and ever like a machine.[149] The unclean desire may be completely unattainable for the soul in its present state, the enjoyment lost, and yet the soul will never remove its attention from it, even for a moment, even to care for itself. Like a zombie clawing at prey through a glass window until its fingers wear away, the damned soul is so consumed that it remains in impotent and unfulfilled desire forever.[150] This is one of the chief pains of hell in Tolkien's *Beowulf*—the damned soul thrusts himself down into the fire forever, with no hope for comfort or change of circumstance.[151] This may be why the Bible (and Tolkien) can also refer to hell as the eternal death[152] or the everlasting darkness.[153]

Tolkien clearly associates hell with the idea of imprisonment and duress.[154] Not only Angband but also Mandos are called prisons for the wicked.[155] The demonic spirits held in prison until the end echo Jude 1:6. When Morgoth is cast down "like thunder" from his throne and lies sprawled upon the floor of hell, we hear an echo of Luke 10:18. But in this he differs from the church: the prisons (all but one) are ruled by Morgoth, Sauron, or some other maleficent entity. Satan, however, does not *rule* hell; it is *his* prison.

These, though, are evidences of Middle-earth's pagan milieu; there is no trace of Satan's rulership in Tolkien's nonfictional works. Indeed, as far as Middle-earth goes, hell is always a physical place, located far in the North and guarded by intimidating gates and (at one point) a deadly wolf.[156] Here is evidence of Tolkien's collocation of various mythological and Christian symbols. A blasted volcanic wasteland in the North calls to mind northern entrances to heathen hells, such as Hekla or the Dimmuborgir, and Carcharoth is clearly a form of Garmr.[157] At the same time, Tolkien is familiar with the distinctive Anglo-Saxon Christian image of the "Hell Mouth." "Hell" is, as he points out, a native Anglo-Saxon word, mixing images of torment with a general hidden realm of death.[158] The various concrete hells such as Angband, Mandos, Utumno, and so forth perhaps echo the sometimes confusing interchangeability of such mythological realms as Hel, Niflhel, and Niflheim.[159]

Tolkien's reading of the *Beowulf*-poet only seems to predicate hell of specially evil individuals—perjurers, murderers, and other malicious villains.[160] How far does this also represent Tolkien's own view? There is no direct published statement to answer this question, but the tenor of Tolkien's thought suggests he is basically optimistic about the fate of all but the most pernicious souls.

PURGATORY

As a Roman Catholic, Tolkien affirms not only heaven and hell but a transitional state of purification in which the soul destined for heaven undergoes preparation for the life of blessedness. This is *purgatory*. He does not address purgatory at length outside of his fiction, but it appears in major ways within it. Tolkien waffles between describing the hobbits' journey from the Grey Havens as a symbol of death or as a transition to a time of healing.[161] Purgatory, of course, combines both of these ideas. Though a place beyond death, it is not a final destination. Tolkien explicitly affirms purgatory even in his earlier fiction[162] and also directly describes "Leaf by Niggle" as a purgatorial story.[163]

"Niggle" is the most detailed account of Tolkien's views on the subject and deserves extended treatment.[164] If "Niggle" is to be trusted here, there seem to be two stages to Tolkien's purgatory: what we might call "the Workhouse" and "the Parish." Neither is a place of torture, and both are fundamentally salubrious, but the former focuses on purification while the latter involves practice in virtue.

When Niggle is discovered not to have any "luggage" (spiritual virtues), he is sent to the Workhouse.[165] He works hard with his hands at simple tasks, takes bitter medicine, and receives no social companionship. At this stage, he is kept in the dark to aid introspection. The windows all look "inwards," symbolizing both self-reflection and the cloister.[166] This process may take hundreds of years, or at least seem so.[167] Niggle dwells at first on the mistakes of his past. But he is weaned from worldly and fleeting pleasures and fed on the bread of satisfaction and diligence. He, who could never focus on his work, finds himself becoming the master of his time; he is able to properly order his tasks, devoting the right amount of effort to the right projects. He loses a sense of rush and gains a sense of quietude.[168] He lives in a little cell full of sunshine.[169] The picture here, evoked by the word "cell," is again one of monastic asceticism: discipline, self-denial, spiritual purity, and wholesomeness. Niggle continues to take Communion.[170]

During the discussion between the Father and Son (the Board of Inquiry from chapter 1), we see that Niggle had a rightly oriented love but did not exercise it. That is, though he is "saved," he has wasted his life.[171] After the reckoning of Niggle's deeds, he is judged ready to move on because it is evident he has become other-centered rather than self-absorbed. He transitions from the Workhouse stage to the Parish stage. This second stage functions less as a place of correction and more as a place for healing and fulfillment.[172] Progress seems not to be guaranteed, and Tolkien holds out the possibility that a soul might even *regress* into the Workhouse stage again.[173] Here, Niggle is granted the reward for his labor: his own Tree, perfected, finished, and real.[174] All his labor is here manifest in its true beauty. But he also sees that he has not labored alone. His irritating neighbor Parish (the indirect cause of Niggle's death) had a hand in his Tree as well.[175]

"Niggle's Parish" (as it comes to be called) is not heaven. God is not there, and while the place is pure and good, with no stain of sin, it is not complete. The task to which God has allotted Niggle as a sub-creator, as a human, cannot now be fundamentally altered after death, nor by God's grace does this realized work contain any flaw, but Niggle still has purgatorial work to do, finishing out the assigned labor of his life. His work is at the same time fixed, sanctified, but incomplete. He needs Parish's help to finish it.[176]

Niggle also apparently plays a role in moving Parish out of the Workhouse stage, though this is a grace and probably for Niggle's benefit.[177] The intercessions of the saint Niggle and perhaps Parish's family on earth shorten his stay in the unpleasant part of purgatory. Anybody familiar with Dante's *Purgatorio* or with medieval church history knows that the prayers of the living have great power to help those in purgatory. Notably, in this second stage, the soul begins to realize the good of community. Tolkien is perhaps unique among thinkers on purgatory in having the pilgrim souls help in sanctifying one another. The Workhouse is a solitary place, but the Parish requires cooperation and complementarity.[178] Each begins to fill up the virtues they once lacked. Niggle learns discipline; Parish learns to appreciate beauty.[179] They have not yet reached the perfection of heaven: they still argue and grow tired. They take nourishment from the theologically symbolic "Spring" at the heart of the realm.[180] Interestingly, even this stand-in for the spiritual life that flows from Christ takes its form from Niggle's imagination. Eventually, Niggle is prepared to enter into heaven ("the Mountains") and the presence of Christ ("the shepherd").[181]

Tolkien holds out hope that, like Niggle's Parish, God might in his mercy give Tolkien's incompletely imagined and rudimentary world a corrected reality.[182] It is a hope that many of Tolkien's readers likely share, and he seems also to have been aware of this. Niggle's Parish, the art that stands in for Tolkien's own, proves very useful as a convalescent home, holiday, or refreshment. It is for many the best introduction to the Mountains—that is, the fantasy world provides the most effective avenue to introduce people to the truth of eternity.[183]

HEAVEN

Tolkien has much more to say about the Mountains than either previous destination. In heaven, the good unfinished, the stories unwritten, and the hopes unfulfilled all find their completion.[184] Here we find a great host of blessed spirits[185] alongside Mary the queen of heaven.[186] One must, however, distinguish between heaven (the place on another plane of existence where God has his throne) and the final unity of heaven and earth depicted at the end of Revelation. Even in its earliest phases, the heaven of Middle-earth is not a place within the world; Valinor is not heaven but Eden. Heaven exists in the timeless halls of Eru beyond the stars.[187] But "glimpses" (a recurrent word) of heaven do exist. Tolkien remarks that Niggle, even while on earth, had some taste of heaven that worked its way into his art, though its true nature is only revealed to those that come there.[188]

Tolkien's Men are ineluctably drawn beyond the world to a contentment unknown (the presence of God).[189] He echoes Augustine, who professes that the human heart is restless until it finds its rest in God. Every human heart thirsts for perfect beauty but can never find it.[190] The human heart is *made* for paradise and only gets brief glimpses of its proper blessedness in this life.[191] The visual terminology here is purposeful, since in heaven the saints and angels enjoy the beatific vision of God: the infinite and infinitely joyful contemplation of God's glory, beauty, and holiness. Their faces become themselves radiant in this contemplation, and this special loveliness of reflected beauty is the final purpose of human existence.[192]

Such a description reinforces the Christian belief that the state of the human being in eternity is a specifically *embodied* one.[193] But Tolkien clearly conforms his thought to 1 Corinthians 15 when he writes that redeemed Man will have a form both like and unlike the fallen one we know.[194] Humans may have bodies, but they are spiritual bodies. Likewise, the body of the resurrected Christ was both similar and dissimilar to a normal body. He models Elvish resurrection directly upon 1 Corinthians 15 and the risen Jesus.[195] Matter is taken up into spirit by passing into knowledge and so becomes timeless and under the spirit's full control. So while resurrected bodies are in a sense incorporeal, they also manifest in the physical world. It can pass physical barriers or vanish, but also be touched. Its spatial position is controlled by its will.[196]

GLIMPSES OF HEAVEN IN *PEARL*

In the introductory essay to his translation of *Pearl*, Tolkien briefly addresses the way in which citizens of heaven are thus more alive than those of earth.[197] In this poem, a father meets his deceased daughter in a vision of heaven. Tolkien's comments focus on the contrast between the narrator and his daughter. The girl, as a glorified and perfected saint, casts the light of her clear intelligence upon her earthly-minded father and chastises him with the unyielding words of truth. Her desire is cleansed of all ungodly affections; she is filled with the spirit of heavenly charity and only desires his eternal good. She refuses him the comfort of pity or the indulgence of a reunion that pretends the death that separates them has no significance. But, rather than mourn, the maiden reminds her father of theological truth: she is redeemed, saved, a queen in heaven and part of the holy host of the 144,000 that follow the Lamb, Jesus Christ. She will not return to earth, but, by resigning himself to the will of God, he can join her in glory.[198]

REVELATION AND THE REIGN OF ARAGORN

Tolkien also offers a picture of the new heavens and the new earth in his own poetry and prose. He is in fact at his most eschatological (and biblical) when he writes of an Eagle that sings a hymn over the rescued city of Minas Tirith. It is here quoted in full, with biblical allusions footnoted:

> And the Shadow departed, and the Sun was unveiled, and light leaped forth[199]; and the waters of Anduin shone like silver,[200] and in all the houses of the City men sang for the joy that welled up in their hearts from what source they could not tell.[201] And before the Sun had fallen far from the noon out of the East there came a great Eagle flying, and he bore tidings[202] beyond hope from the Lords of the West,[203] crying: Sing now, ye people of the Tower of Anor, for the Realm of Sauron is ended for ever,[204] and the Dark Tower is thrown down.[205] Sing and rejoice, ye people of the Tower of Guard, for your watch hath not been in vain,[206] and the Black Gate is broken,[207] and your King hath passed through, and he is victorious.[208] Sing and be glad, all ye children of the West, for your King shall come again,[209] and he shall dwell among you all the days of your life.[210] And the Tree that was withered shall be renewed, and he shall plant it in the high places,[211] and the City shall be blessed. Sing all ye people![212]

Every clause of this beautiful hymn is rich with meaning, and it might be sung as part of the liturgy of any Christian church at Eastertide. It is Tolkien's own picture of the heavenly Jerusalem. Minas Tirith under the reign of the christotypical king Aragorn is a foreshadowing of Christ's rule over the city which is the unity of heaven and earth. Aragorn's coronation is explicitly blessed by the angelic Gandalf and tied to the reign of the heavenly powers. Once crowned, he rises in a new majesty: "Tall as the sea-kings of old, he stood above all that were near; *ancient of days* he seemed and yet in the flower of manhood; and wisdom sat upon his brow, and strength and healing were in his hands, and a light was about him. And then Faramir cried: 'Behold the King!' "[213] Most notable here is the phrase "ancient of days," an unusual name lifted directly from the messianic Daniel 7:9–10. Outside the walls of the holy city, the Shire's year of plenty in 1420 also foreshadows the abundance of heaven.[214]

The typologically heavenly denouement of *The Lord of the Rings* highlights Tolkien's focus on the transience of earthly life. Some things are truly gone and will not return. One cannot pretend that evil has never happened.[215] But there is also a way in which, in a memorable phrase, everything sad comes untrue.[216] Sadness is transubstantiated into joy.[217] Not all tears are evil, says Gandalf, and it is possible to be filled with a sadness blessed without bitterness.[218]

HEAVEN AS FINAL EUCATASTROPHE

And so we return to Tolkien's brilliant neologism "eucatastrophe": the sudden turn that brings a piercing joy.[219] This happens because, as we noted in chapter 1, it is a glimpse of ultimate truth. Our nature chained in the materialistic cause and effect ending in biological death feels a sudden relief upon its perception that this happy ending is the way the world really works. Our nature is made for it.[220] The joy of heaven is therefore not an epicurean hedonism or a staid formalism. Christian joy produces tears because it comes from the moments when joy and sorrow are united and reconciled.[221] The Eucharist, for example, is the central foretaste of heaven here on earth, and it is inseparably bound with death.[222] But it is also the guarantee of resurrection. The joy of heaven is an imprint of the joy of the resurrected Christ. The beatific vision above seems for Tolkien to be specifically the vision of the Crucified One, God in his supreme union of love and suffering. Heaven is not an escape from sorrow but sorrow's *redemption*.

In heaven we look from the mirrored truth of the physical creation to the truth itself, and this transforms not just creation but our creativity as well. Salvation does not change or destroy nature, but completes and corrects it. Evil does not exist in God's design, so when our crooked natures are set straight and we are able to continue our natural drive toward making art, we will do so faultlessly and in full accord with God's infinite variety.[223]

CONCLUSION

After addressing the tension between viewing death as gift or curse, we touched on the end of the world as a catastrophe leading to recreation, in which the original unmarred design will be lifted up into an even greater beauty by the marring of sin and its redemption. Tolkien is hesitant to ascribe an explicit or certain hope of eternal life to those before Christ but allows them some faith in the character of God. Tolkien has a doctrine of final judgment in which other human beings can affect their fellows' sentence. He affirms the punishment of the damned—whoever they may be—in a hell of their own making. His allegorical "Leaf by Niggle" narrativizes his views on purgatory as both hospital and training ground. Finally, Tolkien strongly affirms a bodily existence in heaven for eternity, in which all hopes are fulfilled.

As is fitting for the father of fantasy, Tolkien's heaven revisits his signature doctrine of sub-creation and finds in heaven a place where our art, the expression of our deepest desires, can partake of reality.

FURTHER READING

This particular locus gathers many of Tolkien's major themes and unique contributions, including eucatastrophe, hope, and death. As such, aside from the resources listed below, readers will find that virtually any thematic or survey treatment of Tolkien's thought will (or should) touch upon these areas to some extent.

Birzer, Bradley J. "The 'Last Battle' as a Johannine Ragnarök: Tolkien and the Universal." In *The Ring and the Cross: Christianity and "The Lord of the Rings,"* edited by Paul E. Kerry, 259–82. Madison: Fairleigh Dickinson University Press, 2011.

Devaux, Michaël, assisted by Christopher Tolkien and Carl F. Hostetter, ed. "Fragments on Elvish Reincarnation." In *J. R. R. Tolkien, L'effigie des Elfes,* edited by Michaël Devaux, 94–161. Paris: Bragelonne, 2014.

Greenwood, Linda. "Love: 'The Gift of Death.' " *Tolkien Studies* 2 (2005): 171–95.

Helen, Daniel, ed. *Death and Immortality in Middle-earth.* Edinburgh: Luna Press, 2017.

McBride, Sam. "Death" and "Eucatastrophe, Estel, and the End of Arda." In *Tolkien's Cosmology: Divine Beings and Middle-earth.* Kent, OH: Kent State University Press, 2020.

Nelson, Charles W. "'The Halls of Waiting': Death and Afterlife in Middle-earth." *Journal of the Fantastic in the Arts* 9, no. 3 (1998): 200–211.

Ordway, Holly. "'Further Up and Further In': Representations of Heaven in Tolkien and Lewis." *Journal of Inklings Studies* 3, no. 1 (2013): 5–23.

Purtill, Richard. "The Sudden Joyous Turn." In *J. R. R. Tolkien: Myth, Morality, and Religion,* 129–54. New York: Harper & Row, 1984.

Testi, Claudio. "Logic and Theology in Tolkien's Thanatology." In *The Broken Scythe: Death and Immortality in the Work of J. R. R. Tolkien,* edited by Roberto Arduino and Claudio Testi, 175–92. Zurich and Jena: Walking Tree Press, 2012.

Thayer, Anna. *On Eagle's Wings: An Exploration of Eucatastrophe in Tolkien's Fantasy.* Edinburgh: Luna Press, 2016.

Whittingham, Elizabeth A. *In The Evolution of Tolkien's Mythology: A Study of the History of Middle-earth,* 123–200. London: McFarland, 2007.

Wood, Ralph C. "Consummation: When Middle-earth Shall Be Unmarred." In *The Gospel according to Tolkien: Visions of the Kingdom in Middle-earth,* 156–65. Louisville: Westminster John Knox, 2003.

GLOSSARY OF NAMES AND TERMS FROM TOLKIEN'S FICTION

This glossary does not include characters, places, or other names from *The Lord of the Rings* or *The Hobbit*, which it must be assumed are already familiar to any reader of this volume. If the spelling of a name changed through various stages of writing, the final spelling occurs first and the earlier spelling second.

Ainulindalë	The first part of *The Silmarillion*; the name of Tolkien's creation myth.
Ainu(r)	Generic term for angels.
Akallabêth	The section of *The Silmarillion* recounting the fall of Númenor.
Aman	The blessed land, the paradise in the West, of which Valinor is a part.
Andreth	A wise woman, one of the main characters in the philosophical tale "The Debate of Finrod and Andreth."
Angband	The hell-like fortress of Tolkien's Satan figure Morgoth.
Aotrou and Itroun	A husband and wife, two characters in Tolkien's eponymous story.

Arda	The earth; sometimes, the solar system.
Ar-Pharazôn	Last king of Númenor who rebelled against the Valar.
Aulë	Vala associated with craftsmanship.
Beleriand	The westernmost region of Middle-earth, later flooded.
Beren	A Man who loved the Elf princess Lúthien and with her won back a Silmaril from Morgoth.
Carcharoth	A fierce wolf who guarded the gates of Angband.
Eä	The universe.
Eärendil	A great mariner who sailed to Valinor to appeal to the Valar for help against Morgoth, now gifted with a Silmaril and sailing the heavens.
Edain	The early tribes of Men who allied with the Elves against Morgoth.
Elbereth	"Star-Queen"; another name for Varda.
Eldar	The Elves.
Eönwë/Fiönwë	Herald of the Valar.
Eriol	In the earliest versions of Tolkien's writings, a human who met Elves and transmitted their stories.
Eru	God.
Estel	Hope, trust, religious faith.
fëa(r)	Elvish term for the soul or spirit.
Fëanor	Greatest artist of the Elves, maker of the Silmarils, rebel against the Valar.
Finrod	An Elf who first discovered Men and had a special relationship with them.
Finwë	One of the Kings of the Noldor, an Elven tribe.
Fíriel	A Númenorean woman, author of "Fíriel's Song."

First Age	The age of the world spanning from its creation to the defeat of Morgoth; an unknown span of time.
Glaurung	A dragon; foe of Túrin.
hröa(r)	Elvish term for the physical body.
Húrin	A human hero captured and tortured by Morgoth; father of Túrin.
Ilúvatar	A name of God meaning "All-Father."
Istari	Wizards.
Legendarium	A term designating the stories and material relating to Tolkien's fictional mythology of the world of Middle-earth.
Lindo	An Elf; Eriol's host.
Lúthien	Elven lover of Beren who with him reclaimed a Silmaril.
Maia(r)	Lesser angelic spirits.
Mandos	Vala of death and fate.
Manwë	King of the Valar and therefore of the world; vice-regent of God.
Melian	A Maia, mother of Lúthien.
Melkor	Original name of Morgoth.
Míriel	First wife of Finwë; her refusal to be reincarnated led to a dispute among the Valar.
Morgoth	The Vala who turned to evil; Satan.
The Music of the Ainur	English translation of *ainulindalë*; the song by which God and the angels make the world and its history.

Nienna	Valië of pity and grief.
Niggle	An erstwhile painter; protagonist of the story "Leaf by Niggle," not part of the legendarium.
Noldor	The largest of the three tribes of Elves, specially gifted with all kinds of crafts, and eventually self-exiled from Valinor.
Númenor	An island kingdom gifted to Men for their service against Morgoth, later corrupted and destroyed.
Olórin	Gandalf's angelic name.
The One	A name for God.
Ósanwe-kenta	A short essay on Elvish telepathy.
oré	Elvish word meaning heart, in the metaphorical sense.
Quenya/Qenya	Name of one of Tolkien's Elvish languages.
Radagast	The Brown Wizard, concerned with the flora and fauna of Middle-earth.
Sauron	Former lieutenant of Morgoth who rises to take his place, primary villain of *The Lord of the Rings*.
Second Age	The age of the world spanning from roughly the founding of Númenor to the first defeat of Sauron; about 3,400 years.
Silmaril	Any of three holy gems made by Fëanor, in which the untainted light of the Two Trees still existed.
Teleri	One of the three tribes of Elves; associated with the sea.

Third Age	The age of the world spanning from the first defeat of Sauron to the destruction of the One Ring; about three thousand years.
Tulkas	Vala of strength and battle.
Túrin Turambar	A hapless human who fights against the curse of his fate, hero of *The Children of Húrin.*
Two Trees	Trees, one gold and one silver, that shone with a pure and holy light, whence the lesser light of the Sun and Moon derive; destroyed by Morgoth and Ungoliant, their light now lives only in the Silmarils.
Undying Lands	See Aman.
Ungoliant	Primeval spider demon; mother of Shelob.
Unseen Realm	The invisible spiritual world.
Ulmo	Vala of water.
Utumno	First hell-like fortress of Morgoth.
Vala(r)	The angelic rulers of the world. Feminine "Valië/ Valier."
Valinor	Home of the Valar, an earthly paradise.
Vanyar	The holiest of the three tribes of Elves.
Varda	Wife of Manwë and Queen of the Valar; kindler of the stars.
Yavanna	Valië of the earth; wife of Aulë.

BIBLIOGRAPHY

TOLKIEN SOURCES

"*Ae Adar Nín*: The Lord's Prayer in Sindarin." *Vinyar Tengwar* 44 (June 2002): 21–30.

"*Alcar mi Tarmenel na Erun*: The *Gloria in Excelsis Deo* in Quenya." *Vinyar Tengwar* 44 (June 2002): 31–38.

Beowulf: A Translation and Commentary together with Sellic Spell. Edited by Christopher Tolkien. Boston: Houghton Mifflin, 2014.

Bodleian Library, Tolkien A 18/1, f. 1–17.

"The Book of Jonah." *Journal of Inklings Studies* 4, no. 2 (2014): 5–9.

The Book of Lost Tales, Part One. Edited by Christopher Tolkien. Boston: Houghton Mifflin, 1984.

The Book of Lost Tales, Part Two. Edited by Christopher Tolkien. Boston: Houghton Mifflin, 1984.

"On Dragons." In *The Hobbit: Facsimile Gift Set*, 1–40. London: HarperCollins, 2018.

"The Devil's Coach-Horses: Eaueres." *The Review of English Studies* 1, no. 3 (1925): 331–36.

Excerpt from Letter to Przemyslaw Mroczkowski, January 20–26, 1946. *Christie's Fine Printed Books and Manuscripts 1 June 2009.*

Excerpt from Letter to Przemyslaw Mroczkowski, 1958. Christie's Fine Printed Books and Manuscripts 1 June 2009.

The Fall of Arthur. Edited by Christopher Tolkien. Boston: Houghton Mifflin Harcourt, 2013.

"Fate and Free Will." Edited by Carl Hostetter. *Tolkien Studies* 6 (2009): 183–88.

The Fellowship of the Ring. Second edition, revised impression. Boston: Houghton Mifflin,1987.

Finn and Hengest: The Fragment and the Episode. New York: HarperCollins, 1998.

The Hobbit. 75th Anniversary edition. New York: Mariner, 2012.

Interview with Denys Gueroult. BBC interview, January 20, 1965.

"Late Notes on Verb Structure." *Parma Eldalamberon* 22 (2015): 141–68.

The Lay of Aotrou and Itroun together with the Corrigan Poems. Edited by Verlyn Flieger. London: HarperCollins, 2016.

The Lays of Beleriand. Edited by Christopher Tolkien. Boston: Houghton Mifflin, 1985.

The Legend of Sigurd and Gudrún. Edited by Christopher Tolkien. Boston: Houghton Mifflin Harcourt, 2009.

Letters from Father Christmas. Edited by Baillie Tolkien. London: HarperCollins, 2015.

The Letters of J. R. R. Tolkien. Edited by Humphrey Carpenter with the assistance of Christopher Tolkien. Boston: Houghton Mifflin, 1981.

Letter to Clyde S. Kilby, ca. July 1966. J. R. R. Tolkien Letter collection, L-Kilby 4, The Marion E. Wade Center, Wheaton College, Wheaton, IL.

Letter to Michael George Tolkien, April 24, 1957. British Library, MS Add. 71657.

Letter to Nevill Coghill, August 21, 1954. Published by Wayne G. Hammond and Christina Scull. "Tom Bombadil Addenda & Corrigenda." Dated December 30, 2014. https://wayneandchristina.wordpress.com/2014/12/30/tom-bombadil-addenda-corrigenda/.

Letter to John Roberts (22 August 19–5). Sale 16204 - Printed Books,
     Maps, Manuscripts and Photogra–hs, 4 Nov 2008 - Lot
     430. Accessed May 20, 2011. http://www.bonhams.com/eur/
     auction/16204/lot/430/.

The Lost Road and Other Writings. Edited by Christopher Tolkien. Boston:
     Houghton Mifflin, 1987.

The Monsters and the Critics and Other Essays. Boston: Houghton Mifflin,
     1984.

Morgoth's Ring. Edited by Christopher Tolkien. Boston: Houghton Mifflin,
     1993.

"The Name 'Nodens.' " *Tolkien Studies* 4 (2007): 177–83.

"Notes on Óre." *Vinyar Tengwar* 41 (July 2000): 11–19.

"Ósanwe-kenta: 'Enquiry into the Communication of Thought.' " *Vinyar
     Tengwar* 39 (July 1998): 21–34.

The Peoples of Middle-earth. Edited by Christopher Tolkien. Boston:
     Houghton Mifflin, 1996.

"Philology: General Works." In *The Year's Work in English Studies, vol.* 4,
     32–66. London: Oxford University Press, 1927.

"Qenya Lexicon." *Parma Eldalamberon* 12 (2011).

The Return of the King. Second edition, revised impression. Boston:
     Houghton Mifflin, 1987.

The Return of the Shadow. Edited by Christopher Tolkien. Boston:
     Houghton Mifflin, 1988.

Sauron Defeated. Edited by Christopher Tolkien. Boston: Houghton
     Mifflin, 1992.

A Secret Vice: Tolkien on Invented Languages. New York: HarperCollins,
     2016.

The Shaping of Middle-earth. Edited by Christopher Tolkien. Boston
     Houghton Mifflin, 1986.

The Silmarillion. Edited by Christopher Tolkien. Boston: Houghton Mifflin, 1977.

Smith of Wootton Major: Extended edition. Edited by Verlyn Flieger. London: HarperCollins, 2005.

The Story of Kullervo. Edited by Verlyn Flieger. Boston: Houghton Mifflin Harcourt, 2016.

"Tolkien in Oxford." BBC2 Archival interview. Original broadcast March 30, 1968. https://www.bbc.co.uk/archive/release--jrr-tolkien/znd36v4.

Tolkien On Fairy-stories. Extended edition. Edited by Verlyn Flieger and Douglas A. Anderson. London: HarperCollins, 2008.

"Tolkien on Tolkien." *Diplomat* 18 (October 1966):197.

The Tolkien Reader. New York: Ballantine, 1975.

The Treason of Isengard. Edited by Christopher Tolkien. Boston: Houghton Mifflin, 1989.

Tree and Leaf, including the Poem Mythopoeia [and] The Homecoming of Beorhtnoth Beorhthelm's Son. London: HarperCollins, 2001.

The Two Towers. Second edition, revised impression. Boston: Houghton Mifflin, 1987.

Unfinished Tales of Númenor and Middle-earth. Edited by Christopher Tolkien. Boston: Houghton Mifflin, 1980.

The War of the Jewels. Edited by Christopher Tolkien. Boston: Houghton Mifflin, 1994.

The War of the Ring. Edited by Christopher Tolkien. Boston: Houghton Mifflin, 1990.

"'Words of Joy': Five Catholic Prayers in Quenya." *Vinyar Tengwar* 43 (January 2002): 5–38.

"'Words of Joy': Five Catholic Prayers in Quenya, Part Two." *Vinyar Tengwar* 44 (June 2002): 5–20.

"Words, Phrases and Passages in Various Tongues in *The Lord of the Rings*." Edited by Christopher Gilson. *Parma Eldalamberon* 17 (2007): 178–79.

SECONDARY SOURCES

Abelard, Peter. *Exposition on the Lord's Prayer*.

"A Dialogue: Discussion by Humphrey Carpenter, Professor George Sayer, and Dr. Clyde S. Kilby, Recorded September 29, 1979, Wheaton, Illinois." *Minas Tirith Evening-Star* 9, no. 2 (January 1980): 16–17.

Agøy, Nils Ivar. "Quid Hinieldus cum Christo? New Perspectives on Tolkien's Theological Dilemma and His Sub-Creation Theory." *Mythlore* 21, no. 2 (1996): 31–38.

Aquinas, Thomas. *Summa Theologica*.

Arendt, Hannah. *Eichmann in Jerusalem: A Report on the Banality of Evil*. New York: Penguin, 2006.

Arthur, Sarah. *Walking with Bilbo: A Devotional Journey through "The Hobbit."* Wheaton: Tyndale House, 2005.

———. *Walking with Frodo: A Devotional Journey through "The Lord of the Rings."* Wheaton: Tyndale House, 2003.

Ateş, Ahmet Mesut. "J. R. R. Tolkien's 'Leaf by Niggle': A Fantastic Journey to Afterlife." *Mallorn* 56 (Winter 2015): 19–21.

Augustine. *De Trinitate*.

———. *Enchiridion*.

Bassham, Gregory, and Eric Bronson, eds. *"The Lord of the Rings" and Philosophy: One Book to Rule Them All*. Chicago: Open Court, 2003.

Bates, Matthew. *Salvation by Allegiance Alone: Rethinking Faith, Works, and the Gospel of Jesus the King*. Grand Rapids: Baker, 2017.

Beal, Jane. "Tolkien, Eucatastrophe, and the Re-Creation of Medieval Legend." *Journal of Tolkien Research* 4, no. 1 (2017): Article 8.

Bergen, Richard Angelo. "'A Warp of Horror' J. R. R. Tolkien's Sub-creation of Evil." *Mythlore* 36, no. 1 (2017): 103–21.

Bernthal, Craig. *Tolkien's Sacramental Vision: Discerning the Holy in Middle-earth.* Lechlade, UK: Second Spring, 2014.

Bertoglio, Chiara. "Dissonant Harmonies: Tolkien's Musical Theodicy." *Tolkien Studies* 15 (2018): 93–114.

Birzer, Bradley. *J. R. R. Tolkien's Sanctifying Myth: Understanding Middle-earth.* Wilmington, DE: Intercollegiate Studies Institute, 2002.

Bossert, A. R. "'Surely You Don't Disbelieve': Tolkien and Pius X; Anti-Modernism in Middle-earth." *Mythlore* 25, no. 1 (2006): 53–76.

Boyd, Craig A. "Augustine, Aquinas, and Tolkien: Three Catholic Views on *Curiositas.*" *Heythrop Journal* 61 (2020): 222–33.

———. "Nolo Heroizari: Tolkien and Aquinas on the Humble Journey of Master Samwise." *Christianity & Literature* 68, no. 4 (2019): 605–22.

———. "The Thomistic Virtue of Hope in Tolkien's 'Leaf by Niggle.'" *Christian Scholar's Review* 48, no. 2 (2019): 131–46.

Caldecott, Stratford. *The Power of the Ring: The Spiritual Vision Behind "The Lord of the Rings" and "The Hobbit."* New York: Crossroad, 2003.

Carpenter, Humphrey. *The Inklings: C. S. Lewis, J. R. R. Tolkien, Charles Williams, and Their Friends.* Boston: Houghton Mifflin, 1979.

———. *J. R. R. Tolkien: A Biography.* Boston: Houghton Mifflin Harcourt, 2014.

Carswell, John. "All Tales May Come True: Tolkien's Creative Mysticism." *Mallorn* 58 (2017): 10–13.

Castell, Daphne. "The Realms of Tolkien." *New Worlds* 50, no. 168 (November 1966): 143–54.

Chance, Jane, ed. *Tolkien and the Invention of Myth: A Reader.* Lexington, KY: University of Kentucky, 2004.

———. *Tolkien, Self, and Other: "This Queer Creature."* New York: Springer, 2016.

———, ed. *Tolkien the Medievalist.* New York: Routledge, 2003.

———. *Tolkien's Art: A Mythology for England.* Revised edition. Lexington, KY: University of Kentucky Press, 2001.

Chant, Joy. "Niggle and Numenor." *Mallorn* 11 (1977): 4–11.

Chapman, Vera. "The Religion of a Hobbit." *Mallorn* 3 (1971): 15–16.

Chausse, Jean. "Icons of Jesus Christ in *The Lord of the Rings.*" *Mallorn* 39 (2001): 30–32.

———. "The Healing of Théoden or 'A Glimpse of the Final Victory.' " *Mallorn* 59 (2018): 49–51.

Chesterton, G. K. *Orthodoxy.* London: John Lane, 1908.

Chisholm, Chad. "Demons, Choices, and Grace in *The Lord of the Rings.*" *Mallorn* 45 (2008): 20–23.

Christopher, Joe. "The Moral Epiphanies in *The Lord of the Rings.*" *Mallorn* 33 (1995): 121–25.

Clark, Craig. "Problems of Good and Evil in Tolkien's *The Lord of the Rings.*" *Mallorn* 35 (1997): 15–19.

Clark, George, and Daniel Timmons, eds. *J. R. R. Tolkien and His Literary Resonances: Views of Middle-earth.* London: Greenwood Press, 2000.

Cook, Irene Tolkien. "Letter to the editor." *Amon Hen* 162 (March 2000): 24–25.

Cook, Simon J. "Fantasy Incarnate: Of Elves and Men." *Journal of Tolkien Research* 3, no. 1 (2016): Article 1.

Costabile, Giovanni. "Stolen Pears, Unripe Apples: The Misuse of Fruits as a Symbol of Original Sin in Tolkien's 'The New Shadow' and Augustine of Hippo's *Confessions.*" *Tolkien Studies* 14 (2017): 163–67.

Cox, John. "Tolkien's Platonic Fantasy." *VII: Journal of the Marion E. Wade Center* 5 (1984): 53–69.

Croft, Janet Brennan, and Leslie Donovan, eds. *Perilous and Fair: Women in the Works and Life of J. R. R. Tolkien*. Altadena, CA: Mythopoeic Press, 2015.

Curry, Patrick. *Defending Middle-earth: Tolkien: Myth and Modernity*. New York: Houghton Mifflin, 2004.

Dawson, Christopher. *Progress and Religion*. Washington, DC: Catholic University of America Press, 2001.

De Armas, Frederick A. "Gyges' Ring: Invisibility in Plato, Tolkien and Lope de Vega." *Journal of the Fantastic in the Arts* 3, no. 3/4 (1994): 120–38.

de Beauvoir, Simone. *A Very Easy Death*. New York: Penguin, 1990.

Devaux, Michaël. "Les anges de l'Ombre chez Tolkien: chair, corps, et corruption." In *Les Racines du Légendaire (La Feuille de la Compagnie no. 2)*, edited by Michaël Deveaux, 191–245. Geneva: Ad Solem, 2003.

Devaux, Michaël, assisted by Christopher Tolkien and Carl F. Hostetter, ed. "Fragments on Elvish Reincarnation." In *J. R. R. Tolkien, l'effigie des Elfes*, edited by Michaël Devaux, 94–161. Paris: Bragelonne, 2014.

Devine, Celia. "Fertility and Grace in *The Lord of the Rings*." *Mallorn* 57 (2016): 10–11.

Dickerson, Matthew. *Following Gandalf: Epic Battles and Moral Victory in "The Lord of the Rings"*. Grand Rapids: Brazos, 2003

———. "Frodo and the Passion in J. R. R. Tolkien's *The Lord of the Rings*." In *Engaging the Passion: Perspectives on the Death of Jesus*, edited by Oliver Larry Yarbrough, 211–24. Minneapolis: Fortress Press, 2015.

———. *A Hobbit Journey: Discovering the Enchantment of J. R. R. Tolkien's Middle-earth*. Grand Rapids: Baker, 2012.

Dickerson, Matthew, and Jonathan Evans, eds. *Ents, Elves, and Eriador: The Environmental Vision of J. R. R. Tolkien.* Lexington, KY: The University Press of Kentucky, 2006.

Drout, Michael D. C., ed. *The J. R. R. Tolkien Encyclopedia: Scholarship and Critical Assessment.* New York: Routledge, 2007.

———. "J. R. R. Tolkien's Medieval Scholarship and Its Significance." *Tolkien Studies* 4 (2007): 113–76.

———. "Toward a Better Tolkien Criticism." In *Reading "The Lord of the Rings,"* edited by Robert Eaglestone, 15–28. New York: Bloomsbury, 2006.

Drout, Michael D. C., and Hilary Wynne. "Tom Shippey's *J. R. R. Tolkien: Author of the Century* and a Look Back at Tolkien Criticism since 1982." *Envoi* 9, no. 2 (Fall 2000): 101–67.

Duriez, Colin. *Bedeviled: Lewis, Tolkien and the Shadow of Evil.* Downers Grove, IL: InterVarsity Press, 2015.

Eaglestone, Robert, ed. *Reading "The Lord of the Rings."* New York: Bloomsbury, 2006.

Egan, Thomas. "Chesterton and Tolkien." *The Chesterton Review* 6, no. 1 (1979): 159–61

———. "Chesterton and Tolkien: The Road to Middle-Earth." *VII: Journal of the Marion E. Wade Center* 4 (1983): 45–53.

———. "Tolkien and Chesterton: Some Analogies." *Mythlore* 12, no. 1 (1985): 28–35.

Ekman, Stefan. "Echoes of *Pearl* in Arda's Landscape." *Tolkien Studies* 6 (2009): 59–70.

Elam, Michael David. "The 'Ainulindalë' and J. R. R. Tolkien's Beautiful Sorrow in Christian Tradition." *VII: Journal of the Marion E. Wade Center* 28 (2011): 61–78.

Ellison, John. "Images of Evil in Tolkien's World." *Mallorn* 38 (2001): 21–29.

Fernandez, Irène. "La vérité du mythe chez Tolkien: imagination & gnose." In *Les Racines du Légendaire (La Feuille de la Compagnie no. 2),* edited by Michaël Devaux, 247–72. Geneva: Ad Solem, 2003.

Ferrández Bru, José Manuel. *"Uncle Curro": J. R. R. Tolkien's Spanish Connection.* Edinburgh: Luna Press, 2018.

———."'Wingless Fluttering': Some Personal Connections in Tolkien's Formative Years." *Tolkien Studies* 8 (2011): 51–65.

Fimi, Dimitra. *Tolkien, Race, and Cultural History: From Fairies to Hobbits.* New York: Palgrave Macmillan, 2008.

Fisher, Jason. "Tolkien's Fortunate Fall and the Third Theme of Ilúvatar." In *Truths Breathed through Silver: The Inklings' Moral and Mythopoeic Legacy,* edited by Jonathan B. Himes, Salwa Khoddam, and Joe R. Christopher, 93–109. Newcastle: Cambridge Scholars Publishing, 2008.

Fisher, Jason, ed. *Tolkien and the Study of His Sources: Critical Essays.* London: McFarland, 2011.

Fisher, Matthew. "Saint Smith: Reading *Smith of Wootton Major* as a Saint's Life." *Orcrist* 9 (2017): 53–57.

Flieger, Verlyn. "The Arch and the Keystone." *Mythlore* 38, no. 1 (2019): 7–19.

———. "But What Did He Really Mean?" *Tolkien Studies* 11 (2014): 149–66.

———. "The Music and the Task: Fate and Free Will in Middle-earth." *Tolkien Studies* 6 (2009): 151–81.

———. *Splintered Light: Logos and Language in Tolkien's World.* Revised edition. Kent, OH: Kent State University Press, 2002.

———. "Whose Myth Is It?" In *Arda Special I: Between Faith and Fiction,* edited by Nils Ivar Agøy, 32–39. Uppsala, Sweden: Arda Society, 1998.

Flood, Alison. "JRR Tolkien Advised by WH Auden to Drop Romance." *Guardian* (online). February 11, 2014. https://www.theguardian. com/books/2014/feb/11/jrr-tolkien-advised-wh-auden-lord-of- the-rings.

Fontenot, Megan N. "The Art of Eternal Disaster: Tolkien's Apocalypse and the Road to Healing." *Tolkien Studies* 16 (2019): 91–109.

Fornet-Ponse, Thomas. "'Strange and Free'—On Some Aspects of the Nature of Elves and Men." *Tolkien* Studies 7 (2010): 67–89.

Fredrick, Candice and Sam McBride. "Battling the Woman Warrior: Females and Combat in Tolkien and Lewis." *Mythlore* 25, no. 3/4 (2007): 29–42.

———. "Women as Mythic Icons: Williams and Tolkien." In *Women among the Inklings: Gender, C. S. Lewis, J. R. R. Tolkien, and Charles Williams*, 29–54. Westport, CT: Greenwood Press, 2001.

Freeman, Austin M. "Celestial Spheres: Angelic Bodies and Hyperspace." *TheoLogica* 2, no. 2 (2018): 168–86.

———. "The Author of the Epic: Tolkien, Evolution, and God's Story." *Zygon* 56, no. 2 (2021): 500–16.

———. "Flesh, World, Devil: Evil in J. R. R. Tolkien." *Journal of Inklings Studies* 10, no. 2 (2020): 139–71.

———. "*Pietas* and the Fall of the City: A Neglected Virgilian Influence on Middle-earth's Chief Virtue." In *Tolkien and the Classical World*, edited by Hamish Williams, 131–63. Zollikofen, Switzerland: Walking Tree Press, 2020.

———. "Critiquing Tolkien's Theology: Three Bad Arguments and Three Good Ones." In *Theology and Tolkien*, edited by Douglas Estes. Minneapolis: Lexington Books, forthcoming.

Friedman, John Block. *Orpheus in the Middle Ages*. Syracuse, NY: Syracuse University Press, 2001.

Fry, Carrol. "'Two Musics about the Throne of Ilúvatar': Gnostic and Manichaean Dualism in *The Silmarillion*." *Tolkien Studies* 12, no. 1 (2015): 77–93.

Gallant, Richard Z. "Original Sin in Heorot and Valinor." *Tolkien Studies* 11 (2014): 109–29.

Garbowski, Christopher. "Eucatastrophe and the 'Gift of Ilúvatar' in Middle-earth." *Mallorn* 35 (1997): 25–32.

———. "Tolkien's Middle-earth and the Catholic Imagination." *Mallorn* 41 (2003): 9–12.

Garde, Judith N. *Old English Poetry in Medieval Christian Perspective: A Doctrinal Approach*. Cambridge: Boydell & Brewer, 1991.

Garnett, Irene. "From Genesis to Revelation in Middle-earth." *Mallorn* 22 (1985): 39.

Garrido, Gerardo Barajas. "Perspectives on Reality in *The Lord of the Rings*." *Mallorn* 42 (2004): 51–59.

———. "Perspectives on Reality in *The Lord of the Rings*: Part II—Nature, Beauty, and Death." *Mallorn* 43 (2005): 53–59.

Garth, John. *Tolkien and the Great War: The Threshold of Middle-earth*. Boston: Houghton Mifflin, 2013.

Greene, Deirdre. "Higher Argument: Tolkien and the Tradition of Vision, Epic and Prophecy." *Mallorn* 33 (1995): 45–52.

Greenwood, Linda. "Love: 'The Gift of Death.'" *Tolkien Studies* 2 (2005): 171–95.

Gupta, Nijay. *Paul and the Language of Faith*. Grand Rapids: Eerdmans, 2020.

Gustaffson, Lars. "Two Swedish Interviews with J. R. R. Tolkien." Translated by Morgan Thomsen and Shaun Gunner. *Hither Shore* 9 (2013).

Hall, Alaric, and Samuli Kaislaneiemi. "'You Tempt Me Grievously to a Mythological Essay': J. R. R. Tolkien's Correspondence with

Arthur Ransome." In *Ex Philologia Lux: Essays in Honour of Leena Kahlas-Tarkka*, edited by J. Tyrkkö, O. Timofeeva, and M. Salenius, 261–80. Helsinki: Société Néophilologique, 2013.

Hammond, Wayne, and Christina Scull. *The J. R. R. Tolkien Companion and Guide*. 3 vols. London: HarperCollins, 2017.

Harrison, W. H. "Éowyn the Unintended: The Caged Feminine and Gendered Space in *The Lord of the Rings*." Master's thesis, University of British Columbia, 2013.

Hart, Trevor, and Ivan Khovacs. *Tree of Tales: Tolkien, Literature, and Theology*. Waco: Baylor University Press, 2007.

Heiser, Michael. *Angels: What the Bible Really Says about God's Heavenly Host*. Bellingham, WA: Lexham Press, 2018.

———. *The Unseen Realm: Recovering the Supernatural Worldview of the Bible*. Bellingham, WA: Lexham Press, 2015.

Helen, Daniel, ed. *Death and Immortality in Middle-earth*. Edinburgh: Luna Press, 2017.

Helen, Daniel, and Morgan Thomsen. "A Recollection of Tolkien: Canon Gerard Hanlon." *Mallorn* 54 (2013): 40–42.

Hemmi, Yoko. "Tolkien's *The Lord of the Rings* and His Concept of Native Language: Sindarin and British-Welsh." *Tolkien Studies* 7, no. 1 (2010):147–74.

Henry, Elisabeth. *Orpheus with His Lute: Poetry and the Renewal of Life*. London: Bristol Classical Press, 1992.

Hibbs, Pierce Taylor. "Meddling in the Mind of Melkor: *The Silmarillion* and the Nature of Sin." *VII: Journal of the Marion E. Wade Center* 33 (2016): 41–56.

Honegger, Thomas. "Tolkien through the Eyes of a Mediaevalist," *Reconsidering Tolkien*. Cormarë Series 8. Zurich and Berne: Walking Tree Publishers, 2005.

Hood, Gwyneth E. "Sauron as Gorgon and Basilisk." *VII: Journal of the Marion E. Wade Center* 8 (1987): 59–71.

———. "Nature and Technology: Angelic and Sacrificial Strategies in Tolkien's *The Lord of the Rings*." *Mythlore* 19, no. 4 (1993): 6–12.

Houghton, John William. "Augustine and the Ainulindalë." *Mythlore* 21 (1995): 4–8.

———. "Neues Testament und Märchen: Tolkien, Fairy Stories, and the Gospel." *Journal of Tolkien Research* 4, no. 1 (2017): Article 9.

———. "Rochester the Renewer: The Byronic Hero and the Messiah as Elements in the King Elessar." *Mythlore* 11, no. 1 (1984): 13–16.

Houghton, John William, and Neal K. Keesee. "Tolkien, King Alfred, and Boethius: Platonist Views of Evil in *The Lord of the Rings*." *Tolkien Studies* 2 (2005): 131–59.

Hyles, Vernon. "On the Nature of Evil: The Cosmic Myths of Lewis, Tolkien, and Williams." *Mythlore* 13, no. 4 (1987): 9–13.

Irenaeus. *On the Apostolic Preaching*. Translated by John Behr. Crestwood, NY: St. Vladimir's Seminary Press, 1997.

Jipp, Joshua. *Christ Is King: Paul's Royal Ideology*. Minneapolis: Fortress, 2016.

Jones, Kathleen. "The Use and Misuse of Fantasy." *Mallorn* 23 (1986): 5–9.

Juriçková, Martina. "Creation and Subcreation." *Mallorn* 57 (Winter 2016): 21–22.

Kane, Douglas C. "Law and Arda." *Tolkien Studies* 9 (2012): 37–57.

Ker, Ian. *Newman on Vatican II*. New York: Oxford University Press, 2014.

Kerry, Paul. *The Ring and the Cross: Christianity and "The Lord of the Rings."* Madison: Fairleigh Dickinson University Press, 2011.

Kilby, Clyde. *Tolkien and the Silmarillion*. Wheaton: H. Shaw, 1976.

Kocher, Paul H. "Ilúvatar and the Secret Fire." *Mythlore* 12, no. 1 (1985): 36–37.

Kowalik, Barbara. "Elbereth the Star-Queen Seen in the Light of Medieval Marian Devotion." In *O What a Tangled Web Tolkien and Medieval Literature: A View from Poland*, edited by Barbara Kowalik, 93–114. Zollikofen: Walking Tree Press, 2013.

Kreeft, Peter. *The Philosophy of Tolkien: The Worldview behind "The Lord of the Rings."* San Francisco: Ignatius, 2005.

Kuteeva, Maria. "'Old Human,' or 'The Voice in Our Hearts': J. R. R. Tolkien on the Origin of Language." In *Arda Special I: Between Faith and Fiction*, edited by Nils Ivar Agøy, 72–89. Uppsala, Sweden: Arda Society, 1998.

Lakowski, Romuald Ian. "The Fall and Repentance of Galadriel." *Mythlore* 25, no. 3/4 (97/98) (2007): 91–104.

Larsen, Kristine. "Medieval Cosmology and Middle-earth: A Lewisian Walk Under Tolkienian Skies." *Journal of Tolkien Research* 3, no. 1 (2016): Article 5.

Lee, Stuart D. "'Tolkien in Oxford' (BBC, 1968): A Reconstruction." *Tolkien Studies* 15 (2018): 115–76.

Lee, Stuart D., ed. *A Companion to J. R. R. Tolkien*. Chichester: Wiley, 2014.

Lewis, Alex. "Splintered Darkness." *Mallorn* 26 (1989) 31–33.

Lewis, C. S. *The Collected Letters of C. S. Lewis, Volume 3: Narnia, Cambridge, and Joy, 1950–1963*. Edited by Walter Hooper. New York: HarperCollins, 2004.

———. *Complete C. S. Lewis Signature Classics*. New York: HarperOne, 2008.

———. "Myth Became Fact." In *God in the Dock*, edited by Walter Hooper, 63–67. Grand Rapids: Eerdmans, 2001.

———. *Perelandra*. New York: Scribner, 2003.

———. "Sometimes Fairy Tales May Say Best What's to Be Said." In *Of Other Worlds*, 35–38. Boston: Houghton Mifflin Harcourt, 2002.

Madsen, Catherine. "Light from an Invisible Lamp: Natural Religion in *The Lord of the Rings*." *Mythlore* 14, no. 3 (1988): 43–47.

Matthews, John. "Reappraising Gawain: Pagan Champion or Christian Knight?" *Mallorn* 31 (1994): 7–14.

Maximus Confessor. *Ad Thalassium*.

McBride, Sam. *Tolkien's Cosmology: Divine Beings and Middle-earth*. Kent, OH: Kent State University Press, 2020.

McClain, Michael. "The Indo-Iranian Influence on Tolkien." *Mallorn* 19 (1982): 21–24.

McIntosh, Jonathan S. *The Flame Imperishable: Tolkien, St. Thomas, and the Metaphysics of Faërie*. Kettering, OH: Angelico, 2017.

Milbank, Alison. *Chesterton and Tolkien as Theologians: The Fantasy of the Real*. London: T&T Clark, 2007.

———. "Tolkien, Chesterton, and Thomism." In *Tolkien's "The Lord of the Rings": Sources of Inspiration*, edited by Stratford Caldecott and Thomas Honegger, 187–198. Zurich and Jena: Walking Tree, 2008.

Mitchell, Philip Irving. "'But Grace Is Not Infinite': Tolkien's Explorations of Nature and Grace in His Catholic Context." *Mythlore* (2013): 61–81.

———. "'Legend and History Have Met and Fused': The Interlocution of Anthropology, Historiography, and Incarnation in J. R. R. Tolkien's 'On Fairy-stories.'" *Tolkien Studies* 8 (2011): 1–21.

Monda, Andrea, and Wu Ming 4. "Tolkien as Catholic Philosopher?" In *Tolkien and Philosophy*, edited by Roberto Arduini and Claudio A. Testi, 85–124. Zurich and Jena: Walking Tree Press, 2014.

Monks, Caroline. "Christianity and Kingship in Tolkien and Lewis." *Mallorn* 19 (1982): 5–28.

Morse, Robert E. "Rings of Power in Plato and Tolkien." *Mythlore* 7, no. 3 (1980): 38.

Murray, Robert. "Sermon at Thanksgiving Service, Keble College Chapel, 23rd August 1992." *Mallorn* 33 (1995): 17–20.

Nagy, Gergely. "The 'Lost' Subject of Middle-earth: The Constitution of the Subject in the Figure of Gollum in *The Lord of the Rings*." *Tolkien Studies* 3 (2006): 57–79.

Neberman, Skyler. "Eucatastrophe: On the Necessity of Sorrow for the Human Person." *Mallorn* 57 (2016): 27–28.

Nelson, Charles W. "'The Halls of Waiting': Death and Afterlife in Middle-earth." *Journal of the Fantastic in the Arts* 9, no. 3 (1998): 200–211.

Nelson, Dale. "*The Lord of the Rings* and the Four Loves." *Mallorn* 40 (2002): 29–31.

Neubauer, Łukasz. "'The Eagles are coming!': A Pneumatological Reinterpretation of the Old Germanic 'Beasts of Battle' Motif in the Works of J. R. R. Tolkien." *Journal of Inklings Studies* 11, no. 2 (2021): 169–92.

Newman, John Henry. *Fifteen Sermons Preached Before the University of Oxford*. New York: Longmans, Green, and Co, 1909.

———. "On the Inspiration of Scripture." *The Nineteenth Century* 15, no. 84 (Feb 1884).

———. *Parochial and Plain Sermons, Vol. 2*. London: Longmans, Green, 1891.

Norman, Philip. "The Prevalence of Hobbits." *New York Times Magazine*, January 15, 1967.

Olszański, Tadeusz Andrzej. "Evil and the Evil One in Tolkien's Theology." *Mythlore* 21, no. 2 (1996): 298–300.

Ordway, Holly. "'Further Up and Further In': Representations of Heaven in Tolkien and Lewis." *Journal of Inklings Studies* 3, no. 1 (2013): 5–23.

————. *Tolkien's Modern Reading: Middle-earth beyond the Middle Ages.* Park Ridge, IL: Word on Fire Academic, 2021.

Pearce, Joseph, ed. *Tolkien: A Celebration.* New York: HarperCollins, 1999.

Pearce, Joseph. *Tolkien: Man and Myth.* New York: HarperCollins, 1998.

Pedersen, Kusmita. "The 'Divine Passive' in *The Lord of the Rings*." *Mallorn* 51 (Spring 2011): 23–27.

Pirson, Ron. "Tom Bombadil's Biblical Connections." *Mallorn* 37 (1999): 15–18.

Plimmer, Charlotte, and Denis Plimmer. "The Man Who Understands Hobbits." *The Daily Telegraph*, March 22, 1968.

Polk, Nicholas J. S. "The Holy Fellowship: Holiness in *The Lord of the Rings*." *Mallorn* 57 (2016): 29–31.

————. "A Holy Party: Holiness in *The Hobbit*." *Mallorn* 59 (2018): 57–63.

Purtill, Richard. *J. R. R. Tolkien: Myth, Morality, and Religion.* New York: Harper & Row, 1984.

Ratliff, John. "'That Seems to Me Fatal': Pagan and Christian in *The Fall of Arthur*." *Tolkien Studies* 13 (2016): 45–70.

Resnik, Henry. "An Interview with J. R. R. Tolkien." *Niekas* 18 (1967): 37–47.

Richmond, Donald P. "Tolkien's Marian Vision of Middle-earth." *Mallorn* 40 (2002): 13–14.

Rosebury, Brian. "Revenge and Moral Judgement in Tolkien." *Tolkien Studies* 5 (2008): 1–20.

Rutledge, Amelia A. "'*Justice* Is Not *Healing*': J. R. R. Tolkien's Pauline Constructs in 'Finwë and Míriel.'" *Tolkien Studies* 9 (2012): 59–74.

Rutledge, Fleming. *The Battle for Middle-earth: Tolkien's Divine Design in "The Lord of the Rings."* Grand Rapids: Eerdmans, 2004.

Ryken, Philip. *The Messiah Comes to Middle-earth: Images of Christ's Threefold Office in "The Lord of the Rings."* Downers Grove, IL: InterVarsity Press, 2017.

Sanford, Len. "The Fall from Grace–Decline and Fall in Middle-earth: Metaphors for Nordic and Christian Theology in *The Lord of the Rings* and *The Silmarillion*." *Mallorn* 32 (1995): 15–20.

Sayer, George. "Recollections of J. R. R. Tolkien." *Mallorn* (1995): 21–25.

Schweicher, Eric. "Aspects of the Fall in *The Silmarillion*." *Mythlore* 21, no. 2 (1996): 167–71.

Scott, Bud. "Tolkien's Use of Free Will Versus Predestination in *The Lord of the Rings*." *Mallorn* 51 (Spring 2011): 31–33.

Scull, Christina. "What Did He Know and When Did He Know It?: Planning, Inspiration, and *The Lord of the Rings*." In The Lord of the Rings, *1954–2004: Scholarship in Honor of Richard E. Blackwelder*, edited by Wayne G. Hammond and Christina Scull, 101–12. Milwaukee: Marquette University Press, 2006.

Seddon, Eric. "*Letters to Malcolm* and the Trouble with Narnia: C. S. Lewis, J. R. R. Tolkien, and Their 1949 Crisis." *Mythlore* 26, no. 1 (2007): 61–81.

Seeman, Chris. "Tolkien's Revision of the Romantic Tradition." *Mallorn* 33 (1995): 73–83.

Shippey, Tom. *The Road to Middle-earth*. 3rd ed. New York: HarperCollins, 1993.

Smith, Mark Eddy Smith. *Tolkien's Ordinary Virtues*. Downers Grove, IL: InterVarsity Press, 2001.

Smith, Thomas W. "Tolkien's Catholic Imagination: Mediation and Tradition." *Religion & Literature* 38, no .2 (Summer 2006): 73–100.

Steed, Robert. "The Harrowing of Hell Motif in Tolkien's Legendarium." *Mallorn* 58 (2017): 6–9.

———. "Tolkien's Preference for an Early Medieval Catholic Sensibility in *The Lord of the Rings* and *The Silmarillion*." Proceedings of Mythmoot III, Signum University, Linthicum, MD, January 11, 2015.

Sterling, Grant C. "'The Gift of Death': Tolkien's Philosophy of Mortality." *Mythlore* 21, no. 4 (1997): 16–38.

Stevenson, Jeff. "A Delusion Unmasked." *Mallorn* 24 (1987): 5–10.

Strauss, Ed. *A Hobbit Devotional: Bilbo Baggins and the Bible.* Uhrichsville, OH: Barbour, 2012.

Tally, Robert T., Jr. "Demonizing the Enemy, Literally: Tolkien, Orcs, and the Sense of the World Wars." *Humanities* 8, no. 1 (2019): 54. https://doi.org/10.3390/h8010054.

Testi, Claudio A. *Pagan Saints in Middle-earth.* Zurich and Jena: Walking Tree Publishers, 2018.

———. "Logic and Theology in Tolkien's Thanatology." In *The Broken Scythe: Death and Immortality in the Work of J. R. R. Tolkien*, edited by Roberto Arduino and Claudio Testi, 175–92. Zurich and Jena: Walking Tree Press, 2012.

———. "Tolkien and Aquinas." In *Tolkien and the Classics*, edited by Roberto Arduini, Giampaolo Canzonieri, and Claudio Testi, 57–71. Zurich and Jena: Walking Tree Press, 2019.

———. "Tolkien's Work: Is It Christian or Pagan? A Proposal for a 'Synthetic' Approach." *Tolkien Studies* 10 (2013): 1–47.

Thayer, Anna. *On Eagles' Wings: An Exploration of Eucatastrophe in Tolkien's Fantasy.* Edinburgh: Luna Press, 2016.

Tneh, David. "The Human Image and the Interrelationship of the Orcs, Elves and Men." *Mallorn* 55 (2014): 35–39.

———. "Orcs and Tolkien's Treatment of Evil." *Mallorn* 52 (2011): 37–43.

Tolkien, Simon. "My Grandfather." *The Mail on Sunday*, February 23, 2003.

Traherne, Elaine. "Speaking of the Medieval." In *The Oxford Handbook of Medieval Literature in English*, edited by Elaine Treharne, Greg Walker, and William Green, 1–16. Oxford: Oxford University Press, 2010.

Vaccaro, Christopher. "'And One White Tree': The Cosmological Cross and the *Arbor Vitae* in J. R. R. Tolkien's *The Lord of the Rings* and *The Silmarillion*." *Mallorn* 42 (2004): 23–28.

———. *The Body in Tolkien's Legendarium: Essays on Middle-earth Corporeality.* Jefferson, NC: McFarland, 2013.

Vanhoozer, Kevin J. *Is There a Meaning in This Text? The Bible, the Reader, and the Morality of Literary Knowledge.* Grand Rapids: Zondervan, 2009.

Vink, Renée. "'Jewish' Dwarves: Tolkien and Anti-Semitic Stereotyping." *Tolkien Studies* 10 (2013): 123–45.

Ward, Michael. *Planet Narnia: The Seven Heavens in the Imagination of C. S. Lewis.* Oxford: Oxford University Press, 2007.

Ware, Kallistos. "Interview with Dean W. Arnold." Metropolitan Kallistos Ware. January 16, 2007. https://soundcloud.com/dean-w-arnold/kallistos-full-interviewmov-aac-audio.

West, Kevin. "Julian of Norwich's 'Great Deed' and Tolkien's 'Eucatastrophe.'" *Religion & Literature* 43, no. 2 (2011): 23–44.

West, Richard C. "A Letter from Father Murray." *Tolkien Studies* 16 (2019): 133–39.

White, Ellen. *Yahweh's Council: Its Structure and Membership.* Tübingen: Mohr Siebeck, 2014.

Whittingham, Elizabeth A. *The Evolution of Tolkien's Mythology: A Study of the History of Middle-earth.* London: McFarland, 2007.

Willhite, Gary L., and John R. D. Bell. "J. R. R. Tolkien's Moral Imagination." *Mallorn* 40 (2002): 7–12.

Wood, Ralph C. *The Gospel according to Tolkien: Visions of the Kingdom in Middle-earth.* Louisville: Westminster John Knox, 2003.

Wolfe, Brendan. "Tolkien's Jonah." *Journal of Inklings Studies* 4, no. 2 (2014): 11–26.

Wytenbroek, J. R. "Apocalyptic Vision in *The Lord of the Rings*." *Mythlore* 14, no. 4 (1988): 7–12.

Yandell, Stephen. "'A Pattern Which Our Nature Cries Out For': The Medieval Tradition of the Ordered Four in the Fiction of J. R. R. Tolkien." *Mallorn* 33 (1995): 375–92.

Zimmer, Mary. "Creating and Re-Creating Worlds with Words: The Religion and the Magic of Language in *The Lord of the Rings*." *VII: Journal of the Marion E. Wade Center* 12 (1995): 65–78.

NOTES

1. J. R. R. Tolkien, *The Letters of J. R. R. Tolkien: A Selection*, ed. Christopher Tolkien and Humphrey Carpenter (Boston: Mariner Books, 2000). The letters will be cited by letter number and then by page number.

2. *Letters*, 49:60–62; 153: 187–96. He does not send the latter because he believes it makes him sound like he takes himself too seriously. The fact that we have these two drafts in itself proves nothing about Tolkien's reticence to speak on matters theological, which we know he frequently did, especially with Lewis. He could have had the same conversation with Lewis in person. And we do not have the actual letter (if any) sent to Peter Hastings, which could have expressed the same concerns in a different tone.

3. Wayne Hammond and Christina Scull, *The J. R. R. Tolkien Companion and Guide, vol. 1: Chronology* (London: HarperCollins, 2017), 63 (hereafter *Chronology*).

4. C. S. Lewis, *The Collected Letters of C. S. Lewis, Volume 3: Narnia, Cambridge, and Joy, 1950–1963*, ed. Walter Hooper (New York: HarperCollins, 2004), 1549. See also the references to the importance of theological discussion in Hammond and Scull, *Chronology*, 185, 337, and Wayne Hammond and Christina Scull, *The J. R. R. Tolkien Companion and Guide, vols. 2–3: Reader's Guide* (London: HarperCollins, 2017), 1284 (hereafter *Guide*). This, despite the fact that he seemed not to have held any works by theologians or philosophers in his library, apart from a copy of the *Summa Theologica* (Claudio Testi, "Logic and Theology in Tolkien's Thanatology," in *The Broken Scythe: Death and Immortality in the Work of J. R. R. Tolkien*, ed. Roberto Arduino and Claudio Testi [Zurich and Jena: Walking Tree, 2012], 185). His daughter-in-law Irene Tolkien Cook writes, on the other hand, "Tolkien was a theological scholar in his own right, by virtue of all he had read" (Irene Tolkien Cook, letter to the editor, *Amon Hen* 162 (March 2000): 24.

5. *Letters*, 213:228.

6. *Letters*, 340:420–21.

7. Priscilla Tolkien, quoted in Andrea Monda and Wu Ming 4, "Tolkien as Catholic Philosopher?" in *Tolkien and Philosophy*, ed. Roberto Arduini and Claudio A. Testi (Zurich and Jena: Walking Tree Press, 2014), 86.

8. *Letters*, 142:172. He tells one correspondent that there is a lot of theology in the book, and that he only realized exactly how much after he read a theological analysis in a magazine (letter to G. S. Rigby described in Hammond and Scull, *Chronology*, 681).

9. *Letters*, 153:194.

10. *The Monsters and the Critics and Other Essays.*

11. Michael D. C. Drout points out a few other internal divisions within the field; see, for example, Michael D. C. Drout, "Toward a Better Tolkien Criticism," in *Reading "The Lord of the Rings,"* ed. Robert Eaglestone (New York: Bloomsbury, 2006), 15–16.

12. Another related but distinct question also arises: Why read Tolkien as a *theologian?* The rest of this book will, one hopes, provide a sufficient answer.

13. Among the most enduring have been Joseph Pearce, *Tolkien: Man and Myth* (New York: HarperCollins, 1998); Bradley Birzer, *J. R. R. Tolkien's Sanctifying Myth* (Wilmington, DE: Intercollegiate Studies Institute, 2002); Verlyn Flieger, *Splintered Light* (Kent, OH: Kent State University Press, 2002); Ralph C. Wood, *The Gospel According to Tolkien* (Louisville: Westminster John Knox, 2003); Stratford Caldecott, *The Power of the Ring* (New York: Crossroad, 2003); Fleming Rutledge, *The Battle for Middle-earth* (Grand Rapids: Eerdmans, 2004); Peter Kreeft, *The Philosophy of Tolkien* (San Francisco: Ignatius, 2005). Others include Alison Milbank, *Chesterton and Tolkien as Theologians* (London: T&T Clark, 2007); Craig Bernthal, *Tolkien's Sacramental Vision: Discerning the Holy in Middle Earth* (Lechlade, UK: Second Spring, 2014); Jonathan S. McIntosh, *The Flame Imperishable* (Kettering, OH: Angelico, 2017); Sam McBride, *Tolkien's Cosmology* (Kent, OH: Kent State University Press, 2020), and a host of devotional works such as Mark Eddy Smith, *Tolkien's Ordinary Virtues* (Downers Grove, IL: InterVarsity Press, 2001); Matthew Dickerson, *Following Gandalf* (Grand Rapids: Brazos, 2003); and its expanded retitled version *A Hobbit Journey* (Grand Rapids: Baker, 2012). This is not an exhaustive survey. Paul Kerry's introduction to *The Ring and the Cross* (Madison: Fairleigh Dickinson University Press, 2011) offers an extended overview of the state of the debate, though it is by now outdated.

14. Michael D. C. Drout and Hilary Wynne, "Tom Shippey's *J. R. R. Tolkien: Author of the Century* and a Look Back at Tolkien Criticism since 1982," *Envoi* 9, no. 2 (Fall 2000): 109–110.

15. Drout and Wynne, "Tom Shippey's," 107.

16. For example, the authors in the first section of Kerry, *Ring and the Cross.* Any Christian scholar of Tolkien must grapple with no less an authority than Verlyn Flieger, "But What Did He Really Mean?" *Tolkien Studies* 11 (2014): 149–54. For a charitable and balanced perspective that cautions against reducing Tolkien to a Christian writer, see Patrick Curry, *Defending Middle-earth: Tolkien, Myth and Modernity* (New York: Houghton Mifflin, 2004), especially chapter 4 ("The Sea: Spirituality and Ethics").

17. Claudio A. Testi, "Tolkien's Work: Is It Christian or Pagan? A Proposal for a 'Synthetic' Approach," *Tolkien Studies* 10 (2013): 1–47. Testi has also produced a monograph on this subject which expands upon his essay *Pagan Saints in Middle-earth* (Zurich and Jena: Walking Tree Publishers, 2018).

18. Testi, *Pagan Saints.*

19. Testi, *Pagan Saints,* 9.

20. Testi, *Pagan Saints,* 10.

21. Testi, *Pagan Saints,* 26. See also Claudio Testi, "Tolkien and Aquinas," in *Tolkien and the Classics,* ed. Roberto Arduini, Giampaolo Canzonieri, and Claudio Testi (Zollikofen, Switzerland: Walking Tree, 2019). McIntosh argues much the same throughout his own work.

22. John Henry Newman, "The Influence of Natural and Revealed Religion Respectively," in *Fifteen Sermons Preached Before the University of Oxford* (New York: Longmans, Green, 1909), 16–36. For Newman's influence on Tolkien, see below.

23. *Beowulf: A Translation and Commentary*, 328–29.

24. Kevin J. Vanhoozer, *Is There a Meaning in This Text? The Bible, the Reader, and the Morality of Literary Knowledge* (Grand Rapids: Zondervan, 2009). Vanhoozer's work responds to some of Drout's concerns (for instance, Drout, "Toward a Better," 15–28) in ways I cannot enter into here.

25. See, for example, *Letters*, 153:190.

26. See, for example, *Letters*, 131:145; *Morgoth's Ring*, 359–60, 370; *The Nature of Middle-earth*, 263.

27. *Letters*, 153:189; 212:286–87.

28. *Letters*, 269:355.

29. *Letters*, 211:283–84.

30. *Letters*, 211:283–84.

31. *Letters*, 153:194–95.

32. *Letters*, 153:189.

33. *Letters*, 153:192; 297:383–84. This has not stopped others from overriding Tolkien's wishes. See, for example, Ron Pirson, "Tom Bombadil's Biblical Connections," *Mallorn* 37 (1999): 15–18.

34. *Tree and Leaf, including Mythopoei*, "Mythopoeia."

35. Clyde Kilby, *Tolkien and the Silmarillion* (Wheaton: H. Shaw, 1976), 172.

36. For *Lembas*, see *Letters*, 210:275. For Mary, see *Letters* 213:288. For threefold office, see Kilby, *Tolkien and the Silmarillion*, 172.

37. *Letters*, 250:340. Emphasis added.

38. Irene Tolkien Cook states that Tolkien did not unquestioningly accept Roman doctrine and dogma. "As he had an enquiring mind, he agonised over his personal beliefs, but kept the faith" (Irene Tolkien Cook, "Letter," 24). In context, Cook is writing about his opinions of the revised Vatican II liturgy.

39. See, however, Drout, "Toward a Better," 20, and Holly Ordway, *Tolkien's Modern Reading* (Park Ridge, IL: Word on Fire Academic, 2021), 12–14 for the dangers in using the *Letters* uncritically. Again, readings based on the theory of Foucault and Barthes will probably disagree with the very basis of my method here, but it is not the purpose of this book to provide a theory of literary criticism. Needless to say, citing Tolkien's letters "at excruciating length" here can be the proper choice when seeking to preserve Tolkien's own voice, and there are numerous references to his fiction and other works that balance my approach.

40. See *The Book of Lost Tales, vol. 1*, 9; *The Book of Lost Tales, vol. 2*, 327.

41. Newman founded the Birmingham Oratory with which the young Tolkien was so intimately involved, not only as a parishioner but also as a self-described junior inmate (*Letters*, 306:395). Father Francis Morgan, Tolkien's de facto father figure (*Letters*, 332:416) and legal guardian after 1904, was a priest of the oratory and at one point Cardinal Newman's personal secretary. For more on Father Morgan, see José Manuel Ferrández Bru, *"Uncle Curro": J. R. R.*

Tolkien's Spanish Connection (Edinburgh: Luna Press, 2018) and "'Wingless Fluttering': Some Personal Connections in Tolkien's Formative Years," *Tolkien Studies* 8 (2011): 53.

42. *Return of the King*, 118.

Chapter I: God

1. For Tolkien, God's existence does not seem to be a significant question. Unlike his friend C. S. Lewis in his youth, he never abandoned or denied his faith, though at times he was less observant (*The Letters of J. R. R. Tolkien*, 250:340). To a man who attended morning mass almost daily, even while on the fields of France in the Great War, it is hard to say what "less observant" might entail, however. The sole point of evidence usually brought forward to prove that Tolkien's faith was not as unruffled as it seemed occurs in a 1949 letter to his son Michael. In speaking about marriage, he writes that if there is a God, then life and circumstances are God's instruments (*Letters*, 43:51). Here Flieger argues that Tolkien tended toward a polarity of hope and despair, and that this letter indicates that his seasons of despair included doubts about God's existence. The evidence for this is scant, however. The "bleak doubt" with which Flieger associates Tolkien's "if" statement is not borne out by the rest of the letter—see, for instance, the end of the letter and its rhapsodic account of the Eucharist! This clearly shows that the force of the "if" here is logical rather than existential. That is, Tolkien suffers no real doubt as to God's existence, but instead offers an "If A, then B" argument. If God exists, then he will use life and circumstances as his instruments. God exists; therefore, he does use them. See Flieger, *Splintered Light*. This is not to disagree with Flieger's excellent assessment in the rest of the chapter, only to note that Tolkien's pessimism did not take the form of religious doubt. Indeed, as Letter 255 (quoted by Flieger on page 4) indicates, his pessimism is actually founded in a Christian anthropology of sin and the fall. In fact, this mixture between rejoicing in the simple goods of the world and sorrowing in inevitable worldly loss—finding contentment only in the eternal—is the characteristically Christian perspective that allows Tolkien to speak so powerfully to us today.

2. In this letter, he renders the word "MIND" in all capital letters, indicating not just any mind but a transcendent one, the prime and first cause of mind as such.

3. *Letters*, 310:399.

4. *Tolkien On Fairy-stories*, 42–43.

5. See also the ascription of "Mythopoeia" in *Tree and Leaf, including Mythopoeia*.

6. Tolkien, "Mythopoeia," in *Tree and Leaf*.

7. *Fairy-stories*, 42–43.

8. *Fairy-stories*, 44.

9. "Mythopoeia," *Tree and Leaf*.

10. *Letters*, 89:101.

11. *Letters*, 89:101.

12. *Fairy-stories*, 44.

13. *Letters*, 89:101.

14. *Letters*, 89:101. Tolkien's talk of a conviction rather than argument recalls Hebrews 11:1, the classic definition of faith, rendered according to the Vulgate as *"argumentum non parentum."* We are reminded here of Cardinal Newman's views on the relationship of faith to reason: "Faith is an instrument of knowledge and action, unknown to the world before, a principle *sui*

generis, distinct from those which nature supplies, and in particular … independent of what is commonly understood by Reason" (Newman, *Fifteen Sermons,* 179). Newman argued that one could distinguish between the intuitive leaps with which the original process of reasoning is often associated and the subsequent systematic reflection undertaken in order to justify those leaps (256–59).

15. *Letters,* 310:400.

16. *Letters,* 310:400.

17. *Letters,* 310:400.

18. *Letters,* 310:400.

19. *Letters,* 156:204; 165:220; 181:235; Charlotte Plimmer and Denis Plimmer, "The Man Who Understands Hobbits," *The Daily Telegraph,* March 22, 1968. When Tolkien says that the Third Age "was not a Christian world" ("Tolkien on Tolkien," *Diplomat* 18 [October 1966]: 197), we note that he says *the Third Age* (a temporal marker) rather than *Middle-earth* (a location). This means that we ought to understand Tolkien to be referring to the fact that Christ has not yet come at the time of these tales, rather than that Tolkien has constructed an alternate, non-Christian universe. See, in corroboration of this point, Plimmer and Plimmer, "The Man." For a very different take on the meaning of natural theology here, see Catherine Madsen, "Light from an Invisible Lamp: Natural Religion in *The Lord of the Rings,*" *Mythlore* 14, no. 3 (1988): 43–47.

20. Philip Norman, "The Prevalence of Hobbits," *New York Times Magazine,* January 15, 1967, 30–31, 97, 100–102. In the first years of Tolkien studies, before so much material had come to light, many people could be forgiven for assuming that hobbit villages must feature a church (see, for example, Vera Chapman, "The Religion of a Hobbit," *Mallorn* 3 [1971]: 15–16).

21. *Letters,* 156:204. When we come later to discuss the church, we shall see that Númenoreans and other denizens of Middle-earth *did* have organized religion, but that this had died out by the time of the Third Age.

22. *Letters,* 156:206. Christopher Dawson's *Progress and Religion* (Washington, DC: Catholic University of America Press, 2001), admired by Tolkien, similarly argues that religion is a natural human impulse, a central element of all culture, and a basic building block for civilization.

23. *Sauron Defeated,* 402.

24. *Letters,* 153:192.

25. Tolkien, "Late Notes on Verb Structure," *Parma Eldalamberon* 22 (2015): 147.

26. Below, we shall see that there is more to the story.

27. Denys Gueroult, BBC interview, January 20, 1965.

28. *Morgoth's Ring,* 311.

29. *Sauron,* 404.

30. *Letters,* 211:283; *The Book of Lost Tales, vol. 2,* 163.

31. *Sauron,* 400. "Heaven" can also mean the (spatiotemporal) abode of the blessed in the presence of God. For this sense, see chapter 10.

32. *The Book of Lost Tales, vol. 1,* 119.

33. *Lost Tales 1,* 49.

34. *Lost Tales 1,* 49.

35. *Letters* 54:66.

36. *Letters,* 153:192.

37. *Letters,* 191:252.

38. *Letters,* 200:259. The hierarchy has only two levels, though, as we will see in chapter 5.

39. *Fairy-stories*, 78.

40. *Letters*, 163:212. The fact that Tolkien here echoes Plato rather than Aristotle should not give us pause. While many scholars like McIntosh and Testi have shown Tolkien's dependence on Thomas Aquinas's Christian Aristotelianism, Aquinas himself was no mere Greek translator. He also worked within the Christian intellectual tradition, especially that of Augustine (whose Neoplatonism is well known). Aquinas (and Tolkien) never adopt secular philosophies or modes of thought wholesale. See also McIntosh, *The Flame Imperishable*; Testi, *Pagan Saints*; Robert E. Morse, "Rings of Power in Plato and Tolkien," *Mythlore* 7, no. 3 (1980): 38; Frederick A. De Armas, "Gyges' Ring: Invisibility in Plato, Tolkien and Lope de Vega," *Journal of the Fantastic in the Arts* 3, no. 3/4 (1994): 120–38; Gergely Nagy, "Saving the Myths: The Re-Creation of Mythology in Plato and Tolkien," in *Tolkien and the Invention of Myth: A Reader*, ed. Jane Chance (Lexington, KY: University of Kentucky, 2004), 81–100; Eric Katz, "The Rings of Tolkien and Plato: Lessons in Power, Choice, and Morality," in *The Lord of the Rings and Philosophy: One Book to Rule Them All*, ed. Gregory Bassham and Eric Bronson (Chicago: Open Court, 2003), 5–20; John Cox, "Tolkien's Platonic Fantasy," *VII* 5 (1984): 53–69.

41. See, for example, *The Shaping of Middle-earth*, 263.

42. *The Silmarillion*, 15; *Letters*, 153:190. Tolkien's remark that the metaphysical distinction between a permissive making (such as the Valar do) and true Creation (which only Eru brings about by an act of will) does not necessarily correspond to the metaphysics of the real world. What could he mean by this? It is perhaps best to read this caveat as merely a hedge against overconfident metaphysical assertion, rather than a backward denial of creation *ex nihilo*.

43. *Morgoth's Ring*, 344.

44. *Morgoth's Ring*, 344.

45. *Lost Tales 1*, 214.

46. *Letters*, 212:287. Even Tolkien's angels, otherwise so involved in creation, only do this indirectly (*The Nature of Middle-earth*, 292).

47. *Silmarillion*, 20. See further the next section and our discussion of the Holy Spirit.

48. *Lost Tales 1*, 59; *Silmarillion*, 15.

49. *Letters*, 54:66.

50. *Sauron*, 401 and so on.

51. *Lost Tales 1*, 209.

52. *Fairy-stories*, 65–66.

53. *Fairy-stories*, 78.

54. *Fairy-stories*, 78; *Letters*, 200:259.

55. *Letters*, 191:252.

56. *Letters*, 131:146.

57. His daughter Priscilla mentions that she cannot recall him ever reflecting on the Trinity in his writings or in her presence (Monda and Wu Ming 4, "Tolkien," 86).

58. *Morgoth's Ring*, 335.

59. *The Tolkien Reader*, 109–12.

60. See, for example, Jane Chance, *Tolkien's Art: A Mythology for England* (Lexington, KY: University of Kentucky Press, 2001), 97. Other readings have been proposed, such as two guardian angels (Ahmet Mesut Ateş, "J. R. R. Tolkien's 'Leaf by Niggle': A Fantastic Journey to Afterlife," *Mallorn* 56 [Winter 2015]: 19). Thomas Honegger proposes a medieval allegorical assignation of the four "daughters of God," Justice, Mercy, Truth, and

Peace in "Tolkien through the Eyes of a Mediaevalist," 10. This was originally published in *Reconsidering Tolkien*. Cormarë Series 8, ed. Thomas Honegger (Zurich and Berne: Walking Tree Publishers, 2005), 45–66. Available at https://www.academia.edu/12159892/_Tolkien_through_the_Eyes_of_a_Medievalist_updated_version_2021_.

61. *Reader*, 109–12.

62. This experience will be dealt with more fully in chapter 7. The idea of light and its association with God is of course a central one for Tolkien. See Flieger, *Splintered Light*.

63. Augustine, *De Trinitate 8*.

64. Thomas Aquinas, *Summa Theologica*, 1.37.1. John Henry Newman, *Parochial and Plain Sermons*, vol. 2 (London: Longmans, Green 1891), 229.

65. *Letters*, 89:99.

66. Newman, *Parochial and Plain Sermons*, 222. Emphasis added.

67. "Tolkien on Tolkien."

68. Aquinas, *Summa* 1.33.1; Augustine, *De Trinitate 8*.20; also Newman *contra* much of Western Catholicism (see Ian Ker, *Newman on Vatican II* [New York: Oxford University Press, 2014], 57–58).

69. The study of the Son is Christology, and the study of the Spirit is pneumatology. The Father's uniqueness is often subsumed under discussions of the oneness of God.

70. *Beowulf: A Translation and Commentary*, 105.

71. *Beowulf*, 149; *Reader*, 111.

72. This is a massive scholarly field in its own right, but for a prime biblical example, see Rev 19–21.

73. Some, like Neubauer, associate the Eagles and their accompanying rushing wind with the Spirit/*pneuma*. See also Łukasz Neubauer, "'The Eagles are coming!': A Pneumatological Reinterpretation of the Old Germanic 'Beasts of Battle' Motif in the Works of J. R. R. Tolkien," *Journal of Inklings Studies* 11, no. 2 (2021): 169–92.

74. Kilby, *Tolkien and the Silmarillion*, 59. McIntosh takes this view, as does Paul H. Kocher, "Ilúvatar and the Secret Fire," *Mythlore* 12, no. 1 (1985): 36–37. One wonders, though, what the logical connections between the two sentences might be. For of course the adjective "holy" is never applied to the Secret Fire.

75. J. R. R. Tolkien, "Qenya Lexicon," *Parma Eldalamberon* 12 (2011): 81.

76. Newman, *Parochial Sermons*, 219 and so on.

77. *The Fellowship of the Ring*, 344.

78. *Silmarillion*, 15; *The Lost Road*, 157.

79. *Silmarillion*, 20.

80. *Silmarillion*, 25. This is clearly the instance Kilby references. There is an instance in the draft text of *The Lord of the Rings* in which Gandalf remarks that the Ring might be destroyed by throwing it through a crack in the earth into the Secret Fire—here clearly a literal term for the earth's molten depths. (*Return of the Shadow*, 83)

81. *Silmarillion*, 15–16.

82. *Silmarillion*, 16.

83. *Silmarillion*, 64.

84. *Silmarillion*, 85.

85. *Morgoth's Ring*, 352.

86. *Morgoth's Ring*, 345.

87. See the citations above.

88. Cf. *Tolkien On Fairy Stories*, 39-40, 44-49

89. *Letters*, 63:75.

90. *Letters*, 250:339.

91. *Letters*, 212:289.

92. *The War of the Jewels*, 402; *Sauron*, 248–49.

93. *Fairy-stories*, 65. See also Flieger, *Splintered Light*.

94. *Lost Tales 1*, 54; *Lost Road*, 157.

95. *Sauron*, 391.

96. Tolkien provides Elvish translations for omniscience, omnipresence, and omnipotence in "Qenya Lexicon," 70.

97. *Lost Road*, 161; *Jewels*, 211; J. R. R. Tolkien, "Ósanwe-Kenta: 'Enquiry into the Communication of Thought,' " *Vinyar Tengwar* 39 (July 1998), 30.

98. *Letters*, 89:101, 181:235.

99. *Lost Road*, 29; *Sauron*, 338.

100. Tolkien, "Ósanwe-Kenta," 31.

101. *Letters*, 312:401; *Lost Road*, 165.

102. *Lost Tales 1*, 233, 236.

103. *Lost Road*, 165; *Sauron*, 364, see also 345–46.

104. *Letters*, 246:326.

105. *Letters*, 246:326.

106. *Letters*, 250:340. We will also touch upon this in later chapters.

107. *Letters*, 153:193; 325:411.

108. *Jewels*, 210. See Flieger's note about Tolkien's conscious choice between the same two pronouns in an exchange between Aragorn and Arwen (Flieger, *Splintered Light*, 7).

109. *Letters*, 209:269.

Chapter II: Revelation

1. *Letters*, 310:400.

2. *The Lost Road*, 72.

3. *Return of the King*, 146.

4. Else Christ's redemption and rescue need not have worked backward in *Beowulf: A Translation and Commentary*, 160. They would already be saved.

5. *Letters*, 250:339.

6. *Letters*, 250:339.

7. Tolkien and the rest of the Inklings (especially C. S. Lewis) often discussed whether and how far pagan myths can substitute for theology (see, for example, Hammond and Scull, *Chronology*, 345).

8. *The Monsters and the Critics and Other Essays*, 45.

9. *The Book of Lost Tales, vol. 1*, 49.

10. *Lost Tales 1*, 45.

11. *Monsters*, 26. The influence may extend into more subtle areas; see, for example, *Monsters*, 47.

12. *Beowulf: A Translation and Commentary*, 160.

13. *Monsters*, 21; *Beowulf*, 304–12.

14. *Beowulf,* 304; *Monsters,* 19–20. In the same way, George Sayer reports that Tolkien believed many pagan prayers to have been naturally replaced by Christian ones (Sayer, "Recollections of J. R. R. Tolkien," *Mallorn* [1995]: 22). For the possibility that Tolkien was influenced by Danish theologian and Anglo-Saxon scholar N. F. S. Grundtvig, see Nils Ivar Agøy, "Quid Hinieldus cum Christo? New Perspectives on Tolkien's Theological Dilemma and His Sub-Creation Theory," *Mythlore* 21, no. 2 (1996): 31–38.

15. *Beowulf,* 160, 162, 169.

16. *Monsters,* 40.

17. *Beowulf,* 308; *Monsters,* 27.

18. *Beowulf,* 160.

19. *Beowulf,* 160; *Monsters,* 27, 44, 46.

20. *Beowulf,* 170–71, 175–76.

21. *Beowulf,* 160.

22. *Beowulf,* 160. The harrowing of hell refers to Christ's visit to the realm of the dead after his crucifixion but before his resurrection.

23. *The Nature of Middle-earth,* 200–201.

24. John Henry Newman, "On the Inspiration of Scripture," *The Nineteenth Century* 15, no. 84 (Feb 1884). Importantly, while Newman allows for error in *obiter dicta*—that is, peripheral statements of fact—he defends the inspiration of both the authors and the text of Scripture.

25. *Letters,* 250:338.

26. *Letters,* 250:338.

27. *Letters,* 250:338.

28. *Letters,* 92:109–110.

29. *Beowulf,* 307. Notably he only calls Genesis mythological in its mode of expression, and he places the word in quotations to indicate a qualified usage.

30. *Letters,* 96:109

31. *Letters,* 96:110.

32. *Tolkien On Fairy-stories,* 78.

33. *Fairy-stories,* 78.

34. *Fairy-stories,* 77–78.

35. See *Tolkien Encyclopedia,* 315. Letter to Michael George Tolkien (April 24, 1957), British Library, MS Add. 71657.

36. Humphrey Carpenter, *The Inklings: C. S. Lewis, J. R. R. Tolkien, Charles Williams, and Their Friends* (Boston: Houghton Mifflin, 1979), 56; *Letters,* 306:395. Tolkien may have been exempted from the Holy Scripture entrance examination due to his previous work, and he later stood on the committee for entrance examinations which included the Holy Scripture exam (Hammond and Scull, *Chronology,* 171, 821).

37. From a French translation, not from the Hebrew original, though Tolkien did work with the Hebrew to some extent (Hammond and Scull, *Chronology,* 532). For his original, unedited translation, see J. R. R. Tolkien, "The Book of Jonah," *Journal of Inklings Studies* 4, no. 2 (2014): 5–9, and the accompanying piece by Brendan Wolfe, "Tolkien's Jonah," *Journal of Inklings Studies* 4, no. 2 (2014): 11–26. He seemed inclined to translate more but politely refused to become an editor (Hammond and Scull, *Chronology,* 536). For a summary of the correspondence between Tolkien and Father Jones on the *Jerusalem Bible,* see Hammond and Scull, *Chronology* 528–32, 535–36, 684.

38. See *The Story of Kullervo*, 123. He particularly bemoaned the loss of a Bible translation into Gothic due to their Arianism (Hammond and Scull, *Chronology*, 813). His own translation projects frequently focus on biblical or religious themes (*Exodus, Ancrene Wisse, Pearl*, etc.). Future linguists might fruitfully explore whether Tolkien's theological views impact the choices he makes in his translation work.

39. See J. R. R. Tolkien, "The Name 'Nodens,' " *Tolkien Studies* 4 (2007): 177–83; *Monsters*, 23, 26. For a list of biblically based translations, poems, or other subject matter studied in the course of his degree or academic work, see Hammond and Scull, *Chronology*, 34–35, 46–47, 821.

40. For example, *Beowulf*, 162. Likewise, he references the Bible in "The Devil's Coach Horses," but at the end says that on this point he is indebted to a man at the Bodleian.

41. Compare *Letters*, 182:238 to *Letters*, 191:252. See also Hammond and Scull, *Chronology*, 577.

42. Letter to Michael George Tolkien (April 24, 1957), British Library, MS Add. 71657.

43. *Letters*, 250:340; 267:353.

44. *Letters*, 310:400.

45. Hammond and Scull, *Chronology*, record discussions on the "narrow way" of salvation (249), the psalms (345), and Bible translations (347, 421).

46. *Letters*, 306:393.

47. *Letters*, 250:339.

48. *Letters*, 306:394.

49. *Letters*, 250:339.

50. *Letters*, 306:394.

51. *Letters*, 250:338.

52. *Return*, 414; see also *The Peoples of Middle-earth*, 51–52.

53. *Letters*, 131:156.

54. Here named "Eruhildi," Sons of God (*Sauron Defeated*, 411).

55. *The Book of Lost Tales, vol. 2*, 196, 214. Three out of four of these cities appear in the Bible. One might especially draw attention to Nineveh as the setting for the book of Jonah, there said to be three days' travel from end to end.

56. None of which appear in the pre-Vatican II *Missale Romanum*. These may therefore be taken as evidence that Tolkien engaged in private Bible readings and was not a mere passive participant in the Mass—if such evidence is needed.

57. Hammond and Scull, *Chronology*, 714.

58. *Return*, 414. See chapter 12.

59. *Unfinished Tales*, 234. Although a coda at the end of each king in Kings and Chronicles, 1 Kings 22:45 is a pert example: "As for the other events of Jehoshaphat's reign, the things he achieved and his military exploits, are they not written in the book of the annals of the kings of Judah?" (NIV). For a few other brief stylistic similarities, see Irene Garnett, "From Genesis to Revelation in Middle-earth," *Mallorn* 22 (1985): 39.

60. *Morgoth's Ring*, 246.

61. *Nature,* 211.

62. *Nature,* 211.

63. *The Fellowship of the Ring*, 96; see also *The Two Towers*, 340, the fulfillment of his vision in the Mirror of Galadriel.

64. *Fellowship*, 75, 288. Ironically, Sauron has wrapped his own land in so much metaphysical shadow that he himself cannot perceive the Ring traveling through Mordor.

65. *Towers*, 303.

66. *Return*, 259. This also implies that other passages in which the world is changed may not mean simple change but also remaking—that is, to the hope of Arda Unmarred. See chapter 12.

67. *Return*, 299.

68. Within *The Lord of the Rings*, see Glorfindel's prophecy about the doom of the Witchking (*Return*, 92, 332); Ioreth's memory that the hands of the King shall be the hands of a healer (*Return*, 136); the prophecy about the Dead Men of Dunharrow and Aragorn's fulfillment of it (*Towers*, 106; *Return*, 71); the Ents' hope that they shall see the Entwives again, but only after they have lost everything (*Towers*, 80). The prophecy of the return of the King under the Mountain is a major plot point in *The Hobbit*.

69. See *Return*, 330.

70. *Fellowship*, 392–94.

71. *Return*, 248.

72. *Fellowship*, 310; *Towers*, 43; *Return*, 248, 365–66; *The Treason of Isengard*, 204.

73. *Fellowship*, 68–69; *Return*, 89.

74. His fate is foretold in *Return*, 152 (by Legolas), 337–38 (by his grandparents), 338 (by Elrond), 339–40 (by his mother and Elrond), and 341 (by Arwen).

75. *Return*, 123, 340.

76. *Towers*, 274–75.

77. *Towers*, 52.

78. *Towers*, 252.

79. *Return*, 27.

80. *Towers*, 221–22.

81. *Towers*, 340.

82. *Fellowship*, 247. See also 2 Cor 12:2–4; Dan 12:4; Rev 10:4.

83. *Gawain and the Green Knight*, 14; see also *Nature*, 211.

84. *Sauron*, 194–95.

85. *Fellowship*, 259.

86. They are, in order: his dream of the Elf-towers and the Sea (*Fellowship*, 118–19); his dream of Gandalf in the house of Bombadil (*Fellowship*, 138–39, 274); his dream of Valinor (*Fellowship*, 146); a dream of the Black Riders attacking Crickhollow (*Fellowship*, 189); a dream of the winged Nazgûl before their unveiling (*Fellowship*, 216); two dreams of peace which gladden his heart in dark times (*Towers*, 242, 263).

87. *Fellowship*, 406; *Return*, 155–56.

88. On Amon Hen, *Fellowship*, 417; the portent of the stone king with a garland of flowers, *Towers*, 311; Sam has a premonition of danger, *Return*, 175; Frodo and Sam are simultaneously urged toward action, *Return*, 219.

89. *Return*, 359.

90. Leaving the brooch to Aragorn, *Towers*, 53; realizing Grishnakh wants the Ring, *Towers*, 58.

91. *Towers*, 21, 350.

92. *Lost Road*, 303; *Nature*, 175–76, 200–201, 211.

93. *Return*, 341. For a more extended treatment, see McBride, *Tolkien's Cosmology*, chapter 4.

94. *Towers*, 338. See also *The War of the Ring*, 226. Tolkien refers to this as "inspiration" twice in *Letters*, 211:278.

95. *Lost Tales, 2*, 44, and the corresponding passage in *Beren and Lúthien*. Tolkien changes this passage to assert even more positively that this is the case. See *Lost Tales 2*, 45, and Christopher Tolkien's examination of the phenomenon on 68.

96. *Return*, 184–85.

97. *Fellowship*, 210 (on Weathertop); *Towers*, 328–29 (in Shelob's lair).

98. *Fellowship*, 284, emphasis added.

99. *Return*, 240.

100. *Fellowship*, 83; *Towers*, 31–32 (this is how he is later available to save Faramir).

101. *Letters*, 328:413.

102. *Letters*, 328:413.

103. *Letters*, 211:283. Note the qualifying, "As far as I know"!

104. *Letters*, 63:75.

105. These two stories are attempts at linking the Middle-earth legendarium with the present-day world through the trope of time travel, and originated in a wager with C. S. Lewis. Tolkien would write a time travel story, and Lewis would write a space travel story. Lewis eventually published his Space Trilogy to much success, while Tolkien, characteristically, never completed his part of the bargain. In both of Tolkien's uncompleted drafts, modern characters gain knowledge of the fall of Númenor through dreams and visions.

106. *Lost Road*, 53.

107. *Sauron*, "The Notion Club Papers," introduction.

108. Gueroult interview, 1964.

109. *Letters*, 211:283.

110. *Letters*, 131:145.

111. Hammond and Scull, *Chronology*, 118.

112. *Letters*, 131:145.

113. *Sauron*, 176–77.

114. *Letters*, 91:104.

115. *Letters*, 163:211, emphasis in original.

116. *Letters*, 153:189.

117. Hammond and Scull, *Chronology*, 646.

118. *Letters*, 66:79.

119. *Towers*, 303.

120. Compare his remarks in *Letters*, 163:211; 180:231; and in Norman, "The Prevalence of Hobbits." In *Letters*, 163:216–17 he also includes Strider(!), Lothlorien, and other (now) key elements in the story.

121. *Letters*, 163:211. See also elements of the appendices as being revealed to his limited comprehension (Hammond and Scull, *Chronology*, 517). For a non-theological summary of Tolkien's authorial inspiration, see Christina Scull, "What Did He Know and When Did He Know It?: Planning, Inspiration, and *The Lord of the Rings*," in *The Lord of the Rings, 1954–2004: Scholarship in Honor of Richard E. Blackwelder*, ed. Wayne G. Hammond and Christina Scull (Milwaukee: Marquette University Press, 2006), 101–12.

122. *Letters*, 163:211.

123. *Sauron*, 195.

124. *Sauron*, 198.

125. *Letters*, 163:213; 180:232.

126. *Sauron*, 203.

127. *Sauron*, 203.

128. *Sauron*, 203.

129. *Sauron*, 181.

130. *Letters*, 89:99.

131. *Lost Road*, 38.

132. *Letters*, 163:217.

133. *Sauron*, 302.

134. *Lost Road*, 41.

135. *Lost Road*, 52.

136. *Sauron*, 185.

137. J. R. R. Tolkien, *A Secret Vice: Tolkien on Invented Languages* (New York: HarperCollins, 2016).

138. *Letters*, 208:267.

139. *Letters*, 211:283.

140. Hammond and Scull, *Chronology*, 781.

141. *Letters*, 211:283.

142. *Letters*, 211:278.

143. Norman, "The Prevalence of Hobbits."

144. Dating perhaps to around or before the "Council of London" with his friends in the Tea Club and Barrovian Society, 1914.

145. John Garth, *Tolkien and the Great War: The Threshold of Middle-earth* (Boston: Houghton Mifflin, 2013), 180.

146. *Letters*, 328:413.

147. *Letters*, 328:413.

Chapter III: Creation

1. *The Letters of J. R. R. Tolkien*, 131:145–46.

2. *Letters*, 153:188. See also 131:145.

3. *Unfinished Tales*, 319; *The Lost Road*, 15, 61; *Sauron Defeated*, 290; Tolkien, "Qenya Lexicon," 35.

4. *Tolkien On Fairy-stories*, 44.

5. *Letters*, 183:243.

6. J. R. R. Tolkien, "Notes on Oré," *Vinyar Tengwar* 41 (July 2000): 27, 30.

7. Jonathan S. McIntosh has helpfully explored the story more fully in *The Flame Imperishable*, 158–67. However, Tolkien here departs from Thomas, who denies any mediatorial creative role to the angels. As John Houghton has pointed out, the "Ainulindalë" shares more similarities with Augustine's reading of Genesis. See John William Houghton, "Augustine and the Ainulindalë," *Mythlore* 21 (1995): 4–8.

8. *Morgoth's Ring*, 330.

9. *Morgoth's Ring*, 42, 50.

10. *The Book of Lost Tales, vol. 1*, 49.

11. The roles of the angels in the music and the discords representing evil will be explored in their proper places.

12. Eru gives the same sort of being to the music as the Ainur themselves possess, who in turn share in his own reality (*Lost Tales 1*, 49).

13. *The Silmarillion*, 15. In an early version, Tolkien even ponders whether God might love Man more than the angels (*Lost Tales 1*, 55).

14. *Letters*, 153:190. Richard Greene reports that upon overhearing Greene had banned the word "creative" from his fiction-writing course, Tolkien left his seat by the fireplace to wring his hand in approval, emphasizing how much he disliked the overuse of the word, and asserting, "There is only one Creator" (Hammond and Scull, *Chronology*, 813–14, citing *Time*, October 8, 1973). Tolkien's impulse to distinguish the creative activity of God from human acts is sound and places Tolkien firmly in the pre-modern camp of aesthetics and imagination, as outlined by M. H. Abrams, *The Mirror and the Lamp* (New York: Oxford University Press, 1953); Richard Kearney, *The Wake of Imagination* (New York: Routledge, 1988); Trevor Hart, *Making Good* (Waco: Baylor University Press, 2014).

15. *Lost Tales 1*, 49. See also the idea of creativity as rearrangement in Stephen Yandell, "'A Pattern Which Our Nature Cries Out For': The Medieval Tradition of the Ordered Four in the Fiction of J. R. R. Tolkien," *Mallorn* 33 (1995): 375–92, 383–84.

16. The Secret Fire or Flame Imperishable; see chapter 1.

17. *Silmarillion*, 15; see also *Lost Tales 1*, 52; *Morgoth's Ring*, 8. The idea that the Ainur had to grow in their understanding of one another in order to accomplish this enters only in later versions.

18. *The Nature of Middle-earth*, 289.

19. Thomas, for example, denies even a ministerial creative power to angels (*Summa* 1.45.5, 1.65.3). See also the (unsatisfactory) discussion on this issue by McIntosh in *Flame Imperishable*, chapter 4. Robert Murray asserts that Tolkien maintained this emphasis on angelic participation in his primary belief as well ("Sermon at Thanksgiving Service, Keble College Chapel, 23rd August 1992," *Mallorn* 33 (1995): 20.

20. *Lost Tales 1*, 52.

21. *Silmarillion*, 15; see also *Lost Tales 1*, 52.

22. *Morgoth's Ring*, 9. But compare *Lost Tales 1*, 53–54, the earliest version, to the surprising reading of a middle manuscript, *Lost Road*, 157, where the Music is said to contain a few flaws.

23. *Morgoth's Ring*, 251.

24. *Morgoth's Ring*, 251.

25. *Silmarillion*, 20, see also 25; *Morgoth's Ring*, 13.

26. *Silmarillion*, 15.

27. *Letters*, 156:147.

28. *Morgoth's Ring*, 11.

29. *Silmarillion*, 18, 28, 49. See also Tolkien, "Late Notes on Verb Structure," 165, where there is an Elvish phrase for the will of God tied to a root sense of the application of force or pressure toward a deliberate end.

30. See also *Lost Tales 1*, 230; *Letters*, 212:284–85.

31. *Lost Road*, 31. In some versions, the Valar are given special permission to change the world themselves (*Sauron*, 258, 311, 316, 336, 409, etc.).

32. *Lost Road,* 63; *Sauron,* 357; *Unfinished Tales,* 210, 406. The role of angels is fully explored in chapter 5.

33. *Lost Tales 1,* 63. While Eriol has heard of and recognizes the Valar as equivalent to his own deities (Odin, Thor, etc.), he admits to never having heard of Eru the One.

34. *Lost Road,* 72.

35. *Sauron,* 333, 398, 403; *Lost Road,* 160.

36. *Sauron,* 290.

37. *Sauron,* 333, 401–2. For more on the "gift of death" and Tolkien's developing views, see chapter 12.

38. *Letters,* 156:203.

39. *Unfinished Tales,* 345; *The Treason of Isengard,* 115.

40. *Letters,* 306:393.

41. *Silmarillion,* 17.

42. *Silmarillion,* 19.

43. *Lost Tales 1,* 55.

44. *Letters,* 61:73.

45. *Silmarillion,* 265; see also *Letters,* 64:76.

46. *Lost Road,* 165.

47. *Letters,* 64:76; see also *The Shaping of Middle-earth,* 269.

48. *Lost Tales 1,* 142, 151, 180.

49. *Letters,* 212:285–86, emphasis added. See also "Notes on Oré," 27.Whether human death was part of God's original design or a punishment inflicted for disobedience, we will have cause to examine below.

50. *Letters,* 94:106–7.

51. J. R. R. Tolkien, "Fate and Free Will," ed. Carl Hostetter, *Tolkien Studies* 6 (2009): 187. Note that the bracketed formatting is from original manuscript.

52. "Fate and Free Will," 186–87.

53. *Unfinished Tales,* 31.

54. *Sauron,* 382.

55. *Letters,* 64:76.

56. *Letters,* 96:110.

57. *Lost Road,* 51.

58. "Fate & Free Will," 184–85.

59. *Letters,* 153:191.

60. *Lost Road,* 213–14.

61. For example, *Silmarillion,* 41–42.

62. *Letters,* 153:195.

63. *Silmarillion,* 44.

64. Nor is this, tempting as it may sound, a mere Calvinist imposition onto Tolkien's Roman Catholic framework; for more on this, see Thomas, *Summa Contra Gentiles,* 3, esp. 75–76.

65. Bud Scott calls the interplay between fate and predestination the two lenses of a binocular vision that paints Tolkien's world in three dimensions, "Tolkien's Use of Free Will Versus Predestination in *The Lord of the Rings," Mallorn* 51 (Spring 2011): 33.

66. *The Peoples of Middle-earth,* 396–97.

67. *Letters,* 156:204.

68. *Letters*, 153:193; 181:234; 297:387.

69. *Lost Road*, 66.

70. *Sauron*, 402.

71. See also Thomas, *Summa* 2a.2.8, 2a.5.5. Thomas's concept of the *desiderium naturale Dei* is a thorny issue, but see Henri de Lubac, *Surnaturel* (Paris: Lethielleux, 1991).

72. *Lost Road*, 303; "Notes on Oré," 13.

73. *Letters*, 200:260. Clark goes too far in assuming that Eru has intervened only twice in the world's history. There could be many other unrecorded instances, and many less explicit recorded ones. See also Craig Clark, "Problems of Good and Evil in Tolkien's *The Lord of the Rings*," *Mallorn* 35 (1997): 15.

74. *Morgoth's Ring*, 329. See also *Morgoth's Ring*, 12.

75. *Lost Road*, 48. See also *Letters*, 156:204.

76. *Lost Road*, 48.

77. *Lost Road*, 48; *Return of the Shadow*, 405; see also a negative example in *Unfinished Tales*, 361.

78. *Fairy-stories*, 268.

79. *Fairy-stories*, 28.

80. *Fairy-stories*, 253.

81. *Letters*, 181:234.

82. *Fairy-stories*, 253.

83. *Letters*, 89:99–100.

84. *Fairy-stories*, 267. This is also true in Middle-earth; see Tolkien, "Late Notes on Verb Structure," 151.

85. *Fairy-stories*, 253.

86. *Fairy-stories*, 252.

87. *Fairy-stories*, 268.

88. *Fairy-stories*, 245–46, 296.

89. *Fairy-stories*, 296. This passage was originally struck out.

90. *Unfinished Tales*, 31; *Lost Road*, 48; *Letters*, 89:100–101.

91. See also Austin M. Freeman, "The Author of the Epic: Tolkien, Evolution, and God's Story," *Zygon* 56, no. 2 (2021): 500–516.

92. *Letters*, 131:146.

93. *Morgoth's Ring*, 329, 382.

94. *Letters*, 131:147.

95. *Letters*, 153:194.

96. *Letters*, 156:203

97. *Morgoth's Ring*, 375. See also *Morgoth's Ring*, 349.

98. *Silmarillion*, 17.

99. *Lost Tales 1*, 55.

100. *Lost Tales 1*, 55; see also *Lost Tales 1*, 56 and *Silmarillion*, 16–17.

101. For more on this idea, see the section on theodicy in chapter 7.

102. *Letters*, 17:24.

103. *Morgoth's Ring*, 402.

104. *Letters*, 17:24.

105. *Letters*, 181:236.

106. *Unfinished Tales*, 345.

107. *Letters*, 93:105–6.

108. *Letters*, 131:161.

109. *Letters*, 94:106.

110. *The Two Towers*, 320–21.

111. *Return of the King*, 199; *Letters*, 94:106.

112. *Fairy-stories*, 47, 78. For ways in which Tolkien's view contrasted with the Liberal Theology of his day, see John William Houghton, "Neues Testament und Märchen: Tolkien, Fairy Stories, and the Gospel," *Journal of Tolkien Research* 4, no. 1 (2017): Article 9.

113. *Fairy-stories*, 78.

114. *Letters*, 109:121. See also 163:212.

115. *Letters*, 109:121.

116. *Letters*, 71:82.

117. *Letters*, 109:121.

118. *Letters*, 94:107.

119. *Fairy-stories*, 40; *Towers*, 37.

120. *Lost Tales 1*, 52.

121. *Fairy Stories*, 71.

122. Here Tolkien is philosophically similar to Plato in his account of art in *Republic*.

123. *Fairy-stories*, 72.

124. *Letters*, 153:195; 156:203. See chapter 5 for more on ontological hierarchies.

125. *Letters*, 200:259.

126. *Letters*, 131:151; *Morgoth's Ring*, 308.

127. *Morgoth's Ring*, 308. See also the brief but telling fragment in Tolkien, "The Creatures of the Earth," *Parma Eldalamberon* 14 (2003): 5–10.

128. *The War of the Jewels*, 405.

129. *Letters*, 131:160. See also Gueroult interview: "Yes, I am wedded to those kind of loyalties because I think, contrary to most people, I think that touching your cap to the Squire may be damn bad for the Squire but it's damn good for you."

130. *Letters*, 310:399. Zimbardo also discusses Tolkien's chain of being but leaves out the Valar and non-sentient creatures. See Rose A. Zimbardo, "Moral Vision in *The Lord of the Rings*," in *Understanding "The Lord of the Rings": The Best of Tolkien Criticism*, ed. Rose A. Zimbardo and Neil D. Isaac (New York: Houghton Mifflin, 2006), 69–73.

131. *Letters*, 144:176; see also the selfish king and the selfless parson in "Farmer Giles," the discussion of kings and priests in chapter 9 below.

132. *Letters*, 165:220.

133. *Letters*, 163:215.

134. *Fairy-stories*, 81. George Sayer relates the experience of hiking with Tolkien, including Tolkien's comments on the Christian properties of certain herbs ("Recollections of J. R. R. Tolkien," *Mallorn* 21, no. 2 [1995]: 22).

135. *Morgoth's Ring*, 251.

136. *Return*, 190.

137. *Letters*, 310:400.

138. *Letters*, 78:90–91.

139. *Fairy-stories*, 71–72.

140. *Letters*, 96:110.

141. *Letters*, 75:87–88.

142. *Morgoth's Ring*, 345.

143. *Return*, 177.

144. *Return*, 30.

145. *Silmarillion*, 45.

146. *Peoples*, 413. For the way in which Tolkien's use of fruit imagery parallels Augustine's, see Giovanni Costabile, "Stolen Pears, Unripe Apples: The Misuse of Fruits as a Symbol of Original Sin in Tolkien's 'The New Shadow' and Augustine of Hippo's *Confessions*," *Tolkien Studies* 14 (2017): 163–67.

147. *Letters*, 328:412; *Morgoth's Ring*, 342–43.

148. Hammond and Scull, *Chronology, 409*.

149. *Silmarillion*, 46.

150. *Morgoth's Ring*, 379.

151. *Letters*, 310:399–400.

152. *Letters*, 310:400.

153. *Letters*, 153:189. He seems in favor of deflating the sometimes over-expanded scientific ego (Hammond and Scull, *Chronology*, 724).

154. *Letters*, 211:282.

155. *Letters*, 310:399.

156. *Letters*, 310:399.

157. *The Nature of Middle-earth*, 250–51.

158. *Nature*, 250–51, 256.

159. *Nature*, 289.

160. *Nature*, 271–72.

161. *Morgoth's Ring*, 338.

162. *Letters*, 153:192.

163. *Letters*, 310:399.

164. *Fairy-stories*, 246. For Tolkien's views on nature and enchantment, see Gerardo Barajas Garrido, "Perspectives on Reality in *The Lord of the Rings*: Part II-Nature, Beauty, and Death," *Mallorn* 43 (2005): 54–55.

165. *Fairy-stories*, 246.

166. *Fairy-stories*, 81. This is the argument picked up by Hood in relation to technological integration with nature; see also Gwyneth Hood, "Nature and Technology: Angelic and Sacrificial Strategies in Tolkien's *The Lord of the Rings*," *Mythlore* 19, no. 4 (1993): 9.

167. Garth, *Tolkien and the Great War*, 121.

168. *Fairy-stories*, 78; *Letters*, 200:259.

169. Tolkien does record brief comments on visual arts and theology. In the journal he kept of his Italian pilgrimage, he comments negatively on churches defaced by monuments to past politicians, and on a painting of the Assumption of Mary by Titian: "It has nothing whatever to say to me about the Assumption: which means that with that in mind it is offensive (to me) … Can a picture concerned with religion be satisfactory on one side only? Spiritual but bad art; great art but irreligious? I find it impossible to disentangle the two. Easier perhaps for the irreligious. I am thinking, of course, only of any one individual beholder. My religious

feelings and ideas are no doubt as ignorant as my artistic ones—to speak of one such beholder" (Hammond and Scull, *Chronology*, 490–91).

170. *Fairy-stories*, 281.

171. *Fairy-stories*, 36. See also chapter 6.

172. *Fairy-stories*, 44.

173. *Fairy-stories*, 67.

174. See also *Fairy-stories*, 66. As Milbank observes, to invent even a fictional world commits the author to metaphysics ("Tolkien, Chesterton, and Thomism," in *Tolkien's "The Lord of the Rings": Sources of Inspiration*, ed. Stratford Caldecott and Thomas Honegger [Zurich and Jena: Walking Tree, 2008], 190).

175. *Fairy-stories*, 281.

176. Priscilla Tolkien, "Leaf by Niggle," *Tolkien Estate*, accessed December 22, 2021, https://www.tolkienestate.com/en/writing/other-tales-and-poetry/leaf-by-niggle.html. Also cited in Hammond and Scull, *Guide*, 663.

177. *Letters*, 153:188. Juriçková also points out that myth can impart religious truths not otherwise palatable ("Creation and Subcreation," *Mallorn* 57 [Winter 2016]: 22). She does not tie this to C. S. Lewis's similar observations in "Sometimes Fairy Tales May Say Best What's to Be Said," in *Of Other Worlds* (Boston: Houghton Mifflin Harcourt, 2002), 35–38.

178. *Letters*, 153:188–89.

179. *Nature*, 263.

180. *Letters*, 153:188–89.

181. *Nature*, 263.

182. *Letters*, 153:194.

183. *Letters*, 131:146. For more on Tolkien's views on creativity, see Trevor Hart, "Tolkien, Creation, and Creativity," in *Tree of Tales: Tolkien, Literature, and Theology*, ed. Trevor Hart and Ivan Khovacs (Waco: Baylor University Press, 2007), 39–54.

184. *Letters*, 153:193–94.

185. *Morgoth's Ring*, 371.

186. *Fairy-stories*, 60. In this sense, Seeman argues that Tolkien transforms the Christian romanticism of his predecessor Coleridge. See Chris Seeman, "Tolkien's Revision of the Romantic Tradition," *Mallorn* 33 (1995): 73–83.

187. *Letters*, 153:194.

188. *Silmarillion*, 43.

189. *Morgoth's Ring*, 360.

190. *Fairy-stories*, 64.

191. *Letters*, 153:195.

192. *Fairy-stories*, 41.

193. *Fairy-stories*, 67.

194. *Fairy-stories*, 69. Here Tolkien seems to draw deeply from Chesterton's argument in "The Ethics of Elfland." For more on Tolkien's connection to Chesterton, see, for example, the work of Thomas Egan, "Chesterton and Tolkien," *The Chesterton Review* 6, no. 1 (1979): 159–61; "Chesterton and Tolkien: The Road to Middle-Earth," *VII* 4 (1983): 45–53; "Tolkien and Chesterton: Some Analogies," *Mythlore* 12, no. 1 (1985): 28–35.

195. *Fairy-stories*, 41. For further treatment on Tolkien's "magical" view of language, see Mary Zimmer, "Creating and Re-Creating Worlds with Words: The Religion and the Magic of Language in *The Lord of the Rings*," *VII* 12 (1995): 65–78.

196. *Fairy-stories*, 41. Simon Cook argues that Tolkien's views on the meaning generated through new combinations of adjectives and nouns has links to his theory of incarnation; "Fantasy Incarnate: Of Elves and Men," *Journal of Tolkien Research* 3, no. 1 (2016): Article 1.

197. *Fairy-stories*, 52.

198. *Fairy-stories*, 52.

199. *Fairy-stories*, 246.

200. *Letters*, 131:145.

201. *Fairy-stories*, 79, 247.

202. *Letters*, 200:259.

203. *Morgoth's Ring*, 345.

204. *Sauron*, 199.

205. *Morgoth's Ring*, 51.

206. *Fairy-stories*, 79, 246.

207. *Lost Tales* 1, 59.

208. *Lost Tales* 1, 209.

209. *Lost Tales* 1, 53.

210. *Lost Tales* 1, 157.

211. *Towers*, 321.

212. *Morgoth's Ring*, 12, 42. Note that here we have an interesting parallel between good and evil artifacts. Sauron has a Ring, while Morgoth's "ring" is Middle-earth itself (*Morgoth's Ring*, 400). Likewise, Fëanor and the Blessed Realm have three jewels, while the cosmos is itself God's jewel.

213. *Morgoth's Ring*, 251.

214. *Morgoth's Ring*, 319. See also *Morgoth's Ring*, 338.

Chapter IV: Humanity

1. For example, *The Letters of J. R. R. Tolkien*, 131:147; 153:189, 195; 156: 203–4; *The Lost Road*, 204; *Morgoth's Ring*, 11–12. In a strange christological echo, the first Elves are called the Unbegotten or Eru-begotten (*The War of the Jewels*, 421), though see Luke 3:38.

2. Apparently this title can also be lost through disobedience (*Sauron Defeated*, 358, 411).

3. The *Silmarillion*, 41–42; *Lost Road*, 162.

4. *Silmarillion*, 41–42.

5. *Letters*, 183:240.

6. Suggestive of Newman's *Essay on the Development of Christian Doctrine*.

7. Tolkien, "Fate and Free Will," 186.

8. Tolkien, "Fate and Free Will," 186.

9. Tolkien, "Fate and Free Will," 182.

10. Apart from God, the angels are the first appearance of willing agents on the stage of the cosmos, but since their wills at first correspond completely to that of God, they create little change in the state of things.

11. Tolkien, "Fate and Free Will," 185.

12. *Letters*, 183:239–40.

13. *Silmarillion*, 41. See also Tolkien's earliest formulation of this passage in *The Book of Lost Tales, vol. 1,* 59; also *Lost Road,* 163; *Morgoth's Ring,* 21, 36.

14. *Lost Tales 1,* 59; *Morgoth's Ring,* 21.

15. *Morgoth's Ring,* 380.

16. *The Peoples of Middle-earth,* 370.

17. *Lost Road,* 165. Because of the divinely bestowed gift of freedom, human beings in Middle-earth are too great to be ruled by angels (*Morgoth's Ring,* 314). The angels still predominantly serve and guide rather than interfere, since it is unlawful to coerce the will of another being, and many times ineffective regardless (*Peoples,* 334; *Lost Road,* 229; *Morgoth's Ring,* 188). Men go their own way, and things become more complex. Compare *Morgoth's Ring,* 244.

18. Tolkien, "Fate and Free Will," 185. For an analysis of Tolkien's language in "Fate and Free Will," alongside his accounts of the Music, see Verlyn Flieger, "The Music and the Task: Fate and Free Will in Middle-earth," *Tolkien Studies* 6 (2009): 151–81.

19. Tolkien *On Fairy-stories,* 65.

20. *The Monsters and the Critics and Other Essays,* 21.

21. *Fairy-stories,* 65.

22. "Mythopoeia," *Tree and Leaf, including Mythopoeia.*

23. "Mythopoeia."

24. *Lost Tales 1,* 232. While Tolkien at one point asserts that the Elves learn speech from the Valar (*Lost Road,* 180), and at another point that the Valar adopt the speech of the Elves, who are especially gifted (*Jewels,* 405), this is not necessarily a contradiction. Much like any geniuses, the Elves learn their skill from masters they later surpass.

25. *Fairy-stories,* 65.

26. *Morgoth's Ring,* 392; *Letters,* 246:326.

27. *Letters,* 131:155.

28. *Morgoth's Ring,* 245.

29. *Letters,* 203:262.

30. See below. For a survey of the final fate of each of Tolkien's fictional races, see Charles W. Nelson, "'The Halls of Waiting': Death and Afterlife in Middle-earth," *Journal of the Fantastic in the Arts* 9, no. 3 (1998): 200–211.

31. *Morgoth's Ring,* 37.

32. *Silmarillion,* 42; *Morgoth's Ring,* 37.

33. *Lost Tales 1,* 59.

34. *Monsters,* 23.

35. *Letters,* 211:280.

36. *The Two Towers,* 112.

37. *Sauron,* 382.

38. *Silmarillion,* 265.

39. *Lost Tales 1,* 59; *Morgoth's Ring,* 43; *Silmarillion,* 42.

40. *Silmarillion,* 41; *Lost Road,* 163.

41. Men *do* love the earth, a desire God has planted within them. But they look forward to the New Earth, when eternity overtakes time (*Sauron,* 365). Thus the Elves call them the Guests or Strangers and envy them (*Silmarillion,* 42).

42. *Letters*, 131:149. See also Irène Fernandez, "La vérité du mythe chez Tolkien: imagination & gnose," in *Les Racines du Légendaire (La Feuille de la Compagnie no. 2)*, ed. Michaël Deveaux (Geneva: Ad Solem, 2003), 262.

43. Quoted in Alaric Hall and Samuli Kaislaneiemi, "'You Tempt me Grievously to a Mythological Essay': J. R. R. Tolkien's Correspondence with Arthur Ransome," in *Ex Philologia Lux: Essays in Honour of Leena Kahlas-Tarkka*, ed. J. Tyrkkö, O. Timofeeva, and M. Salenius (Helsinki: Société Néophilologique: 2013), 271 and 274. Tolkien notes here that this is not the case in his own mythology, however.

44. *Towers*, 40–41.

45. *Letters*, 156:203; see also 181:234–35.

46. *Letters*, 181:235.

47. *Silmarillion*, 16.

48. *Morgoth's Ring*, 358.

49. Tolkien, "Qenya Lexicon," 35. Emphasis added.

50. *Letters*, 153:194. Emphasis added.

51. *Letters*, 131:147.

52. *Letters*, 181:235.

53. *Letters*, 153:189.

54. *Fairy-stories*, 257–58.

55. *Letters*, 144:176; 181:235.

56. *Morgoth's Ring*, 160.

57. *Morgoth's Ring*, 21.

58. *Letters*, 181:235.

59. *Letters*, 131:146.

60. *Jewels*, 405.

61. *Letters*, 131:146.

62. *Lost Tales 1*, 97.

63. *Morgoth's Ring*, 316.

64. *Morgoth's Ring*, 37.

65. *The Fellowship of the Ring*, 94.

66. *Fairy-stories*, 75.

67. *Letters*, 131:155.

68. *Letters*, 131:147.

69. *Letters*, 144:176. Tolkien says that tracing one's bloodline to an Elvish strain is the only real claim to nobility.

70. *Letters*, 153:194.

71. *Letters*, 131:147.

72. *Unfinished Tales*, 235.

73. *Morgoth's Ring*, 37.

74. *Letters*, 131:147.

75. *Jewels*, 217.

76. *Lost Tales 1*, 59.

77. *Lost Tales 1*, 97.

78. *Return of the King*, 149.

79. *Unfinished Tales*, 66.

80. *Silmarillion*, 210.

81. *Lost Tales 1*, 97.

82. *Morgoth's Ring*, 340.

83. *Letters*, 131:149.

84. *Morgoth's Ring*, 342.

85. *Morgoth's Ring*, 343.

86. *Letters*, 131:158.

87. *Letters*, 131:160.

88. *Letters*, 131:158.

89. *Unfinished Tales*, 345. See also Tom Shippey's discussion of smiling despair in *The Road to Middle-earth*, 3rd ed. (New York: HarperCollins, 1993), 179.

90. *Letters*, 131:158.

91. *Letters*, 131:159.

92. *Letters*, 246:329.

93. *Return of the Shadow*, 281.

94. *Shadow*, 281.

95. *Return*, 146.

96. *Lost Road*, 191.

97. *Jewels*, 203.

98. *Jewels*, 211.

99. *Morgoth's Ring*, 244.

100. *Lost Road*, 178; see also 129.

101. *Lost Road*, 146.

102. *Silmarillion*, 44; see also *Jewels*, 204.

103. *Peoples*, 391.

104. *Silmarillion*, 46.

105. *Letters*, 153:191, 195; *The Nature of Middle-earth*, 248.

106. *Morgoth's Ring*, 419.

107. See the solid work of David Tneh on this subject in multiple publications, such as David Tneh, "The Human Image and the Interrelationship of the Orcs, Elves and Men," *Mallorn* 55 (2014): 35–39.

108. *Fairy-stories*, 254–55.

109. *Fairy-stories*, 254–55. For more on the question of the existence of fairies, see Dimitra Fimi, *Tolkien, Race, and Cultural History: From Fairies to Hobbits* (New York: Palgrave Macmillan, 2008), part one.

110. *Morgoth's Ring*, 330.

111. *Morgoth's Ring*, 250.

112. *Silmarillion*, 67.

113. *Lost Road*, 246.

114. *Fairy-stories*, 155.

115. *Morgoth's Ring*, 337.

116. *Nature*, 289.

117. *Nature*, 263.

118. *Morgoth's Ring*, 337.

119. *Morgoth's Ring*, 241–42.

120. *Morgoth's Ring*, 233, 349.

121. *Morgoth's Ring*, 331.

122. *Fairy-stories*, 42–43.

123. *Morgoth's Ring*, 330.

124. *Morgoth's Ring*, 220, 336.

125. *Morgoth's Ring*, 221.

126. *Morgoth's Ring*, 315, 317, 330.

127. *Morgoth's Ring*, 337.

128. *Morgoth's Ring*, 317. Aristotle and Thomas thus speak of the soul as the "form" of the body, meaning it is what constitutes the individualized identity of this particular material object.

129. *Morgoth's Ring*, 317.

130. *Morgoth's Ring*, 225.

131. *Letters*, 156: 204,205.

132. *Morgoth's Ring*, 330.

133. *Morgoth's Ring*, 221. Tolkien elaborates on a sort of psychic communication in "Ósanwe-Kenta," but as it is unclear whether he would affirm this in the primary world, I have left it aside. It is worth noting, however, that Tolkien depicts both physical bodies and physical speech as dulling the ability for direct mind-to-mind communication (24–26).

134. *Jewels*, 405.

135. *Morgoth's Ring*, 219; see chapter 7 on demonic influence and possession.

136. *Morgoth's Ring*, 222–23. See also Garth, *Tolkien and the Great War*, 35; Hammond and Scull, *Chronology*, 40, 53, 302. It is also at least possible that he believed in psychic phenomena (Hammond and Scull, *Chronology*, 344–45).

137. *Morgoth's Ring*, 232.

138. *Morgoth's Ring*, 216.

139. *Morgoth's Ring*, 349.

140. *Morgoth's Ring*, 349.

141. *Sauron*, 178.

142. *Sauron*, 177.

143. *Sauron*, 177.

144. *Sauron*, 180–81.

145. *Sauron*, 194–95.

146. *Sauron*, 194.

147. *Morgoth's Ring*, 353.

148. *Morgoth's Ring*, 342.

149. *Morgoth's Ring*, 333.

150. *Letters*, 211: 280; *Morgoth's Ring*, 330.

151. We follow Tolkien's usage here, in which "Man" is a name for the species as a whole.

152. For example, Candice Fredrick and Sam McBride, "Battling the Woman Warrior: Females and Combat in Tolkien and Lewis," *Mythlore* 25, no. 3/4 (2007): 29–42; "Women as Mythic Icons: Williams and Tolkien," in *Women Among the Inklings: Gender, C. S. Lewis, J. R. R. Tolkien, and Charles Williams* (Westport, CT: Greenwood Press, 2001), 29–54; W. H. Harrison, "Éowyn the Unintended : The Caged Feminine and Gendered Space in *The Lord of the Rings*" (master's thesis, University of British Columbia, 2013). See my own more extensive response

to this charge in "Critiquing Tolkien's Theology: Three Bad Arguments and Three Good Ones," in *Theology and Tolkien*, ed. Douglas Estes (Minneapolis: Lexington Books, forthcoming).

153. *Letters*, 43:49.

154. *Morgoth's Ring*, 227.

155. *Morgoth's Ring*, 216.

156. *Letters*, 43:48.

157. *Morgoth's Ring*, 216.

158. *Morgoth's Ring*, 234.

159. *Morgoth's Ring*, 225.

160. *Morgoth's Ring*, 233.

161. *Morgoth's Ring*, 225–27.

162. *Morgoth's Ring*, 211.

163. *Morgoth's Ring*, 211.

164. *Morgoth's Ring*, 211.

165. *Morgoth's Ring*, 334.

166. *Letters*, 49:61.

167. *Letters*, 43:51.

168. *Letters*, 43:48.

169. *Letters*, 43:50.

170. *Letters*, 43:50.

171. *Letters*, 43:49.

172. *Letters*, 43:49.

173. *Letters*, 43:50.

174. *Letters*, 43:50–51.

175. *Letters*, 43:49.

176. *Letters*, 43:50.

177. *Jewels*, 421. He is critical of the modern liberated woman. Usually female economic independence means subservience to employer rather than father or husband (*Letters*, 43:50)

178. C. S. Lewis, *Complete C. S. Lewis Signature Classics* (New York: HarperOne, 2008), 96.

179. *Unfinished Tales*, 226.

180. *Towers*, 40–41; *Morgoth's Ring*, 224.

181. *Monsters*, 21.

182. *Letters*, 310:400.

183. *Morgoth's Ring*, 11–12.

184. *Letters*, 45:55.

185. *Fairy-stories*, 58. See also 152–54 on the danger of an "older" society.

186. Garth, *Tolkien and the Great War*, 58.

187. See also Tolkien's qualifications of patriotism and nationalism as personal, non-imperialist commitments in Hammond and Scull, *Guide*, 1399.

188. Hammond and Scull, *Chronology*, 26–27, 38.

189. Hammond and Scull, *Guide*, 1286–87.

190. Hammond and Scull, Garth, *Tolkien and the Great War*, 251. For an exposition of Tolkien's turn to tradition in order to recover a Christian sense of divine presence, see Thomas Smith, "Tolkien's Catholic Imagination," in *Jerusalem, Athens, and Rome: Essays in Honor of James V. Schall, S.J.*, ed. Marc D. Guerra (South Bend, IN: St. Augustine's, 2013), 4–36.

191. Garth, *Tolkien and the Great War*, 256.

192. *Sauron*, 402.

193. *Silmarillion*, 45.

194. *Fairy-stories*, 44.

195. *The Treason of Isengard*, 24.

196. *Fairy-stories*, 44.

197. *Fairy-stories*, 55.

198. *Letters*, 269:355.

199. *Fairy-stories*, 155. For Tolkien's views on the evolution of culture, including the way in which Christ acts as the focal point of history, see Philip Irving Mitchell, "'Legend and History Have Met and Fused': The Interlocution of Anthropology, Historiography, and Incarnation in J. R. R. Tolkien's 'On Fairy-stories,'" *Tolkien Studies* 8 (2011): 1–21.

200. Letter 29. For a rebuttal of the charge of anti-Semitism in Tolkien's depiction of Dwarves, see Renée Vink, "'Jewish' Dwarves: Tolkien and Anti-Semitic Stereotyping," *Tolkien Studies* 10 (2013): 123–45.

201. *Letters*, 61:73. See also his opposition to the Boer War in Hammond and Scull, *Guide*, 1399.

202. *Letters*, 78:90.

203. *Sauron*, 93.

204. *Letters*, 78:90; see also 269:355.

205. *Towers*, 269.

206. *Letters*, 96:111.

207. *Letters*, 186:246.

208. See, for example, Hammond and Scull, *Chronology*, 39. Douglas C. Kane, for instance, points out how legal concepts are inherently tied to philosophical and other concerns; see "Law and Arda," *Tolkien Studies* 9 (2012): 37–57. Kane neglects the ways in which legal theory, inseparable as it is from ethical theory, also relies on implicit or explicit theological assumptions.

209. *Letters* 52:63–64. See also the record of his deeply moving meeting with the queen and Prince Philip (Hammond and Scull, *Chronology*, 798, 800, 810–11).

Chapter V: Angels

1. *The Book of Lost Tales, vol. 2*, 267. On analyzing the poem, Tolkien believes Earendel to be a title for John the Baptist, and the term "angel" to refer to John's role as messenger.

2. *The Letters of J. R. R. Tolkien*, 54:66.

3. *Letters*, 156:205; 211:280.

4. *Letters*, 89:99. In analyzing this letter, we see that Tolkien denies individual rays coming from the Light because God's activity is perfectly simple and one. God is simple act. He does not will individual things discretely, but everything at once, in a single unified whole. It is rather our perception and relation to God which give the appearance of multiple acts.

5. *Letters*, 89:99.

6. *Letters*, 89:99.

7. *Letters*, 54:66.

8. *Letters*, 89:99.

9. See also Tolkien, "Ósanwe-Kenta," 31.

10. See also Tolkien, "Ósanwe-Kenta," 31.

11. *Sauron Defeated*, 177.

12. *The Peoples of Middle-earth*, 396.

13. The most prominent work in this area is that of Michael Heiser, though the field is wide. See Michael Heiser, *The Unseen World* (Bellingham, WA: Lexham Press, 2015); Heiser, *Angels* (Bellingham, WA: Lexham Press, 2018). For a critical exegetical approach, see Ellen White, *Yahweh's Council* (Tübingen: Mohr Siebeck, 2014).

14. Gueroult interview, emphasis in original.

15. *Letters*, 211:283.

16. C. S. Lewis, *The Screwtape Letters* (*Complete C. S. Lewis Signature Classics*), 276.

17. Lewis, *The Screwtape Letters*, 276.

18. Lewis, *The Screwtape Letters*, 276.

19. Gueroult interview.

20. See here Michael Ward's essential book on Lewis, *Planet Narnia* (Oxford: Oxford University Press, 2007).

21. *The War of the Jewels*, 405; by contrast, see *Morgoth's Ring*, 398.

22. *Morgoth's Ring*, 398. See also Tolkien, "Ósanwe-Kenta," 24.

23. *Letters*, 200:259.

24. *Letters*, 181:232–37.

25. *Morgoth's Ring*, 36.

26. *Sauron*, 401. At one point Tolkien refers offhandedly to the saints as "lesser angels" (Gueroult interview), but it is unclear whether he means this to be a metaphysical claim or a claim of functional equivalence.

27. *The Silmarillion*, 41; *Morgoth's Ring*, 36.

28. *Letters*, 131:143–61.

29. *The Return of the King*, 232.

30. *Peoples*, 381.

31. *Unfinished Tales*, 413.

32. *The Two Towers*, 200. Gandalf fights and defeats the balrog (another Maia) after a long battle, but as he was already greatly exhausted, we can assume the confrontation could have been much more decisive. A battle between Sauron and Gandalf might not be as one-sided as expected.

33. *Jewels*, 405.

34. *Morgoth's Ring*, 9.

35. *The Lost Road*, 350.

36. *The Book of Lost Tales*, vol. 1, 52.

37. *Sauron*, 357.

38. *Silmarillion*, 15.

39. *Silmarillion*, 20.

40. *Morgoth's Ring*, 378.

41. *Morgoth's Ring*, 338.

42. *Morgoth's Ring*, 378.

43. *Letters*, 200:259; *Lost Road*, 204; *Sauron*, 357; *Morgoth's Ring*, 337–38. In the published *Silmarillion*, however, we read only that "many" chose to enter the world, and the idea that the mightiest Ainur became the Valar disappears (*Silmarillion*, 25).

44. *Silmarillion*, 20, emphasis added; *Letters*, 200:259.

45. *Lost Road*, 350.

46. *Morgoth's Ring*, 330; *Sauron*, 400. The name "Enkeladim" is late and rare and takes as its source a giant of Greek myth, Enceladus, whose name refers to the sound of the trumpet that orders the march. Enceladus is defeated by Athena in the titanomachy. He appears in *Aeneid*, book 3. This name therefore connotes great spiritual stature and the power of ordering and command. The other greater spirits mentioned here are probably the more powerful Maiar.

47. *Morgoth's Ring*, 405.

48. Tolkien, "Ósanwe-Kenta," 24.

49. Tolkien, "Ósanwe-Kenta," 24. See also Tolkien, "Ósanwe-Kenta," 30: "Some say that Manwë, by a special grace to the King, could still in a measure perceive Eru; others more probably, that he remained nearest to Eru, and Eru was most ready to hear and answer him."

50. *Morgoth's Ring*, 330.

51. *Morgoth's Ring*, 147.

52. *Letters*, 200:259.

53. *Letters*, 200:259.

54. *Morgoth's Ring*, 49, 147.

55. *Morgoth's Ring*, 273.

56. *Morgoth's Ring*, 19, 34.

57. *Morgoth's Ring*, 145.

58. *Silmarillion*, 187.

59. *Morgoth's Ring*, 339, 402.

60. *Letters*, 153:193–94; 200:259, though not necessarily of the same rank. A distinction between Valar and Maiar was late in coming (*Lost Tales 1*, 63).

61. *Silmarillion*, 30.

62. *Silmarillion*, 30.

63. *Peoples*, 388; *Unfinished Tales*, 406.

64. *Letters*, 200:259; 325:411; *Morgoth's Ring*, 425; *Unfinished Tales*, 406, 411; *Peoples*, 388; Tolkien, "Ósanwe-Kenta," 23.

65. *Unfinished Tales*, 413.

66. *Peoples*, 363.

67. *Silmarillion*, 234. She is described as being of the "divine" race of the Valar, though she is explicitly a Maia. Tolkien frequently includes both Valar and Maiar in the same ontological category, only differentiated in terms of power and authority.

68. *Silmarillion*, 46; *The Nature of Middle-earth*, 308.

69. *Lost Tales 1*, 66; see also 99.

70. *Lost Tales 1*, 219.

71. *Letters*, 156:205.

72. *Letters*, 131:146.

73. *Morgoth's Ring*, 34, 145; *Sauron*, 357.

74. *Silmarillion*, 20.

75. *Morgoth's Ring*, 425.

76. *Morgoth's Ring*, 392.

77. *Letters*, 153:193–94.

78. *Letters*, 181:234.

79. *Silmarillion*, 15; see also *Morgoth's Ring*, 8; *Lost Tales 1*, 53.
80. *Silmarillion*, 15.
81. *Morgoth's Ring*, 11. As is mentioned in the final chapter, there will be another, fuller Music at the end of time.
82. *Morgoth's Ring*, 144.
83. *Morgoth's Ring*, 51.
84. *Morgoth's Ring*, 362.
85. *Morgoth's Ring*, 334.
86. *Morgoth's Ring*, 350.
87. *Morgoth's Ring*, 330.
88. *Morgoth's Ring*, 144.
89. *Lost Road*, 213. But, now that Satan has ruined the creation through his malice, they are not only to rule but to redress the marring of the world, restoring or rectifying it as best they can (*Morgoth's Ring*, 223).
90. *Letters*, 156:206.
91. *Morgoth's Ring*, 246.
92. Tolkien, "Ósanwe-Kenta," 29.
93. *Morgoth's Ring*, 405.
94. *Morgoth's Ring*, 405.
95. *Sauron*, 373.
96. *Morgoth's Ring*, 405.
97. *Morgoth's Ring*, 404.
98. *The Fellowship of the Ring*, 279; see also *The War of the Ring*, 401.
99. *Morgoth's Ring*, 400.
100. *Morgoth's Ring*, 404.
101. *Letters*, 153:193; 156:206; *Towers*, 269; *Peoples*, 390; *Lost Tales 2*, 77.
102. *Letters*, 181:235; 297:387; *Nature*, 232–33.
103. *Letters*, 153:193.
104. *Silmarillion*, 74–75; *Lost Tales 1*, 144; *Morgoth's Ring*, 99, 286.
105. *Sauron*, 373.
106. *Letters*, 153:193; *Nature*, 292.
107. *Morgoth's Ring*, 314; see also *Nature*, 293.
108. *Silmarillion*, 187; *Letters*, 153:194; 156:204; *Sauron*, 403; *Morgoth's Ring*, 427.
109. *Letters*, 156:206.
110. *Return*, 317.
111. *Lost Road*, 15–16.
112. *Morgoth's Ring*, 145.
113. *Lost Road*, 160.
114. Tolkien, "Ósanwe-Kenta," 31–32.
115. *Letters*, 131:147.
116. *Letters*, 156:203; *Morgoth's Ring*, 425; Tolkien, "Ósanwe-Kenta," 31–32.
117. *Morgoth's Ring*, 399.
118. *Silmarillion*, 74.
119. *Morgoth's Ring*, 425.
120. *Morgoth's Ring*, 337.

121. *Morgoth's Ring*, 12.

122. *Peoples*, 388.

123. *Morgoth's Ring*, 340.

124. *Silmarillion*, 21; *Morgoth's Ring*, 218; *Letters*, 200:259; 325: 411.

125. *Silmarillion*, 21; *Jewel*, 397.

126. Tolkine, "Ósanwe-Kenta," 29.

127. *Letters*, 200:259; 212:285; 325:411.

128. *Morgoth's Ring*, 15–16.

129. *Nature*, 242.

130. *Silmarillion*, 29.

131. *Nature*, 245. This echoes patristic and medieval speculation on the nature of angelophanies; see also Austin M. Freeman, "Celestial Spheres: Angelic Bodies and Hyperspace," *TheoLogica: An International Journal for Philosophy of Religion and Philosophical Theology* 2, no. 2 (2018): 172–74.

132. *Peoples*, 364; Tolkien, "Ósanwe-Kenta," 25, 30–31. Though, of course, see the contested question about the identity of Tom Bombadil summarized in *Encyclopedia*, 670–71. Tolkien seems to have toyed with ranking Melian among the Istari in some sense (*Nature*, 95, 101).

133. *Letters*, 200:260.

134. *Letters*, 200: 260; 211:280.

135. *Letters*, 200:260.

136. *Letters*, 246:332. Note his explicit caveat about reasoning by narrative necessity here.

137. *Morgoth's Ring*, 99, 286.

138. Tolkien, "Ósanwe-Kenta," 31.

139. Tolkien, "Ósanwe-Kenta," 30.

140. *Morgoth's Ring*, 69.

141. *Silmarillion*, 21. See also C. S. Lewis, *Perelandra* (New York: Scribner, 2003), 200–201. Lewis is well known for differentiating between male/female and masculine/feminine. The former is a created reflection of the latter.

142. *Jewels*, 397; Tolkien, "Ósanwe-Kenta," 25, 27.

143. *Lost Road*, 185.

144. *Letters*, 211:282. But compare *Jewels*, 400–401, where it is said that the Valar do have proper names among themselves. This is a curious contradiction, as both sources date to the period 1958–1960.

145. *Morgoth's Ring*, 129.

146. This is the main subject of the short essay "Ósanwe-Kenta," meaning thought-transference.

147. *Sauron*, 202.

148. *Sauron*, 203.

149. Tolkien, "Notes on Oré," 13, 15.

150. *Morgoth's Ring*, 380.

151. *Letters*, 156:202.

152. *Letters*, 183:243.

153. *Letters*, 156:203.

154. Tolkien, "Ósanwe-Kenta," 29.

155. *Morgoth's Ring*, 245.

156. *Morgoth's Ring*, 362.

157. *Morgoth's Ring*, 138.

158. See *Morgoth's Ring*, 427.

159. *Morgoth's Ring*, 392.

160. *Morgoth's Ring*, 93.

161. *Morgoth's Ring*, 273.

162. *Morgoth's Ring*, 273.

163. *Letters*, 212:287; *Jewels*, 210. Interestingly, Tolkien vacillates between a formal and intimate tone in this scene between God and an angel. He eventually settles on having Aulë and God speak formally, using the second-person pronoun "you" rather than the intimate "thou."

164. See *Morgoth's Ring*, 405.

165. *Lost Tales 1*, 220.

166. J. R. R. Tolkien, "Words, Phrases and Passages in various tongues in *The Lord of the Rings*," *Parma Eldalamberon* 17 (2007): 178–79. See also *Morgoth's Ring*, 362.

167. Tolkien, "Words, Phrases and Passages," 178–79; *Nature*, 234.

168. See *Lost Tales 1*, 223; Tolkien, "Ósanwe-Kenta," 28–29; *Nature*, 307, 309.

169. *Morgoth's Ring*, 401.

170. *Morgoth's Ring*, 402.

171. Tolkien, "Ósanwe-Kenta," 27–29.

172. Tolkien, "Ósanwe-Kenta," 28–29.

173. Tolkien, "Ósanwe-Kenta," 28.

174. Tolkien, "Ósanwe-Kenta," 28.

175. *Morgoth's Ring*, 402.

176. *Morgoth's Ring*, 162.

177. Though the truth of the Wizards' origin was only revealed in the appendices, we see Pippin ponder Gandalf's true nature in the throne room of Gondor (*Return*, 29).

178. *Letters*, 89:99; 156:202; *The Treason of Isengard*, 422; Hammond and Scull, *Chronology*, 749, where Gandalf's sternness and gentleness in his guardianship are said to be particularly comforting.

179. *Morgoth's Ring*, 203; see also 147. *Letters*, 200:250, however, states that Olórin (Gandalf) was a Maia of Manwë.

180. *Return*, 365.

181. His staff breaks at Gandalf's command. He casts him from the White Council and from the order of Wizards (*Towers*, 189).

182. *Towers*, 98.

183. *Unfinished Tales*, 364, 406.

184. For example, *Letters*, 144:180; 145:182; 153:192; 156:202, 205. There are more instances.

185. *Letters*, 156:207.

186. *Unfinished Tales*, 408.

187. *Letters*, 246: 327; 268:354.

188. *Letters*, 131:159.

189. *Return*, 365.

190. *Letters*, 156:202.

191. *Letters*, 131:147.

192. *Unfinished Tales*, 406; *Letters*, 131:159; 145:182; 156:202; *Return*, 365. Once Saruman's spirit leaves his body, it withers instantly (*Return*, 300). See also Tolkien, "Ósanwe-Kenta," 30–31.

193. *Unfinished Tales*, 406; *Letters*, 131:159; 145:182; 156:202; *Return*, 365–66. Once Saruman's spirit leaves his body, it withers instantly (*Return*, 300).

194. *Letters*, 131:159; 145:182; *Return*, 365.

195. *Unfinished Tales*, 407.

196. *Letters*, 181:237; *Unfinished Tales*, 407.

197. *Letters*, 153:192.

198. *Letters*, 156:202.

199. *Unfinished Tales*, 407.

200. *Letters*, 156:203.

201. *Unfinished Tales*, 344, 365.

202. *Unfinished Tales*, 344, emphasis added.

203. Tolkien devotes a short note to the way the heart can communicate truth: see "Notes on Oré."

204. According to the Council of Chalcedon, Jesus Christ, as truly God and truly man, is a single divine person with two complete natures, divine and human. This means the single person Jesus possesses, among other things, two wills and two minds—one, omniscient and eternal, and the other, limited and finite. When Jesus became incarnate, it seems that he undertook a sort of self-limiting, not always accessing his omniscient divine mind but relying for the most part upon his limited human mind. Thus, he can ask, "Who touched me?" (Luke 8:45 NIV), or admit that not even he knows when the end of the world will come (Matt 24:36; Mark 13:32). And yet, underneath this truly human mind, Jesus' divine nature knows the answers to these questions.

205. *The Treason of Isengard*, 422; *Unfinished Tales*, 364, 406, 408.

206. *Letters*, 210:271; *Unfinished Tales*, 406.

207. *Towers*, 98.

208. *Return*, 29.

209. *Towers*, 95.

210. Tolkien points out that this is nowhere more true than in the much-anticipated confrontation between Gandalf and the Witch-king: the resistance that Gandalf has kindled is in fact so powerfully effective that no actual confrontation is necessary. The wraith is destroyed through human agency (*Letters*, 156:203). Gandalf is victorious but has not met power with power.

211. *Letters*, 156:202–3.

212. *Return*, 94.

213. *Return*, 128.

214. *Towers*, 98.

215. With Sauron (*Towers*, 101); with Shadowfax (108).

216. *Fellowship*, 417.

217. *Towers*, 99. We are not told what this high place has to do with things, but the term "high place" is a term for a location of spiritual power.

218. *Unfinished Tales*, 361.

219. *Letters*, 156:203; 144:180.

220. *Letters*, 144:180.

221. *Letters*, 156:203.

222. *Letters*, 156:203.

223. *Letters*, 156:202.
224. *Letters*, 156:202.
225. *Letters*, 156:203.
226. See Moses' shining face in Exodus 34:35, or the unbearable brightness of the angels' faces in Dante's *Divine Comedy*.
227. *Letters*, 156:203; see also 156:202.
228. *Letters*, 156:202.
229. *Treason*, 422.
230. *Unfinished Tales*, 344, emphasis added.
231. *Towers*, 98; see also *Treason*, 426.
232. *Towers*, 98; see also *Treason*, 426.
233. *Towers*, 98.
234. *Towers*, 97.
235. *Return*, 233.
236. *Towers*, 97.
237. *Towers*, 99.
238. *Return*, 31.
239. *Return*, 230.

Chapter VI: The Fall

1. *The Letters of J. R. R. Tolkien*, 153:203.
2. Tolkien's favorite adjective for the fall is "inevitable."
3. *Tolkien On Fairy-stories*, 265.
4. *Letters*, 131:147.
5. *Morgoth's Ring*, 402.
6. *Letters*, 131:155; 153:204; Tolkien, "Notes on Oré," 14.
7. *Morgoth's Ring*, 340; *Letters*, 131:151.
8. *Letters*, 153:190.
9. *Morgoth's Ring*, 344. Tolkien here also provides an amusing pseudo-scholarly rationalization for the dating and source of the legends and an explanation for their similarity, with an eye toward academic folklorists and their overeager subsumptions. See also the story soup in *Fairy-stories*, 39–40.
10. *Letters*, 131:147.
11. *Sauron Defeated*, 397.
12. *Letters*, 212:286.
13. *Letters*, 181:237.
14. *Letters*, 153:195.
15. Theologically, the fall of angels and their presence in Genesis 1–3 is a disputed topic, but it was not so for Tolkien.
16. *Letters*, 181:235; 186:246.
17. *Letters*, 200:259.
18. For more on this, see chapter 8.
19. *The Lost Road*, 63.
20. *Sauron*, 341, 357–58; *Morgoth's Ring*, 12, 379.

21. *The Silmarillion*, 16–17; *Morgoth's Ring*, 9.

22. *Morgoth's Ring*, 344, 405, 420, 422.

23. *The Return of the King*, 317; *Silmarillion*, 280.

24. *Silmarillion*, 31. Sauron, too, falls in stages: after the destruction of Númenor, for instance, he loses the ability to appear beautiful.

25. *Morgoth's Ring*, 394.

26. *Sauron*, 397; see also *The Fellowship of the Ring*, 60.

27. *Morgoth's Ring*, 392; see also 344.

28. *Morgoth's Ring*, 344.

29. *Morgoth's Ring*, 344.

30. *Letters*, 96:109–10.

31. *Letters*, 156:204; see also 131:154–56.

32. *Fairy-stories* 49, and the alternate version at 229. Also see 36–37.

33. *Fairy-stories*, 265.

34. *Letters*, 96:110.

35. *Fairy-stories*, 73–74; *Silmarillion*, 281; *The Book of Lost Tales, vol. 2*, 159, 321.

36. *The Book of Lost Tales, vol. 1*, 97.

37. *Letters*, 43:51.

38. *Letters*, 96:110.

39. *Lost Tales 1*, 97; *Sauron*, 259; *Fairy-stories*, 81.

40. *Letters*, 96:110.

41. *Fairy-stories*, 265.

42. Cf. *Letters*, 96.

43. *Sauron*, 398, 402, 409; *Silmarillion*, 76; *Lost Tales 1*, 179; *The Shaping of Middle-earth*, 98.

44. *The War of the Jewels*, 399.

45. As a toponym, *Aman* can be correlated with the name of Jerusalem, *Shalem*. Both are places of peace from which holiness radiates.

46. *Letters*, 131:148.

47. *Silmarillion*, 279.

48. *The Two Towers*, 286.

49. *The Fellowship of the Ring*, 392. While the Elves are passing into a sort of exile, Tolkien is clear that the Elves never "fell" as a race, never denied God and received a curse for doing so (see, for example, *The Nature of Middle-earth*, 36, 88). They could sin as individuals, of course, due to their existence in a fallen world (*Nature*, 88). Tolkien explicitly ties this uncursed state to the Genesis account, writing, for example, that Elvish childbirth occurs without pain; compare Gen 3:16 (*Nature* 23, see also 27).

50. *Fellowship*, 353.

51. *Fellowship*, 393.

52. *Lost Tales 1*, 220, 223.

53. *Morgoth's Ring*, 354.

54. *Letters*, 297:387.

55. *Silmarillion*, 141, 259; *Unfinished Tales*, 65; *Jewels*, 293; *Morgoth's Ring*, 305. In *Nature*, 39, 42, Tolkien notes that this fall must have taken place at a time in which the Elves and Valar are otherwise occupied, else they would have interfered.

56. *Beowulf: A Translation and Commentary*, 161. See Tolkien's cursory attempt to tie the three original clans of Men to the three sons of Noah in *Sauron*, 411.

57. *Morgoth's Ring*, 329.

58. *Morgoth's Ring*, 359–60.

59. "Now having made the man ... lord ... of the earth, and of everything that is in it, He secretly appointed him as lord over those who were servants in it. But they, however, were in their <full-development>, while the lord, that is, the man, was very little, since he was an infant, and it was necessary for him to reach full-development by growing in this way ... But the man was a young child, not yet having a perfect deliberation ... and because of this he was easily deceived by the seducer." Irenaeus, *On the Apostolic Preaching*, trans. John Behr (Crestwood, NY: St. Vladimir's Seminary Press, 1997), 47.

60. Since Tolkien frequently calls Morgoth Satan in his letters, I therefore take the liberty of referring to Morgoth as Satan when it seems appropriate.

61. *Morgoth's Ring*, 347.

62. *Morgoth's Ring*, 347. Note the transition to a more merciful portrayal from an alternate version found in the notes where God speaks in wrath (*Morgoth's Ring*, 351; bracketed text taken from *Morgoth's Ring*, 354).

63. *Morgoth's Ring*, 351.

64. *Letters*, 131:154.

65. *Letters*, 131:155. Tolkien himself calls the fall of Númenor an Atlantis myth, so the fall of a great city through pride is not exclusive to the Christian religion, although Tolkien might say that Atlantis is simply another type of the primeval fall. We might also see echoes of Virgil's *Aeneid* in the story, dealing as it does with fathers, sons, and sailing in exile to a new homeland (Straubhar, 248–49 in *The Tolkien Encyclopedia*).

66. *Unfinished Tales*, 266.

67. *Silmarillion*, 270; *Sauron*, 348, 368, 401; *Letters*, 153:155.

68. *Silmarillion*, 271–72; *Sauron*, 347–348, 367, 383, 401; *The Peoples of Middle-earth*, 182–83; *Letters*, 153:155–56.

69. *Return*, 317.

70. *Unfinished Tales*, 266.

71. *Morgoth's Ring*, 245.

72. *Morgoth's Ring*, 344. See the most primitive form of this myth in *Lost Tales 1*, 236.

73. *Morgoth's Ring*, 95, 189, 275, 279.

74. *Lost Tales 1*, 147; *Sauron*, 358.

75. *Towers*, 125–26. See Austin M. Freeman, "Flesh, World, Devil: Evil in J. R. R. Tolkien," *Journal of Inklings Studies* 10, no. 2 (2020): 139–71, 154–56.

76. *Towers*, 185. See also John 8:44.

77. *Towers*, 184. One is reminded of Isaiah 5, "Woe to those who draw iniquity with cords of falsehood ... Woe to those who call evil good and good evil, who put darkness for light and light for darkness, who put bitter for sweet and sweet for bitter! Woe to those who are wise in their own eyes, and shrewd in their own sight" (Isa 5:18, 20 ESV). There are many other parallels in this chapter, which includes a tower in the midst of a garden whose walls are broken down in judgment and multiple instances of "devouring" imagery (Gandalf remarks below that Saruman's fate is to be "devoured").

78. *Towers*, 185.

79. *Towers*, 186.

80. *Return*, 258.

81. *Towers*, 183. Note the double sense of the word "enthralling," meaning both fascinating and enslaving.

82. *Letters*, 210:276–77.

83. *Towers*, 118.

84. *Towers*, 119, 124.

85. *Towers*, 124–25.

86. *Towers*, 125.

87. See *Morgoth's Ring*, 187, 275.

88. *Lost Tales 1*, 140–41.

89. *Lost Tales 1*, 140–41. Even more remarkably, Tolkien implies that even *Manwë* is not unaffected by the wicked thoughts Melkor introduces (*Lost Tales 1*, 142).

90. Tolkien does provide an example of inherited *grace*, noting that the repentance of the Númenóreans led to a special grace by which they had little inclination to the sins of lust, greed, hate, and domination (*The Nature of Middle-earth*, 409). For a further exploration of Tolkien's beliefs about the origin of language, see Maria Kuteeva, "'Old Human,' or 'The Voice in our Hearts': J. R. R. Tolkien on the Origin of Language," in *Arda Special I: Between Faith and Fiction*, ed. Nils Ivar Agøy (Uppsala, Sweden: Arda Society, 1998), 72–89.

91. J. R. R. Tolkien, "Philology: General Works," in *The Year's Work in English Studies*, vol. 4 (London: Oxford University Press, 1927), 60.

92. *Letters*, 165:220; *Sauron*, 201. See Garth, *Tolkien and the Great War*, 51–52 and several studies on Tolkien's concept of native language such as Yoko Hemmi, "Tolkien's *The Lord of the Rings* and His Concept of Native Language: Sindarin and British-Welsh," *Tolkien Studies* 7, no. 1 (2010):147–74.

93. *Sauron*, 203.

94. For a fictional example, see *Unfinished Tales*, 38, where Voronwë activates the sea-love and ship-lore of his mother's kin within his mind.

95. *The Treason of Isengard*, 24. We should not place too much weight on this, however, as this mostly seems to have been due to artistic necessity for the scene.

96. *Treason*, 24.

97. *Return*, 190; *Letters*, 153:190–91.

98. *Morgoth's Ring*, 410, 414.

99. *Letters*, 186:246.

100. *Morgoth's Ring*, 133.

101. *Letters*, 212:286.

102. *Morgoth's Ring*, 405–6.

103. For example *Letters*, 153:190, 195.

104. *Fellowship*, 281; *Letters*, 153:190.

105. *Morgoth's Ring*, 396–97.

106. *Morgoth's Ring*, 419. It should be noted that the origin of the Orcs is a fraught question, as we see above.

107. *Morgoth's Ring*, 186, 273.

108. Norman, "The Prevalence of Hobbits"; see also *Letters*, 78:90. The matter-of-fact way in which Tolkien expects the interviewer to know his opinion on this question because of

a statement in his fiction should give us more confidence in reasoning from the legendarium to Tolkien's actual views.

109. *Letters*, 312:401.

110. *Fairy-stories*, 67.

111. "Mythopoeia" in *Tree and Leaf, including Mythopoeia*.

112. *The Monsters and the Critics and Other Essays*, 23.

113. *Letters*, 64:76.

114. *Letters*, 69:80.

115. *Letters*, 250:337.

116. *Silmarillion*, 41–42; *Lost Tales 1*, 59.

117. *Morgoth's Ring*, 379, though this seems to contradict other places such as *Fellowship*, 381 which give evil, once begun, a self-propagating character.

118. *Silmarillion*, 36; *Return*, 316, 328; *Lost Tales 1*, 166. It may even be the case that the corruption can be lessened in a certain area through special effort (*Morgoth's Ring*, 307), although the different relation between Morgoth and the material world may not allow this to translate into the primary world.

119. Garth, *Tolkien and the Great War*, 48.

120. *Letters*, 195:255.

121. *Fairy-stories*, 276.

122. *Letters*, 64:76.

123. *Letters*, 2285.

124. For example, *Letters*, 71:82; 153:191; 191:252.

125. *Silmarillion*, 255. See also *Morgoth's Ring*, 203; *Return*, 228.

126. *The Tolkien Reader*, 159.

127. *Sauron*, 402.

128. *Sauron*, 402; *Peoples*, 436–37.

129. *Return*, 285.

130. *Return*, 297.

131. *Peoples*, 370.

132. See chapter 12, below.

133. *Letters*, 212:286, emphasis added; see also *Morgoth's Ring*, 333.

134. *Monsters*, 23; *Letters*, 131:154.

135. *Letters*, 212: 286.

136. *Silmarillion*, 36; see also *Morgoth's Ring*, 18, 32, 53.

137. *Morgoth's Ring*, 255; see also *Morgoth's Ring*, 217.

138. *Silmarillion*, 279, 281; see also *Sauron*, 351, 373.

139. *Morgoth's Ring*, 428.

140. *Peoples*, 370.

141. *Morgoth's Ring*, 259.

142. *Fellowship*, 381.

143. *Letters*, 191:252.

144. *Peoples*, 411.

145. *Letters*, 212:286–87.

146. *Morgoth's Ring*, 399–400.

147. *Morgoth's Ring*, 400. See further in this passage for explanations of the mythological alignment of certain substances, such as gold, silver, and water.

148. *Morgoth's Ring*, 344.

149. Tolkien clearly holds that the fall results in a curse on our natures, since he reasons fictionally that the Elves, being unfallen, are also uncursed (*The Nature of Middle-earth*, 32, 88).

150. *Lost Tales 1*, 166.

151. *Morgoth's Ring*, 353.

152. *Sauron*, 195; *Morgoth's Ring*, 211.

153. *Lost Tales 1*, 209.

154. *Morgoth's Ring*, 351.

155. *Morgoth's Ring*, 351, 410.

156. *Morgoth's Ring*, 410.

157. *Sauron*, 180–81.

158. *Morgoth's Ring*, 222, 241.

159. *Letters*, 96:111.

160. *Fairy-stories*, 69.

161. *Letters*, 89:102.

162. *Fellowship*, 364–65.

163. *Morgoth's Ring*, 334.

164. *Sauron*, 401.

165. *Monsters*, 170.

166. *Fairy-stories*, 74. We should note that some aspects of nature are hostile to Mankind apart from the Devil's provocations, e.g. *Lost Tales 1*, 67, 99; Caradhras in *Fellowship*, 302 (but see *Return of the Shadow*, 424, where these voices are called demons).

167. *Fairy-stories*, 67.

168. *Fairy-stories*, 257.

169. *Fairy-stories*, 41.

170. *Letters*, 131:145.

171. *Letters*, 131:145.

172. *Letters*, 131:146.

173. *Fairy-stories*, 42.

174. *Letters*, 153:194.

175. Letter to Nevill Coghill, published by Wayne G. Hammond and Christina Scull in their addenda and corrigenda to the *J. R. R. Tolkien Companion and Guide*; see "Tom Bombadil Addenda & Corrigenda," *Too Many Books and Never Enough* (blog), December 30, 2014, https://wayneandchristina.wordpress.com/2014/12/30/tom-bombadil-addenda-corrigenda/.

176. *Fairy-stories*, 65–66; "Mythopoeia."

177. *Peoples*, 413.

178. *Peoples*, 420.

179. *Letters*, 43:48.

180. *Letters*, 43:48.

181. *Morgoth's Ring*, 392.

182. *Letters*, 43:51.

183. The Reformers deny this; for most Protestants, such desires are themselves sin and the result of the fall.

184. *Letters*, 153:190.

185. *Morgoth's Ring*, 341.

186. *Letters*, 212:287.

187. *Letters*, 131:146.

188. *Silmarillion*, 286–87; *Morgoth's Ring*, 9; *Letters*, 153:151.

189. *Letters*, 181:237.

190. *Unfinished Tales*, 178. Pride is also mentioned here.

191. *Towers*, 203–4.

192. *Fellowship*, 414.

193. *Sauron*, 156, 187.

194. *Return*, 177.

195. *Fellowship*, 382.

196. But it is also clear that sometimes temptation can be construed as an actual force, external to the one being tempted. The two clearest examples are Frodo's repeated impulses to put on the Ring and Pippin's theft of the *palantír* (*Towers*, 196–200, 204). In the climactic scene at Mount Doom, Frodo is literally overwhelmed, with no possibility of resistance.

197. *Letters*, 153:195.

198. *Letters*, 153:195. For an in-depth analysis of this problem, see Robert T. Tally Jr., "Demonizing the Enemy, Literally: Tolkien, Orcs, and the Sense of the World Wars," *Humanities* 8, no. 1 (2019): 54.

199. *Letters*, 153:195.

200. *Letters*, 153:191.

201. *Morgoth's Ring*, 304, 312.

202. For example, *Morgoth's Ring*, 334, 409; *Letters*, 153:195. Elsewhere he expresses less confidence in such matters (for example, *Morgoth's Ring*, 411).

203. *Letters*, 153:195; *Morgoth's Ring*, 409, 419.

204. *Letters*, 78:90. He acknowledges that some cultures may produce more of such people on average, though none has a monopoly.

205. *Towers*, 301; *Return*, 285. At one point, even many of the ruffians that had oppressed the Shire are reformed (*Sauron*, 93). This is a fact (unsurprisingly) missed by Kathleen Jones in her atheist critique of Tolkien's ethics (Kathleen Jones, "The Use and Misuse of Fantasy," *Mallorn* 23 [1986]: 8–9). See the response by Jeff Stevenson in "A Delusion Unmasked," *Mallorn* 24 (1987): 5–10.

206. *Silmarillion*, 269.

207. *Sauron*, 402, 411; *Morgoth's Ring*, 355; *Letters*, 156:204.

208. *Unfinished Tales*, 71–72.

209. For more on the Orcs as more complex than they are usually taken, see David Tneh, "Orcs and Tolkien's Treatment of Evil," *Mallorn* 52 (2011): 37–43.

210. *Morgoth's Ring*, 308.

Chapter VII: Evil and Sin

1. *Morgoth's Ring*, 334.

2. The debate over an alleged polarity in Tolkien's concept of evil is longstanding. Verlyn Flieger directly calls it a "contradiction." See Flieger, "The Arch and the Keystone," *Mythlore*

38, no. 1 (2019): 11. For a full survey and bibliography, see Austin M. Freeman, "Flesh, World, Devil: Evil in J. R. R. Tolkien," *Journal of Inklings Studies* 10, no. 2 (2020): 139–71.

3. Others have attempted to read Tolkien's mythology as dualistic, but for reasons explored below, these arguments are unpersuasive. See Michael McClain, "The Indo-Iranian Influence on Tolkien," *Mallorn* 19 (1982): 24; Carrol Fry, "'Two Musics about the Throne of Ilúvatar': Gnostic and Manichaean Dualism in *The Silmarillion*," *Tolkien Studies* 12, no. 1 (2015): 77–93; and a rebuttal in Richard Angelo Bergen, "'A Warp of Horror': J. R. R. Tolkien's Sub-creation of Evil," *Mythlore* 36, no. 1 (2017): 103–21.

4. *Morgoth's Ring*, 406.

5. See Lewis, *Perelandra*, 132. Fleming Rutledge has also pointed out this connection; see *The Battle for Middle-earth*, 86–87. Note too that Lewis somewhat modeled Ransom on Tolkien, as can be seen by Ransom's shouting lines from *The Battle of Maldon* in the midst of the fight.

6. *Enchiridion*, 11–15. Interestingly, Tolkien has the Elves define goodness and beauty in an essentially negative mode as well—as being more or less free from the corruption Morgoth foists upon the world's design (*The Nature of Middle-earth*, 173–74). But this is because of the special situation of the world after the fall, and not truly a metaphysically rigorous definition anyway.

7. *The Letters of J. R. R. Tolkien*, 183:243.

8. See Alex Lewis, "Splintered Darkness," *Mallorn* 26 (1989): 31–33.

9. *Morgoth's Ring*, 405.

10. This concept is well-explored by C. S. Lewis, but also by Hannah Arendt, *Eichmann in Jerusalem: A Report on the Banality of Evil* (New York: Penguin, 2006).

11. *The Silmarillion*, 17.

12. Sam observes that Gollum switches between "we" and "I" when referring to himself, and that the first-person pronoun seems to be a sign that his good side is winning out (*The Two Towers*, 251). Gollum's individual personhood is directly tied to his good rather than his evil personality. Sam begins to kill Gollum, but the realization of Gollum's decline stops him short (*The Return of the King*, 222). Gollum's use of personal pronouns as a window into his psychology has been fruitfully explored by Gergely Nagy, "The 'Lost' Subject of Middle-earth: The Constitution of the Subject in the Figure of Gollum in *The Lord of the Rings*," *Tolkien Studies* 3 (2006): 57–79. Interestingly, Faramir several times refers to Sauron as "the Nameless." He too has lost even his name, though this is to him a sign of power (*Towers*, 18).

13. *Letters*, 211:279.

14. The degenerating aspect of evil does not rest in the spiritual realm alone. The lifespan of the Númenoreans wanes in direct connection with the coming of the Shadow (*Unfinished Tales*, 228, 235–36). The same holds true for their later descendants. "They *fell* into evils and follies," explains Faramir (*Towers*, 286, emphasis added). He gives three reasons for his people's decline, all three phrased in passive constructions to emphasize a fall away from being and activity. Either they become obsessed with the Darkness and black magic (both images of negation and absence), or they slide into idleness and sloth (an explicit loss of active agency), or they engaged in civil wars until becoming so weak as to be conquered by wild men. Even Gondor is the agent of its own decay, falling by degrees into decrepitude. This decay is characterized by death, hunger, tombs, old kingdoms, and names (of their *descent*, no less). Lords are childless, aged, withered men in secret chambers and cold towers. The final blow is the lack of an heir, a denial of procreation and the impulse toward life, which is the duty of all people

but especially of kings. See Chance's analysis of the imagery of age as a sign of evil in *Tolkien's Art*, 41 and following.

15. *Morgoth's Ring*, 70; see also 110, 133; Tolkien, "Ósanwe-kenta," 31.
16. *Morgoth's Ring*, 391.
17. *Morgoth's Ring*, 403–4.
18. *Morgoth's Ring*, 407.
19. *Letters*, 131:153.
20. *Unfinished Tales*, 407.
21. *Towers*, 190.
22. *Towers*, 172; see also *The War of the Ring*, 53.
23. *War*, 63–64; *Towers*, 187. This is a shift from Tolkien's previous work. Manwë had, due to his innocence, failed to understand the depths of Morgoth's malice, whereas now it is the enemy who has lost understanding because of his rejection of true wisdom.
24. *Towers*, 126.
25. *Towers*, 172.
26. *Unfinished Tales*, 289.
27. *Towers*, 190.
28. *Towers*, 189.
29. *Towers*, 124.
30. *Towers*, 125.
31. *Return*, 299.
32. *Return*, 263.
33. *Return*, 300.
34. *Return*, 300.
35. Peter Abelard, *Exposition on the Lord's Prayer*, sixth petition, author's translation.
36. For a further exploration of this issue, see Freeman, "Flesh, World, Devil: The Nature of Evil in J. R. R. Tolkien," *Journal of Inklings Studies*, 10, no. 2 (2020): 139–71.
37. *Morgoth's Ring*, 297.
38. As Jane Chance observes, "Wormtongue, Grishnákh, and Saruman all display aspects of the higher sins of pride, avarice, envy, and wrath through their incomprehension or manipulation of language. Gollum and Shelob both illustrate the lower sins of gluttony, sloth, and lechery." Chance, *Tolkien's Art*, 164.
39. Conversely, Númenoreans have a specially graced inclination away from lust, greed, gluttony, hate, cruelty, and tyranny (*Nature*, 319–409).
40. *The Tolkien Reader*, 110.
41. *Reader*, 110.
42. See *Morgoth's Ring*, 344–45. Tolkien notes that all things in Arda Unmarred (the unfallen world) should be beautiful, and that death and decay are not (*Nature*, 270). They are the results of fall and sin. But he also clarifies that natural imperfections such as mutations are not necessarily evil or sinful, but the divinely designed way the physical world functions (*Nature*, 250–51).
43. In a basic sense this includes enemies like Orcs, but in a fictional world Tolkien is also free to embody the conflict of man against nature in good and evil terms as well. Boromir murmurs that there are fell voices amidst the winds of Caradhras. Aragorn responds that there are many evil and unfriendly things not in league with Sauron (*The Fellowship of the Ring*, 302). Elsewhere, frustrated that readers assumed Old Man Willow is working for Sauron, Tolkien

fumes that people cannot seem to imagine things hostile to humans that are not servants of the devil (*Letters*, 175:228; see also Hammond and Scull, *Chronology*, 506).

44. *Letters*, 312:401–2; *Reader*, 159.

45. *Letters*, 96:110.

46. *Letters*, 66:78.

47. *Letters*, 49:61.

48. *Letters*, 49:61.

49. *Letters*, 49:61.

50. *Letters*, 312:402. Certain cultures, such as wartime Germany and Japan, can be so structurally corrupted that they produce many people more like Orcs than men, though they hold no monopoly on such a sad lot (*Letters*, 78:90). Tolkien laments that Oxford too deserves to be wiped out in a fiery bloodbath like Sodom because of the abominations perpetrated there (*Letters*, 69:80).

51. Morgoth, Tolkien's fictional version of Satan, is called Lord of this World, a clear reference to 2 Corinthians 4:4, where Satan is also called the god of this world (or "this age"; the Greek is *aionos*). He is not the only reason why the world sets itself against the good. Even if Morgoth leaves the world, his evil remains (*Morgoth's Ring*, 322). The tree of evil will never be slain while this world endures, and God himself must come in to tear it up by the roots (*The Peoples of Middle-earth*, 411).

52. *Letters*, 212:287.

53. *Return*, 305.

54. *Towers*, 155. See also *Fellowship*, 381; *War*, 45. Similarly, Morgoth's evil power and will remain as an independent force to work within his servants, even after he has been cast out of the world (*Morgoth's Ring*, 259; *Silmarillion*, 260). Not even he himself can stop them now.

55. *Morgoth's Ring*, 395.

56. *Fellowship*, 366; *Towers*, 172–73, 187–88. There is one instance where this asymmetry is actually reversed: Manwë is so free from evil that he does not understand Melkor's treachery (*Silmarillion*, 65).

57. *Morgoth's Ring*, 397, emphasis added.

58. *Silmarillion*, 251; *The Shaping of Middle-earth*, 155, 157.

59. *The Monsters and the Critics and Other Essays*, 34.

60. *Monsters*, 83.

61. *Monsters*, 34.

62. *Monsters*, 86.

63. *Monsters*, 89.

64. For Tolkien, temptation and confession lie at the heart of the Gawain poem, where the peril Gawain faces inside the castle is just as real and perilous on the moral plane as is his fight with the Green Knight on the physical plane (*Monsters*, 73–74, 83).

65. *Tolkien On Fairy-stories*, 37, 229.

66. *Fairy-stories*, 49.

67. See Frodo's growth in spiritual discernment below. *Sauron Defeated*, 5–6.

68. *Sauron*, 5; the second version of this passage emphasizes less Frodo's benevolence and more his desire for political power.

69. *Return*, 177.

70. *Return*, 188.

71. *Return*, 143.

72. *Letters* 246:332; for Sam's temptation to transform Mordor into a garden paradise, see *Return*, 177.

73. *Towers*, 204. For the ways in which the *palantír* acts as a symbol for the sin of *curiositas*, see Craig A. Boyd, "Augustine, Aquinas, and Tolkien: Three Catholic Views on *Curiositas*," *Heythrop Journal* 61 (2020): 222–33.

74. *Fellowship*, 414.

75. *The Treason of Isengard*, 327.

76. *Fellowship*, 414.

77. *Fellowship*, 413.

78. *Treason*, 327.

79. *Letters*, 246:328.

80. *Letters*, 246:332.

81. *Fellowship*, 382.

82. *Fellowship*, 70–71.

83. *Fellowship*, 278; *Silmarillion,* 301; *War*, 72.

84. *Towers*, 203.

85. *Letters*, 153:190.

86. Aragorn chastises Frodo for jesting that he will grow thin enough to be a wraith (*Fellowship*, 196–97). Glorfindel tells Aragorn not even to handle the Morgul blade if he can avoid it (*Fellowship*, 223). Saruman could put a spell on the company if they approach him without the proper seriousness (*Towers*, 181–82).

87. *Letters*, 131:160.

88. *Morgoth's Ring*, 401.

89. *Morgoth's Ring*, 95; Tolkien, "Ósanwe-Kenta," 32. Tolkien more often writes of lies using a botanical metaphor and speaks of liars sowing seeds of falsehood, which take root and last long after their sower has departed (*Morgoth's Ring*, 189; *The Book of Lost Tales, vol. 1*, 140, 147). The one that sows lies will not lack a harvest, Tolkien warns (*Morgoth's Ring*, 95). Morgoth gives the Noldor much hidden (and true!) knowledge, which deceives and destroys them on another front. It is not good to know some things, which kill happiness for being only half-understood (*Lost Tales 1*, 141). Morgoth does not deceive the Elves in what he says, but in the perlocutionary effect of his speech—that is, what they think he wants to occur by means of his speech. Morgoth is no helper to the Elves, as they think, and gives them only so much truth as they can destroy themselves with.

90. *Morgoth's Ring*, 279; *Unfinished Tales*, 355; see also *Silmarillion*, 227. This is what happens to Húrin: seeing through Morgoth's eyes, he sees all things crooked (*Silmarillion*, 231; *The War of the Jewels*, 259). In a less supernatural way, Wormtongue's false counsel performs the same function with Théoden.

91. *Fairy-stories*, 72–73.

92. *Fellowship*, 183.

93. See *Monsters*, 34.

94. *Peoples*, 182.

95. For example, *Lost Tales 1*, 142.

96. *Towers*, 181–82, 184. Saruman knows the truth but suppresses it in unrighteousness (Rom 1:18). He recognizes that the Valar are helping Gandalf but resists him anyway, deceiving himself and others (*Unfinished Tales*, 361).

97. *Letters*, 210:277.

98. *Letters*, 210:277.

99. *Return*, 298, where Saruman's voice can still deceive only if it is allowed to do so; *Morgoth's Ring*, 189, 279; *Jewels*, 259 (and the parallel passage in *Silmarillion*, 231).

100. Sauron is master of treachery and faithless (*Return*, 166–67).

101. *Towers*, 165.

102. *Towers*, 188.

103. Remember the sad and lonely hell of C. S. Lewis's *The Great Divorce*.

104. *Towers*, 171.

105. *Return*, 89.

106. *The Book of Lost Tales*, vol. 2, 27.

107. *Lost Tales 1*, 103.

108. *Morgoth's Ring*, 399.

109. *Letters*, 131:160; 155:200.

110. *Letters*, 181:237. Indeed, unless applied to the Valar, "power" is always an ominous word for Tolkien (*Letters*, 131:152). The realm of the will is specially singled out by Tolkien over and over again. Sauron's will is so strong that if any but the strongest will uses the *palantír*, it will immediately turn toward the Dark Lord (*Towers*, 204). Denethor's mind is too great for Sauron to subdue, and so he is instead manipulated and broken (*Return*, 132). Frodo cannot be Ringlord until his will and pride grow enough to be able to dominate the will of others, especially enemies (*Letters*, 246:331). He instead resists, and complains that he is instead falling under its power and would go mad if it were taken (*Return*, 214). Gollum, who carries the Ring much longer than Frodo, has completely succumbed to its pressure upon him. He both hates and loves it, as he does himself. But he has no will left in this regard (*Towers*, 64).

111. *Morgoth's Ring,* 399. Tolkien clarifies that any being can of course interfere in evil purposes, denying other creatures the means to achieve their aims, without being considered to dominate the will. The Valar, who clearly know God's will, are the most reliable of such interpositors (*Nature*, 248).

112. *Morgoth's Ring*, 12; *Silmarillion*, 18.

113. *Morgoth's Ring*, 411; *Letters*, 153:195; see also 212:287.

114. *Letters*, 131:145.

115. *Letters*, 131:145.

116. *Letters*, 155:200.

117. *Letters*, 131; Tolkien seems to leave the door open for a proper use of magic, as Lewis did with his Merlin in *That Hideous Strength*. See *Letters*, 131:152, where he speaks of magic as easily corruptible into evil. That it is *corruptible* rather than *corrupt* implies that one might resist the temptation.

118. *Letters*, 131:146.

119. *Letters*, 53:65.

120. *Letters*, 53:65.

121. *Letters*, 131:146.

122. *Letters*, 181:237. This, says Tolkien, would have been Gandalf's error if he had taken the Ring. He would have erased the line distinguishing good from evil (*Letters*, 246:333). Much like a modern dictator, Gandalf would disguise domination in innocuous names. His version of charity would be tyranny; concern would conceal absolute control. But the old Rohirric proverb states that evil is often its own worst enemy (*Towers*, 200). Unity, cooperation, and even success are goods which a being approaching absolute evil must ultimately lose.

123. *Letters*, 75:87–88. See also *Letters*, 181:236.

124. *Letters*, 75:88.

125. *Letters*, 155:200.

126. *Morgoth's Ring*, 395–96. *Morgoth's Ring*, 396 (to which compare the behavior of the demons in Lewis's *Screwtape Letters*). Tolkien is careful not always to blame the victims of such domination. Torture and brainwashing, for example, are physical processes for which a person cannot necessarily be faulted for capitulating. Moral failure only occurs if one did not make the best effort possible relative to one's own limitations, and the closer one comes to those limits, the more blame may be mitigated (*Letters*, 246:326). Tolkien equates Frodo's "failure" to destroy the Ring after demonic mental torture with a physical failure as would have occurred through being stopped by bodily violence (*Letters*, 246:327).

127. *Morgoth's Ring*, 394; *Nature*, 239.

128. *Morgoth's Ring*, 396.

129. *Morgoth's Ring*, 397.

130. *Letters*, 183:243–44.

131. *War*, 401. For more on the Ring as a symbol of power, see Gerardo Barajas Garrido, "Perspectives on Reality in *The Lord of the Rings*," *Mallorn* 42 (2004): 54–58.

132. *Return*, 213.

133. *Silmarillion*, 270.

134. *Towers*, 301.

135. *Unfinished Tales*, 353, 358.

136. *Return*, 97.

137. *Silmarillion*, 289.

138. *Fellowship*, 286.

139. *Fellowship*, 210, 234.

140. *Letters*, 131:151.

141. *Towers*, 76.

142. *Towers*, 204.

143. *Towers*, 188.

144. *Towers*, 190.

145. *Return*, 291.

146. *Return*, 292.

147. *Fellowship*, 58.

148. John Rateliff notes the clash between Christian and heathen in Tolkien's *The Fall of Arthur*, see also John Rateliff, "'That Seems to Me Fatal': Pagan and Christian in *The Fall of Arthur*," *Tolkien Studies* 13 (2016): 45–70.

149. *Morgoth's Ring*, 397.

150. *Morgoth's Ring*, 334.

151. *Peoples*, 370.

152. *Letters*, 183:244.

153. *Morgoth's Ring*, 344. Tolkien briefly calls Morgoth/Satan the rightful ruler of earth, though his right may have been revoked by his rebellion (*Sauron*, 342). The phrase was ejected at once, but it is still highly significant that Tolkien even considered this concept, for it is of course similar to Lewis's Space Trilogy cosmology, and both ideas derive from a brief mention in the New Testament, in which Satan is called "god of this world" (2 Cor 4:4) and "prince of the power of the air" (Eph 2:2 ESV).

154. *Morgoth's Ring*, 354; *Nature*, 253.

155. *Sauron*, 341, 358, 411; *Silmarillion*, 259.

156. *Morgoth's Ring*, 398.

157. *Morgoth's Ring*, 348.

158. See, for instance, besides, *Beowulf: A Translation and Commentary*, Aelfric's homily *De falsis diis* (On false gods) and Wulfstan's adaptation of it, commonly referred to as *De falsis deis*.

159. *Beowulf*, 170–71.

160. *Monsters*, 44.

161. *Shaping*, 233; *Morgoth's Ring*, 344; *Peoples*, 182, 306, 438.

162. *Lost Tales 1*, 236; *Sauron*, 402. Tolkien creates an imaginative picture of the development of false theologies, which parallels the work of Christopher Dawson's *Progress and Religion*, which Tolkien cites throughout *Fairy-stories*. Rather than a myth of progress toward truth, humanity instead abandons the truth it already had at the first (see *The Lost Road*, 17). Here he begins to blend the latter stages of his mythological prehistory with the earliest stages of known history. Here in *Lost Road*, 17, especially we see Tolkien's fictional rationale for ancient ship burials in later generations.

163. *Monsters*, 48.

164. *Beowulf*, 172.

165. *Beowulf*, 172.

166. *Reader*, 14–15.

167. *Letters*, 131:146.

168. *Letters*, 183:243–44.

169. *Letters*, 183:244.

170. *Letters*, 156:206.

171. *Letters*, 156:207.

172. *Unfinished Tales*, 71.

173. *Lost Road*, 69.

174. *Letters*, 183:244.

175. *Towers*, 332–33.

176. *Return*, 129.

177. *Return*, 164.

178. *Morgoth's Ring*, 397.

179. *Letters*, 131:156; see also *Sauron*, 348, 367–68, 383; *Silmarillion*, 271–72.

180. *Sauron*, 335.

181. *Silmarillion*, 271–72.

182. *Letters*, 156:205. Note that only evil men serving Sauron make temples or sacred sites (*Nature*, 393).

183. *Sauron*, 347, 367; *Peoples*, 182–83.

184. *Silmarillion*, 273–74.

185. *Silmarillion*, 273–74.

186. *Sauron*, 401; *Peoples*, 427.

187. *Silmarillion*, 274; *Peoples*, 183.

188. *Silmarillion*, 276.

189. *Silmarillion*, 277.

190. *Sauron*, 371; *Silmarillion*, 277.

191. *The Book of Lost Tales, vol. 2*, 62.

192. *The Lays of Beleriand*, 59.

193. *Lays of Beleriand*, 59. These may be the last remnants of the strange beings in *Lost Tales 1*, 99, in which three classes of spirits haunt the pine woods of the world. Later, of course, Nan Dungortheb becomes the haunt of Ungoliant's spider spawn.

194. *Letters*, 312:402.

195. *Lost Road*, 12.

196. *Morgoth's Ring*, 397.

197. *Lost Road*, 25.

198. *Lost Road*, 18. In earlier phases, this included the race of Dwarves as a whole, reported to be atheists (*Lost Tales 2*, 223).

199. See Tolkien's original interview with Lars Gustaffson, published in English as "Two Swedish Interviews with J. R. R. Tolkien," trans. Morgan Thomsen and Shaun Gunner, *Hither Shore* 9 (2013).

200. Hammond and Scull, *Chronology*, 349.

201. *Morgoth's Ring*, 318. For more on the role of music in Tolkien's theodicy, see Chiara Bertoglio, "Dissonant Harmonies: Tolkien's Musical Theodicy," *Tolkien Studies* 15 (2018): 93–114.

202. Augustine, *Enchiridion* viii; Aquinas, *Summa Theologica* 3.1.3.3.

203. *Morgoth's Ring*, 245.

204. *Morgoth's Ring*, 129.

205. *Lost Tales 1*, 54–56. We have discussed the other examples Tolkien gives in the section on divine providence, but in a very late version of *The Silmarillion*, in which Morgoth makes the Moon (Ithil) as a sort of evil watchtower before being driven from it, we find again the way in which God creates beauty from evil. The moon catches the light of the sun when she is invisible, and silver moonlight now comes from golden sunlight, and the world is enriched (*Morgoth's Ring*, 42).

206. *Morgoth's Ring*, 402.

207. Michael David Elam, by way of the "Ainulindalë," helpfully explores the way in which sorrow can be considered beautiful in Christian tradition. See "The 'Ainulindalë' and J. R. R. Tolkien's Beautiful Sorrow in Christian Tradition," *VII* 28 (2011): 61–78. In a more limited way, Neberman also notes the necessity of sorrow for character formation in "Eucatastrophe: On the Necessity of Sorrow for the Human Person," *Mallorn* 57 (2016): 27–28.

208. *Fellowship*, 363; see also *Treason*, 232.

209. *Fellowship*, 203.

210. *Gawain and the Green Knight*, 18.

211. *Silmarillion*, 28.

212. *Return*, 149.

213. *Letters*, 153:195. Allowing Orcs into the network of God's good creation both adds the goodness of being and allows Orcs to participate in the possibility of redemption. For Orcs as able to repent, see *Morgoth's Ring*, 419.

214. *War*, 195.

215. *Lost Tales 1*, 142, 151, 180.

216. *Letters*, 153:194.

217. *Lost Tales 1*, 55, see also *Morgoth's Ring*, 11; *Lost Tales 1*, 142, 151.

218. *Silmarillion*, 41–42.

219. *Morgoth's Ring*, 21.

220. *Letters*, 153:194.

221. *Morgoth's Ring*, 411.

222. *Letters*, 153:195.

223. *Letters*, 153; see also *Morgoth's Ring*, 411.

224. *Morgoth's Ring*, 244–45; *Nature*, 270.

225. *Letters*, 153:191.

226. *Letters*, 131:147.

227. *Peoples*, 418.

228. *Letters*, 181:235.

229. *Morgoth's Ring*, 211.

Chapter VIII: Satan & Demons

1. Work could also be done on the particular words Tolkien deploys around these ideas. The term "devil" or "devilry" appears sixteen times in *Lord of the Rings*, usually in reference to actual demons like Sauron or Saruman, or to the Orcs doing their will (*The Fellowship of the Ring*, 191, 342, 378; *The Two Towers*, 142, 144, 157, 177, 198, 235, 351; *The Return of the King*, 95, 105, 119, 137, 175, 191, 209). By contrast, there is only one occurrence of the word "god" (*Return*, 113). This use of "devilry" is likely linked in Tolkien's mind to the word "bedevil," which the fourth definition listed in the *Oxford English Dictionary* defines as "to transform mischievously or bewilderingly, to corrupt, spoil, confound, or muddle" (see also Hammond and Scull, *Chronology*, 497, 499, 774). Once, Tolkien can casually reference the "demon" of creativity (Hammond and Scull, *Chronology*, 781).

2. Interestingly, there is no significant mention of Satan in "The Devil's Coach-Horses," which is instead about a particular word in Old English.

3. *The Letters of J. R. R. Tolkien*, 153:195; 156:202, 205–6; 175:228; 211:283; 294:376; *Sauron Defeated*, 314; Stuart D. Lee, "'Tolkien in Oxford' (BBC, 1968): A Reconstruction," *Tolkien Studies* 15 (2018): 154.

4. *The Shaping of Middle-earth*, 166; *Sauron*, 314.

5. *Letters*, 156:206.

6. *Letters*, 183:214.

7. *Letters*, 200:259.

8. *Sauron* 341; *The Lost Road*, 63, 157, 206; *Sauron*, 401; *Morgoth's Ring*, 144, 378–79.

9. *Morgoth's Ring*, 9; *The Silmarillion*, 16.

10. *The Nature of Middle-earth*, 344.

11. *Lost Road*, 157; *The Book of Lost Tales, vol. 1*, 54; see also *Lost Road*, 63. The darkness here is simply the physical cold, dark emptiness of space, and not any sort of evil element inherent

in nature. But it serves as a primeval symbol of otherness in a sub-created universe centered upon light (see Verlyn Flieger, *Splintered Light*).

12. *Morgoth's Ring*, 379.

13. *Silmarillion*, 31.

14. *Shaping*, 271.

15. *Morgoth's Ring*, 330, 375.

16. *Morgoth's Ring*, 355; see *Sauron*, 401–2.

17. *Letters*, 156:202. Tolkien's Satan suffers five of the seven deadly sins: covetousness, pride, envy, lust, and wrath (*Lost Road*, 206). Being proud, he covets and lusts after the world and all it contains, and grows jealous of its rightful regent Manwë. His frustrated desires turn to wrath and destruction.

18. *Sauron*, 341, 358; *Shaping*, 233; *Morgoth's Ring*, 379.

19. *Nature*, 344.

20. *Letters*, 153:190; see also *Fellowship*, 281.

21. *Morgoth's Ring*, 404.

22. *Silmarillion*, 285.

23. *Letters*, 153:190.

24. *Letters*, 183:243.

25. *Letters*, 183:243–44; 131:151; *Shaping*, 164, 166.

26. *Letters*, 131:151.

27. *Morgoth's Ring*, 273. See also Tolkien, "Ósanwe-Kenta," 29.

28. *Morgoth's Ring*, 391.

29. *Morgoth's Ring*, 391. Tolkien notes in a letter to Nevill Coghill that several characters either fall or repent on a knife's edge (Hammond and Scull, *Chronology*, 461).

30. *Morgoth's Ring*, 273.

31. *Morgoth's Ring*, 391.

32. *Morgoth's Ring*, 403.

33. *Morgoth's Ring*, 391.

34. Tolkien, "Ósanwe-Kenta," 28.

35. *Letters*, 131:152.

36. *Morgoth's Ring*, 390. We may be reminded of Zeus, the Greek god of power and lightning, who is also the chief and eldest of the gods and stronger than all of them put together.

37. *Morgoth's Ring*, 395.

38. *Morgoth's Ring*, 395.

39. *Morgoth's Ring*, 395; *Nature*, 294.

40. *Nature*, 294.

41. *Morgoth's Ring*, 9–10.

42. *Morgoth's Ring*, 9–10.

43. Tolkien indeed frequently equates Morgoth's power with his will (*Morgoth's Ring*, 403). He speaks of Morgoth's will working at a distance, even from outside the universe (see, for example, *Nature*, 239). But it is unclear whether this can be applied to spiritual forces in the primary world or whether this is merely narrative convenience (*Lost Road*, 24). Sauron's hostile will can be felt as a physical presence (*Towers*, 238). It too acts at a distance, invading Minas Tirith through the *palantír* (*Return*, 133). It is Sauron's will at work in the conflict over Faramir, says Gandalf (*Return*, 126).

44. *Morgoth's Ring*, 334, 403.

45. *Morgoth's Ring*, 395.

46. *Nature*, 294.

47. *Morgoth's Ring*, 397.

48. *Morgoth's Ring*, 420.

49. *Morgoth's Ring*, 396; see also 395.

50. *Morgoth's Ring*, 395.

51. *Morgoth's Ring*, 395.

52. *Morgoth's Ring*, 396.

53. *Morgoth's Ring*, 395.

54. *Morgoth's Ring*, 391.

55. *Nature*, 344.

56. *Morgoth's Ring*, 390–91.

57. *Morgoth's Ring*, 391.

58. *Morgoth's Ring*, 390–91; *Nature*, 238–39.

59. *Morgoth's Ring*, 403, 422.

60. *Silmarillion*, 153, 181.

61. And yet he still possesses vast mental power. Morgoth's thought is nigh-measureless, perceiving deeply and widely, weighing all things in his plots (*Silmarillion*, 205). This is a strange statement to synthesize with Tolkien's portrayal of nihilistic, planless rage. But it in fact highlights the vast power Tolkien grants his devil in his unfallen state. If, being reduced to a mere shadow of his former self, he is yet counted among the most cunning of created beings, how great then must have been his intellect at the first?

62. *Morgoth's Ring*, 403.

63. *Morgoth's Ring*, 395.

64. *Morgoth's Ring*, 394.

65. *Morgoth's Ring*, 400.

66. *Unfinished Tales*, 266. This is a summary by Christopher Tolkien of a note written by his father. The exact line between the elder and younger Tolkien's thoughts is fuzzy here.

67. *Silmarillion*, 31, 145.

68. *Silmarillion*, 285. As both Morgoth and Sauron advance in evil, they lose the ability to change forms or even to appear without a body (*Morgoth's Ring*, 15; *Letters*, 153:190; *Nature*, 242).

69. *Letters*, 43:48.

70. Tolkien's devil is successful in tempting Men directly and as a whole, but not so successful with Elves, who only fall individually (*Morgoth's Ring*, 334; *Nature*, 88). They have too much spiritual knowledge to ever accept offers of power and domination. So Sauron tempts the Elves not with wickedness but with beauty. He persuades them that they can recreate paradise here, under their control, away from the prying hands of the gods. Thus the three Elven Rings are made (*Letters*, 131:152). Even in the primary world, the attempt to escape time and change can make one a victim to the deceits of the devil, who offers a cheap substitute in limitless serial time instead (*Letters*, 181:236; 208:267).

71. *Morgoth's Ring*, 392.

72. *Morgoth's Ring*, 275.

73. *Lost Road*, 331.

74. *Morgoth's Ring*, 275.

75. Tolkien, "Ósanwe-Kenta," 32.

76. Letters, 156:205.

77. See Lost Road, 30.

78. Letters, 131:155; 156:205.

79. Sauron, 347.

80. Letters, 156:207.

81. Return, 131.

82. Morgoth's Ring, 334, 355.

83. Letters, 210:277.

84. Towers, 183; see also The War of the Ring, 62.

85. Towers, 183; see also War, 62.

86. Morgoth's Ring, 397.

87. Morgoth's Ring, 395–96; see also 379; Tolkien, "Ósanwe-Kenta," 28.

88. The Book of Lost Tales, vol. 2, 27. Notably, the narrator takes pains to exonerate Lúthien for lying in order to get into Angband.

89. The Monsters and the Critics and Other Essays, 34.

90. Monsters, 34.

91. J. R. R. Tolkien, "On Dragons," in The Hobbit: Facsimile Gift Set (London: HarperCollins, 2018), 60. Hammond and Scull note that in a letter to Nevill Coghill, Tolkien discusses "medieval thinking in regard to fallen angels and the rebellion of peoples against their chief, in connection with Sauron and the Black Riders," but we are not told what this connection signifies (Chronology, 461).

92. Morgoth's Ring, 404. Tolkien creates his own fictional justifications for the physical manifestations of evil in his legendarium. Morgoth, decreased by evil, incarnates himself permanently as a Tyrant King, losing the majority of his angelic powers of mind and spirit in exchange for vast physical power (Sauron, 402; Morgoth's Ring, 399). As such, he must be fought in the physical realm. His demonic servant Sauron is likewise a sorcerer weaving dark spells, master of werewolves, vampires, ghosts, and misshapen monsters (The Lays of Beleriand, 228; Lost Road, 283; Silmarillion, 156. For Sauron's place among the classic monsters of literature, see Gwyneth E. Hood, "Sauron as Gorgon and Basilisk," VII 8 (1987): 59–71.

93. Letters, 131:154; Morgoth's Ring, 404.

94. Letters, 312:402.

95. Road, 166–70.

96. Nature, 242.

97. Silmarillion, 32.

98. Silmarillion, 280–81.

99. Return, 212.

100. Return, 214; Morgoth's Ring, 399.

101. Silmarillion, 304.

102. Return, 155.

103. Letters 212:286; Lost Tales 1, 142–43.

104. Morgoth's Ring, 53. Note that even at their beginning these spirits are associated with darkness, silence, cold, and emptiness—the nothingness between the stars.

105. Silmarillion, 32.

106. Morgoth's Ring, 420.

107. *Lost Road*, 24, 65.

108. *War*, 331.

109. *Monsters*, 34–35.

110. *Monsters*, 36.

111. *Return*, 155.

112. *Beowulf: A Translation and Commentary*, 159.

113. *Sauron*, 196. As explained in chapter 2, I take Tolkien's characters' comments in "The Notion Club Papers" to be virtually his own beliefs on this score.

114. *Sauron*, 197.

115. *Sauron*, 197.

116. *Sauron*, 197.

117. *Sauron*, 197.

118. *Letters*, 45:55.

119. *Letters*, 45:55.

120. *Unfinished Tales*, 295.

121. *Sauron*, 196.

122. *Sauron*, 37–38; *Return*, 223. It is peculiar that Chad Chisholm would stress the freedom of Frodo's choice not to destroy the Ring in the face of direct evidence to the contrary in Tolkien's letters (for example, *Letters*, 246:325–27). See Chisholm, "Demons, Choices, and Grace in *The Lord of the Rings*," *Mallorn* 45 (2008): 20–23.

123. *Towers*, 347.

124. *Return*, 116.

125. *Letters*, 210:272. Of course, demons *are* ghosts, in the technical sense of spirits (*Sauron*, 196).

126. *Return*, 115; *Letters*, 210:272.

127. See *Lost Tales 1*, 67.

128. *Lost Tales 2*, 216.

129. *Lost Tales 1*, 99.

130. *Lost Tales 1*, 236.

131. *Letters*, 156:207.

132. *Beowulf*, 160. For example, Tolkien equates Norse dwarves with demons in his lecture on dragons to a group of schoolchildren ("On Dragons," 54). While this is most likely due to a desire to simplify things for his young audience, it is possible that Tolkien subscribed to the theory that traces the etymology of "dwarf" to Old Indian *dhvaras*, "demonic spirit"' of death.

133. *Monsters*, 20.

134. *Nature*, 242. This is in contrast to the pleasant odors associated with saintliness in Catholic folklore.

135. Rateliff, "'That Seems to Me Fatal,'" 123; *Letters*, 297:381.

136. Rateliff, "'That Seems to Me Fatal,'" 123; *Letters*, 144:177–78.

137. *Morgoth's Ring*, 109.

138. *Beowulf*, 159.

139. *Beowulf*, 159.

140. *Towers*, 328.

141. *Towers*, 329.

142. *Lost Road*, 24, 65.

143. *The War of the Jewels*, 150.

144. *Morgoth's Ring*, 414.

145. *Return*, 178.

146. This is a frequent demonic symptom, especially famous for its role in the development of folk traditions such as the incubus/succubus, nightmare, and night hag.

147. *Return*, 179.

148. *Towers*, 328–29; see also *Return*, 179.

149. *Fellowship*, 302.

150. *Return of the Shadow*, 424.

151. *Letters*, 156:207.

152. While spiritual warfare may be fought for souls, it takes place external to the soul itself. All maleficent spiritual forces attack from the outside. No being whatsoever can read minds (Tolkien, "Ósanwe-Kenta"). Intelligent inquirers might be able to deduce quite a bit from circumstances, personal proclivities, and so forth, but one's thoughts remain between oneself and God. Even when Tolkien's Elves and angels practice "thought-transference," this is more like a nonverbal conversation. A thought is intentionally sent and received; the mind itself cannot be read like a book. The temptation of greater minds is to force weaker minds to reveal themselves (*Morgoth's Ring*, 399).

153. *Fellowship*, 211.

154. *Towers*, 313.

155. *Towers*, 313.

156. *The Treason of Isengard*, 374. Emphasis added.

157. *Fellowship*, 417.

158. *Treason*, 373.

159. *Return*, 141.

160. *Return*, 213.

161. *Towers*, 238.

162. *Fellowship*, 234.

163. *Fellowship*, 208, 210; *Return*, 305.

164. Joe Christopher characterizes these and other moments as moral epiphanies ("The Moral Epiphanies in *The Lord of the Rings*," *Mallorn* 33 (1995): 121–25.

165. *Return*, 221. Emphasis added.

166. *Shadow*, 81. Alternatively, he would have become enslaved under the Necromancer (*Shadow*, 264).

167. *Fellowship*, 223.

168. *Return*, 190.

169. *Letters*, 328:413.

170. *Return*, 178–79.

171. *Fellowship*, 226–27.

172. *Letters*, 191:252.

Chapter IX: Christ & Salvation

1. As already discussed in chapter 1, Jesus appears in "Leaf by Niggle," acting as the merciful intercessor on Niggle's behalf. Jesus is not only the generous king but the shepherd that guides Niggle into the mountains of deep heaven (*The Tolkien Reader*, 116–17). This is not to

say shepherd images, drawn as they are from the New Testament, are absent in Old English theology. See, for instance, Aelfric of Eynsham's *Sermones Catholici, Homily XVII*, On the Second Sunday after Easter, 239–45. His appearance in "Niggle" and the style of Tolkien's "Noel" (see below) offer good evidence that Tolkien's Anglo-Saxon Christology is not merely a thematic fluke. *Of course* the style and tone of ideal leaders in an ostensibly English epic like *The Lord of the Rings* will wear Old English garb. But given these two extra-legendary documents, as well as Tolkien's sparse epistolary remarks, we can make the case that such christological tendencies are not authorial affectations but genuine beliefs.

2. *The Letters of J. R. R. Tolkien*, 297:387.

3. *Letters*, 181:237. Emphasis in original.

4. *Letters*, 181:237.

5. *Letters*, 297:387.

6. Tolkien, "Fate and Free Will," 186–87.

7. Tolkien, "Fate and Free Will," 187.

8. *Morgoth's Ring*, 332.

9. *Morgoth's Ring*, 356.

10. *Letters*, 209:269. See also Simon J. Cook, "Fantasy Incarnate: Of Elves and Men," *Journal of Tolkien Research* 3, no. 1 (2016): 5–6.

11. Indeed the only other religious references in *The Father Christmas Letters* are to a few feast days of the saints.

12. The poem was rediscovered in 2013 by Hammond and Scull.

13. Note that both Morgoth and Sauron are said to have power over cold.

14. *Unfinished Tales*, 406–7.

15. *Unfinished Tales*, 410.

16. *Unfinished Tales*, 407.

17. *Unfinished Tales*, 407, 410.

18. While it may be tempting to read into Tolkien's comments above a position on whether Christ assumed a fallen or unfallen human nature, we must resist. First, this debate would have been beyond the pale of Tolkien's theological concerns (so far as we know); second, the peril of embodiment in Arda arises from Morgoth's corruption of the intrinsic nature of the material world—the explicit difference that Tolkien himself points out between our world and his mythology. The situation is fundamentally disanalogous.

19. Gueroult interview; Henry Resnik, "An Interview with J. R. R. Tolkien," *Niekas* 18 (Spring 1967): 43.

20. Resnik, "An Interview," 43.

21. Letter from J. R. R. Tolkien to Clyde S. Kilby, ca. July 1966. J. R. R. Tolkien Letter collection, L-Kilby 4, The Marion E. Wade Center, Wheaton College, Wheaton, IL.

22. Philip Ryken expands on this in his own work, *The Messiah Comes to Middle-Earth: Images of Christ's Threefold Office in "The Lord of the Rings"* (Downers Grove, IL: IVP Academic, 2017). For older approaches to messianic archetypes, see John Houghton, "Rochester The Renewer: The Byronic Hero and The Messiah as Elements in The King Elessar," *Mythlore* 11, no. 1 (1984): 13–16; Jean Chausse, "Icons of Jesus Christ in *The Lord of the Rings*," *Mallorn* 39 (2001): 30–32.

23. See "A Dialogue: Discussion by Humphrey Carpenter, Professor George Sayer, and Dr. Clyde S. Kilby, Recorded September 29, 1979, Wheaton, Illinois," *Minas Tirith Evening-Star* 9, no. 2 (January 1980): 16–17.

24. For more on Tolkien's images of kingship, see Caroline Monks, "Christianity and Kingship in Tolkien and Lewis," *Mallorn* 19 (1982): 5–28.

25. *The Fall of Arthur*, V.35–47.

26. *The Legend of Sigurd and Gudrún*, 62–63.

27. We noted in chapter 1 that generosity is the key characteristic of the Anglo-Saxon king.

28. *The Return of the King*, 330.

29. *Return*, 323.

30. *The Two Towers*, 36. Perhaps of interest, this statement of Jesus occurs directly after a reference to his defeat of Satan, further strengthening the *Christus Victor* motif.

31. *Return*, 150.

32. *Return*, 142. In a search for applicability rather than allegory, we might say that Faramir represents the role of the good pope as vicar of Christ, eagerly awaiting his return and pointing others there. See Robert Steed, "Tolkien's preference for an early medieval Catholic sensibility in *The Lord of the Rings* and *The Silmarillion*," Proceedings of the 3rd Mythgard Institute Mythmoot (2015), 4–8.

33. *Letters*, 250:340.

34. *Return*, 139.

35. *Return*, 139.

36. *Return*, 142.

37. *Return*, 147.

38. The same is true when Gandalf meets Denethor. See *Return*, 29.

39. *Towers*, 104.

40. Compare *Return*, 31 (Gandalf) and 341 (Aragorn).

41. *Return*, 31.

42. *Return*, 233.

43. G. K. Chesterton, *Orthodoxy* (London: John Lane, 1908), 299. Notably, this chapter is titled "Authority and the Adventurer."

44. *Return*, 246.

45. For example, *Return*, 248–49.

46. *Return*, 250.

47. *Return*, 250.

48. *Return*, 338. For the use of hope as a specifically religious concept, see chapter 10. Christopher Vaccaro outlines an extensive theological history of similar trees in "'And One White Tree': The Cosmological Cross and the *Arbor Vitae* in J. R. R. Tolkien's *The Lord of the Rings* and *The Silmarillion*," *Mallorn* 42 (2004): 23–28.

49. *Unfinished Tales*, 213.

50. *Letters*, 250:338.

51. *Morgoth's Ring*, 203. Recall that for Tolkien, hope often equates to trust in God or faith.

52. *Letters*, 212:286. Technically, the Bible never speaks of Jesus raising himself from the dead, but of the Father raising the Son.

53. *Tolkien On Fairy-stories*, 78. See below for the resurrection's role in salvation.

54. In his personal life, he seems to have taken Easter seriously. Once Tolkien apologizes to Rayner Unwin for not working during the liturgical events of Holy Week (Hammond and Scull, *Chronology*, 552). He visited his son John rather than be alone for Holy Week after Edith's death (Hammond and Scull, *Chronology*, 810).

55. *Towers*, 98.

56. *Towers*, 98.

57. *Towers*, 98.

58. *Towers*, 98.

59. *Fairy Stories*, 77.

60. *Fairy-stories*, 75.

61. Fairy-stories 75. There are almost too many eucatastrophes, of smaller or larger scale, to name in Tolkien's writing. His own favorites include the arrival of the Eagles at the climax of *The Hobbit* and the horns of the Rohirrim at the battle of the Pelennor Fields. For ways in which, even outside of Middle-earth, Tolkien seems to rewrite legends to give a eucatastrophic ending, see Jane Beal, "Tolkien, Eucatastrophe, and the Re-Creation of Medieval Legend," *Journal of Tolkien Research* 4, no. 1 (2017): Article 8.

62. *Fairy-stories*, 75.

63. *Fairy-stories*, 75. See also note 62 of this chapter.

64. *Fairy-stories*, 75.

65. *Fairy-stories*, 78.

66. *Fairy-stories*, 78. C. S. Lewis not the least among them. For Tolkien's rejection of Liberal Protestant demythologization of the resurrection and other miracles, see John William Houghton, "Neues Testament und Märchen: Tolkien, Fairy Stories, and the Gospel," *Journal of Tolkien Research* 4, no. 1 (2017): Article 9.

67. *Fairy-stories*, 78.

68. *Letters*, 89:100. See also *Fairy-stories*, 76.

69. *Fairy-stories*, 75.

70. *Fairy-stories*, 78.

71. *Fairy-stories*, 78.

72. *Fairy-stories*, 78, also 155; *The Book of Lost Tales, vol.* 2, 252.

73. *Fairy-stories*, 78.

74. *Fairy-stories*, 75.

75. *Letters*, 89:100.

76. Since biblical history begins with the creation, as Tolkien's myths do, it is inaccurate to say that Tolkien's legendarium is completely prior to a history of redemption. He himself leaves space in his narrative of earliest human history for the biblical account. It is likely that most of the recorded history of Men in Middle-earth is set sometime around Genesis 10–11.

77. *The Book of Lost Tales, vol.* 1, 220.

78. *Morgoth's Ring*, 355. While this may mean that Tolkien incorrectly believed (along with many lay Christians) that humans in heaven become angels, it more likely refers to the escha-tological elevation of Men above the angelic "Powers" (the literal translation of Valar). See, for example, 1 Corinthians 6:3. This was Origen's position, for example: humans were created to replace the fallen angels.

79. *Morgoth's Ring*, 333.

80. *Letters*, 246:327.

81. *Return*, 152.

82. *Morgoth's Ring*, 322.

83. Again, this is not to say Tolkien *denies* substitutionary atonement, or other models of atonement in general, only that this is the only position for which we have documentation. Rarely, Tolkien refers to absolution (*Silmarillion*, 275–76) or cleansing (*Towers*, 123; *Return*, 144).

84. *Letters*, 192:253.

85. *Fellowship*, 328; *Return*, 341, emphasis added.

86. *Morgoth's Ring*, 344; see also 350–51, and, laconically, 404. In the very late stages, documented by Christopher Tolkien in "Myths Transformed," earth is the most important site in the universe because it is the location of the main drama of the conflict of Satan with God and the children of God (*Morgoth's Ring*, 375). Again, Tolkien is in harmony with an Irenaean theology of creation.

87. Tolkien's other writings do contain the word. The *History of Middle-earth* cites several other uses of atonement language, most often in a commonplace setting. Note, however, that at one point Morgoth is said to be imprisoned for seven thousand Valian years, after which he is offered grace for repentance and atonement (*Lost Road*, 112).

88. *Return*, 164.

89. *Sauron Defeated*, 92.

90. *Fellowship*, 153–54.

91. *Towers*, 99.

92. *Return*, 82–83. See also Vernon Hyles, "On the Nature of Evil: The Cosmic Myths of Lewis, Tolkien, and Williams," *Mythlore* 13, no. 4 (1987): 13.

93. *Return*, 82.

94. *Return*, 102.

95. *Return*, 132.

96. This is a widespread rhetorical trope found in the writings of church fathers from Irenaeus of Lyon to John Damascene. For a representative passage, see Maximus Confessor, *Ad Thalassium* 64.

97. *Return*, 156.

98. *Fellowship*, 282.

99. *Fellowship*, 282.

100. *Towers*, 121.

101. *Silmarillion*, 303, 301 (where the "strange chance" decreed by God takes a more prominent role).

102. *Return*, 155.

103. *Return*, 156.

104. *Towers*, 121.

105. For an overview with relevant literature, see Judith N. Garde, *Old English Poetry in Medieval Christian Perspective: A Doctrinal Approach* (Cambridge: Boydell & Brewer, 1991), 113–30.

106. Elisabeth Henry, *Orpheus with His Lute: Poetry and the Renewal of Life* (Bristol Classical Press, 1992), 38, 50–53, 81, etc.; Elaine Traherne, "Speaking of the Medieval," in *The Oxford Handbook of Medieval Literature in English* (Oxford: Oxford University Press, 2010), 10; John Block Friedman, *Orpheus in the Middle Ages* (Syracuse University Press, 2001), 125–26.

107. *Beowulf: A Translation and Commentary*, 160.

108. For a more extended treatment of this motif, see Robert Steed, "The Harrowing of Hell Motif in Tolkien's Legendarium," *Mallorn* 58 (2017): 6–9.

109. *Towers*, 106.

110. *Return*, 57.

111. *Return*, 71.

112. *Return*, 61–62

113. *Sauron*, 15.

114. *Return*, 62.

115. *Sauron*, 15.

116. *Return*, 152.

117. *The Silmarillion*, 252.

118. In Roman Catholic theology, the Mass is a true representation of the sacrifice of the cross, but depends wholly and completely on the cross for its efficacy. It is therefore an application of the single act of salvation rather than a separate instance of it.

119. The first Elves had predestined spouses, for instance (*The Nature of Middle-earth*, 62).

120. *Towers*, 268.

121. *Towers*, 290.

122. *Fellowship*, 384. Fleming Rutledge sees here a reference to Ephesians 5:20. See Fleming Rutledge, *The Battle for Middle-earth: Tolkien's Divine Design in "The Lord of the Rings"* (Grand Rapids: Eerdmans, 2004), 134.

123. *Fellowship*, 284; *Return of the Shadow*, 406–7; *The Treason of Isengard,* 105, 115, 121.

124. *Return*, 340; *Treason*, 114.

125. *Unfinished Tales*, 345; *Treason*, 114.

126. *Return*, 337–38 (by his grandparents).

127. *Fellowship*, 384–85.

128. *Towers*, 106.

129. *Unfinished Tales*, 32.

130. For example, *Towers*, 210, 276; *Return*, 52; *Treason*, 82.

131. Notably, the *Oxford English Dictionary* locates *dom* in this sense in works such as the West Saxon Gospels and the Lindisfarne Gospels. The phrase "crack of doom," originally tied to the loud crack of judgment day, is given a new interpretation by Tolkien. He playfully transfers an audible crack of doom into a physical crack in the earth where doom is decided.

132. For Tolkien's thoughts on precisely how fate and human free agency interact, see "Fate & Free Will."

133. Frodo is not the only person unconditionally elected—Gandalf says that he himself was only a subsidiary means by which Bilbo should find the Ring. Bilbo was "chosen," and Gandalf chosen only to choose him (*Unfinished Tales*, 345). Aragorn also thinks the *palantír* comes to him for a purpose, but this seems far from unconditional (*Return*, 155).

134. See *Fellowship*, 70–71, 284: *Return*, 214; *Shadow*, 406–7; *Treason*, 105, 115, 121.

135. *Fellowship*, 70–71.

136. *Shadow*, 407.

137. Tolkien, "Fate & Free Will," 184–85.

138. *Letters*, 250:337.

139. *Morgoth's Ring*, 338.

140. Joshua Jipp, *Christ Is King: Paul's Royal Ideology* (Minneapolis: Fortiress, 2016); Matthew Bates, *Salvation by Allegiance Alone* (Grand Rapids: Baker, 2017); Nijay Gupta, *Paul and the Language of Faith* (Grand Rapids: Eerdmans, 2020).

141. *Arthur*, V.16–17.

142. *Unfinished Tales*, 70.

143. *Silmarillion*, 275.

144. *Letters*, 250:338–40.

145. *Letters*, 250:338.

146. Letter to Przemyslaw Mroczkowski, January 20–26, 1964. Excerpts published in *Christie's Fine Printed Books and Manuscripts* 1 *June 2009.*

147. *Letters*, 86:97.

148. Contra Donald P. Richmond, "Tolkien's Marian Vision of Middle-earth," *Mallorn* 40 (2002): 13.

149. *The Hobbit*, 81–82. Emphasis added.

150. *Hobbit*, 81–82.

151. *Return*, 206.

152. *Return*, 206.

153. *Return*, 207.

154. *Return*, 209.

155. *Return*, 212.

156. *Return*, 220.

157. *Return*, 219.

158. *Return*, 177.

159. See Tolkien, "Fate and Free Will," where Tolkien says that God respects free will by working through the chances of the world.

Chapter X: The Church

1. *The Letters of J. R. R. Tolkien*, 250:339.

2. *Letters*, 250:337–38.

3. *Letters*, 79:91.

4. *Letters*, 79:91.

5. A gloomy thought, he says (*Letters*, 79:91).

6. *Letters*, 63:75. In terms of artistry in religion, Tolkien frequently appreciates and comments upon the musical artistry of a service (see especially Hammond and Scull, *Chronology*, 497). He finds a trumpet fanfare at the elevation of the Host very fitting for high religious ceremony, for example (Hammond and Scull, *Chronology*, 497). He envisions his own Elvish hymns as Gregorian chants (Hammond and Scull, *Chronology*, 667–68). In terms of church art and decoration, he finds that he cannot disconnect artistic merit from spiritual meaning (Hammond and Scull, *Chronology*, 490–91). He approved of the Giotto frescoes and Bassano's San Jerome but not of Titian's Assumption or the monuments to past rulers (Hammond and Scull, *Chronology*, 491, 494–96).

7. *Letters*, 89:100.

8. *Letters*, 63:75.

9. Hammond and Scull, *Chronology*, 779.

10. This shaped his life in numerous ways both major and minor, involving not only theological but cultural concerns. For example, it seems that he abstained from meat on Fridays in commemoration of Jesus' sacrifice on the cross on Good Friday, as the organizers of an honorary dinner in Tolkien's honor obtained a special dispensation from the diocese for their event (Hammond and Scull, *Chronology*, 551). He was a longtime member of Catenian Association of Catholic businessmen and professionals, of which he served as president for one year (Hammond and Scull, *Chronology*, 129, 304). He made many submissions to Roman Catholic magazines and journals (Hammond and Scull, *Chronology*, 150, 181–82, 193). He sent his children to Catholic schools. Hammond and Scull list several other mentions of Tolkien's Catholic involvement (e.g., *Chronology*, 156, 163, 170–71, 181, 197–98, 243, 351).

11. Thanks to his mother. After her death Tolkien was integrally connected to the Birmingham Oratory as a youth, usually serving Mass before school and talking with many of the residents there (*Letters*, 250:340; 306:395). He soon discovered and admired Francis Thompson, a Catholic mystical writer (Garth, *Tolkien and the Great War*, 13–14).

12. *Letters*, 250:340; 267:354.

13. *Letters*, 250:337. This is not to say that Tolkien disdained the clergy. His eldest son John was ordained as a priest, and his admiration for his surrogate father Francis Morgan was unbounded, as evident in the same letter. Aside from his affection for Father Francis, Tolkien cultivated close friendships with several other priests like Robert Murray, Vincent Reade (*Letters*, 66:78; Hammond and Scull, *Chronology*, 60, 187), Father Augustin Emery or "Uncle Gus" (Hammond and Scull, *Guide*, 334–35), and Father Douglas Carter. Carter, it may also be noted, starred in a film on Newman with script written by Tolkien's son John (Hammond and Scull, *Chronology*, 213, 802). He also had other friendly relations with priest-scholars such as Father Hugh Maycock of Pusey House (Hammond and Scull, *Chronology*, 717) and Father Martin D'Arcy (Hammond and Scull, *Guide*, 290). Tolkien furthermore had close connections to several nuns, including Sister (later Mother) Mary Michael, a lifelong friend (Hammond and Scull, *Chronology*, 109, 122, 312, 367, 837), Mother St. Teresa Gale of Cherwell Edge and the Society of Oxford Home-Students (Hammond and Scull, *Chronology*, 178, 1289), and Reverend Mother Mary St. John, sister of Tolkien's childhood friend Christopher Wiseman and headmistress of Priscilla's Catholic school (Hammond and Scull, *Chronology*, 216–561). Aside from Cherwell Edge, Tolkien was also involved with the Oxford Convent of the Sacred Heart (Hammond and Scull, *Chronology*, 181–82). There are a few other scattered letters to nuns (Hammond and Scull, *Chronology*, 707, 796), as well as a few comments on the name Coventry as *not* derived from "convent" (*Letters* 97:112; Hammond and Scull, *Chronology*, 305–6).

14. *Letters*, 250:337.

15. *Letters*, 250:337. This is likely a good point to mention Tolkien's possible firsthand experience of such behavior with his son John. John came to stay with his parents at the beginning and end of January 1968 (Hammond and Scull, *Chronology*, 750–51). This second time he stayed on indefinite sick leave, but the time period corresponds to the archbishop being made aware of a note from January 15 that alleged Father Tolkien sexually abused a group of Boy Scouts, and to which Father Tolkien is suggested to have admitted. It is unclear how much his father or mother knew of what was occurring; Tolkien's writing mentions that John came to them as an "invalid" because he had "collapsed" on the verge of a "nervous breakdown" (Hammond and Scull, *Chronology*, 753, 774). A fuller treatment of the history of Father Tolkien's alleged abuse may be found in "The Roman Catholic Church Case Study: Archdiocese of Birmingham

Investigation Report" published by Independent Inquiry into Child Sexual Abuse, particularly section C.3: "Father John Tolkien: an example of safeguarding response pre and post-Nolan." The document notes that several such allegations were made over the course of time, including earlier than 1968. "C.3: Father John Tolkien: an example of safeguarding response pre and post-Nolan," *Independent Inquiry Child Sexual Abuse,* accessed January 4, 2022, https://www.iicsa.org.uk/reports-recommendations/publications/investigation/birmingham-archdiocese/part-c-post-nolan-safeguarding-archdiocese/c3-father-john-tolkien.

16. *Letters,* 49:62.

17. *Letters,* 306:394.

18. A. R. Bossert, " 'Surely You Don't Disbelieve': Tolkien and Pius X: Anti-Modernism in Middle-earth," *Mythlore* 25, no. 1 (2006): 53–76.

19. Cook, letter to the editor, 24.

20. Simon Tolkien, "My Grandfather," *The Mail on Sunday,* February 23, 2003; see also Daniel Helen and Morgan Thomsen, "A Recollection of Tolkien: Canon Gerard Hanlon," *Mallorn* 54 (2013): 41.

21. Sayer, "Recollections," 24–25.

22. See his analogy with the tree in *Letters,* 306:393–94.

23. *Letters,* 306:393.

24. *Letters,* 250:339.

25. *Letters,* 250:339.

26. *Letters,* 250:338.

27. Sometimes this is only by way of a passing choice of words. Once Tolkien mentions the "hymn" of the ocean and its "organ," both evocative of a church service and the praise of God but placed within the natural context of the trackless sea so dear to him (*The Shaping of Middle-earth,* 217).

28. Garth, *Tolkien and the Great War,* 112–13.

29. *The Lay of Aotrou and Itroun,* 16, 19, etc.

30. We find early church attendance with Edith (Hammond and Scull, *Chronology,* 49, 86), though we know that Edith eventually stopped going to Mass while remaining active in the parish (Humphrey Carpenter, *J. R. R. Tolkien: A Biography* [Boston: Houghton Mifflin Harcourt, 2014], 152–53). Carpenter dates Edith's growing anti-Catholic resentment to the second decade of their marriage (thus, the mid-1920s) and states that Edith even began to disapprove of Ronald's taking the children to church (153). This apparently bore no fruit, as by 1939 he was attending Mass with the children but not Edith (Hammond and Scull, *Chronology,* 246). Overall, Tolkien kept regular habits of weekly church attendance (Hammond and Scull, *Chronology,* 798–99). This includes rising early (Hammond and Scull, *Chronology,* 282, 292) and, when away from home, overcoming various practical inconveniences (Hammond and Scull, *Chronology,* 398, 477, 489, 496). He consistently attended Mass during his pilgrimage to Italy (Hammond and Scull, *Chronology,* 494–97), despite the fact that many tourists will give themselves some leeway on Sunday mornings. Once he even attended both Mass and (in the evening) Benediction (Hammond and Scull, *Chronology,* 495–95). Prioritizing Mass was a longstanding behavior for Tolkien, as he even attended Mass (and possibly confession) while deployed in the Great War (Hammond and Scull, *Chronology,* 89, 92–93, 97). See the summary of his church attendance during wartime in Hammond and Scull, *Chronology,* 830.

31. *Letters,* 176:229.

32. *Letters*, 267:354. See Sayer's story of Tolkien telling stories of Mary to some young children during Mass (Sayer, 23–24).

33. *Letters*, 43: 49.

34. *Letters*, 212: 286. Emphasis removed.

35. *Letters*, 212: 286. However this process occurs, we can be sure that Tolkien did *not* envision it as Titian did, with all twelve apostles looking on in awe as the heavens part and God places a crown upon Mary's head. He writes that Titian's Assumption has nothing to say to him about the actual assumption of Mary, and is therefore offensive to him (Hammond and Scull, *Chronology*, 491). We do not know his opinion of another famous Marian image he viewed on his trip to Italy, the Madonna del Pianto ("weeping virgin")—now stolen (Hammond and Scull, *Chronology*, 494).

36. *Gawain and the Green Knight*, 6.

37. *Gawain*, 5.

38. *Aotrou*, 21/104. Similar images appear in *Pearl*.

39. *Chronology*, 97.

40. *The Lay of Aotrou and Itroun*, 35. This poem, "Corrigan I," is based on an earlier poem by Villemarqué.

41. *Gawain*, 5.

42. *The Story of Kullervo*, 111.

43. Gueroult interview. See also *Letters*, 213:288.

44. *Letters*, 156:207.

45. *The Silmarillion*, 26. Ingwë, high king of all Elves, appears specially devoted to Varda and her loveliness (*The Nature of Middle-earth*, 98).

46. *The Lost Road*, 240.

47. *Letters*, 213:288. For an analysis of the way in which Marian titles from the Litany of Loreto may be applied to Galadriel, see Michael W. Maher, S.J., "'A Land without Stain': Medieval Images of Mary and Their Use in the Characterization of Galadriel," in *Tolkien the Medievalist*, ed. Jane Chance (New York: Routledge, 2003), 225–36. See also Barbara Kowalik, "Elbereth the Star-Queen Seen in the Light of Medieval Marian Devotion," in *O What a Tangled Web Tolkien and Medieval Literature: A View from Poland*, ed. Barbara Kowalik (Zollikofen: Walking Tree Press, 2013), 93–114.

48. *The Fellowship of the Ring*, 373. Note that this was written many years before—the idea of Galadriel's purity was not a new one.

49. *The Two Towers*, 288.

50. *The Return of the King*, 259, 360. It should be noted that Celeborn is included in this reverence (for Treebeard at least).

51. *Return*, 362.

52. *Return*, 195.

53. Nor was Varda in earlier versions of *The Silmarillion*. Fiönwë (later Eönwë) was her son. Later, the idea that the Valar have children was abandoned.

54. *Unfinished Tales*, 240. She is still a penitent in 1971 (*Letters*, 320:407). For an overview of what Christopher Tolkien has called the trickiest problem in the legendarium, see Romuald Ian Lakowski, "The Fall and Repentance of Galadriel," *Mythlore* 25, no. 3/4 (97/98) (2007): 91–104.

55. *Unfinished Tales*, 244.

56. *Letters*, 353:431.

57. *Towers*, 329.

58. *Return*, 191.

59. *Return*, 195.

60. *Letters*, 309:397; Carpenter, *Inklings*, 51–52.

61. *Letters*, 153:193. Matthew Fisher theorizes that "Smith of Wootton Major" follows the shape of a saint's life; see "Saint Smith: Reading *Smith of Wootton Major* as a Saint's Life," *Orcrist* 9 (2017): 53–57.

62. *Towers*, 278.

63. *Nature*, 273.

64. Tolkien himself, on a vacation to Italy, visited Assisi with his daughter, presumably for the purpose of pilgrimage while in the area. He noted that the frescoes in the Basilica of St. Francis moved him deeply. He also visited the Basilica of St. Clare (Letter 167). In Venice at the Byzantine church of Santa Fosca he reports, "The feeling that haunted me during the rest of my short visit to Italy: that of having come to the heart of Christendom; an exile from the borders and far provinces returning home, or at least to the home of his fathers ... I felt a curious glow of dormant life and Charity—especially in the chapels of the Blessed Sacrament" (Hammond and Scull, *Chronology*, 489). This, he says, despite the overlay of neglect or tourism or the occasional incongruities of the juxtaposition of the quotidian with the elevated (Hammond and Scull, *Chronology*, 489, 496–97). From Venice the Tolkiens make their way to Assisi, where they visit the relics such as the body of St. Clare and the cross that spoke to St. Francis (Hammond and Scull, *Chronology*, 495). Apparently Tolkien also accepts that God spoke to Francis in a vision and commanded him to repair a chapel, the first house of the Poor Clare nuns (Hammond and Scull, *Chronology*, 496). He enjoys reading St. Francis's Canticle of the Sun (paraphrased in the English hymn "All Creatures of our God and King") in the sunshine of the gardens of San Damiano (Hammond and Scull, *Chronology*, 496). He also derides the superstitious habits of graffitiing the walls with names and agrees that, far from attracting the attention of the saints, it will provoke them to anger (Hammond and Scull, *Chronology*, 496). This is to treat holiness as some sort of mechanism to be manipulated. Depressed by the commodification of the once-beautiful churches (Hammond and Scull, *Chronology*, 490–91), he finds San Damiano—simple, lacking in Baroque adornment—soaked with the personality of Clare and Francis more than any other site (Hammond and Scull, *Chronology*, 496).

65. *Unfinished Tales*, 323.

66. *Unfinished Tales*, 314, 317–18. Note the transition from awe to holiness. The numinous property of the tomb is objective, noticed and remarked upon even before its reason is known.

67. *Unfinished Tales*, 317–18, 322.

68. *Unfinished Tales*, 316, 324.

69. *Aotrou and Itroun*, 18–20 (contrasting the church bell with the silver fountain of Faerie), 21/104 (prayer for God to keep their souls).

70. Carpenter, *Biography*, 68. This comes in the emotionally fraught context of persuading Edith to convert to Catholicism so they can marry, so perhaps his phrasing is unusually hostile here. Compare his remarks about Lewis's Ulster Protestantism, 148.

71. Hammond and Scull, *Chronology*, 286, 292, 313. This is a far cry from his earlier experiences as a student. When Tolkien went up to Oxford, Catholic students were only a small minority, and older Catholic students were set by the local chaplain to mentor him and ensure he settled in (Hammond and Scull, *Chronology*, 34, 826). Much later, as a senior academic, Tolkien

returned the favor when he was elected to the Oxford and Cambridge Catholic Education Board, responsible for appointing chaplains to the universities (Hammond and Scull, *Chronology*, 190).

72. Hammond and Scull, *Guide*, 1311.

73. *Letters*, 306:394.

74. *Letters*, 250:339.

75. *Letters*, 250:339.

76. *Letters*, 250:339. The phrase "blasphemous fable of the Mass" is lifted from the Thirty-Nine Articles, the central document of Anglicanism.

77. Here we once more hear the influence of Newman's *Essay on the Development of Christian Doctrine*.

78. *Letters*, 306:394.

79. *Letters*, 306:394.

80. Garth, *Tolkien and the Great War*, 251.

81. Garth, *Tolkien and the Great War*, 256.

82. Garth, *Tolkien and the Great War*, 256.

83. *Letters*, 89:102.

84. Garth, *Tolkien and the Great War*, 19, 251; see also Tolkien's letter on marriage, Carpenter, *Inklings*, 51–52. Differences between Roman Catholic and Anglican theologies were a major factor in the disagreements between Tolkien and Lewis.

85. Testi, *Pagan Saints*, 97.

86. *Finn and Hengest*, 14.

87. See *Letters*, 72:84; Sayer, "Recollections," 24; Hammond and Scull, *Chronology*, 51, 289.

88. Garth, *Tolkien and the Great War*, 157.

89. *Letters*, 306:395.

90. *Nature*, 94.

91. *Nature*, 95.

92. *Nature*, 96.

93. *Silmarillion*, 74–75.

94. *The Book of Lost Tales, vol. 1*, 144. See also *The Book of Lost Tales, vol. 2*, 165, where head coverings and manner of dress seem to be an indication of reverence.

95. *Silmarillion*, 261; *Unfinished Tales*, 192.

96. *Unfinished Tales*, 174; see also Exodus 20:22, 25.

97. *Silmarillion*, 266; *Sauron Defeated*, 400.

98. *Unfinished Tales*, 174.

99. *Unfinished Tales*, 174, 192.

100. *Letters*, 183:243; *Sauron*, 400.

101. *The Lost Road*, 66.

102. *Letters*, 211:281.

103. *Sauron*, 400.

104. *Return*, 68.

105. *Nature*, 394.

106. There was no restriction on worship of the One or ban on constructed temples prior to the removal to Númenor. But afterward, the Meneltarma was the sole permitted place of worship and temples are only built by evil men. Tolkien's good men would never use such a

heathen site for their own sacred purposes without completely destroying any man-made structures first (*Nature*, 393).

107. *Letters*, 156:206; *Silmarillion*, 272; *Sauron*, 335; *Lost Road*, 30, 67–68.

108. *Silmarillion*, 266.

109. *Silmarillion*, 269; *Unfinished Tales*, 234.

110. *Nature*, 393.

111. *Letters*, 154:206 and 211:281, in which it is said to be mostly a memorial of their dead relatives, and where theology too is said to be greatly reduced. Some traces beside "grace at meat" still exist. Weekdays are named after religious figures (the day of the Valar corresponding to Sunday in importance). For more on the religious practice of Third Age peoples, see Michael R. Hickman, "The Religious Rituals of the Dúnedain of Gondor," *Mallorn* 27 (1990): 15–23. Hickman also has a companion piece, "The Religious Ritual and Practise of the Elves of Middle-earth at the Time of the War of the Ring," *Mallorn* 26 (1989): 39–43.

112. *Letters*, 154:206, 165:220.

113. *Letters*, 211:281.

114. *Letters*, 154:207.

115. *Letters*, 154:207.

116. *Lost Road*, 21–22.

117. *Lost Road*, 28.

118. *Lost Road*, 38.

119. *Tolkien On Fairy-stories*, 74.

120. *Unfinished Tales*, 317–18.

121. *Unfinished Tales*, 321.

122. *Unfinished Tales*, 319. Cirion's oath to God which hallowed the Halifirien was specifically not an attempt to restore the worship of God, for that would have been seen as sacrilegious. Tolkien also notes that the trilithon "monument" spoken of in the oath cannot have been of a religious nature, and that the Halifirien became hallowed only at the time of the oathtaking. Even so, monuments such as Stonehenge, etc., play no part in the religious customs of either good or evil men (*Nature*, 392–93).

123. *Lost Road*, 234; *Silmarillion*, 83; *Shaping*, 97.

124. *Silmarillion*, 83; *Morgoth's Ring*, 112.

125. *The Tolkien Reader*, 115.

126. *Letters*, 246:328.

127. *Letters*, 89:99. Tolkien can speak of a feast of reason and a flow of soul between the Inklings (Hammond and Scull, *Chronology*, 300).

128. *Return*, 156.

129. *Return*, 155.

130. *Towers*, 311.

131. *Return*, 199.

132. *Towers*, 321.

133. *Towers*, 322.

134. Garth, *Tolkien and the Great War*, 36. See also Tolkien's comments on Thompson in Hammond and Scull's *Chronology*, 58 and *Guide*, 1293–94.

135. Garth, *Tolkien and the Great War*, 36. For the way in which Tolkien's fiction may be read as mediating divine meaning, see Thomas W. Smith, "Tolkien's Catholic Imagination: Mediation

and Tradition," *Religion & Literature* 38, no. 2 (Summer 2006): 75. More briefly, see Christopher Garbowski, "Tolkien's Middle-earth and the Catholic Imagination," *Mallorn* 41 (2003): 9–12.

136. Especially Craig Bernthal, *Tolkien's Sacramental Vision: Discerning the Holy in Middle-earth* (Angelico Press, 2014).

137. *The Hobbit*, 205.

138. *Fellowship*, 155.

139. *The Treason of Isengard*, 378, 385.

140. *The Hobbit*, 262–63.

141. George Sayer, "Recollections of J. R. R. Tolkien," in *Tolkien: A Celebration*, ed. Joseph Pearce (London: Fount, 1999), 10; *Letters*, 306:392.

142. Hammond and Scull, *Chronology*, 110, 164.

143. *Letters*, 43:53–54.

144. *Letters*, 43:53–54.

145. *Letters*, 43:53–54.

146. *Letters*, 250:338–39. We know that he frequently took Communion daily, at least as an adult. He notes that he almost ceased going to Communion in Leeds and Northmoor (*Letters*, 250:330). Perhaps not every day during his time at university, as he makes special note to Edith that he had attended (Hammond and Scull, *Chronology*, 43), though it is not an entirely unusual occurrence, as he attends Mass even when touring Europe with some young wards (Hammond and Scull, *Chronology*, 51).

147. *Letters*, 250:338.

148. *Letters*, 250:339.

149. *Letters*, 250:338.

150. *Letters*, 250:338.

151. *Letters*, 250:338.

152. *Letters*, 250:338. Though Tolkien, as is common, also reminds us that God alone knows the circumstances of each soul.

153. *Letters*, 250:339.

154. *Letters*, 250:339; Sayer, "Recollections," 24. One of the liturgical reforms of Vatican II, of course, was approving a liturgy in the vernacular rather than in the traditional Latin. He disapproved of this revised liturgy, preferring to continue to recite in Latin (Hammond and Scull, *Chronology*, 801). He notes that he was pleased with having rosary and the Litany of Loretto said in Latin at San Pietro during his pilgrimage in Italy (Hammond and Scull, *Chronology*, 494). But he could not have wholly disapproved of a liturgy in the vernacular, since we find him commenting on the tragedy of losing a vernacular liturgy in Gothic which would have served as a model for all Germanic peoples and thereby provided a native Catholicism that should have endured (Hammond and Scull, *Chronology*, 813; see also *Letters*, 272). Tolkien likely, as did many people, disliked the exact style of the liturgy rather than its being written in the vernacular.

155. Kilby, *Tolkien and the Silmarillion*, 172.

156. *Letters*, 213:288.

157. *Letters*, 210:275.

158. *Letters*, 210:274.

159. *Towers*, 231.

160. *Return*, 213.

161. *Sauron*, 11; see also *Letters*, 328:413.

162. See, among the examinations of the other loves in Tolkien's fiction, Dale Nelson, "*The Lord of the Rings* and the Four Loves," *Mallorn* 40 (2002): 29 and 31.

163. McIntosh, *The Flame Imperishable*, 20–21n52; *Letters*, 49:60–62; Hammond and Scull, *Chronology*, 277.

164. *Letters*, 49:60.

165. *Letters*, 49:61.

166. *Letters*, 49:60.

167. *Letters*, 49:60.

168. *Morgoth's Ring*, 259.

169. *Letters*, 43:51; 49:62.

170. *Letters*, 43:51.

171. *Letters*, 43:52.

172. *Letters*, 43:52.

173. *Morgoth's Ring*, 234.

174. *Letters*, 49:61.

175. *Letters*, 49:61. Lewis's marriage to divorcee Joy Davidman Gresham was greatly troubling to Tolkien (Hammond and Scull, *Chronology*, 559).

176. *Letters*, 49:62.

177. *Letters*, 49:62.

178. *Letters*, 49:62.

179. *Letters*, 49:62. Tolkien does not, however, deny the validity of civil marriages or of marriages to non-Christians (Hammond and Scull, *Chronology*, 559).

180. *Letters*, 49:62.

181. One might extend this to being a grandfather as well. Joanna Tolkien reports that he took his grandchildren to midnight Mass on Christmas and crossed his granddaughter's forehead before hugging her for bed (Hammond and Scull, *Chronology,* 232).

182. Hammond and Scull, *Chronology*, 43.

183. Tolkien pressured Edith to convert to Catholicism as soon as possible rather than wait until closer to their marriage, which meant she was ejected by her landlords (Hammond and Scull, *Chronology*, 42–43). Even before being allowed by Father Francis to see her again, he sent (with his permission) some Catholic devotional pamphlets about the stations of the cross and the seven saying of Jesus from the cross (Hammond and Scull, *Chronology*, 23).

184. Hammond and Scull, *Chronology, 56*. He had previously also begun a journal also marked "ad maiorem Dei gloriam" upon their informal betrothal (Hammond and Scull, *Chronology*, 43).

185. Hammond and Scull, *Chronology*, 84, 86; *Guide*, 334.

186. Dean W. Arnold, "Interview with Dean W. Arnold," Metropolitan Kallistos Ware, January 16, 2007, https://soundcloud.com/dean-w-arnold/kallistos-full-interviewmov-aac-audio.

187. *Morgoth's Ring*, 217.

188. *Nature*, 16, 20.

189. See for this discussion *Morgoth's Ring*, 207–14; *Return*, 340.

190. *Morgoth's Ring*, 221.

191. *Morgoth's Ring*, 234. Nor does Elvish death end the marriage vow (*Nature*, 258–59).

192. *Morgoth's Ring*, 212.

193. *Morgoth's Ring*, 225–27; *Nature* 23.

194. *Nature*, 289.

195. *Nature*, 23, see also 27.

196. *Nature*, 26.

197. *Morgoth's Ring*, 225–27. In case anyone wondered, Tolkien tells us that Elvish sex is longer and more pleasurable than human sex—too intense, in fact, to endure for long (*Nature*, 26–27)

198. *Morgoth's Ring*, 233–34; *Nature*, 16, 20. Some loves such as friendship include no desire for procreation, though differences in gender also create differences in the emotion even apart from romantic considerations. Elves speak also of a love for objects or ideas, such as give rise to the arts or sciences. This includes a concern for the other for its own sake, and thus a study or service of the beloved (*Nature*, 16).

199. *Morgoth's Ring*, 226–27.

200. *Letters*, 43:49.

201. *Letters*, 43:49

202. *Gawain*, 5, 9. John Matthews argues for an originally very different version of Gawain's romantic relationships ("Reappraising Gawain: Pagan Champion or Christian Knight?" *Mallorn* 31 [1994]: 7–14).

203. *Aotrou and Itroun*, 14–15.

204. *Letters*, 131:161.

205. Unpublished Letter to Rayner Unwin (May 12, 1955).

206. *Letters*, 43:52.

207. Carpenter, *Biography*, 46, 126.

208. *The Monsters and the Critics and Other Essays*, 73. Michael D. C. Drout notices that Tolkien's focus on sin and confession remains diametrically opposed to the wider scholarly conversation ("J. R. R. Tolkien's Medieval Scholarship and Its Significance," *Tolkien Studies* 4 [2007]: 144–45).

209. *Monsters*, 87.

210. *Monsters*, 78.

211. *Monsters*, 100.

212. *Monsters*, 107.

213. *Monsters*, 88.

214. *Monsters*, 101.

215. *Monsters*, 102.

216. *Monsters*, 103–4.

Chapter XI: The Christian Life

1. *The Letters of J. R. R. Tolkien*, 250:337.

2. Tolkien, "Fate and Free Will," 185–86.

3. Much more could be said about Tolkien's narrative depiction of such life, and this has already given rise to many devotional books such as Sarah Arthur, *Walking with Frodo: A Devotional Journey through "The Lord of the Rings"* (Wheaton: Tyndale House, 2003); Sarah Arthur, *Walking with Bilbo* (Tyndale House, 2005); Ed Strauss, *A Hobbit Devotional: Bilbo Baggins and the Bible* (Uhrichsville, OH: Barbour, 2012).

4. Sayer, "Recollections," 24.

5. *The Return of the King*, 305. Joy Chant describes Frodo as possessing a "threshed and winnowed holiness"; see Joy Chant, "Niggle and Numenor," *Mallorn* 11 (1977): 4–11.

6. Carpenter, *Biography*, 68.

7. Sayer, "Recollections," 23.

8. Hammond and Scull, *Guide*, 663.

9. See, for example, *Letters*, 246:326. He finds this illustrated in *Gawain and the Green Knight*, and his comments there are apt for evaluations of his own work: "Such comfort and strength as he has beyond his own natural courage is derived only from *religion*. It is no doubt possible to dislike this moral and religious outlook, but the poet has it; and if one does not (with or without dislike) recognize this, the purport and point of the poem will be missed, the point at any rate that the author intended." *The Monsters and the Critics and Other Essays*, 103, emphasis in original.

10. *Letters*, 246:326. Though the conjunction could be read as correlative rather than subordinating, the context seems to indicate the latter.

11. *Tolkien On Fairy-stories*, 281.

12. *Fairy-stories*, 265. See Thomas Aquinas *Summa* 1–2.109.1: "And thus the act of the intellect or of any created being whatsoever depends upon God in two ways: first, inasmuch as it is from Him that it has the form whereby it acts; secondly, inasmuch as it is moved by Him to act."

13. *Letters*, 246:326. Philip Irving Mitchell uses this passage as a jumping-off point to situate Tolkien in the fascinating debate between the natural and supernatural ends of man prior to Vatican II; see "'But Grace Is Not Infinite': Tolkien's Explorations of Nature and Grace in His Catholic Context," *Mythlore* (2013): 61–81.

14. *Letters*, 109:120–21. Aside from those more realistically grounded examples discussed below, we see two generations of Eärendil's descendants will receive a special grace of long and delightful youth and the choice to belong to either Elves or Men (*The Nature of Middle-earth*, 78). There is also a grace of the Valar that specially protects a land against sickness and misfortune and makes all of nature friendly (*Nature*, 321–22, 336).

For the way in which grace appears in more thematic ways in the narrative, see Celia Devine, "Fertility and Grace in *The Lord of the Rings*," *Mallorn* 57 (2016): 10–11.

15. *Letters*, 246:326.

16. *Return*, 184–85. See the discussion on inspiration in this passage above.

17. *Return*, 217.

18. *Return*, 206.

19. *Return*, 207.

20. *Return*, 209.

21. *Return*, 217.

22. *Return*, 218.

23. *Return*, 215.

24. *Return*, 198.

25. *Letters*, 192:253.

26. *Letters*, 181:233; 191:252; 192:253; 246:325–26.

27. *Letters*, 191:251–52; 192:253; 246: 326.

28. *Letters*, 192:253.

29. *Letters*, 192:252–53; 246:326.

30. Both Frodo and Sam had many opportunities to kill Gollum. Frodo's mercy is well-known, but Sam too has his moment of charity on the slopes of Mount Doom. Prior to this, Aragorn, Gandalf, and the Elves spared the creature while in captivity, and of course Bilbo spared him at the first.

31. See *Return*, 225.

32. *Letters*, 246:326.

33. *Letters*, 246:326.

34. *Letters*, 191:252.

35. Sotheby's, *English Literature, History, Children's Books and Illustrations*, London, 12 July 2016, p. 148, quoted in Hammond and Scull, *Chronology*, 503.

36. Quoted in Shippey, *Road*, 164.

37. *Return*, 261.

38. *Return*, 280, 285. Frodo's tone in the former instance shows that he is no mere milksop but a mature and reflective soul.

39. *Return*, 285.

40. *Return*, 298.

41. *Return*, 299. See also Romans 12:19–20; Proverbs 25:22.

42. *Letters*, 191:252.

43. *Letters*, 86:97.

44. *Letters*, 112:126–27.

45. *Letters*, 86:97.

46. Unpublished letter to John Roberts, August 22, 1955.

47. *Letters*, 192:253.

48. *Letters*, 131:151; 153:190.

49. *Letters*, 113:126.

50. *Letters*, 131:154.

51. *Fairy-stories*, 265.

52. *Letters*, 191:252.

53. *Letters*, 165:221; 191:252; 246:330.

54. *Letters*, 165:221. See also Resnik, "An Interview," 39.

55. Quoted in Daphne Castell, "Realms of Tolkien," *New Worlds* 50, no. 168 (November 1966).

56. *The Silmarillion*, 278.

57. See *Return*, 217.

58. *Return*, 217.

59. *Letters*, 191:252. Had Gollum succeeded, he would have found himself in a battle between his repentant love for Frodo and his compulsive slavery to the Ring (*Letters*, 246:330).

60. *Letters*, 96:110.

61. *Monsters*, 100.

62. *Letters*, 246:330; 165:220.

63. *Letters*, 163:215.

64. *Letters*, 89:101.

65. Nicholas Polk ties holiness to humility and patience in "The Holy Fellowship: Holiness in *The Lord of the Rings*," *Mallorn* 57 (2016): 29–31. Why he subsumes holiness beneath humility is unclear.

66. *Letters*, 328:413.

67. *The Hobbit*, 276.

68. *Letters*, 163:215. Tolkien's admiration for "the indomitable courage of quite small people against impossible odds" is not always of a religious nature (Gueroult interview). Craig Boyd argues that Tolkien's concept of humility owes a debt to Thomas Aquinas; see "Nolo Heroizari: Tolkien and Aquinas on the Humble Journey of Master Samwise," *Christianity & Literature* 68, no. 4 (2019): 605–22.

69. *Return of the Shadow*, 281.

70. *Hobbit*, 262–63. See Nicholas Polk's discussion of Thorin's parting as a sign of his sanctification in "A Holy Party: Holiness in *The Hobbit*," *Mallorn* 59 (2018): 57–63.

71. *The Fellowship of the Ring*, 281.

72. *Fellowship*, 284.

73. As noted by others, such as Kusmita Pedersen, "The 'Divine Passive' in *The Lord of the Rings*," *Mallorn* 51 (Spring 2011): 23–27. Pedersen is much more reticent to give reasons as to why Tolkien might employ such a construction.

74. *Fellowship*, 282.

75. *Letters*, 246:328.

76. In *Beowulf: A Translation and Commentary*, Tolkien's immediate context for this quotation, Hrothgar does find Beowulf on his doorstep, after all. In *Monsters*, 77, Tolkien also stresses the normalcy of the Christian belief in the efficacy of prayer, as expressed here fictionally. See Carpenter, *Biography*, 46; Hammond and Scull, *Chronology*, 22. Hammond and Scull list several records of prayers by Tolkien (*Chronology*, 22, 300, 314, 337, 699).

77. *The Lay of Aotrou and Itroun*, 8.

78. *Letters*, 312:401. He asks for prayer from his son Michael for time to work (*Letters*, 315:404).

79. J. R. R. Tolkien, Letter to Przemyslaw Mroczkowski, 1958.

80. *Aotrou and Itroun*, 10.

81. *Monsters*, 44. Gawain, for example, finds shelter in the castle of Bertilak as an answer to prayer, but this is also the scene of his temptation (77).

82. *Letters*, 265:352. For the specific passages Tolkien may have found objectionable, see Eric Seddon, "*Letters to Malcolm* and the Trouble with Narnia: C. S. Lewis, J. R. R. Tolkien, and Their 1949 Crisis," *Mythlore* 26, no. 1 (2007): 61–81. Tolkien will write in his copy of the book that it is not "about prayer, but about Lewis praying." Despite his theological detestation, however, he also writes that "the whole book is always interesting. Why? Because it is about Jack, by Jack, and that is a topic that no one who knew him well could fail to find interesting even when exasperating" (quoted in Hammond and Scull, *Chronology*, 649).

83. See Seddon, "*Letters to Malcolm*."

84. *Letters*, 54:66.

85. "Glory to the Father, and to the Son, and to the Holy Spirit, as it was in the beginning, and now, and ever shall be, world without end. Amen."

86. "Glory to God in the highest, and on earth peace to people of good will. We praise You, we bless You, we adore You, we glorify You, we give You thanks for Your great glory, Lord God, heavenly King, O God Almighty Father. Lord Jesus Christ, Only-Begotten Son, Lord God, Lamb of God, Son of the Father, You take away the sins of the world, have mercy on us; You take away the sins of the world, receive our prayer. You are seated at the right hand of the

Father, have mercy on us. For You alone are the Holy One, you alone the Lord, you alone the Most High, Jesus Christ, with the Holy Spirit in the Glory of God the Father. Amen."

87. Psalm 117: "O praise the Lord, all ye nations: praise him, all ye people. For his merciful kindness is great toward us: and the truth of the Lord endureth for ever. Praise ye the Lord" (KJV).

88. "My soul doth magnify the Lord, and my spirit hath rejoiced in God my Saviour, because He hath regarded the humility of his handmaid: for behold from henceforth all generations shall call me blessed. Because He that is mighty hath done great things to me, and holy is His name. And His mercy is from generation unto generations to them that fear Him. He hath shewed might in His arm: He hath scattered the proud in the conceit of their heart. He hath put down the mighty from their seat, and hath exalted the humble. He hath filled the hungry with good things, and the rich he hath sent empty away. He hath received Israel His servant, being mindful of His mercy. As He spoke to our fathers; to Abraham and his seed forever. Glory be to the Father, and to the Son, and to the Holy Ghost, as it was in the beginning is now, and ever shall be, world without end. Amen."

89. The litany is a call-and-response focused on Mary. After each title, there follows the request "pray for us." I have omitted these frequent repetitions in the interest of space. Several titles in the modern version had not yet been added in Tolkien's day, and have been excluded here. The litany reads: "Lord, have mercy. Christ have mercy. Lord have mercy. Christ hear us. Christ graciously hear us. God the Father of heaven, have mercy on us. God the Son, Redeemer of the world, have mercy on us. God the Holy Spirit, have mercy on us. Holy Trinity, one God, have mercy on us. Holy Mary, pray for us. Holy Mother of God … Holy Virgin of Virgins … Mother of Christ … Mother of divine grace … Mother most pure … Mother most chaste … Mother inviolate … Mother undefiled … Mother most amiable … Mother most admirable … Mother of good Counsel … Mother of our Creator … Mother of our Savior … Virgin most prudent … Virgin most venerable … Virgin most renowned … Virgin most powerful … Virgin most merciful … Virgin most faithful … Mirror of justice … Seat of wisdom … Cause of our joy … Spiritual vessel … Vessel of honor … Singular vessel of devotion … Mystical rose … Tower of David … Tower of ivory … House of gold … Ark of the covenant … Gate of heaven … Morning star … Health of the sick … Refuge of sinners … Comforter of the afflicted … Help of Christians … Queen of Angels … Queen of Patriarchs … Queen of Prophets … Queen of Apostles …Queen of Martyrs … Queen of Confessors … Queen of Virgins … Queen of all Saints … Queen conceived without original sin … Queen of the most holy Rosary … Queen of peace … Lamb of God, Who takest away the sins of the world, spare us, O Lord. Lamb of God, Who takest away the sins of the world, graciously hear us, O Lord. Lamb of God, Who takest away the sins of the world, have mercy on us. Pray for us, O holy Mother of God. That we may be made worthy of the promises of Christ. Let us pray. Grant, we beseech Thee, O Lord God, that we thy servants may enjoy perpetual health of mind and body, and by the glorious intercession of blessed Mary, ever Virgin, may we be freed from present sorrow, and rejoice in eternal happiness. Through Christ our Lord. Amen."

90. The oldest known hymn to Mary as God-bearer. "We fly to Thy protection, O Holy Mother of God; do not despise our petitions in our necessities, but deliver us always from all dangers, O Glorious and Blessed Virgin. Amen."

91. *Letters*, 54:66 (his listing of the prayers). The *Laudate* is a setting for Psalm 113. "Praise the Lord, ye servants: O praise the Name of the Lord. Blessed be the Name of the Lord: from

this time forth for evermore. The Lord's Name is praised: from the rising up of the sun unto the going down of the same. The Lord is high above all heathen: and his glory above the heavens. Who is like unto the Lord our God, that hath his dwelling so high: and yet humbleth himself to behold the things that are in heaven and earth? He taketh up the simple out of the dust: and lifteth the poor out of the mire; that he may set him with the princes: even with the princes of his people. He maketh the barren woman to keep house: and to be a joyful mother of children."

92. *Fairy-stories*, 257, 263–64.

93. *Letters*, 54:66.

94. Hammond and Scull, *Chronology*, 197, 376, 653; *Guide*, 33; Bodleian Library, Tolkien A 18/1, f. 1–17, partially published in *Vinyar Tengwar* volumes 43 and 44. Tolkien's grandson Simon also recalls that he was once given a farthing on which Tolkien had inscribed the whole Lord's Prayer in circular script ("My Grandfather").

95. Carpenter, *Biography*, 207; Sayer, "Recollections," 23.

96. *Nature*, 232.

97. *Nature*, 232.

98. *Nature*, 175–76, 200–201.

99. *The War of the Jewels*, 283.

100. *Nature*, 393. See the section on church in Middle-earth, above, for more on Númenorean prayer.

101. *Nature*, 330.

102. *Letters*, 156:206, though see *The War of the Ring*, 136.

103. *The Two Towers*, 284–85. The draft in *War*, 164, explicitly names the Blessed Realm. The final draft is much more vague.

104. *Letters*, 246:327.

105. *The Book of Lost Tales, vol. 2*, 76–77; *Silmarillion*, 50–51; *The Lost Road*, 303; *Morgoth's Ring*, 161.

106. *Letters*, 312:401.

107. *The Peoples of Middle-earth*, 390.

108. Aside from two unrecorded general prayers for success (Hammond and Scull, *Chronology*, 337, 699). The number is obviously not very large, so the data set is probably not representative.

109. *Return*, 195.

110. *Letters*, 54:66.

111. *Letters*, 183:240.

112. *Letters*, 142:171.

113. Tolkien, "Qenya Lexicon," 12, 73. See also Garth, *Tolkien and the Great War,* 112–13. Since it is merely given as a gloss on a lexicon entry, it is impossible to determine the context of the saying, though Tolkien says it was a common one.

114. *Fellowship*, 235. See also *Towers*, 260, 342–43.

115. Hammond and Scull, *Chronology*, 551.

116. *Fellowship*, 235.

117. *Fellowship*, 235.

118. Gueroult interview.

119. *Letters*, 109:120.

120. Tolkien, "Qenya Lexicon," 35.

121. *Letters*, 246:327.

122. Any survey of the year's work in Tolkien studies provided annually by *Tolkien Studies* will demonstrate this point.

123. *Letters*, 310:400.

124. *Letters*, 310:399–400.

125. *Monsters*, 106; *Fairy-stories*, 254–55, 257, 270. This means that in some cases, moral absolutes can be easily laid down. Cannibalism is not permissible under any circumstances whatsoever (Hammond and Scull, *Chronology*, 344–45).

126. *Letters*, 49:60.

127. *Monsters*, 93. Hammond and Scull's *Chronology* records Tolkien debating with his friends on The Nuremberg Nazi trials (318), the atom bomb and total war (324), the education of the poor (344), cannibalism (344), liberal theology (345), and infant death (349).

128. *Letters*, 310:399.

129. *Letters*, 310:399–400.

130. *Fairy-stories*, 53.

131. *Fairy-stories*, 53.

132. *Morgoth's Ring*, 392.

133. "Mythopoeia."

134. *Letters*, 246:326.

135. *Letters*, 246:326; *Monsters*, 97, 108. Tolkien himself was inclined to be scrupulous in recounting his sins, says Sayer, "Recollections," 23.

136. *Monsters*, 108.

137. *Letters*, 246:326.

138. *Letters*, 246:326.

139. *Letters*, 181:233.

140. *Letters*, 181:233; 191:252; 192:253.

141. *Letters*, 191:252.

142. *Letters*, 191:252.

143. *Letters*, 186:246.

144. *Monsters*, 86.

145. Hammond and Scull, *Chronology*, 344–45.

146. *Monsters*, 89.

147. Gueroult interview.

148. Gueroult interview.

149. *Monsters*, 107.

150. *The Fall of Arthur*, V.8–11.

151. *Arthur*, V.23–25.

152. *Monsters*, 78; *Aotrou and Itroun*, 14–15, 20–21.

153. Garth, *Tolkien and the Great War*, 251.

154. *Letters*, 43:48. We do have record that Tolkien wrote a poem about the Crusader-King Richard I, titled "A Fragment of an Epic: Before Jerusalem Richard Makes an End of Speech," but no indication of its specific content (Hammond and Scull, *Chronology*, 30). This indicates Richard entering combat and would no doubt be illuminating, and perhaps modeled after Chesterton's "Lepanto" and similar to his own *The Fall of Arthur*.

155. See *Letters*, 186:246.

156. *Letters*, 76:89.

157. See Thomas Smith, "Tolkien's Catholic Imagination," 76 and following.

158. Romans 13.

159. *Fairy-stories*, 57.

160. "Mythopoeia"; see *Letters*, 312:401; *Lost Road*, 69. Tolkien joined in the mass protest of the arrest of Cardinal Mindszenty by the communist Hungarian government on exactly this issue (Hammond and Scull, *Chronology*, 365).

161. *Monsters*, 73.

162. *Fairy-stories*, 257; see *Monsters*, 83.

163. *Fairy-stories*, 104.

164. *Towers*, 317.

165. If we accept the judgments of Tom Shippey and Christopher Tolkien that the Rohirrim are based on the Anglo-Saxons, then Éowyn's spirit echoes that Northern courage displayed in *The Battle of Maldon* and softened by Tolkien in "Homecoming." For an overview of this parallel, see Thomas Honegger, "The Rohirrim: 'Anglo-Saxons on Horseback'? An inquiry into Tolkien's use of sources," in *Tolkien and the Study of His Sources: Critical Essays*, ed. Jason Fisher (London: McFarland, 2011), 116–32. For the way in which the Anglo-Saxons (and thus the Rohirrim) represent a deficient, Homeric glory in contrast to Tolkien's more moderated Virgilian duty, see Freeman, "*Pietas* and the Fall of the City: A Neglected Virgilian Influence on Middle-earth's Chief Virtue," in *Tolkien and the Classical World* (Zollikofen, Switzerland: Walking Tree Press, 2020).

166. *Return*, 57–58.

167. *Towers*, 40–41; see *Morgoth's Ring*, 224.

168. See chapter 9 on "faith."

169. *Morgoth's Ring*, 224. Tolkien is also willing to discuss moral counterfactuals, stating that had Fëanor assented to letting Yavanna destroy the Silmarils to rekindle the Trees, it would have cleansed his heart and averted the wickedness that was to come (*Morgoth's Ring*, 295). Had Gollum not fallen back into sin, his partial healing through love would have granted him a clearer vision that would motivate him to sacrifice himself and the Ring for Frodo's sake (*Letters*, 246:330).

170. *War*, 96. For more on the ethics of revenge in Tolkien, see Brian Rosebury, "Revenge and Moral Judgement in Tolkien," *Tolkien Studies* 5 (2008): 1–20.

171. *Towers*, 350.

172. This leads Willhite and Bell to conclude that Tolkien's narrativized moral imagination is not explicitly Christian, though based in Christianity ("J. R. R. Tolkien's Moral Imagination," *Mallorn* 40 [2002]: 12). This section, especially as it stresses the centrality of hope in Eru, seems to imply the opposite.

173. *Morgoth's Ring*, 343.

174. *Morgoth's Ring*, 343.

175. *Towers*, 350–51.

176. *Return*, 222.

177. *Letters*, 246:327.

178. See also *The Tolkien Reader*, 100, 111.

179. *Reader*, 111.

180. *Reader*, 100, 106; *Letters*, 310:400.

181. *Letters*, 246:329.

182. *Towers*, 99.

183. *Fellowship*, 413; Proverbs 14:12; John 2:23–25.

184. *Towers*, 280.

185. *Towers*, 272.

186. *Towers*, 280.

187. *Towers*, 280.

188. *Towers*, 280.

189. *Fellowship*, 371.

190. *Return*, 214.

191. *Letters*, 246:327–28.

192. *Letters*, 246:327.

193. *Letters*, 246:327.

194. *Monsters*, 77.

Chapter XII: Last Things

1. *The Lost Road*, 63.

2. *The Letters of J. R. R. Tolkien*, 203:262; *Tolkien On Fairy-stories*, 74.

3. *Letters*, 153:189. Emphasis added.

4. *Letters*, 208:267.

5. *Morgoth's Ring*, 424; *Letters*, 154:197; 186:246.

6. *Morgoth's Ring*, 382.

7. *The Silmarillion*, 261; *Morgoth's Ring*, 246–47, 376, 426–27.

8. *Morgoth's Ring*, 342–43

9. *The Silmarillion*, 74; *Morgoth's Ring*, 99; *Lost Road*, 65. This includes an End.

10. *The Silmarillion*, 264; *Sauron Defeated*, 408; *Morgoth's Ring*, 427.

11. *Morgoth's Ring*, 333.

12. *Morgoth's Ring*, 330–35.

13. *Letters*, 156:204–5; 212:285–86. This is in a certain sense the impulse behind the new age (but not the Hindu or Buddhist) emphasis on reincarnation, about which Tolkien spoke derisively (Hammond and Scull, *Chronology*, 538).

14. Simone de Beauvoir, *A Very Easy Death* (New York: Penguin, 1990), quoted approvingly in "Tolkien in Oxford." Emphasis altered.

15. *Letters*, 156:201. Emphasis added. See also an entry in *Lost Road*, 371, where passing through death is the precondition for holiness.

16. *The Tolkien Reader*, 118.

17. We can also see this in Tolkien's treatment of funeral practices. As a Roman Catholic, he objected strongly to cremation, for example (Hammond and Scull, *Chronology*, 253). There are several recorded instances in which Tolkien attended or participated in religious funerals. He served at a requiem Mass for Charles Williams (Hammond and Scull, *Chronology*, 310), attended a requiem Mass for John Fraser (Hammond and Scull, *Chronology,* 310), and though himself unable to attend, had his son John represent him at Father Francis's funeral (Hammond and Scull, *Chronology*, 841). He attended the Anglican funeral of C. S. Lewis, and then also had a requiem Mass said in which he served (*Letters* 251:341; Hammond and Scull, *Chronology*, 644).

18. *The Lay of Aotrou and Itroun*, 15.

19. *Aotrou and Itroun*, 21.

20. *Silmarillion*, 42, 187, 265; *Lost Road*, 25, 65; *Sauron*, 345–46, 365, 382; *Morgoth's Ring*, 20–22.

21. *Letters*, 156:205. See *Letters*, 181:235.

22. *Unfinished Tales*, 235–36; *Lost Road*, 66; *Morgoth's Ring*, 330–35.

23. *Silmarillion*, 267; *Unfinished Tales* 235–36; *Sauron*, 347–48, 367–68.

24. *Morgoth's Ring*, 340.

25. *Morgoth's Ring*, 365–66.

26. *Morgoth's Ring*, 341

27. *Morgoth's Ring*, 309, 428.

28. *Morgoth's Ring*, 337.

29. *Letters*, 156:205; *Sauron*, 382; *Morgoth's Ring*, 330–35; *Lost Road*, 68.

30. *Silmarillion,* 265; *Morgoth's Ring*, 364.

31. *Morgoth's Ring*, 365.

32. *Fairy-stories*, 58.

33. *Letters*, 153:189. Emphasis added. For a summary of the natural span and destiny of each of Tolkien's fictional races, see Grant C. Sterling, "'The Gift of Death': Tolkien's Philosophy of Mortality," *Mythlore* 21, no. 4 (1997): 16–38.

34. *Letters*, 212:285.

35. *Letters*, 208:267.

36. *Letters*, 153:189.

37. *Letters*, 156:205. Emphasis added.

38. It must be said that this letter was only written a very short time after letter 153. We do not need to assume a decisive transition, only an uneasiness.

39. *Morgoth's Ring*, 233, 245. Though see also *The Nature of Middle-earth*, 270.

40. Both found in *Morgoth's Ring*. Amelia A. Rutledge argues for a Pauline attitude toward law and grace in this passage; see "'*Justice* is not *Healing*': J. R. R. Tolkien's Pauline Constructs in 'Finwë and Míriel,' " *Tolkien Studies* 9 (2012): 59–74.

41. See the discussion in chapter 7.

42. *Morgoth's Ring*, 312.

43. *Morgoth's Ring*, 310.

44. *Morgoth's Ring*, 315.

45. *Morgoth's Ring*, 314. Emphasis in original.

46. *Morgoth's Ring*, 317.

47. *Morgoth's Ring*, 317.

48. *Morgoth's Ring*, 309.

49. *Morgoth's Ring*, 311.

50. *Morgoth's Ring*, 318.

51. *Morgoth's Ring*, 318.

52. *Letters*, 156:205, 245:325. See also *Lost Road*, 21–22, for an earlier discarded form of mystery.

53. *Fairy-stories*, 75; *Letters*, 245:325.

54. *Letters*, 212:285–86. Emphasis added. See *Silmarillion*, 264–65. For the competing perspectives as to the (fictional) origins of this account, see Verlyn Flieger, "Whose Myth is

it?" in *Arda Special I: Between Faith and Fiction*, ed. Nils Ivar Agøy (Uppsala, Sweden: Arda Society, 1998), 32–39.

55. *Sauron*, 364.

56. *Letters*, 212:286.

57. This fact is made even more poignant by his friend Robert Murray's characterization of him as "a very complex and depressed man" whose fiction "projects his very depressed view of the universe at least as much as it reflects his Catholic faith"; quoted in Richard C. West, "A Letter from Father Murray," *Tolkien Studies* 16 (2019): 133–39, 135.

58. *Morgoth's Ring*, 321.

59. *Fairy-stories*, 58. Tolkien here subverts a quote from Robert Louis Stevenson.

60. *Letters*, 195:255. Jean Chausse argues that Théoden's healing by Gandalf is a glimpse of such a final victory over evil in that it parallels Pentecost and the descent of the Holy Spirit, but the analogy is a strained one. See Chausse, "The healing of Théoden or 'a glimpse of the Final Victory,' " *Mallorn* 59 (2018): 49–51.

61. See *Morgoth's Ring*, 286–87.

62. *Morgoth's Ring*, 260. For the way in which "Leaf by Niggle" demonstrates a Thomistic understanding of hope as a journey of endurance toward heaven, see Craig A. Boyd, "The Thomistic Virtue of Hope in Tolkien's 'Leaf by Niggle,'" *Christian Scholar's Review* 48, no. 2 (2019): 131–46.

63. *Letters*, 181:237.

64. *Beowulf: A Translation and Commentary*, 271.

65. *Morgoth's Ring*, 338.

66. *Morgoth's Ring*, 240.

67. *Morgoth's Ring*, 320.

68. *Morgoth's Ring*, 338.

69. *Morgoth's Ring*, 320.

70. *Morgoth's Ring*, 320.

71. *Beowulf*, 68.

72. *Morgoth's Ring*, 332.

73. *Morgoth's Ring*, 332.

74. *Morgoth's Ring*, 43.

75. *Sauron*, 345–46, 364.

76. *The Return of the King*, 98–99, 129. This is the only time the word "heathen"—a religious judgment—appears in *The Lord of the Rings*. See John R. Holmes, "'Like Heathen Kings': Religion as Palimpsest in Tolkien's Fiction," in *The Ring and the Cross: Christianity and "The Lord of the Rings,"* ed. Paul E. Kerry (Madison: Fairleigh Dickinson University Press, 2011), 119–44.

77. *Return*, 129.

78. *Return*, 169.

79. *Return*, 199. Note also that hope can take many forms, sometimes unconscious. Sam, for instance, is given a steel will that despair cannot conquer (*Return*, 211).

80. *Morgoth's Ring*, 341; *Sauron*, 398. Capitalization thus.

81. *Return*, 343–44. Emphasis added. See also *The Peoples of Middle-earth*, 270. Note a significant contrast between this and *Return*, 342: Aragorn is unsure whether Sauron will be defeated but certain that there is hope after death. This is also a contrast between youth and old age.

82. Compare Tolkien's comments on Genesis, in which he references Lewis and the person who draws nourishment from the beauty of the story alone (*Letters* 96:109–110, quoting C. S. Lewis, "Myth Became Fact," in *God in the Dock*, ed. Walter Hooper [Grand Rapids: Eerdmans, 2001], 63–67).

83. *Morgoth's Ring*, 351.

84. *Morgoth's Ring*, 321.

85. Men do undergo a process of waiting and reflection in Mandos but depart thence to an unknown place, perhaps directly to God (*Morgoth's Ring*, 340, 429). The Dwarves likewise have faith that God will make them holy and give them a part with Aulë in the remaking of the world (*Silmarillion*, 44; see also *Letters*, 5359, 5586). Until then they partake of an intermediate state of conscious waiting, just as the Elves do (*The Hobbit*, 262).

86. *The Book of Lost Tales, vol. 1*, 59; *The Shaping of Middle-earth*, 100; *Lost Road*, 247, 305, 381; *Sauron*, 364.

87. *Morgoth's Ring*, 232, 235–36; see also *Sauron*, 196. Likewise, the appearance of this idea in a more autobiographical work lends credence to its status in Tolkien's primary belief. Hammond and Scull, *Guide*, 872–73.

88. *Morgoth's Ring*, 222, 235. Given what we see in "Leaf by Niggle," we can safely assume that this represents Tolkien's actual thought on the matter, in purgatory at least.

89. *Morgoth's Ring*, 235–36.

90. The *Beowulf*-poet does not allow his non-Christian characters to speak of heaven, says Tolkien, because he explicitly denies an understanding or hope of heaven to pagans (*Monsters*, 38). Nevertheless, he displays knowledge of it: heaven is a joyful and peaceful place, the bosom of the Father, the guardian of the heavens, the King of glory (*Beowulf*, 173).

91. *Monsters*, 99.

92. *Monsters*, 333.

93. *Monsters*, 339, 342. There is a sort of naturalistic image of the end in the song of the barrow-wights (*The Fellowship of the Ring*, 152). For more on Tolkien's apocalypse imagery, see Megan N. Fontenot, "The Art of Eternal Disaster: Tolkien's Apocalypse and the Road to Healing," *Tolkien Studies* 16 (2019): 91–109.

94. *Monsters*, 336.

95. *Lost Road*, 158.

96. *Return*, 224; *Morgoth's Ring*, 339, 341, though here by direct intervention of God.

97. *Return*, 224, 225. J. R. Wytenbroek examines other apocalyptic overtones in the book in "Apocalyptic Vision in *The Lord of the Rings*," *Mythlore* 14, no. 4 (1988): 7–12, though the book of Revelation is consistently misspelled as "Revelations."

98. *Return*, 259. Gandalf compares the fulfillment of his good designs to a feast, in keeping with the wedding feast of the Lamb, Revelation 19 (*Return*, 248).

99. *Lost Tales 1*, 92, see also 179.

100. Though some hope lies in the future, see *Morgoth's Ring*, 68.

101. Though see *Lost Tales 1*, 219.

102. The Silmarils were meant to survive the end (*Morgoth's Ring*, 274).

103. *Shaping*, 165; *Lost Road*, 331–32. See the excision of this passage noted in *The War of the Jewels*, 247.

104. *Lost Road*, 161.

105. *Morgoth's Ring*, 342.

106. *Silmarillion,* 255; see also *Morgoth's Ring,* 203.

107. *The Treason of Isengard,* 82.

108. *Morgoth's Ring,* 319, 332, 343. On 251, Tolkien has some say Elves and Men will unite into one race; others, that Men can visit or join Elves in the new creation. But Tolkien at this point gives the greatest fictional weight to the idea that Men are not ultimately concerned with the world at all—a marked contrast to Catholic orthodoxy.

109. *Lost Tales 1,* 53; *Lost Road,* 157; *Morgoth's Ring,* 21–22, 37, 43; *Silmarillion,* 15–16, 41–42.

110. Note that the Elves are explicitly excluded in some of the passages above, though in others mention is made of the Children of Ilúvatar—presumably Elves and Men together.

111. *Morgoth's Ring,* 343.

112. *Morgoth's Ring,* 343. In Tolkien's drafts for *Tolkien On Fairy-stories,* he affirms of fairies in the primary world (if they exist) exactly what he will go on to affirm of the Elves in Middle-earth. They are immortal while the world lasts but will perhaps be annihilated at its end, never to escape this world or its cycle of story and time (*Fairy-stories,* 255). See also 274 in a different context.

113. *Morgoth's Ring,* 333, 342, 405; *Nature,* 233.

114. *Morgoth's Ring,* 333.

115. *Morgoth's Ring,* 351–52. Emphasis added.

116. *Monsters,* 23. See also Len Sanford, "The Fall from Grace—Decline and Fall in Middle-earth: Metaphors for Nordic and Christian Theology in *The Lord of the Rings* and *The Silmarillion,*" *Mallorn* 32 (1995): 15–20.

117. *The War of the Ring,* 45; *Morgoth's Ring,* 237.

118. *Silmarillion,* 49.

119. *Morgoth's Ring,* 399. The remark is about Middle-earth, but he notes that even in the real world, this battle is still to come. See also *Morgoth's Ring,* 71, and *Letters,* 131:149, where he implicitly denies a biblical influence.

120. *Letters,* 156:207.

121. *Letters,* 156:207.

122. *Hobbit,* 262; *Fellowship,* 154; *Return,* 259; *Silmarillion,* 254, 301; *Shaping,* 166; *Return of the Shadow,* 128. Particularly notable is *Silmarillion,* 301, which appears to reference Revelation 21:1. This may again be referenced in *Return,* 259.

123. *Letters,* 96:110.

124. The Elves, for instance, hope for a life that stands in clear, recognizable, and continuous relation to the present one (*Morgoth's Ring,* 332).

125. *Morgoth's Ring,* 405. These are not, he notes, mutually exclusive.

126. *Morgoth's Ring,* 252.

127. *Morgoth's Ring,* 251, 405.

128. *Morgoth's Ring,* 351.

129. *Morgoth's Ring,* 37.

130. *Reader,* 108–9.

131. *Letters,* 96:110.

132. *Letters,* 96:110. Kevin West offers a more hopeful (though less textually-based) reading of Tolkien as optimistic universalist, while acknowledging the problems with such a view, in "Julian of Norwich's 'Great Deed' and Tolkien's 'Eucatastrophe,' " *Religion & Literature* 43, no. 2 (2011): 23–44. Olszański ("Evil and the Evil One in Tolkien's Theology," *Mythlore* 21, no. 2

[1996]: 298–300) and Garbowski ("Eucatastrophe and the 'Gift of Ilúvatar' in Middle-earth," *Mallorn* 35 [1997]: 29) also gesture toward this.

133. *Letters*, 113:128.

134. *Letters*, 269:355.

135. *Fairy-stories*, 53.

136. *Letters*, 181:234; see also 246:326.

137. *Letters*, 113:126–27.

138. *Letters*, 113:126–27.

139. *Monsters*, 41; *Beowulf*, 170–73, 297–98.

140. See *Morgoth's Ring*, 235.

141. *Morgoth's Ring*, 236.

142. *Return*, 300. Does this mean annihilation? Probably not, as Tolkien elsewhere says explicitly that souls are indestructible even by God (*Letters*, 211:280; *Morgoth's Ring*, 330).

143. *Unfinished Tales*, 240.

144. Hammond and Scull, *Chronology*, 249, reporting a conversation among the Inklings. Note, though, that we do not know Tolkien's position during this conversation.

145. *Letters*, 181:234.

146. *Letters*, 113:127.

147. *Letters*, 181:234–35. See also *Silmarillion*, 180.

148. *Letters*, 181:235.

149. *Morgoth's Ring*, 407. The example is from C. S. Lewis, *The Great Divorce* (1949). Tolkien clearly echoes Lewis in this passage.

150. *Morgoth's Ring*, 407. The transformation and fulfillment of all desire is, likewise, one of the chief characteristics of heaven.

151. *Beowulf*, 173.

152. *Monsters*, 36; see also Saruman's apparent fate in *Return*, 300.

153. *Silmarillion*, 253; *Lost Road*, 234, 330; *Morgoth's Ring*, 112.

154. *Lost Road*, 371.

155. *Jewels*, 15; *Morgoth's Ring*, 411. One is tempted to think that Tolkien shifted from explicitly calling Angband "hell" just as he shifted from calling the Valar "gods," but the usage still occurs, see for instance the early *The Lays of Beleriand*, 6, 16; the late *Jewels*, 29, 275. These may be editorial omissions, however. There seems to be another association of Mandos with hell in the early version of the poem "The Last Ark" recorded in *Monsters*, 221.

156. Such that Tolkien can play with it in highly symbolic ways. While the Elves besiege Angband, they bring life; green things grow at the door of hell (*Silmarillion*, 118).

157. The three significant wolves in the Lay of Leithian (Draugluin, the Sauron-wolf, and Carcharoth) may likewise evoke the three-headed Cerberus and the Greco-Roman underworld.

158. *Beowulf*, 298.

159. See also Garth, *Tolkien and the Great War*, 127.

160. *Monsters*, 39, 41, 43.

161. *Morgoth's Ring*, 365–66; *Unfinished Tales*, 240; *Letters*, 246:327–28. The difference here is that Frodo and Bilbo must still die, though they may partake of a sort of death cleansed from the taint of the fall (*Letters*, 325:410–11).

162. *Lost Tales 1*, 92.

163. *Letters*, 153:195. Tolkien may also refer obliquely to purgatory in the "Notion Club Papers." When discussing the detachment of soul from body, Ramer speculates that many people must pass through the "lonely Cold" before they can finally reach their destination (*Sauron*, 195).

164. As mentioned in chapter 1, the story is most likely quite close to Tolkien's own actual beliefs.

165. *Reader*, 108.

166. *Reader*, 108.

167. *Reader*, 108.

168. *Reader*, 109.

169. *Reader*, 112.

170. *Reader*, 112.

171. *Reader*, 109–110.

172. See Frodo's "purgatorial" experience in Valinor, *Letters*, 246:328.

173. *Reader*, 120.

174. *Reader*, 112.

175. *Reader*, 113–14.

176. *Reader*, 114.

177. *Reader*, 115–16.

178. *Reader*, 115, 117. This cooperation is also tied to the important relationships of the bodily life—to the same neighbors and spouses. Parish waits for his wife (117).

179. *Reader*, 115.

180. *Reader*, 116. The Spring flows into a lake; compare the lake imagery at the end of Newman's purgatorial poem, "The Dream of Gerontius." Interestingly, the Old Took's given name is also Gerontius.

181. *Reader*, 116–17.

182. *Letters*, 153:189. For more on Tolkien's beliefs about God bestowing reality on our artistic creations, see John Carswell, "All Tales May Come True: Tolkien's Creative Mysticism," *Mallorn* 58 (2017): 10–13.

183. *Reader*, 120.

184. *Letters*, 45:55. See also *Letters*, 96:110–111, where Tolkien compares the possibilities of unwritten stories to mountains in the distance and ties this view to the line in "Niggle." The hope of an endless experience of tales as moving as those we now see only in unwritten glimpses must have greatly affected Tolkien.

185. *Silmarillion*, 40. Tolkien also notes that earthly relationships may be continued into eternity (*Letters*, 45:55; *Reader*, 118; *Gawain and the Green Knight*, 17–18).

186. *Aotrou and Itroun*, 21/104.

187. Garth, *Tolkien and the Great War*, 127.

188. *Reader*, 114, 118.

189. *Unfinished Tales*, 235.

190. *Lost Tales 2*, 321.

191. *Lost Road*, 80.

192. *Sauron*, 199.

193. See *Sauron*, 180–81

194. *Fairy-stories*, 79; see also *Morgoth's Ring*, 332–33. See also 1 John 3:2.

195. This chapter will not explore the fraught problem of Elvish reincarnation; here Tolkien speaks of the resurrection of an Elvish body after its physical form has faded from the world due to long life. It is not specifically an eschatological event. But the parallel is explicit.

196. *Morgoth's Ring*, 364.

197. For ways in which Tolkien adopts and adapts elements of *Pearl* into Middle-earth, see Stefan Ekman, "Echoes of *Pearl* in Arda's Landscape," *Tolkien Studies* 6 (2009): 59–70.

198. *Gawain*, 17–18. Here, Tolkien chides commentators for misunderstanding the difference between the intermediate state and the resurrection body. He is not afraid to correct others on theological points. Here, and in all his other commentaries on his translation work, he speaks as one with authority on theological matters. This belies his repeated claims to theological reticence.

199. Revelation 22:5.

200. Revelation 22:1.

201. Revelation 21:4. The people do not know the source of their joy because Christ has not yet been revealed.

202. Revelation 8:13; 21:3.

203. The saints. For example, Revelation 19:14.

204. Satan is finally conquered. Revelation 20:1–3, 10.

205. Revelation 12:10.

206. Matthew 24:42; Mark 13; 1 Peter 5:8, and many more places.

207. Matthew 16:18.

208. The King Jesus passes through death and hell and in so doing conquers them. Eph esians 4:8–9; Hebrews 2:14; 1 Corinthians 15:15, 54, and many more.

209. The second coming. Zechariah 9:9; Matthew 16:27; 1 Corinthians 4:5, and many more.

210. Revelation 21:3.

211. The tree of life from Genesis is restored in the new Jerusalem. Hebrews 10:37; Revelation 22:7, 20.

212. Zechariah 9:9. The whole passage: *Return*, 241. See also Shippey, *Road*, 226–27; and Vaccaro, "'And One White Tree,'" 23.

213. *Return*, 246, emphasis added.

214. *Return*, 303–4.

215. *Fellowship*, 363, 392; *The Two Towers*, 155. How does this relate to Tolkien's thoughts on new creation and the restoration of all things? We may suggest that it may be a case of never stepping in the same river twice: such things may continue to exist and be enjoyed in memory but will never return to a state of being comparable to the "present reality" of the future blessedness.

216. *Return*, 229–30.

217. See *Return*, 232. Compare similar passages of overwhelming joy when Sam sees Gandalf alive again (*Return*, 230) and at the celebration feast on the field of Cormallen (*Return*, 232).

218. *Return*, 309–10.

219. *Letters*, 45:55. Compare *Return*, 232. This is a prime instance in which Tolkien's actual beliefs work themselves into his fiction—even down to the metaphors.

220. *Letters*, 45:55. The resurrection, remember, is the greatest eucatastrophe.

221. *Letters*, 45:55. Emphasis added.

222. *Letters*, 43:53–54.

223. "Mythopoeia," in *Tree and Leaf, including Mythopoeia*.

Name Index

SUBJECT INDEX

461

Scripture Index

Old Testament

New Testament